Praise for
Heidi Wessman Kneale

All romance stories need a little magic, and Heidi Kneale has told us a romantic story brilliantly…. [MARRY ME] deserves to be on the top of your TBR pile.

—Kayden Claremont,
author "Timeless Passion"

"I enjoyed [AS GOOD AS GOLD], well written and with well-rounded characters."

—Long and Short Reviews

"…Kneale succeeds in reversing reader expectations in more ways than one."

—Chris Butler, The Fix:
Short Fiction Review

"Heidi Kneale has so much imagination. She's one of the best I've seen."

—Anne Wingate, author
Deb Ralston series

"…the world introduced [in AS GOOD AS GOLD] was intriguing and there seem to be more possibilities to be explored, always a sign of a strong tale."

—Margaret Fisk, author
Uncommon Lords & Ladies series

Dedication

For their Ladyships,
Lady Sarah and Lady Amy.
Go forth and be mighty.

House of the Dark

by
Heidi Wessman Kneale

Of The Dark—Book 3

Enjoy.

House of the Dark
COPYRIGHT © 2018 by Heidi Wessman Kneale
Book 3 of "Of The Dark" series.

Other titles in the **Of The Dark** series:
- God of the Dark (Book 1)
- Bride of the Dark (Book 2)

Cover Design: HW Kneale and SR Kneale
ISBN: 978-0-6484228-5-3
IngramSpark version 1.0—08 Dec 2018

Printed on planet Earth by human beings.

This book is also available in a digital edition for those who adore carrying hundreds of books on their smartphones.

License Statement

Table of Contents

❧❦☙

Our Story So Far...

To save the village of Sacred Spring, Adrastea Healer agreed to marry Mor-Lath, God of the Dark. They exchanged their vows on a hill, surrounded by war.

The first thing Mor-Lath did was take her to the great city of Feown. There, he showed the vast Cithran Army, a half-million strong, which had laid siege to Feown, and was the same army that destroyed Crossroads and nearly destroyed Sacred Spring.

Now in possession of a wife, Mor-Lath accomplished two mighty miracles—through Adrastea, he sacrificed the lives of the Cithran Army to make Adrastea immortal and through this, also saved her village and all of the Duchy of Feown. But in this dark fait accompli, he tears the Lines of Deeper Power that hold Creation together, nearly tearing the world apart. He manages to bring the world back together, but his actions have left the Lines more fragile than he realized.

Mor-Lath was also faced with another problem; apparently contrasting prophecies dog his heels. Without a wife, his other half, Mor-Lath is only a demi-god, doomed to fail at the final confrontation with the Light. But with a wife, another prophecy threatens to destroy him. Mor-Lath believes if he fathers a son, that son will destroy him. Thus, he leaves Adrastea untouched.

Adrastea accustoms herself to her new life. While not the wedding she'd hoped to have, she accepted her new married fate and was determined to do her best in her new life.

Mor-Lath turns his attention to the state of the world. While he had been hunting and courting Adrastea, Mor-Lath had neglected the world, especially the Cithran Empire. There, a new power had arisen, one that also could read prophecy and discover that the woman known as The Bride was the key to the ultimate triumph over Creation. He wants to get to the bottom of the mystery of why the Cithrans have such an interest in Adrastea. This leads him to the Cithran High Council who claim to follow the commandments of a god they call The One True. Mor-Lath scoffs at this, for he knows there is no such god, or even a mortal of great power that answers to the name of One True.

Nevertheless, this insistence on making trouble for the neighboring nations must be stopped. Mor-Lath starts plans for a war. Time to put the Cithrans back into their place.

Meanwhile, Adrastea frets about the state of her marriage. By Feowan customs, a marriage isn't complete without consummation, that act that would, potentially, conceive children and thus ensure the next generation. But Mor-Lath never approached Adrastea in that manner. This baffled her; why would someone as determined as Mor-Lath was to acquire a bride, refuse to make her a wife? Mor-Lath was very clear about her purpose to be by his side in the final confrontation. Shame he had not explained the rest.

Worried that the act of marriage has remained incomplete, Adrastea comes up with a successful plan to achieve consummation—much to her grief. Angry at being deceived and fearful of a possible child, he sears her belly so that she can never conceive.

Adrastea flees to Sacred Spring and the comfort of family and home. Later she discovers about the Son of Mor-Lath prophecy and wonders why he did not share this with her. Could have saved them both much pain. Nevertheless, she resolved to accept her new infertile status as she would accept her husband's celibacy.

Only he wasn't being celibate. When Adrastea learned that Mor-Lath's *laissez-faire* policy only applied to her, and he had no compunction over tumbling other women, her fury takes over.

One by one she locates and kills every woman with whom Mor-Lath had had intimate relations, taking their souls into her possession. Mor-Lath caught up with her at the final death. In his fury, he banished her to Dom-al-gol, that dark purgatory where dead souls are imprisoned to ponder upon the sins of their lives and wait to be shriven.

Time moved differently in Dom-al-gol. From the damned souls, she learns that Mor-Lath hadn't been doing his godly duty. Souls had been sent there, languishing without salvation. Adrastea vowed to do something about that, once she figured out how to escape.

And she did. Once she returned to the mortal world, Adrastea pins Mor-Lath to a table with a rather wicked knife, one that only she can remove. This was the best revenge she could imagine. As long as he remained there, they are not united, and they will surely lose at the final confrontation with the Light. Adrastea is more than happy for them to lose, if it means the end of Mor-Lath.

But much to her surprise, Phyl and Lucea, the God of the Light, do not want this to happen. While preventing her from committing further damage, They leave Mor-Lath to ponder on his actions that led him to being pinned to a table. Meanwhile, They command Adrastea to let go of her anger. If she professes to be a Daughter of the Light, then she needs to act as one, and do her best to set things right—including making Mor-Lath do his duty as God of the Dark and shrive the forgotten souls.

Mor-Lath is also given an ultimatum: if he does not do right by his bride, the Light are willing to grant her request for a divorce, an act that would lead to his ultimate defeat.

Adrastea was shocked to learn that she'd been gone for fifteen long years. So much time had passed, so many things had happened, including war. The world she once knew had changed much. Only way to go was forward. She listened to the counsel of the Light and released her anger, while also bringing Mor-Lath to account by making him shrive the souls of the undead.

He did so. When all are done, he made her another offer, to heal her belly and undo that dreadful hurt he'd committed against her. No bargains, no conditions.

His efforts failed. Having pinned all her hopes on this one gesture, all her rage flooded back. Thoughtlessly, she removed the knife that had pinned him to the table, intending on killing him with it.

The moment he was free, Mor-Lath turned her rage against her, redirecting it to sensual passion, for half her rage came from physical unfulfillment. Thus, he beguiled her from dismembering him and rechanneled her fury before it destroyed them both.

News of war reached them the next morning as Feown is attacked. While Adrastea's rage had been spent, she hadn't exactly been reconciled to Mor-Lath. But that was business for later. Mor-Lath took Adrastea to Feown to see what could be done to help. There, she found a young mother in labor. Adrastea helped ease the child into the world but was unable to save the mother's life. Harianne was the name the mother gave her daughter before she departed for the Light.

Chapter 1

Adrastea lowered the sleeping baby on her bed in the Temple of Mor-Lath. The infant didn't stir—the pinkness of her cheeks and the slow movement of her chest the only signs that she was a living thing. How soft the skin felt when Adrastea stroked it. Could she be a parent?

She studied the new life. What was she going to do? She'd never been a parent—had never given it much thought, really. She always figured if she did get married and had a family, she'd have Ari there and her own mother to help her. She never thought she'd parent alone.

Aril trusted her in life. She gave her approval in death for Adrastea to take care of her child.

Adrastea knelt beside the bed and stroked the baby's downy head. So much to consider. The past two days since releasing Mor-lath felt like riding on the cart behind a runaway horse. And here came the bottom of the hill.

The baby's eyes pinched up. The little shoulders squirmed before settling back into sleep.

What should she do next? Surely the baby couldn't stay here in the Temple. The Light had said Harianne belonged at Sacred Spring. There, at least, she could be safe.

What about herself? Should she stay here, or should she leave? She had promised Berengaria and Radelisa she'd stay and make things right.

What to do?

And then, there was Mor-Lath. He'd changed his tune quickly when faced with utter destruction.

She was still married to him. Probably always would be.

He said he wanted to make everything better—make a new start.

Did he?

He'd tricked her into releasing him from the table. Really, it was her own fault. She should have known he'd never have healed her. And she should not have let him goad her into such rage as to snatch the closest weapon, despite the fact it was already buried in his chest. And then she—

Not that it mattered now. She needed to stop letting Mor-Lath push her into anger. He couldn't control her if she wasn't angry. Anyhow, she had more important considerations in her life.

Adrastea pushed her finger into the fist of the baby. Look at the tiny fingernails. She ran her thumb tip over them. Someone had to take care of this baby. Adrastea had promised Aril and had stood up to Mor-Lath. He'd relented, calling the child a 'plaything'.

She sighed and looked about the luxurious bedroom. This was no place for an infant. She could not stay here, not permanently. Even if it meant deserting the priestesses for the time being.

She would have to return to Sacred Spring.

Mor-Lath appeared at the foot of the bed, startling her.

He wore a brown robe, hood thrown back. He looked very much like a Light priest. He leaned on the wooden bedpost. "There you are. Come on, we've got things to do—"

Her rage flared up; she had thought it dead. Her mind reached out to find the nearest weapon she could use.

Her thoughts settled on one of the fashionably long and wickedly sharp hat pins scattered on the dressing table. It had to be as long as a butcher knife and as thick as a leather needle. She'd emptied them out of their wooden box, so she'd have somewhere to dump Desmone's and the others' souls. It would do.

In one fluid movement, a hat pin flew to her hand. She drove it through his hand and into the wood.

"Aaah! Damn!" He hissed in pain. "What was that for?" He grabbed the pin and pulled.

It wouldn't come out. A small well of shimmery blood dripped from where the pin emerged from his hand.

Adrastea simply folded her arms. "You tricked me into releasing you from that table. You said you'd heal me. You failed. So back you go."

"What?" His temples pulsed with his quickened heartbeat. "Adrastea?"

She went to the wardrobe. She'd need clothing. The fine dresses would do until she could get sensible things again. One of the fine shawls would make an adequate sling for the baby. And this time, Adrastea planned on taking every single jewel on which she could lay her hands. It's not like he'd wear them. If there was another woman in his life (best not to think upon't), Adrastea did not want her to be decked in these. These were hers. Really, they were. At least, until she sold them.

Would any of the priestesses go with her? She'd grown used to their company, especially Radelisa and Berengaria.

Mor-Lath attempted to free himself. "You can't leave me here forever," he pleaded.

She didn't even glance back. "The hell I can." She returned with an armful of clothes chosen not so much for their cut, but for their fabric. So what if she'd grown accustomed to their fine softness? Recut the gowns to suit country styles, and she would have the best of both worlds. And make baby clothes from the scraps. She dumped her load on the other side of the bed from the baby, who, despite the noise, slept on. Did he even realize the child was there?

He snarled at his failed attempts. "You expect me to stand here for the rest of my existence?"

Adrastea shrugged as she folded the gowns. "According to you and the Light, that's not such a long time. Anyhow, I'm going back to Sacred Spring."

"I thought we were going to make things right." Pain tinged his voice.

She folded her arms and regarded him. "Are we?"

"I thought—" He drew in a breath. "I was. I..." He wilted. "You're still angry, aren't you?"

The remains of her rage simmered in her heart. She beat at them, hoping to snuff their embers. Phyl told her to release her anger, forgive. "I... I don't trust you. Because of that, I can't stay here."

He bowed his head. "What about last night?"

Oh, he had to bring that up. What had she done? How could she have given in like that? There she had been, so furious at him that, had she the power, she would have killed him on the spot. How had he turned her rage around like that? He had broken her control and, once freed, she had ravaged him. Thoughts of her pinning him down on this very bed flooded her head. She rode him hard, demanding every last scrap of satisfaction.

She plonked her fists on her hips. "Well? What about it?" It still echoed in her traitorous blood.

He stared at her, momentarily at a loss for words. He gave his head a shake. "Didn't it mean anything?"

Her jaw dropped in astonishment. "Oh, it had meaning alright. It means you're a selfish, manipulative bastard. Gives me one more reason to add to the rest as to why I should leave. If you think I'm going to fall into your arms after one night of passion and pretend that you're not the mongrel you are, then you're a greater fool than before."

He kept his head down and didn't meet her gaze. "You can't lie to a god. I know you enjoyed it."

"You played me."

"You wanted it. You always did."

"You're fifteen years too late." Do not be drawn into an argument. That's how he got freed in the first place; he provoked her to shed her reason and fly into passion. He wasn't going to do that to her again.

She had only a moment's notice when he drew on the Deeper Power. She had just enough time to call on it herself when he stretched forth his hand. By the Power lifted her up and across the bed.

"Stop that," she scolded as he placed her in front of him. He stroked her cheek with the back of his free hand. She slapped it away. "I'm not falling for your tricks again." His arm snaked around her wrist and drew her closer. She put her hands on his chest and pushed away from him.

"You would willingly give up passion for the rest of your life?" he murmured.

"I would willingly give up frustration, loneliness and aggravation. If passion must be sacrificed in the name of a peaceful life, then so be it." She gave him a cold shoulder. "Anyhow, you had no problems seeking other women for your bed. Nothing says I cannot find another man to warm mine." She glanced over her shoulder. "Someone who will give me not just the passion you seem to think I want, but fidelity, respect and love."

He reached out and grabbed her by the arm. His eyes burned with intensity. "You love me?"

She drew in a breath, measured it and returned his gaze. "No." She gave that word cautiously.

The wry expression on his face told her he didn't accept her answer.

She stared him down a while longer before turning away. She didn't love him. Should she have loved him? Was that what the Light expected of her? If so, They were sadly mistaken. Mor-Lath hadn't done one single thing to make her love him. You're manipulative, she thought. You're cruel...

"...you're selfish, you ignore me, and expect me to jump when you say boo." She shook her finger in his face. "Just because you had a hand in creating my soul doesn't mean you can dictate how I live my life. You disregard my hopes and opinions and..." Was she speaking out loud? No matter. He needed to know her thoughts. "And all you've ever thought of is yourself. Never me. This isn't a marriage. It's a farce. It doesn't matter if I keep my vows or not. A marriage is more than an agreement. It's actions. It's intent. It's a living thing, that must be tended and nurtured or it will die." Her eyes flickered to the baby still asleep on the bed.

He grabbed her arm and turned her back. This time he would not let go, no matter how hard she tried to pull away. Even without the Deeper Power, he had the physical advantage. "I know. I've done wrong by you."

"What do you want?" She glared at him, studying him. No anger, remember? she chided herself.

"To make things right."

"Really? Why?"

Uncertainty flickered across his face.

"You don't know, do you?" she said. "You thought you did. You thought you needed a bride. Never thought she might not want a husband. You wanted full godhood. Never thought there might be, oh, I don't know, something else you have to do?" She threw her free hand out in a gesture of frustration. "See all this time we've been married? What did you do with it? While I've spent most of it condemned to the nadir of Creation, you've been out and about and have had plenty of time to think. You *still* don't know what it is that will make us a god."

His eyes tightened. He blinked. He turned his head away.

She sighed. "It no longer matters, because I can't give you what you want if you don't know what it is you want."

Mor-Lath's fingers pressed painfully into her arm. His voice came out tight. "I have hopes and dreams, too, you know. There are things I want, but I'm not getting. You think you're the only one who's little sparrow-wishes are caught in a net?" He drew upon the Deeper Power and flooded it into her.

He hit her with the full force of millennia of frustration and anger. The lines on her face flared with the intensity of his emotions. He shared with her all the pain he'd collected through the years. Almost-memories bumbled through her brain, the flickers of images that could have been people, could have been events. They flickered by her so fast she couldn't get one to stay long enough to identify what—or who—it was. But the emotional results, they lingered. With the impressions came disappointment. Frustration. Anger and despair. Thousands of them, millions of them. Far more than any one mortal lifetime could hold.

They were Mor-Lath's memories. While he did not share their exact contents with her, he made sure she felt every single last shred of emotional pain.

It rocked through her body like a wave. Once she had burned her arm on a stove as a child, a careless moment of letting it sweep by the hot iron. How it stung and stung and stung the moment Ari's cold compress stopped being cold. It had taken a long time before that burningness went away.

This felt very much like that, only all through her whole soul. She cried out. She didn't know if she stood or had fallen, or if he still held her. The only thing she knew was her awareness of self. Everything else was pain.

But it was not hers.

Instead of fighting it, she gave in and let it all flow through her until it left. Once she did that, she found his presence there too. He was there like he had been there last night via her emotions, feeding his passion, his desperation, his need, and not just for physical satiety. He'd opened himself up, perhaps unwittingly.

He did so now. She knew he meant her pain. It was his last, final bid to regain control over her. He wanted her to hurt, because she'd frustrated his greatest desire—godhood. It hadn't been her fault. She hadn't known what to do.

Now she knew.

It came to her in a flash of inspiration wholly and completely separate from what Mor-Lath inflicted upon her. With the pain burning away all other sensations, it came to her like the rays of sunrise breaking over the horizon. If she'd not been carried away on waves of passion the night before, she might have noticed the answer then as well. And then there were other times—when she forced the consummation of their marriage, their wedding day when he'd made her immortal, when she pinned him to the table—she'd seen echoes.

It made sense. It could not be any simpler.

So that's what it is.

Oh, the poor fool. He didn't see it. Probably never would.

Time to complete the circuit. She took the pain and gave it back to him, sharing all, withholding nothing. Frustration, shattered dreams, loneliness, the sting of shame.

The shock of the returning pain broke Mor-Lath's concentration. His sharing ceased. The flood of relief erased the last traces of the burning pain. But that didn't mean the agony stopped. She kept the thought of pain turned on him until her vision cleared from pink spottiness. Only then did she let it go.

They lay on the stone floor together, her spread out on her back, him writhing in a fetal position.

He was no longer pinned to the post. In his surprise and agony, he'd torn his hand free of the hat pin. The pin remained embedded in the bedpost. It would remain there forever until Adrastea released it. Down the bedpost ran a streak of his luminescent immortal blood. It stained the sleeve of his brown robe where he clutched his hand. The pin had torn out between the fingers. Even though he'd stopped feeding her the agony, the faint echoes of his pain rippled under her skin.

For the first time, she let herself freely feel an emotion other than anger regarding Mor-Lath—pity. She sat up, folding her legs underneath her.

With a gentle touch, she took his hand. "Let me see that," she murmured.

He let her take it. She held it between her palms. The calming sense of the Deeper Power flowed through her, manifesting through her will to heal his hand. As it healed, she reflected upon the pain they'd shared and the passion the night before.

That was the secret—a complete sharing of one's self, of giving up one's sense of selfishness for the sake of the other.

Mor-Lath had taken the pain of his life and had given it to her. But he hadn't relinquished the memories behind it. Pride had been the drive behind his action, and pride was also what held it all back.

When the tear had mended itself, she laid the hand back on the floor as gently as she had picked it up. "Don't think this means I'm growing soft. I'm not. I never will be."

He pushed up to sitting as she rose to her feet. "You don't have to leave."

"Yes, I do." She let the Deeper Power flow through her to give her inner strength and to calm her heart. "I was more than willing to be a wife, albeit reluctantly at first. But you never meant to be a husband. Not completely. It would have taken us both together to..." She hesitated. He didn't really need to know what it would have taken. That would have required sacrifice on his part.

"To what?" he demanded. The old stubbornness was back.

"We both have to want a marriage in order for it to work."

"I'm willing to do that now." He cradled his hand.

On the bed the baby stirred and stretched, her little face puckering up again and turning purple. Adrastea ran a hand over the tiny face. She relaxed again. She'd want feeding soon.

That was something she'd have to think about—the needs of this child. Here was something worth sacrificing for. Adrastea wanted motherhood. She wanted family. At least, in that, she could succeed.

As soon as the child quieted, Adrastea looped the shawl around her.

Mor-Lath rose to his feet. He drew a breath. "I promise I'll be a better husband. Just don't leave me."

Adrastea's hands did not slow as she knotted her sling. "I'll believe it when I see it." She lifted the child and settled her in the sling. "Don't bother following me. I doubt you'll get a warm greeting at Sacred Spring."

Adrastea picked up the bundle of clothing. Mor-Lath flicked it out of her arms. "Don't go."

"I'm going." She bent down to pick it back up, but he knocked it out of her reach. It slid across the floor. She couldn't be bothered with his games.

He held out his arms. "Stay?"

Adrastea straightened, hands protectively around the small bundle next to her chest. "No."

He hesitated for a moment then let the unaccustomed word escape his lips. "Please?"

She didn't respond. Leaving the bundle, she went to the dressing table and gathered what jewelry was there. She wrapped it in a scarf and tucked it into the sling.

He laid a hand on her shoulder. She shrugged it off. He laid it on her back. She moved away from it. "Come on," he pleaded. "I can do better."

"You certainly can't do any worse," she snapped. But that would not do. She would not let him get a rise out of her. Calmness. "I don't fear you anymore. There is nothing you can do to intimidate me. And all these sweet words and the lovely-dovey act... you don't fool me. I know what you're really like. That's why I'm leaving."

"I will follow you. I will show you. I'll show everyone how much I need you." His voice cracked as he begged her.

Adrastea looked back at him with slightly annoyed ennui.

"You're selfish, Mor-Lath. Stop thinking about yourself all the time." She hitched up a squirming baby, who broke out into the newborn wail of hunger and frustration. "If only you'd stop thinking about how I could make you a god and started thinking about how you could make me a god, you might have found the answer by now." She gave Harianne a bounce.

"Don't. Follow. Me, Mor-Lath. I'm quit of you. If you think you can come pester me, just remember: yes, I can stop you."

She called on the Deeper Power and summoned the bundle of clothing to her. Before he could reach out to her again, she willed herself away from the temple.

Mor-Lath can stay with his own thoughts. Adrastea had a life to live.

Chapter 2

Mor-Lath, God of the Dark, stood on the broken walls of the city of Feown. He looked down upon the Avelian army to the south. They lay across spoilt farmland, their tents and horses and cannon scattered across a once-fertile plain. How had their king, Wasson, called up so many men to lay siege? Dirty, tired, and weary from ten days enforced march, the army were not at their best. They could easily be defeated, had anyone had the strength to stand up to them.

Feown was in no condition to offer much resistance. Most of the Duchess' armies were engaged across the Great River in Cithra. What few forces remained were not in best form, the old, the weary, the one sent home because they were too spent to be any good abroad.

Granted, it was a clever strategy, attacking Feown, a city weakened by war with the Cithrans. Wasson's generals had not surrounded the city to starve them out. Instead, in the middle of the night, they sent in sappers and spies, to sabotage and terrorize the Feowan citizens.

Nobody had seen this coming. The entire city had been caught by surprise.

This displeased Mor-Lath. He had given warning through his priests to Wasson to leave Feown alone. If he hadn't been so angry with their disobedience, he could admire their clever strategy.

But Mor-Lath was in no mood to be merciful. His heart still ached—literally—from his confrontation with his wife, as did the memory of his hand. She had healed his flesh but refused to heal his soul. He'd let himself become distracted. Now the world was falling apart around him.

Time to set things right.

Wasson, king of Avelia, held out his goblet for more wine. The serving wench, draped in diaphanous scarves and chained by the ankle to the throne, tilted her jar to fill it. The court of Wasson in Avelia was a debauched and decadent place—just the way he liked it. This second son of the old king was not a thoughtful or wise ruler. But oh, he loved a good time! Musicians followed him everywhere, playing at his very whim. Food and wine were offered by servants at all times, so that he would never hunger. Courtiers, painted and bejeweled, followed him to simper and offer platitudes. Not that he went farther than his throne room or bedroom.

It was good to be the king.

He drained his goblet and issues forth a belch. He patted his lips with the edge of his silken robe. His courtroom seemed a bit tedious today. Some rather uninteresting dancers sported about the middle of his throne room. Oh, why did people have to be boring? Why couldn't something interesting happen?

A loud knock came at the doors, interrupting the musicians and startling the dancers. Before the servants could hasten forward to respond, the doors flew open to clamor against the walls, the sound of the impact silencing the merriment of Wasson's court. The force knocked the footmen back, scattering them across the floor. As one, the pomaded heads turned to the disturbance. Wasson rose from his throne and cursed. "Close the damn doors!"

Footmen scurried forward to do his bidding but stopped, dropping to the ground. A murmur of surprise rose among the courtiers, only to be silenced when a figure came through the doors. Dancers scattered out of the way.

It appeared to be a man, cowled and robed in dark brown and carrying a tall staff. He stood in the doorway as if to wait for silence. When it arrived, he ventured forth in measured footsteps, the tip of his staff tapping on the floor in a slow rhythm.

A few courtiers leaned towards each other to whisper their opinions concerning the stranger's purpose and identity. They used words like 'stranger' and 'pauper' then eventually 'priest', the last murmured so low it was barely audible.

When he reached the center of the room, surrounded by fallen footmen, he stopped. By now he had the full attention of the courtiers.

"Wasson, son of Wacifice." His baritone voice filled the court. "I bring a message to you from your god."

Wasson settled back to his divan and waved a handkerchief before his nose. Now this was interesting. "I was not aware I had one." This sent titters through the court, their laughter more of a nervous sort, rather than of amusement.

The cowled man leaned on his staff, both hands wrapped around it. "Your ignorance does not preclude his presence." This brought a faint sigh from the courtiers. "I bring you a message. Withdraw all your troops from Feown."

Wasson's lip curled in a sneer. He looked the stranger up and down. "No. Feown is weak and will soon fall. I'm simply finishing what the Cithrans couldn't."

"Feown is not yours; it belongs to your god. Withdraw your troops from Feown."

At this, Wasson laughed. A few of the stupider courtiers joined him. For the most part, the rest remained silent.

Wasson slammed his fist on his chair. "Feown is mine now! I have done what no other Avelian king has done. I've crushed the Glasskissers." He clutched the handkerchief and pressed his knuckles to his lips. "There is no authority here greater than me. I certainly don't recognize yours."

"You ignore me at your peril. Withdraw your troops from Feown. If you do not obey your god, you and your great city shall be destroyed. Your god is most displeased with your actions."

Again, Wasson laughed, but nobody joined with him.

"You have one night," the priest warned.

Wasson's laugh turned to a scoff. He picked up the nearest item he could find—a goblet—and hurled it at the man. It flew through the air, its scarlet contents flinging out in drops, spattering across people and the floor.

The goblet never reached its intended target. It stopped a meter from the man and fell to the ground with a clatter. The murmur of the courtiers turned to a buzz.

"One night," the man said, before he departed. Unaided, the doors swung closed behind him.

"Shut up, you fools," shouted Wasson to his court. "He's just a crazy old man. The gods are superstitious legends."

Courtiers shuffled nervously. Slowly, they backed away.

"He's just an old fool."

Montrof had discovered, in his old age, how pleasant courtyards were when warmed by the morning sun. This temple garden had a few trees, several flowers and benches drenched in sunlight. It felt good on his bones that had sat too long within the cold confines of stone walls. A few priestesses passed across the other side of the courtyard, murmuring to themselves about business Montrof had no interest in.

As he grew older, his interests had changed. He no longer wandered as a priest of Mor-Lath. He chose to remain here at the temple where he was guaranteed a bite to eat, a place to sleep and a sunny spot in the courtyard. It was a comfortable, if a dull life, certainly the duller since Chamque had passed away a few years ago. Her replacement, Benadon, was not the same. She, unlike her predecessor, did not rise to his baiting.

Ah well. He leaned back against the warm stone and sighed, his eyes closing in pleasure. Perhaps it was for the best he sought to retire.

A shadow fell across his face, bringing an instant coolness. He sat up and opened his eyes. Who disturbed his peace? "What do you want?"

Mor-Lath threw back his dark brown cowl and leaned against the staff in his hands. "Your life is about to get interesting, Montrof."

Montrof sat upright. "Apologies, Holiness. I did not realize it was you."

"Nor did Wasson. But then, he wasn't terribly bright."

"Clever enough to take the throne from his brother."

Mor-Lath grunted his opinion of Wasson's brother. "He wasn't terribly bright either to get himself killed like he did."

Montrof shrugged. "After the 'untimely death' of Wacifice there was a vacancy."

"Yes. Between the ears of his sons."

Montrof eased himself back to the bench. "You should have thought of that before the removal of Wacifice. The sons weren't that great of fools to each hold the throne as long as they did."

"No," conceded Mor-Lath. "But it did prevent a war." He sat down beside Montrof with a sigh. "Or only delayed it."

"You said my life was about to get interesting. Are you thinking of removing Wasson?"

The god nodded. "Yes, I am. Wasson has been an ambitious fool. This morning his troops attacked Feown."

"Ah," sighed Montrof. "He is a bigger fool than his brother. At least his brother had the sense enough to listen to us, at first. Wasson was too young to recognize that his father's death was for a reason."

"At least he'll understand the reason for his own."

Montrof perked up. "Oh? How are you planning on removing Wasson?"

"I have given Wasson one night to remove the troops from Feown. If he complies, all will be well. If he fails, it will be his doom." Mor-Lath looked sideways at his priest. "You are a man of insight, Montrof. I'm sure you know what will happen."

Montrof inclined his head in respect. "You have given me many gifts, but prophecy was not one of them."

"Obedience was. Listen to me, Montrof, and warn the faithful. They are to leave Avelia within three days. They may take with them what they wish, but only what they can carry. If they remain in the city after the evening of the third day, they shall share Wasson's fate."

Montrof grew still. Then he gasped as the shock of realization jolted his body. "We must... leave?"

"You could stay, but I strongly advise against it."

Montrof's eyes rolled back in his head. He leaned against the wall. "Oh, Holiness... must it be this way?"

"Yes." Mor-Lath's voice was cold and uncompromising.

Montrof's brain began to tick over. "But where will we go?"

"Far away from here." He laid a hand on Montrof's shoulder. "Do you trust me?"

Montrof nodded. "You are my god, Holiness."

"Then leave your fate in my hands. Now, go. Warn the others. I will visit other priests and priestesses in Avelia and warn them the same. Do not worry about them. Preach my warning to the people. Then be gone yourself as soon as possible."

Mor-Lath rose and covered his head with the cowl. "I always did like you, Montrof." Then he was gone.

Montrof sat back against the wall one last time. The sunshine fell warm across his skin and glistened off the two tears that streamed down his wrinkled old face.

drastea appeared on the hill in front of the sacred spring. The grass crunched beneath her feet. Behind her the breeze stirred the quakies, their leaves rustling gently against each other. The light of dawn was quite a change from the dark closeness of her bedroom—former bedroom. She turned her face eastwards to enjoy the moment when the sun peeked over the edge of the world.

The baby Harianne fussed and squirmed. Adrastea dropped her bundle of clothing. She tutted to the baby and gave her a bounce until Adrastea could get a sense of what to do next.

The environs around the Spring had changed. Across the pool of water that welled deep from the earth, she saw a brand-new structure. The little temple had been rebuilt. It wasn't much of a building, being little more than several columns and a roof, restored with granite from the foothills. A path that did not exist before led from the temple to the spring. Granite steps descended into the water.

What else had changed in fifteen years? Her heart caught in her throat. What about the people she left behind?

Harianne burst out into full cry, signaling her hunger. When Adrastea stroked the baby's cheek, the baby latched on to her finger to suck. She spat it out when no milk came forth.

"I'm sorry, little one. I wish I could nurse you."

Adrastea dismissed the idea of giving Harianne to a wet nurse. She remembered how her mother mourned when Mikal was handed over to Marta. And hadn't she promised Aril she would take care of her baby?

Adrastea could think of only one Person left to ask. Unslinging the baby, she lowered her to the ground to writhe in hunger while Adrastea sank to her knees.

"Oh Light," she prayed. "What do I do? How do I feed this baby?"

Another brightness grew until it rivaled and surpassed the sun. Lucea's feet touched the grass. It stroked Her ankles in joyful welcome. She knelt and scooped up the wailing infant. She didn't soothe the child but let her fuss. "As Creation provides for each birth mother to suckle her child, so will it provide for you. All you need to do is ask."

"Ask?"

Lucea smiled fondly. "You are an immortal, daughter of the Light. You could be a god. Creation wants to serve you. Now, this is what you need." She explained, in details Adrastea couldn't begin to grasp, of the delicate balance of chemicals in the body that made a mother lactate.

"I can't remember all that." She didn't recognize half the words that tumbled forth from Her lips.

"Creation knows what to do. Just request what you need. It will take care of the rest."

Adrastea nodded. She closed her eyes and made her request of Creation. When she opened her eyes, she didn't feel any different. "Now what?"

Lucea chuckled. "That's all right. It will take time for your body to respond. Now, go drink deeply from the Spring. I shall see the infant fed for now. In a few hours you shall be ready."

While Adrastea drank of the cold water, Lucea Herself suckled the child and murmured things to her that Adrastea couldn't hear.

Lucea breached the one subject that made Adrastea squirm. "We should speak of your husband."

Adrastea stiffened and turned away. "I don't wish to talk about him." If she faced the god, she'd break out crying.

Lucea let out a soft sigh. "I'm sorry your marriage didn't turn out for the better."

Adrastea, still kneeling by the Spring, wrapped her arms around herself. Hot tears spilled out her eyes into the cold water.

Lucea let her cry while She finished feeding Harianne. Her tummy full, the baby fell asleep. Lucea settled her down in the grass by the Spring before holding Her arms out to Adrastea.

Adrastea fell into Lucea's arms. Let the grief pour out of her. "Why did I agree to marry him?"

"You gave of yourself so that others would benefit." Lucea smoothed Adrastea's dark, curly hair. "It was a sacrifice. Sacrifices aren't easy. If they were, they wouldn't be real sacrifices."

Adrastea felt petulant. "But what about me? Can't I have what I want sometimes?" She pushed away from Lucea.

"Should your desires be considered greater than his?"

These words pricked at her soul. Hers had been the whine of selfishness. "I am sorry. I shouldn't have said that."

"Well?" the god asked. "What do you want?"

"I'm sick of him. I want to be free."

"So, say you were divorced from him and he bothered you no more. Then what? After that, what do you want?"

Adrastea unfolded her legs and placed her hands on her belly. "If I was healed, I could have had children of my own."

"You're thinking of others," Lucea replied, her tone patient. "Forget husbands. Forget children. You're on your own, out in the world. You wake up in the morning. What would you do?"

What would she do? What did she do before Mor-Lath? "I could see the world. I was trained as a healer. Ari made me journeyman. They used to travel, You know. I could do that.

"I know they make new discoveries all the time at the university in Feown—assuming that's still there." She frowned. "I really don't know much about what's happened since I was gone. I have a lot to catch up on."

"Yes," the god agreed. "The whole world has changed in fifteen years."

Almost half her life. "I'm..." she did some quick math. "I'm thirty-seven now?"

"Time and age don't mean much to an immortal."

Adrastea felt alone and left behind. "It does to me." Fifteen years was a long time to her. Fifteen years. There had been a war and who knows what else? The need to cry again tugged at her insides.

"That's in the past and you're in the present. And then there's your future to consider. Think upon that instead."

Adrastea had already taken the first step by coming back to Sacred Spring. Maybe she could live here, with Ari or with Uncle Natan and Mikal until she figured out what she would do with herself. Healing would be nice, especially with her talents, or—"

"Do you want to be a god?"

Lucea's question startled Adrastea. "What?" The question stirred memories of her recent argument with Mor-Lath and of last night. The thought of the passion they shared brought a blush to her cheeks before she could stuff it away. He'd tricked her. She wasn't too happy about it after the fact. She willed herself to think about the argument instead. The answer had been in the pain as well as the passion they shared.

Adrastea knew what it took to become a god—they had to give in to the other and share everything, not just passion and pain, but hopes and fears and thoughts and...

"No...?" she replied, hesitant and unsure. If she said yes, would Lucea have made her go back to him?

Why was She on his side anyhow?

Lucea shook her head. "I'm not on his side, not as you're thinking. I don't want the Dark to prevail. It's Mor-Lath I'm concerned about. After all, he was born a son of the Light and a natural mashiah. It's a shame how he's formed his destiny." Lucea sighed. "I am an optimistic creature. I keep hoping he'll change back to what he once was, even if that was a very, very long time ago. Well, maybe not change back, but change forward into something better than he is now.

"You will understand that feeling soon enough." Lucea looked over to the sleeping baby.

"Now," Lucea commanded Adrastea, "Stop whining. You sound like a petulant child.

"I must go now. Pilgrims come to visit the spring. Ere I go, I leave you with this: If he was a better person, a worthier husband, would you want to be a god?"

Adrastea's heart ached. That was cruel. How could She expect her to dwell on something like that? "He's not going to change just like that. Not him."

"Give him a chance. Consider this: for as long as you've known him, when he says he's going to do something, hasn't Mor-Lath accomplished it? He won your hand. Give him a chance to win your heart."

"What if I don't want to?"

"Then he shall have to work all the harder to win you over. He broke your heart; let him fix it.

"Now go visit Ari. She's missed you these long years. Let her know you're all right and that you've come to stay permanently."

Adrastea bowed her head. The god departed.

She was not terribly pleased with Lucea at the moment. Why was it so important to Her for Mor-Lath to succeed? It made no sense!

Chapter 3

Adrastea's feet touched down on the soil of the garden behind Ari's home. She dropped her bundle of clothing and patted the sleeping baby's bottom. The garden hadn't changed much since she last saw it. The familiarity wrapped around her like a warm, wet towel. The same old rosemary hedge, no higher than her waist, separated the garden from the house. Squares and triangles of plots ready for seedlings of food and medicines filled the spaces between the narrow walkways. Sunlight shone across the garden with promise of a lovely spring day. The scent of trimmed rosemary filled the air, mingling with newly-turned earth. Oh, she'd missed that scent. To her, it meant home.

Nearby, Ari Healer pulled early spring weeds ignorant of her former journeyman's arrival. Adrastea took a moment to study her one-time mistress and de-facto aunt. Ari had aged in the fifteen years. More silver than dark touched her hair. Her skin furrowed with the lines of experience. She toiled away in the garden, focused on nothing farther than her hands could reach.

"Hello, Ari."

Ari lifted her gaze and squinted against the light. She blinked before rising. Her fingers, dirt-crusted and gnarled, covered her mouth. "Adrastea?" she whispered.

Adrastea gave her a timid smile, unsure what to do with herself.

"Adrastea!" Ari shrieked. The older woman threw herself at her once-journeyman. Adrastea had barely enough time to turn sideways, otherwise Ari's enthusiastic hug might have crushed the baby. Still, Harianne squeaked as Ari hugged Adrastea tightly. "You're alive!"

Ari pulled back enough to shout back to the house. "Natan? Natan! Adrastea's back! Natan!"

A young woman on the cusp of adulthood stepped to the door of Ari's home. She looked at them, then popped back inside. Adrastea had only a glimpse of her. One of the Innkeeper brood? She wore the usual blouse and bodice. Instead of the full skirts Adrastea would have worn at her age, she wore the bloomers of current Feowan fashion, but no overskirt.

Ari was dressed the same way, only she had an apron over her clothes.

Adrastea shifted the baby out of the way and wrapped her arm around Ari, returning in earnest the hug. As the woman who raised her and loved her as much as any mother could, Ari's significance in Adrastea's life hit her hard. She returned fifteen years of hugs. "I missed you."

Tears streamed down Ari's wrinkled old face. "We thought you were gone forever. We thought he'd killed you. After you left, we didn't hear anything for years. We had no idea what happened to you." She sniffed and wiped her nose with her sleeve.

"I'm sorry, Ari. I promise I'll tell you everything."

Ari looked in Adrastea's eyes, then down at the newborn baby snuggled in the sling. "Oh," she uttered, laying a gentle hand to her own chest. "Did you—?"

"No," Adrastea hastened to answer. "She's adopted. I'm still quite barren."

Concern and maybe fear darkened Ari's face. "So, where is..."

Adrastea stiffened. Ari would have to bring up Mor-Lath. "I don't know, and I don't care. If he's smart, he'll not show his face here." She didn't mean to say it as sharply as she did.

Ari released Adrastea. "What happened?"

Before she could answer, another voice called her name. Uncle Natan, albeit looking older and plumper, appeared in the doorway to Ari's home.

"It is you," he crowed. "You're alive." He hobbled down the pathway, his movements ginger. The young woman who had peeked out before followed. As Natan slowed and she hurried to his side and took his arm. "Salle," he said to her, "run and get Mikal. Tell him to drop everything and come immediately."

"Okay." Salle eyed Adrastea curiously. She hurried around the house and out of sight.

Adrastea watched the retreating young woman. Salle? Salle Innkeeper? Little Salle?

Another girl, a bit younger than Salle, perhaps eleven or twelve, poked her head out of Ari's home. "Ari?"

Ari beckoned. "Come on, Bits." She took the baby from Adrastea and settled the sling around her own thin shoulders.

Bits wandered out, possessing no enthusiasm, just a mild curiosity.

Her uncle had reached Adrastea. He gathered her up in a great big bear hug, growl and all. "I thought we'd lost you for good!" Tears streamed down his craggy face.

Adrastea didn't know what to say to that.

Natan finally released her and set her down. "Where have you been?" He wiped at the moisture on his cheeks.

"I have been to hell and back. It wasn't a pretty journey."

A flash of gold on Natan's hand caught Adrastea's eye. Adrastea pointed to it. "Natan, what is that...?"

Natan proudly held out his hand. "It's a wedding band."

"But that's a Feowan custom." Nobody in Sacred Spring had bothered with such frivolity before. She looked between Ari and her uncle. "You two got married?"

Natan put his arm around Ari and beamed. "Ten years ago." Ari, too, sported a ring, in spite of the garden dirt that encrusted her hands.

"Ten! But what about being Mayor?"

Natan's smile faded a little. "Sometimes it's more important to take care of one person than it is a whole village." He wrapped both arms protectively around Ari.

Adrastea nodded. She understood that. Her gaze lingered on Harianne, still in Ari's arms.

"It's something I should have done many, many years ago." He looked at Ari and his smile returned. "So, my timing was bad. It all came good in the end."

Adrastea had a sudden memory of the taste of brandy.

Natan noticed the bundle in Ari's arms. "Oh, hello, you. Where did you come from?"

The girl Bits stood by, looking awkward at the adults' display of affection. "Ari, can I go now?"

"What?" replied Ari. "That's a small curiosity." To Adrastea she said, "This is Bitsy, Tam and Marta's youngest, and my apprentice. And Salle's my journeyman. The village is getting too big for one healer alone."

That lifted Adrastea's heart. "Is it big enough for three healers?"

Puzzlement crossed Ari's face. "You want to work while you're visiting?"

Adrastea began to fidget. "I'm not visiting. I'm here to stay for good."

Ari and Natan stared at her while Bitsy squirmed. "You can go back to the house, if you want," Adrastea said to Bitsy. She remembered what it was like being an apprentice.

Bitsy looked to Ari who nodded. Bitsy ran off.

Ari left Natan's embrace and came close to Adrastea, as if afraid of being overheard. "What do you mean you're here to stay for good?"

"I've come back," Adrastea said. "He and I... we need some space, though he might disagree. I'd have gotten a divorce if he'd agree to it, but he won't. Still, he knows better than to come bothering me."

"Uh..." began Natan, not sure what to say.

Then Adrastea remembered. "Oh, Ari, I'm sorry. I borrowed your big butcher knife and forgot to return it."

"What? The big one I lost a few weeks ago?"

Adrastea nodded.

"*You* borrowed that?" Ari's forehead creased. "Oh dear." She looked up at Natan. "I think I owe everyone an apology. Sorry."

Natan snorted and looked away as if insulted, clearly teasing Ari. "All right," he sighed with a dramatic roll of the eyes. "You're forgiven."

"Uh, why," said Ari to Adrastea, "did you borrow my butcher knife?"

"I needed something nasty at the moment. That was the scariest thing I could think of." She gave her head a scratch. "Even if I could find it, I don't know if you'd want it back."

"Why? What did you do with it?"

Adrastea grinned apologetically. "I'll tell you later. You'll like this story."

Natan uttered a noise. "You've got a lot of thing you say you'll tell us later."

Ari bounced the sleeping baby and stuck her finger in the infant's tiny fist. "She's an awfully good baby."

Adrastea shrugged. "She's been blessed by the Light. Anyhow, it's a big story I've got to tell you, too much for now. Maybe at dinner?"

"Oh, you're inviting yourself to dinner, are you?" asked Natan.

"Well," replied Adrastea, wringing her hands, "I don't have a place of my own to invite you to.

"And that's another thing. I'll need a place for us to stay, at least until

I can get a place of my own. Say, is—"

A man's voice, deep and urgent, called from inside the house. "Natan!" Everyone in the garden looked up. A moment later, "Ari?" Bitsy must have said something, for the voice cried out, "Oh!" The man burst out the back door, flying into the garden and hopping the rosemary hedge.

A small shock ran through Adrastea. For a moment, she saw her father again. She hadn't given his memory much reflection since the death of her mother. She didn't expect it to come back as sharply as it did.

As the man approached, his sharp eyes, creased with a frown, looked at Natan, then Ari, then finally settled on Adrastea. He studied her for a moment. A huge smile erased all his worry.

"Adrastea!" he shouted and enveloped her in a great big hug. Her tender breasts protested.

"Mikal?" she squeaked. Her brother had grown. He stood tall, almost as tall as Natan, though not as large. He tended closer to their father's slim build.

He released her and held her out at arm's length. "We thought you were never coming back!" And he hugged her again.

"I see you've met the Mayor," said Natan.

Bitsy came trailing out and watched the scene. Mikal called out to her. "Do me a favor. Find Jake and tell him to tell the strangers—nicely, of course—they'll have to wait." He smiled fondly at Adrastea. "Tell them I've had something very important crop up."

Bitsy rolled her eyes but did the Mayor's bidding. She clumped back through the house.

Mikal put his hand on Adrastea's head. "Look, I'm finally taller than you." His grin faded. "Say, where's that husband of yours?"

Adrastea wrinkled her nose. "Far away if he's smart. He's not in my good books at the moment."

Suddenly Mikal was not her excited brother but the concerned Mayor. His countenance changed in an instant. Watching him swap roles was like seeing him swap clothes. Natan had done that when he was Mayor. "He's not going to show up and cause trouble, is he?"

Adrastea wanted to tell him no, but she reflected on her husband's stubborn nature. She sank inside. Lucea was right. She knew Mor-Lath and his single-mindedness. He would pursue her here. Would he cause trouble for the village, for Mikal?

"Probably not," she hedged, wanting to cross her fingers, "but if he does, I'm more than capable of dealing with him. He won't be here for long. Anyhow, forget him. I'm trying to." She turned him towards Ari. "Look, I've adopted you a niece. Her name is Harianne."

Mikal leaned over with a soft expression on his face. "Ooh," he cooed at the baby. "She's so sweet. How long have you had her?"

"She can't be more than a few days old," Ari added.

"Born yesterday, actually," Adrastea admitted. "Her mother was injured when Feown was attacked—" Adrastea put her hand over her mouth. "Oh, you haven't heard. Feown was attacked by Avelia and—"

Mikal laid a hand on her shoulder. "We know. We got the news a little while ago."

Adrastea stared at him. "But how?"

Mikal returned her puzzled look. "Telegraph, of course. We've had a station for a few years now."

"Tele-graph?" Adrastea rolled the unfamiliar word around. Her head ached. Then she remembered. It didn't make much sense when she first heard of it from the priestesses, but then she also had her mind on other things. No doubt someone would explain later.

"Yeah. They're thinking of putting a rail spur through as well. It's mostly for the woodcutters up the canyon, but as it'll come past here, we'll put in a station."

Salle burst through the back door. She, too, leapt the rosemary hedge. Her footsteps slowed as she approached the Mayor. "I'm sorry, Mikal. He insisted on coming. I don't think he's too happy." She tried to catch her breath.

Bitsy dashed out of the house and backed up to the hedge, watching the door.

Two men came through the door. They approached the growing crowd out in Ari's garden. Their clothes said they were not country men. They were dark haired and bronze-skinned like most Feowans and might have been brothers.

"Aw, Bits," Mikal moaned.

Bitsy turned around and gave him the evil eye. "It's not my fault. They were already on their way here."

One of them pointed to Bitsy. "You, go make milord comfortable."

Bitsy folded her arms and looked to Ari. Adrastea could almost hear the unvoiced whine, *do I have to?*

Ari did nothing. She frowned at the men, then turned as if to protect the baby.

"It is not good to keep milord waiting," said one of the men. "He is an old man and—"

"And I do not have much time." The old man of whom they spoke came forth from Ari's door. He was stooped and required a cane to walk. White hair drifted on his head and his fine clothes hugged his body, as fine as a tailor could make them and keep within the sumptuary laws. His voice, once strong, wavered when he spoke. Yet the steel had not departed entirely. This was a man used to being obeyed.

A young woman, dressed in the height of Feowan fashion, helped him along the garden path.

Adrastea knew her; it was Dassie Pennexter. So intent was she on aiding the old man that the young woman did not notice Adrastea.

Mikal folded his arms. He was going to be stubborn. She didn't blame him. A cold feeling crystallized inside her as she put things together. Stick a priest's robe on him, give him less hair, and a slimmer build...

To give Mikal some time to think, Adrastea stepped forward. "I know you. Or, at least I know of you. You're Stobol Pennexter, head of House Pennexter. The priest Jonathan is your brother."

Dassie looked up in startlement, her young hands tightening on Lord Pennexter's arm. Her mouth gaped in surprise, then she grinned in delight at having recognized someone.

"I would have your name from your lips," he demanded of Adrastea.

Adrastea folded her arms. She gave a small shrug of her shoulders. He wouldn't get far with this sort of attitude.

Dassie saved her the problem of answering. She leaned over and whispered into Lord Pennexter's ear. "Oh. You're the village witch, then."

This surprised Adrastea. She looked to Dassie, a question in her eyes. Dassie cringed and offered a silent apology, then whispered again in Lord Pennexter's ear. Adrastea chose to forgive her. "Witch" was probably not the words she'd used. No doubt Lord Pennexter had been speaking with his brother as well.

Mikal cleared his throat. "She is not the village witch; she is my sister."

To Mikal he said, "Any other siblings I must know about?"

"No. Just us."

Lord Pennexter slumped in a moment of weakness. Dassie swooped to hold him up. The two men returned to his side and helped him. "Please, may I sit down?"

Perhaps the old man did have manners after all. Ari directed Salle to guide them back inside the house, to a comfortable chair and out of the sun.

Ari's house had changed much since she was here last. The table and the stove remained the same, but everything else was different. The curtains were different colours. The cupboard where Ari kept everything was gone.

Salle and Dassie helped Lord Pennexter into a chair. Ari gave him a small pillow for his back and went to put on the kettle. This familiar hospitable gesture comforted Adrastea.

Mikal sat down opposite Lord Pennexter. "Is your business so pressing that you must follow me here?"

Adrastea joined her brother. The old, familiar benches of her youth were gone. Nice, new chairs replaced them. The wicker creaked as Adrastea settled next to Mikal.

Lord Pennexter replied with a question of his own. "Is your business here more pressing than mine?"

At first, Mikal didn't understand. Then he let an amused smile play his lips. "If you knew my business, then you would certainly agree it was." Under the table, his hand sought Adrastea's knee. He gave it a squeeze. Adrastea slipped her hand under the table and gripped her brother's hand. Oh, she missed him! And here he was, Mayor of Sacred Spring.

Lord Pennexter presented Mikal with a painted miniature of a dark-haired young man. "You did not properly answer my original question."

Mikal took the picture and handed it straight to Adrastea.

Adrastea's world spun. Mikal, was her first impression. But then the eyes were different, as was the mouth. Sorrow for a lost parent welled in her heart and threatened to spill out her eyes. This is what the portrait told her.

"This," Mikal explained, "Is a portrait of Lord Pennexter's son Josephus. He set out west a long time ago and never came back. All he left was a note saying 'Goodbye'. Since then, no letter, no messages, nothing."

"I must find him," Lord Pennexter said. He leaned across the table, longing and desperation making him abandon his dignity.

"Our father was named Joe," Adrastea said. "But everyone knew him as Joe Weaver. If his real name was Josephus, none of us ever knew." She looked to her uncle. "Uncle Natan, would you know?"

Mikal tapped her leg. "I was looking it up in the book when Salle came with your news."

Lord Pennexter clasped his hands on the table and looked at the two before him. "You say 'was'. Is my son dead?"

Both Adrastea and Mikal drew breath at the same time. She glanced at her brother. He returned her gaze. "If our father," said Adrastea, "is the same as your son, then yes, he's dead. I'm sorry."

The mask of a lord fell away, leaving a sad little old man behind. He stared past them, his brown eyes growing soft with tears. He cried, unashamed, with soft little sobs and years of grief. Dassie laid a hand on his shoulder and didn't know where to look.

Adrastea's hand stole to Mikal's under the table. They sat there, not sure what to say. Ari shooed Bitsy and Salle out to the still room while Natan strongly suggested to the two men that they step out for some fresh air. That left the four family members together to experience their awkward grief in private.

Lord Pennexter did not hide his face but turned it heavenwards.

Adrastea wondered. Had her father gone to the Light? Her mother had. Surely, she would have known, possibly have even met him, had he not.

Dassie clasped her hands tightly and looked away. Mikal sat, as awkward as Dassie. Mikal couldn't remember his father. He let Adrastea hug him.

Adrastea remembered. Joe was the first person in her life to die. She remembered missing him terribly, and then the pain faded as it so often does for the young. Her mother, on the other hand, never forgot. Her father must have been some kind of wonderful for a wife to grieve so and for a parent to search for him now.

The kettle whistled. Adrastea rose to make tea. Ari peeked out briefly from the stillroom, then closed the door softly when she saw her former journeyman had matters in hand.

The cupboard was gone, but a few items remained on the little table that took its place. Adrastea recognized the old tea canister. The teapot and the honey pot were different. Teacups hung on pegs imbedded in the wall.

Soon everyone at the table had a nice hot cup of tea. Dassie helped Lord Pennexter drink his.

"So, tell me," he said after he'd managed a few sips, "when did my son die?"

"About ten— no, um..." Adrastea paused. The fifteen years she was gone didn't feel like fifteen. She did some quick calculations. "It must be nearly thirty years."

"So long? Small wonder we never heard from him." His voice grew low and husky. "And we thought he didn't want to..." The grief washed over him, thick and palpable. All Adrastea could do was cling to Mikal's hand. Dassie squirmed and looked somewhere other than Lord Pennexter or her newfound cousins.

When he could speak again, Lord Pennexter asked, "How did he die? He would have been rather young."

Mikal looked to Adrastea. "He was ill. I don't know anything other than that. We were only children." She nodded her head to her brother. "But it tore our mother apart. She was never the same again."

Now Mikal looked away.

"Could... could I speak with your mother?"

"No," replied Adrastea. "She's dead too, these fifteen years."

"Oh." Lord Pennexter looked down at his folded hands. They shook. Was that because of his sorrow or simply because he was old?

"I was hoping your father still lived, that he would have returned." He looked up at Mikal. "You might be the next best thing. Lord Mayor, I've forgotten your name."

Her brother straightened. "It's Mikal."

The old man nodded his head in approval. "Mikal Pennexter. It'll do."

Mikal shook his head. "No, Mikal Mayor."

But Lord Pennexter wouldn't have it. "You're the son of a nobleman."

A small shock rolled through Adrastea. A nobleman. Their father? Of course. Did Mor-Lath know this?

"Noble blood runs in your veins. You're not a simple country lad. I wouldn't have my grandson behave as such."

Mikal released Adrastea's hand. He rose to his feet. "Now see here, old man. Until thirty minutes ago we didn't even know you existed. Now you expect us to play the country hick and be all delighted in our gratitude that you bothered to come condescend to us poor relations? If you cared so much, why didn't you come seeking us before? Even five years before. Why wait so long?"

A blue vein stood out on Lord Pennexter's forehead. "Because I didn't have any idea you existed! How could I? Your father was a priest of the Light! They don't marry, and they certainly don't have children."

Brother and sister gaped at their grandfather as he delivered this revelation. "He was what?" they said together. First a nobleman...

"You heard me. He was a priest. It was his duty. If the family was to survive, one child of every generation was to be dedicated to the Light." He slumped back in his chair. His words exhausted him.

"But why?" If this was so, it would explain Jonathan.

Dassie, who had been quiet all this time spoke up. "Because of a covenant one of our ancestors made a long time ago."

Lord Pennexter put a hand to his mouth as if to hold back his bitterness. "But it seems that my son has broken that covenant. He forsook his priesthood and took a country wife."

Mikal sank back to his seat, but Adrastea rose up. "Our father was a good man. He loved our mother and we're proof of that. He did everything he could to protect her and us, even after he died..." Adrastea's throat choked up at the mention of her mother. "His protection lasted up to her death."

"Hmm," mused Lord Pennexter. "And don't think I don't know about you, Adrastea. I've heard many stories about you. It took me a while to piece things together, but I know about you. The name, the face, your talents. You've cursed the family, haven't you?"

Adrastea leaned back, alarmed. "What? What do you mean?"

He shook his finger at her. "Oh, you look young, but I wager you're older than you appear. This is the Dark side, isn't it?"

Adrastea drew in a breath. "You know nothing."

"I know you're a Dark priestess, a witch. I've heard tales of you consorting with the Dark One himself. You're the same Country Adrastea that confronted my brother fifteen years ago."

Mikal scooted around to look at his sister. "Ad, is this true?" His voice was more curious than shocked.

She crossed her arms. Her breasts ached. "I wasn't doing anything wrong," she told Mikal. "I was helping Her Grace, nothing more. It was just after—" She rose from her chair and turned away from them all. "I was only healing her. She'd been tortured, hurt."

She heard a baby cry. A burst of pain like hot needles ran through her breasts as it triggered letdown. Milky wetness soaked through the front of her shirt. "Oh, look what—" She pulled her arms tighter around her. "Look," she spat at them all. "I'm not a bloody witch. I'll thank you kindly to not speak of the Dark again. I'm just a simple country woman who plans on living a simple country life. And now, if you'll excuse me, I've got a baby to feed."

She stormed out of the kitchen into the stillroom. Before the door closed, she heard Dassie ask, softly but not too soft she couldn't hear: "What's wrong with her?"

Mikal's reply: "She just got out of a bad marriage."

Adrastea hoped Mikal had enough sense to keep the details of that to himself. Lord Pennexter didn't really need to know just how far his family connections went; he might tell his brother Jonathan.

Adrastea found Ari trying to soothe the hungry baby in the stillroom. Salle poked at the small stove, to stir up the fire. Bitsy returned from the cellar with a bottle of milk.

"Don't bother," Adrastea said as she waved Bitsy back. "I'm capable of feeding her."

That surprised Ari. "Can you? How?"

"Gift of the Light." Adrastea settled herself and Harianne into the nearest chair. She bared her breast, then fumbled with the baby. Ari nodded to Bitsy to take the milk back.

As Bitsy had returned to the cellar, Ari turned to Salle. "Could you pop out and get some fresh water from the pump outside, dear? She'll be thirsty." After her journeyman left, Ari said to Adrastea, "First time?"

"Yeah," Adrastea admitted. She stopped and remembered. In the course of her healer career, she'd shown the occasional new mother how to latch on a baby and give it suck. She'd forgotten.

Soon Arianne was feeding happily. It took a while later until the needlepricking pain of letdown eased up. "Does it have to hurt like that?" Not that Adrastea minded. The physical pain distracted her from the pain in her soul. Just how much did Lord Pennexter know about her? What facts, what fictions, had he gathered? How much did Jonathan know?

"It'll stop hurting. You'll get used to it." Ari fetched a cup. "Might even like it, eventually. Most mothers do."

Salle soon returned and Bitsy dawdled up from the cellar. Ari dipped a cup in Salle's bucket of cool water and held it for Adrastea to drink.

Adrastea was thirstier than she thought.

Ari pulled up a chair. "Now, where have you been for fifteen years?"

Adrastea glanced at Bitsy and Salle. "It's not a tale for children."

Salle let out a squeak of indignation. "I'm not a child."

"She is," replied Adrastea, indicating Bitsy.

The younger apprentice protested. "But I want to hear the story."

"Elissabit," replied Ari. "You will get the tale later. I need to know the details now. Take the afternoon off and go hang around with your cousins."

Bitsy whined a bit more but Ari brought her up sharply. "If I hear you complain about getting free time off, I'll not give any to you ever again."

Bitsy wasn't stupid. She quickly assessed the situation, weighed her options and left. Adrastea looked at Salle, who remained. "If you stay, you're sworn to secrecy."

"Okay." Salle straddled a chair, eager for a good story.

There was that word again. Was it a form of agreement?

"So," said Ari. "Start from the beginning. Last time I saw you was fifteen years ago. You left here, having decided you were going to confront him. So what happened?"

"The whole village doesn't need to know. I will tell Mikal and Natan myself."

She related her story to them, of how she, in her anger, went and killed all the other women who had had sexual relations with her husband. Salle didn't dare breathe. Ari only shook her head. "Oh, Adrastea..."

"I'm sorry." Adrastea's head began to ache. "I was just so angry. I have much I needed to repent of.

"The last must have been a favorite, for he had shown up just in time to watch her die." In turn, he punished Adrastea by banishing her.

Salle, who had been listening the whole time with her hands over her mouth, gasped. "He damned you to Dom-al-gol?"

Adrastea nodded. "And I was there for fifteen years."

Ari looked pale. "Couldn't you have done anything?"

Harianne drained one side, so Adrastea adjusted her to the other. Once she was latched on—and it took a few tries—Adrastea continued her story. "You have to understand that time moves differently in Dom-al-gol. You really don't know how long things take.

"So yes, he may have put me there, but I got myself out as soon as I could." Her voice dropped. "I'm sorry it was fifteen years. I had no idea."

Ari didn't move but waited for her to finish the tale.

"When I returned, I was so furious I tried to kill him as well."

Salle squeaked. "You killed him!"

Adrastea shook her head. "Only a mashiah can kill a god. I'm not a mashiah."

"So, find one."

Both Ari and Adrastea stared at Salle after her bold statement. Salle looked from one to the other. "Wouldn't that be the best solution to the problem?"

Adrastea agreed. "But the problem with mashiahs is he finds them before they're capable of killing him and he kills them first."

Salle's jaw dropped. "There is a lot of death where he is concerned."

Adrastea watched the young woman. Lucky her, with her simple life. She wished for her old life before she met the God of the Dark. "Am I any different? I've killed so many people, some of them for reasons I—" She shook her head. No good dwelling on things she couldn't fix.

She continued her story, relating how she'd pinned him to the table with Ari's knife. "I'll get you a new one as soon as I'm re-established." She spoke of how he'd tricked her into releasing him (though not every detail). "He's lied to me, he's betrayed me, and he's done pretty much everything a man could do to a woman, short of killing me.

"That, he refuses to do, because he needs me. So now he's promising to be a better husband."

Ari sniffed. "Certainly couldn't be a worse one."

"Will keep his promise?" Salle asked.

A nag of doubt chewed at Adrastea's insides. "Just... just let me deal with one thing at a time."

The stillroom door opened. Mikal and Natan came in. Lord Pennexter was not with them. "I've sent him back to the inn," Mikal said. He put his hand to his forehead. "I'm afraid he's not going to leave without getting the answer he wants."

He looked to his sister. "Adrastea, could I—" Then he saw her dishabille while she nursed. He shaded his eyes. "Oh, sorry."

"S'alright." She pulled herself together one-handed. "I'm almost done."

Natan leaned against the big stone bench, casually looking somewhere else. Mikal turned around completely and continued his conversation. "I was going to say we need to go somewhere and talk alone. Lord Pennexter's gone back to the inn. He's... the strain of travel, of us, of everything is a bit much for a man his age."

Adrastea nodded. "That reminds me; I'm gonna need a place to stay. Ari looks like she's full up."

"Oh," Mikal replied, still turned away. "Oh, that is a problem. The inn's full. Has been the past few days. I wish you could stay with me, but I don't have the room and Jacob's up in the loft."

Harianne fell asleep nursing, so Adrastea eased her off the nipple. Ari took the baby while Adrastea put herself back together. "Okay, you can look now."

Mikal turned around with relief.

"I was thinking, Mikal, of staying in mother's old house."

"You can't. I've rented that out."

Adrastea's hands fell from the buttons of her blouse. "Rented it? To who?"

"A weaver couple from Crossroads. They've been there for years. They tend to keep to themselves—not terribly social pair. But they pay their rent regular." Mikal scrubbed his hands through his hair. "You didn't think I'd let it sit empty, especially if we didn't know if you were ever coming back.

"Anyhow, let's go for a walk." He held out the crook of his elbow. Adrastea rose and took it. She held it snugly, hoping to draw strength from her grown-up brother.

Together, they left the stillroom, with Ari's promise that the baby would be all right in her care. "You've got much to catch up on."

Adrastea sighed. "Lord Pennexter," she started without preamble. "What are we going to do about him?"

Mikal patted her arm. "Let us talk about that later. I've got a few things I need to think about first." Adrastea caught the glimmer of the mayorial mask. "I need to know about you for now."

Mikal took her out to the front and brought her through the village. Change was rampant. The village commons out front of Ari's house, where wild grass and the occasional tree once grew, was gone. Houses of one and two stories stood there, with small yards and fences.

"Where's the creek?" she asked.

"Oh, that. We channeled it underground and put it through pipes to everyone's house here in the village." He pointed up the hill, towards where their mother's house stood. "Up there, they had to bring their own pipe around." Mikal pointed back down to the north, where Adrastea could barely see the Taylor's house. "It eventually comes out way out there. There's a few new families who know what to do with such waste water. They make some sort of fertilizer out of it."

But Adrastea wasn't looking where he pointed. Her gaze was still up the hill towards her mother's house. The trees were gone. No other buildings inhabited the hill between the village and there, so she could see clearly. Her mother's house, from this distance, looked the same as it ever was. Behind it, where she remembered the Little Crossroads cabins, there were better dwellings, larger and more permanent. "How big is the village now?"

Mikal thought for a moment. "Oh, a good four hundred souls, give or take. We have some families that come in during the summer season then move back to Crossroads during the winter.

"Oh, Crossroads is huge now. You should see it." He seemed as proud of that town as he was his own village. "They've got the rail line through and the road 'tween here and there's been paved mostly, and they've completely rebuilt it and it's much bigger than before. Ely's still the mayor and he and I get together all the time and..." He looked at his sister who stared up the hill. "I'm sorry. I'm boring you."

She broke from her reverie. "Oh, no. Please. Tell me everything. I was gone for so long that I really have no idea what the world is like now." Her gaze returned to her mother's house. "Can we go see that?"

Mikal looked up. He nodded. They crossed the street and went up what Adrastea had known as the back way. There was a road now instead of a trail, cut into the hill and zigging and zagging. While they hiked up the hill, she related her story to him pretty much as she'd shared it with Ari and Salle. He listened quietly, taking in every word. At the end, he asked, "Is he going to show up here?"

Adrastea sighed. "I told him not to. Not that he would listen to me." She laid her free hand on Mikal's arm. "Believe me, if he does show up, I am more than capable of taking care of him."

Mikal let out a chuckle of astonishment. "Well, if you can pin him to a table with a butcher knife, I'm not going to have to worry about you. Just..."

"What?"

Mikal was silent for a moment. "I worry about everyone else in the village."

Adrastea hadn't thought of that. "You think he'll do the same thing he did in the early days?"

"Threaten us? He's done it before. I don't see why he couldn't do it again if it means it'll help him get what he wants."

Adrastea considered this. True, she had thought of this before, when choosing where to go to. "I have to live somewhere," she explained to Mikal. "I can't stay at the Temple. If he's going to threaten those around me, I thought it best that it be people who've dealt with him before. Besides, back then I was helpless. I'm not exactly helpless now."

"That doesn't reassure me."

Adrastea sighed. Mikal may have been her brother, but he was also

Mayor. His first allegiance was to Sacred Spring. "He doesn't dare offend me now. Sacred Spring is safe because I am here."

"Mmh," was all he said.

They reached the top of the hill and followed the road that led to what was once Lillybet's house. They passed copses of quakies. The gentle morning breeze set their leaves shimmering like the susurrus of soft rain on the roof. "Oh, I missed that sound," she said. "I've missed everything. I'm so glad to be back home."

Mikal didn't say anything. They stopped at the fence before the house. It was new, a properly-constructed picket fence, not the rough-hewn log fence Adrastea remembered. The house was whitewashed, the door was different, and the windows had glass, but it was the same house.

Adrastea opened the gate and approached the porch. She remembered everything that happened here, from early childhood memories to Mor-Lath's courtship. Her eyes flickered to a corner of the porch. He'd kissed her there and she hadn't refused him.

She pushed those thoughts out of her head. Why is it if she had a weakness it would be that one? Why couldn't she not-want to be loved?

Instead she closed her eyes and focused on whatever other faint traces of the Deeper Power were there.

She found them. Very weak, no more than memories, really, but they were there. She recognized them. They were the remains of her father's work. He'd been a priest, if Lord Pennexter could be believed. A priest who'd run away from Feown and came here. A priest who went against his vows, fell in love and remained for the rest of his life. In his traces she felt his love. She felt more than just that. She felt his very essence, still here after decades.

Why is that? she asked Creation. Creation gave her a thorough answer. Adrastea learned more about her father in that moment than she had in a lifetime.

Her eyes flew open. "I know how our father died."

Adrastea came away from the house. "He was Josephus Pennexter, of that I am sure. He was a priest of the Light." She closed the gate behind her. Things she remembered reading came up out of her memory and she shared them with her brother. "See, priests of the Light believe they are subject to the Light and to Creation, to serve and do Their will. They can call upon the Deeper Power as need be, to serve Their—the Light's—purpose. They aren't supposed to call upon it for personal gain.

"The Dark, on the other hand, have no compunction against pulling whatever Lines of Creation are available to them.

"And that's the difference. Our father, being a Light priest, didn't want to work against Creation by calling upon Creation's Deeper Power, so he called upon it from within himself. He used himself to cast protection upon this house and who knows what else." Adrastea sagged against the fence. It creaked against her weight but did not give entirely. "He did it to protect our mother and us." Her throat tightened. "He knew of the demons that haunted her—probably could see them. He tried to protect her. In doing so, by pulling from his own life force, it weakened him so much that when he fell sick, he couldn't fight it off and he died." Adrastea slid to the ground. "I never knew."

"Oh." Mikal stood there, not sure what to do with his hands, so he clenched them, then tried to put them in the pants pockets he didn't have. "But it didn't do any good in the end."

"He tied the protection of the house to our mother as well. That lasted as long as she was alive."

"Shame he didn't tie it to us as well."

Adrastea shrugged. Her fingers played with the tall grass that grew next to the fence. "It's in the past. There's nothing we can do about it."

Mikal finally settled on folding his arms. "You going to tell Lord Pennexter?"

Adrastea shrugged again. "Dunno. Don't know if I care. So what if our long-lost grandfather, one we didn't know about, suddenly shows up to find us, but not his son?" She looked up at her brother, whose dark hair was framed by the halo of golden sunlight glinting off it.

His forehead creased in thought. "There's more going on here than Lord Pennexter coming to find a missing heir. For instance, how did he know to look here? How did he know about you?"

She sighed and heaved herself to her feet, brushing stray grass seeds from her skirt and pantaloons. "Fifteen years ago, I met Lord Pennexter's brother Jonathan. He's a priest of the Light and advisor to Her Grace."

"Who? The Duchess of Feown?"

Adrastea nodded.

"Did you meet her too?"

Again, she nodded. "It wasn't under the best of circumstances. I don't know if she's that favorably disposed to us—me." Adrastea mused. Saraym wasn't terribly pleased to see them earlier. Adrastea was tempted to quit herself of any affair outside of Sacred Spring.

Mikal let the subject drop. He had more pressing matters to mind. "While you were in the stillroom, I spoke further with Lord Pennexter. He's come seeking his heir."

"Why?" She took his arm. They walked away from the house they'd been born in.

"His only son is dead. We're the only living grandchildren."

"So, what about Dassie?"

"Grandchild of his sister."

"Well, why not her?" If Adrastea had to select an heir for Lord Pennexter, she would have said Dassie.

"Because he's a stubborn and old-fashioned man. Can you believe he wants a male heir?"

Adrastea shook her head. "But that's stupid. Lady Pen before him was a woman."

Mikal stopped. "Who?"

Oh, those stupid fifteen years! "Lady Adrastea Pennexter was head of House Pennexter before him. I never met her, but I heard stories."

"Another Adrastea?"

Adrastea lifted her shoulders. "It's a family name. Young Dassie there is also an Adrastea. Oh." A bit of trivia floated to the surface of her memory. "The Pennexters weren't always nobility. They started out a merchant family. When they had vast wealth, they married impoverished nobility. The nobility stopped being impoverished and the Pennexters gained noble titles."

Mikal took all this in. He weighed it. "I still don't want to be his heir. I'm happy enough being mayor."

They came to the head of the road leading down the mountain.

Adrastea looked over the village. "Where's the smithy?"

The smithy, once one of the tallest and sturdiest buildings on Sacred Spring, was gone. Another building, smaller, yet not too small, stood in its place. It was no smithy.

"Oh yeah. During the battle when you— well, when you got married..."

"Battle day, wedding day... same thing," Adrastea snarked.

"Well, that day, the smithy had taken quite a beating. Oh, it withstood it, mostly. Nobody inside was killed, but something knocked the forge's chimney about, so when Peter Smith refired it up a week later, the smithy burned to the ground. We had a bucket brigade, 'cause the tank hadn't been replaced, but it wasn't enough.

"They rebuilt the smithy that way." He pointed south. "They're closer to the creek and have a ready water supply. That's also where we diverted the creek underground and piped water to everyone. We've got it going through privies, so everything gets washed away into the sewers. It's one of the war inventions."

"I missed the war. You'll have to tell me more later." She pointed to the new building where the old smithy had stood. "First, whose house is that?" It was extremely fancy, unlike the other village homes.

Mikal chuckled. "That's the house of the Light."

Adrastea gave him a funny look.

"It's a church."

Adrastea blushed. She should have known.

Across the street from the church was the Inn. It looked very much like it always had, three stories, weathered boards, broad porch. A large-bosomed woman leaned out a window and shook a blanket out. Dust, crumbs and curses came flying out that window.

Adrastea made the mistake of looking up. "That's not Marta."

Mikal tried to hurry her along. "That's Martine."

But it was too late. Adrastea's eyes met Martine's. They stared at each other for a moment before Adrastea was hurried along by her brother.

"Good morning to you, Mayor!" Martine called out. By her tone, Adrastea could tell she was provoking Mikal. "I do hope you'll drop by later."

Mikal did not stop but raised a hand in acknowledgement. "Oh dear," he muttered to his sister. "What are the odds she's recognized you?"

"Very good. Listen, if you didn't want anyone recognizing me, then why did you take me for a walk of the village?"

Mikal's footsteps slowed, to Adrastea's relief. She was at a near trot trying to keep up with him. "Fair enough. If it was anyone else, that would have been fine. But Martine's tongue is becoming as sharp as her mother's, although she's not as bad tempered. She does, however, keep tabs on what happens in the village. Sometimes that's useful, other times it's a nuisance."

Adrastea glanced over her shoulder. Martine remained at the window, albeit inside, watching them depart. "She's not going to create trouble, is she?"

"Nah. But I know my si— um, Martine. She'll want answers. She'll nag me until she gets them."

"Maybe it's better I don't stay at the inn."

Mikal looked at her. "Why would you stay at the Inn?"

"I've got to have some place to stay until I can find more permanent lodgings."

Mikal nodded. "So, you are planning on staying permanently? You really have left him, have you?"

"Mm hmm."

"Hmm..." Mikal replied.

Adrastea hadn't convinced him. This was not the boy she saw last. This was a man, a Mayor, who'd learned to think deeply and keep his own council when he saw fit. He was used to looking at a problem from all angles and looking ahead to the future.

What tact to take with him? "Assuming I do stay and live a perfectly dull country life for the rest of... well, whenever, where could I live?"

They stopped outside Ari and Natan's home. "Remember the old Poulter place behind my—the mayor's—house?"

"Oh no." She remembered it too clearly. Too many deaths. "I do not want to live there."

Mikal waved his hand dismissively. "No, no. The Constables live there now. But remember the lower property where the chickens were kept? The cottage's gone, but the lot's vacant. I might be able to convince the Constables to sell it to you. I assume, that is," he stuttered awkwardly, "assuming you have money?"

"Oh." Gods did not have much need of money. "I have fine jewelry, if they're willing to take that in trade. But that's about it, really."

"I see. Well, they'd prefer money, but I'll see what we can do."

Adrastea thought about it. "I could sell some of the jewelry. It's not like I'm attached to it."

Mikal shook his head. "I doubt you'd find a buyer here. You'd have to go to Crossroads."

She gave him a pointed look. "I'm the Bride of the Dark. Distance doesn't mean much to me."

He stared at her, pondering. "I'd forgotten about that. I mean, it's silly, but sometimes I look at you, and all I see is my sister."

"Even if you haven't seen me for fifteen years?"

"It's as if you've never been gone. Well," he conceded, "You don't look quite the same. There's a hardness behind your eyes. But I hear your voice and it's..." He shrugged. "I just hope things work out here. I'm not looking forward to having my village threatened again."

Guilt blossomed within her. She had returned with some heavy baggage, but in the whole wide world, there wasn't anywhere else she wanted to be. This place sang 'home' to her. Mor-Lath had taken her away from it once; he would never do so again. She gave her brother a spontaneous hug. "I promise I'll keep him away. But please, let me stay."

He didn't respond right away. He accepted his sister's hug and held her for a moment while he thought.

"All right," he said eventually. "You can stay for the meantime. You can sleep at my place until we can find something better. I'll even pull out the trundle bed."

"You mean, a place of my own?"

He gave in with a sigh. "Yes, a place of your own. As soon as possible. I grew up with babies in the house. That was enough to know I value my peace."

She hugged him tightly.

"So," he said, "all you've got to do is secure some property and build a house."

Adrastea smiled at him. "That won't be a problem."

As the sun set in the west, Mor-Lath moved through the Avelian army, still cowled in brown. In his hand he clutched a plainly-worded telegram, encrypted, as legitimate telegrams would be.

The army occupied the southern fields of Feown, having oppressed the villages and towns between their lands and here.

The tent of the Avelian general was easy to spot, for all its ostentation. No doubt while all the lower soldiers were picking at their meager rations, the general and his colonels would be dining well.

Meanwhile, a captain and a lieutenant sat in a smaller tent, smelling the dinner they wouldn't get to sample.

Mor-Lath popped into the tent. "Telegram," he announced, handing it to the lieutenant. The lieutenant, a scrawny, fussy officer, scowled at the brown-robed figure. "Since when does a priest run telegrams?"

"Since he drew the short straw."

The captain couldn't be bothered to rise from his camp chair.

"Where's it from?"

Mor-Lath shrugged. "Priests don't get told where they come from, only where they are going."

"Yeah, all right." The captain settled back. "Well, Lieutenant? What's it say?"

The lieutenant had opened it and scowled at the encryption. It'd take him a while to decode it.

"Think you can get it done just before the end of dinner?"

"Why?" The lieutenant sniffed, his thin nose waggling back and forth.

A huge grin spread across the captain's face. "Here's a trick I learned a long time ago. If we take it to the General just as he's finished eating, then when we mingle with the corporals who come to clear the plates away, we can snag something nice to eat. You like that idea?"

The lieutenant lifted an eyebrow. He got to work decoding the telegram. So busy was he at his work, he didn't notice the cowled figure slip away. In the end, the captain slipped off to deliver orders straight from Avelia advising him to hold for the night and await new orders in the morning.

As the general read the decoded message, he did not notice his half-full plate being whisked away. Instead, his focus and his fury dwelt on the telegram being crushed in his hand. "Wasson is a fool," he declared. To his colonels, he said, "Carry on as planned."

Outside the tent, Mor-Lath sighed. He'd tried the easy way. Ah well. It's a shame all the Avelian gunpowder would be terribly damp and unlightable that night. And if the general insisted on doing things his way, maybe all the barrels of the rifles and the cannons would melt. Or maybe a plague of fleas would distract the soldiers.

Anything, to slow the army until the real news from Avelia reached them.

Then things would change.

Chapter 4

That evening, while Ari and her apprentices prepared a special family dinner, Adrastea sat in the darkened stillroom and nursed Harianne until she fell asleep. The letdown still stung but once the milk was flowing, nursing was quite pleasant. Also, it was better not to stroke the soft cheek of her child while she fed. Babies turned towards touch and away from the nipple, sometimes without releasing the nipple. Not a preferred action on the mother's part.

She listened to the laughter in the other room. Mikal recounted his day's adventures with Adrastea to Salle and Bitsy. After he'd negotiated a purchase price with the Constables for the property she wanted, she'd taken him to Crossroads to trade some of the jewelry for sufficient money. Adrastea acquired a few needful things for the baby before she whisked Mikal away in the manner of immortals to the woodcutters up the canyon for building supplies.

Mikal had nearly thrown up the first time she'd relocated him. He swore he'd never get used to traveling like that.

At least he'd gotten a laugh out of her bargaining with the woodsmen. Now he shared the joke with the others: "So she says to them, 'How much wood does he chop when his hand isn't injured?' They told her, 'Fifteen cords a day.'

"Now, I'm pretty sure they were exaggerating. Adrastea knew it. But she wasn't going to pay the exorbitant price they named, and she couldn't get them to bargain down. She never was one for 'woe is me' stories.

"'So how long will he be out of work?' she asked. They told her about three weeks. She does some quick thinking and says, 'So that's about two hundred cords, more or less? I only need fifty cords.'"

Someone exclaimed over that amount. How big a house was Adrastea planning?

She knew—something bigger than her mother's house, but not quite as big as Ari's. Double-stories. Harianne would have her own room, when she was old enough. No loft for her.

Harianne had fallen asleep and fallen off the nipple. Adrastea tucked herself together and cuddled the sleeping baby for a while longer.

Mikal continued his story. "So, she says, 'If I can heal him so he can return to work tomorrow, would you give me the fifty cords of wood?' Well, they laughed and said yes." Mikal laughed himself. "If only they knew."

"So, what did she do?" It sounded like Salle.

"She took the man's hand and healed it just like that." Mikal snapped his fingers. "Well, they were quite astonished. They all put their heads together. Then they came back and told her she could have as much wood as she could carry away with her own two hands. So, she agreed, picked out the best fifty cords of wood they had there, and magically sent it all away to here. Then, while they all stood there and gawped, she said, 'Thank you. Please call on me again if you need healing.' Then one of them said, 'I don't think we'll bother. We can't afford you.'"

Everyone broke into laughter. It was nice to hear everyone enjoying the story. Adrastea clung to that tiny piece of normality. Perhaps she could belong to this place she called home once more.

Adrastea's arms ached. She placed Harianne in the little box Ari had lined with blankets.

Now free, she moved to the far door of the stillroom, looking out into the garden.

Ari was out there, with a lantern, picking herbs for dinner. To her left, Adrastea saw the kitchen door open, spreading a warm glow of light out to the rosemary hedge. Natan came out, closed the door behind him and made his way to Ari.

Adrastea watched them in the gloom, little more than silhouettes against the lamplight under the starry night. Natan's hand touched Ari's shoulder. He stroked her cheek. They murmured something together that Adrastea couldn't hear. She didn't want to hear what they said. That belonged to them.

Her heart ached as she watched them. They had always loved each other, even when it seemed impossible to be together. Their separation caused Ari grief the whole time Natan was Mayor. In the end, it worked out. Did Ari grieve she never had children? She had felt that pang in her own heart, one only erased with Harianne.

Still, she yearned for someone to love her the way uncle Natan loved Ari. Her heart wrenched when she thought that she would never know such love.

"Well," said a familiar voice next to her, "I see you've found your long-lost grandfather."

Adrastea jumped. Her face burned in embarrassment. She didn't want Mor-Lath to see her pining.

She grabbed the front of his black shirt and whisked him away to the first place she thought of—the temple at the sacred spring. She'd promised Mikal the Dark God wouldn't cause trouble if she could help it.

An anger born of her loneliness erupted within her. She slammed him into the granite column. "Ow!" he complained. "What was that for?"

"Because I hate you," she shrilled at him. "I hate you because you've ruined everything I've ever wanted. I never asked to be your wife. I never wanted to be a—" she hesitated. A god? That wasn't quite true. Ever since the Light had suggested the possibility, it sat in the back of her head. Oh, how different it could have been to be a benevolent god like the Light, to bless mankind and bring them to joy.

She'd never have that with Mor-Lath. There were a lot of things she wouldn't have with him. Her hand went to her cheeks. She saw how Natan touched Ari. It was gentle and loving. Where was the man who could love her that much? Who would hold her every night and promise that he'd be there for the rest of his life? She felt the lines her husband had seared into her flesh.

"I told you to stay away from me." She jabbed a finger into his chest to emphasize her point. "I want nothing more to do with you. And you couldn't even stay away a day."

His hand closed over her finger, enveloping her hand in his. "Well, now, my Bride. You didn't think I'd truly stay away once I realized you'd discovered the secret to godhood, did you?" A pleased smile lit his face. There was something predatory in his eyes.

Adrastea's newly-erupted fear chased away her anger. "What do you mean?" She took an involuntary step back.

He advanced. "Do the words, '*so that's what it is*,' mean anything to you?"

She stopped herself from taking another step. She had to stand her ground, even if it meant his nose touched hers. She had no reason to be afraid of him. She put her other hand up to push him away, but he captured that as well, bringing them close to his chest.

"I don't know what you're talking about," she protested, her voice higher than usual.

"Oh, yes you do. I felt something click in you." His thumbs stroked the back of her hands. "You realized something very, very important. There is only one thing I know of that would be more important to you than anything else, even your own life. You said you wanted me to be miserable with the secret just out of reach. And then I realized you'd figured it out."

"And it took you a whole day to realize this?"

"It took you fifteen years."

She tried to jerk her hands away, but he wouldn't let go. She called on the Deeper Power, but he matched her. "It took you five thousand years," she countered. "Even then, it was someone else who figured it out."

Through her captured hands she could feel his heartbeat accelerating. "But you know." He started breathing harder. "You know, and you could make me a god."

Adrastea fought her fear. Surely, he wouldn't try taking the secret from her, ripping it painfully from her memories.

But he couldn't. That was the whole point of the secret. It couldn't be taken, only shared.

Her fear evaporated. She laughed at him. "Aye, I know the secret. It wasn't that hard to guess. And the best thing about it is that if you stole it away, it would be useless to you.

"You can't handle it. That's why Creation would never let you see it. I'm not stopping you from becoming a god. You're stopping you." She drew herself up. "Now let me go."

He didn't. He held onto the Deeper Power.

She deliberately let hers go; no sense in overtly provoking him. He studied her. She merely waited for him to finish. She feigned more interest in the stars in between the pale columns of the temple.

"You hate me that much?"

"What is there to like?"

He didn't respond, so she simply waited. If she left now, he'd pursue her. She didn't want that. Best to deal with the situation here and now.

He held her hands and didn't say anything for a long time. What was he was thinking? The lines on her face hummed along with his thoughts, their message just out of reach. Was he trying to figure out a way to get her to tell him? Would he trick her, force her, ravish her memory?

It was too dark for her to fathom his thoughts from his eyes. Her stomach reminded her of dinner. Did anyone realize she was missing? Would they come looking for her, or even know where to look? She tried to pull her hands from his grip but he wouldn't let go.

"Adrastea?"

"Hmm?"

"Will you give me the secret? Please?" he added as if it was painful. He drew her hands to his lips.

Adrastea drew in a breath. Did he think it was that easy? And then she considered again. Would he know what to do with it? Either he would, or he wouldn't. If he didn't, then she will have lost nothing. If he did…

For the first time, she looked at her husband, truly looked at him. What he would be like if he were good? Maybe not as Phyl was, as God of the Light; Adrastea just couldn't see Mor-Lath like him. But what if…

Adrastea shook her head. No good dwelling on what-ifs. Even she was not so naïve to think that she could change a man, especially after marriage. Only he could change himself.

His hands tightened, not to cause pain, but out of desire. "Please. I beg you. Tell me." The buzzing of the lines resolved into concrete emotions. Desperation. Yearning.

"Give me everything," she said. "I want you to give everything you are to me. Stop being cruel and sarcastic and nasty. Speak kindly to me, touch me softly, and think about how I feel. Make me happy. Don't hurt me. Love me the way Natan loves Ari. Be there for me when I need you. Tell me things and not just when I ask. Open yourself to me and share your memories. Tell me stories. Spend lazy afternoons with me under the quakies. Make me laugh when I'm near and keep me in mind when I'm not. Don't shove me aside because I'm inconvenient. Consider that I am your wife and I should be your equal. Ask my opinion on things and listen to my counsel." She stopped to take a breath.

He waited to see if she would continue. "Share everything with me. And I do mean everything."

He turned this over in his mind. "So," he said eventually, "I do all that and you'll give me the secret?"

Adrastea closed her eyes. All the hope she had drained out of her. She leaned her head forward until it came to rest on his chest and whimpered in frustration.

He sighed, released her hands and pushed her back. "I should have known." His voice dropped low in disappointment. "I know you wouldn't have given me the secret straight out." He ran his hands through his hair. "It's my fault. Look. I'll do all those things. You'll see." He lifted her face. "Give me a chance. All I ask is that if I do all that, that you give me the secret. Please?"

Adrastea had nothing to lose. "All right."

"Promise?"

She nodded. Before she could pull away, he leaned over and gave her a gentle kiss. "I'll hold you to that."

Then he was gone, leaving nothing but a soft eddy of breeze where he'd once stood.

"Oh…" she whimpered. Adrastea leaned against a stone column. He just didn't get it. And for that very reason, the secret would remain safe. "You are a fool, God of the Dark. I just told you the secret, simply because you asked."

❧❦❧

When Adrastea returned to the garden, Ari was looking for her, lantern opened fully and raised high. "Where have you been?" A touch of panic tinted her question.

Adrastea stood there, arms crossed over her chest. The canyon breeze rolled through. She shivered. "I had something to take care of."

Ari lowered the lantern. "Nothing serious, I hope?"

Adrastea allowed herself a little laugh. "Just the fate of the world."

The breeze ruffled a tendril of Ari's hair. "Was it him?"

"Nothing to worry about," Adrastea reassured her. She followed Ari inside for dinner. While the food and company were most enjoyable, her thoughts kept straying back to her husband.

After dinner, they returned to Mikal's home. After he and his apprentice had long sought their beds, she sat by his banked stove and held a wakeful baby. She tried to think of everything else she could—anything but Mor-Lath.

He would blame her when things went wrong in the end. Would his last thoughts of her, just before he was destroyed, be ones of bitterness?

Should she care? No, she told herself, rather forcefully. She would not care.

Dawn brightened the windows. The moment Adrastea woke, she didn't recognize where she was. Her sleep had been broken by a baby wanting nursing every few hours. Was it going to be like this every night?

It took her a few moments to recognize Natan's, or rather, Mikal's ceiling. Above her in the attic Mikal's apprentice Jacob stirred. She heard his footfalls back and forth across the floor then listened as he climbed down the outside ladder. That must be terribly cold in winter. What happened if he woke up ill? There wasn't any room inside the small house for a stairway. Surely there was a better way?

She'd met Jacob Mayorprentice—Big Peter and Sheelagh Smith's youngest lad—last night. He was a skinny boy and didn't have much to say. He'd stared at her all through dinner. Had he been raised on the stories of how she'd rescued his brother Peter from drowning? Or was that how it had been told? Just because he was silent didn't mean he was a dull boy. What thoughts tumbled through his head?

Jacob came in the back door, sniffed when he saw her, then started his chores around her.

"Good morning," she said.

He nodded without looking at her and went back outside with the water bucket.

Later she obliged him by moving away from the stove, so he could stir up the fire and start breakfast: bacon and eggs. Was that extravagance because they had a visitor or because Mikal could afford to eat like that every day?

Ari once explained to her how hard a Mayor's life was. He had little income, therefore he couldn't afford luxuries like meat for breakfast every day. He certainly couldn't afford a family. She'd taken Ari's words at face value as a child. As an adult she read far more into them now.

Still, bacon and eggs. Good old country fare.

While he prepared the meal, Jacob kept looking at her. He'd put four eggs in the frypan and two slices of bacon.

When the smell permeated the house, Mikal stirred. He came out clad in nothing but trousers and tousled hair. "Hey, Jacob, what's—"

Then he saw Adrastea. "Oh," he said, surprised to see his sister there. He rubbed the sleep out of his eyes and scrubbed at his hair. "Hang on one moment." He ducked back into the bedroom and came out clad in a shirt, which he tucked into his pants. "Sorry 'bout that. I'd forgotten you were here."

Adrastea gave Mikal a one-armed hug. "If only all the men in my life were prone to forget me like that."

"Oh, serpent's tooth."

Adrastea gave him a coy look. Jacob, at the stove, simply rolled his eyes.

Mikal inhaled deeply. "At least I can offer you some breakfast." He peeked into the frypan and then gave Jacob a pointed glance.

Resigned, Jacob slithered off to fetch more eggs.

"If it's not too much trouble." Adrastea watched the silent apprentice leave. "Doesn't he like me?"

"He just met you. Until yesterday, you were stuff of legend. Maybe he's resentful of his brother. See, Peter and Sheelagh dote on Little Peter most shamefully. Jacob sometimes gets forgotten."

When he saw her look of embarrassment, he hastened to add, "Oh, it's not because of you, not directly. When Little Peter nearly drowned, his parents realized just how valuable their son was to them. They haven't forgotten it since, even though they had three daughters and this second son. It's 'Peter this' and 'Peter that'. He'll be running the family business soon."

Mikal leaned close to whisper to Adrastea. She wondered if Jacob had Mikal's old habit of eavesdropping. "Even so, I think his resentfulness helps him be a better mayorprentice, because as my apprentice, that makes him somebody. He's also good at keeping secrets."

"I noticed."

"Well, yeah. He picked that up from being chastised too often for expressing his opinion as a boy."

Jacob returned. Mikal quickly swapped the subject without missing a beat. "So, now that you've got more wood than you know what to do with, who are you going to get to build your house? You should have chosen planked wood instead of the logs, no matter how seasoned they are." He still spoke close and low to Adrastea, but not so low that Jacob couldn't overhear.

Adrastea thought he wanted Jacob to hear. Regarding the wood, "That doesn't matter. As for building the house, I thought I'd do it."

Mikal straightened. "You?"

Adrastea patted sleeping little Harianne on the bottom to give her hands something to do. "It shouldn't be that hard. All I need is a good look at someone else's house. I can copy that. Maybe our mother's house, if the Weavers will let me."

Mikal pulled a chair up to the table and plunked down in it. Jacob returned to the pantry for plates. "So you're going to split the logs into planks, lay your foundation and put the whole thing together by yourself? You don't have to do that. I'm sure the Carpenters would be willing to lend a son to help you."

She joined him at the table in the chair she'd just recently vacated. "Thank you, but no. I don't need the help." Noticing there wasn't a chair for Jacob, she beckoned to one of the spare chairs that lined the wall. It slid forward until it hit the edge of the table with a soft clunk. Mikal jumped. "My ways aren't always mortal ways."

Breakfast was ready. Jacob put a plate down in front of Natan, then one before the empty chair. Then he served Adrastea.

Ah. Eating with a baby in one's arms was quite tricky. Best to put Harianne down.

One of the items she purchased at Crossroads was a small wooden cradle. With a flick of her hand, the contents—cloth diapers, layette, blankets—lifted up and settled themselves down on a spot on the floor. Then she commanded some of the blankets back in before settling Harianne.

A plate of bacon and eggs clattered to the floor, the crockery breaking in half. Jacob had frozen when he saw the baby's things flying about.

"Oh, dear," muttered Adrastea. With a wave of her hand, the plate restored itself to wholeness. The food left the floor to return to the plate. It settled down on the table before her, as perfect as when Jacob first served it.

"That is so strange," Mikal remarked before he took a bite.

Jacob could only stare, jaw open. Adrastea reached out, touched his chin. He quickly closed his mouth.

"Sorry. I forgot. I guess it is strange when you're not used to that sort of thing." Adrastea thought of the priestesses back at the temple. They never batted an eye, being so used to the ways of a god. Were they all right without her? She had promised things would change, then she abandoned them. She vowed she'd visit them later, if only to reassure them.

"Until we get used to the idea of you around, could you please refrain from, um... things? I need my apprentice with unscrambled brains." He spoke as the mayor and not her brother.

"I'll try and keep 'things' to a minimum." She gave the impact of that promise some more thought. "Perhaps it is best that I wait until nighttime to build my new home?"

"If you're going to be quiet about it." He hesitated. "How were you planning on building your new home?"

Adrastea smiled at him. "I was going to ask Creation to indulge me."

Mikal snorted. "You sound like Chloe."

Jacob had retreated to the chair against the wall to eat his breakfast. His eyes never left Adrastea. He watched her intently in case she looked to swallow him whole.

"Chloe Priestess? Is she still here?"

Mikal swallowed a bite of eggs and nodded. "She stayed because we needed her. She's mellowed a bit, but she's still very much a priestess of the Light."

"As she should be. I'm quite fond of The Light myself."

Jacob fumbled his fork. It hit the plate with a clatter, startling Arianne. She let out a fuss. With a thought, Adrastea set the cradle to rocking.

Jacob blurted, "But you're the Dark One!"

Adrastea cupped her chin in her hand. What kind of stories have people been telling about her? "No, that's my husband. I'm just his wife. I was raised in the Light. I openly confess myself a follower of Them, mostly to spite my husband, but also because They've been so good to me." Her voice trailed off. The Light had been kind and forgiving. They'd comforted her when things went so wrong. "I may be the Bride of the Dark, but I do not follow his ways. I'm better than that."

Mikal polished off his breakfast. "Good luck convincing Chloe." He rose from the table. At that cue, Jacob quickly shoved the last bits of bacon and eggs into his mouth and took Mikal's plate.

Adrastea hovered protectively over hers. While Jacob washed the dishes, she finished her breakfast. She willed her empty plate clean, thus saving the apprentice the effort. She did not want to do anything to outstay her welcome.

She looked at the clothes she'd been wearing for the past twenty-four hours. "I'll have hunt down Truesie and see if she can get me something practical to wear. This fine cotton is no good for hard work."

Mikal's hands slowed as he lowered his teacup. "Oh, I guess you wouldn't know. Truesie died in the war."

Adrastea sat back down with a thump. "What? Which war?"

Jacob stared at her as if she's sprouted daisies from her ears.

She continued. "Please remember I know absolutely nothing of the past fifteen years. Nothing."

Mikal put the last plate away. "After you left the second time, Feown went to war. The Duchess gathered an army. She recruited from all over. Not just men, but women too. Unless you were married or had young children, you were fair game to be recruited.

"A lot of people jumped at the chance. First of all, you were paid a wage if you went, plus a death benefit if you were killed.

"And Truesie was one of those who went and didn't return. Tom was another." His memory caught in his throat.

Adrastea remembered Mikal's foster brother. He and Mikal had been close growing up. "I'm sorry."

"They went away to war. They went to fight the Cithrans. After..." he hesitated, studying his sister, choosing his words carefully, "after the fall of the Cithran army, I guess the Duchess thought it a good time to counterstrike. She pulled together an army and they crossed the river and..." Mikal put his head in his hands. "Could we please speak of something else?"

"I'm sorry," she said again. "I didn't know."

Mikal drew a deep breath. "Not your fault. You'd do better asking someone else, preferably someone who knows what happened. I'm the Mayor of Sacred Spring. I have had other things that demanded my attention." He cleared his throat and sniffed. "So, what do you have planned for today?"

Adrastea accepted the change of subject. "Put together a plan of my new house." She rose, licking her lips that had gone dry. "I wanted to thank the Constables for their generosity in letting me buy their land. Thanks for interceding for me." Her eyes flickered to Jacob. "I assume they're Crossroaders?"

Mikal nodded.

"How much do they know about me? About..."

"Don't worry. They're sensible people. They may seem a little gruff at first, but that's their job. They know what everyone has said—"

Adrastea grimaced.

"And they know what I and Natan have told them. Believe me; they'll reserve their judgment until you do something stupid."

Then she groaned. "That's what I was afraid of."

He poured the wash water into the still-warm frypan. "Why? You planning on doing something stupid?"

"Does breathing count?"

Adrastea surveyed her new property. It stood next to what had been the Poulters' home, which now belonged to the Constables. Their stone house didn't look much different from what she remembered, but there were three apple trees in the back yard. They would provide some shade to her property in the late afternoon. Perhaps she would plant some more trees later.

Across the street was an empty field that Mikal said belonged to the public stables. The stables were far enough away across that field, he said, that the smell and noise wouldn't bother Adrastea.

A waist-high stone wall surrounded the property. It would need a gate installed.

"So it is you," said a familiar voice.

Adrastea looked over her shoulder. Martine leaned on the stone wall. She didn't look too much like her mother. The expression on her face was softer, her hips weren't as wide. The new style of her blue pantaloons with no skirt did not suit her at all. Her breasts were full, and she wore her black bodice laced too tightly.

"Yes, it's me."

Martine nodded. She watched her, which made Adrastea squirm. "What?"

Martine shrugged. "I was just curious. You know, I remember what you did."

"What I did?"

"You know, how you saved us in the beginning. I remember that. But since then…" She shrugged. "I've heard lots of rumors and things."

Adrastea sighed. "What do people think of me here?"

"It depends."

Frustration wrinkled Adrastea's forehead. "You're not giving me much to go on."

Martine looked both ways before lifting one leg, then another over the wall. She slunk along until she stood next to Adrastea. Then she leaned against the stone wall, her back to the neighbors and the village. "It depends who you talk to. At the time some were grateful for your sacrifice. Others cursed you for bringing the Dark One's luck here. Then there were the rumors that you'd come back, terribly abused and abandoned. Everyone had something to say about that. Natan Mayor tried to quench that. Then those few who said they'd seen you—they were Crossroaders—refused to say anything more, and that was that. Occasionally stories of you would crop up, for good or ill. Sometimes people ask after you, even people who weren't here when it happened.

"But now here you are. I... I can't believe I'm looking at you." She sounded wistful. She smoothed her hair with her hands. Adrastea noticed the glint of gold on her left hand.

"You're married?"

She nodded. "Willem. Got married not too long after you did— uh, I mean..." She wiped her hands on her pantaloons. "Was yours a real marriage?"

Adrastea wrinkled her nose. "Unfortunately, yes."

"Oh. Why unfortunately?"

Adrastea gave her a very pointed look. "You didn't think he'd make a good husband, did you?"

Martine shrugged. "How would I know? He's the God of the Dark. I mean, all I remember were Chloe— that is, Mira's lessons. She always preached. Chloe said the same. She kept telling us how evil he was and things." Martine leaned close. "Is he?"

Adrastea slowly nodded. "He is—" she wanted to say how he was as cruel and rotten as the stories made him. An image of a disappointed Phyl entered her thoughts. "He can be."

Martine sucked in a breath. "Oh." She gripped the cotton fabric of her pantaloons. "He's not going to come back, is he?"

"Light, no. Not if he's smart. I'll give him another hiding if he does."

Martine stared at her. Then to Adrastea's surprise, she burst out laughing. "You mean you can do that to— to him?"

Adrastea didn't feel so amused. "If he annoys me enough." The thought of Phyl frowning filled her head again. "Lately he's been... not so bad." If 'lately' meant yesterday and not the day before.

Martine's laughter dropped into nervous, self-conscious natters.

"You saying you're here for good?"

"Yes. I've come home. I plan on living a quiet life here for a very long time."

Martine's gaze rested on the bundle in the sling around her shoulder. "Is it because of...?" She gestured subtly to the sleeping infant.

Adrastea opened her mouth to explain then realized they weren't alone.

Chloe Priestess, flanked by two apprentices, stood at the stone wall. When did she show up? Chloe hadn't changed much. She was still blonde, skinny and had a pinched look about her face. Unlike the other women Adrastea had seen in the village, Chloe wore full skirts, as did her apprentices. Even so, her blouse sleeves were short. Her thin arms crossed firmly over her not-much-of-a-chest and her fingers grasped her upper arms. The two apprentices, mid-adolescents whose familial resemblance Adrastea couldn't pick, stood behind her, awkward and squirmy. Briefly, Adrastea saw the flash of several guardian angels hovering over the trio.

"You are not welcome here, Bride of the Dark."

Martine scooted away from Adrastea. She slunk to the stone wall, hopped over and left after shooting a guilty look at Chloe.

Chloe ignored her. She uncrossed her arms, put her hands on the wall and leaned forward. "I remember how badly the Dark One wanted you. I don't think that has changed. I do hope you will leave soon."

Adrastea squared her shoulders, wrapped her arms around the baby and approached the wall.

Chloe hissed in surprise and backed away, not because of Adrastea, but because of the baby. Chloe watched it in case it might send nasty tentacles shooting from its swaddling to wrap around her neck and pull her in for an unholy meal. "You brought the spawn of the Dark to our village?" She made a sign to ward away evil. The apprentices copied her.

Adrastea rolled her eyes. "Kindly don't do that. It's rude."

"Anyhow, this is not Mor-Lath's child." When she spoke his name, the apprentices flinched, and Chloe's frown deepened. "I saved this child from certain death to raise as my own. Believe me, my husband has no desire to claim her." She hitched Harianne closer. "And to answer your questions, whether you meant to ask them or not, yes, I've come to stay for good. I am going to live here." She jabbed a finger towards the land on which she stood.

Then she gestured to the fifty cords of wood. "I'm going to build a house and I'm going to live a nice, quiet life. I'd appreciate if you would leave me alone. I don't mean you, or anyone else in this village, harm. Despite the horrid destiny thrust upon me, I'm not such a bad person. But if you insist on annoying me, I can make life difficult for you. So, go away and let me be."

Chloe shook her head. "I can't do that. You know I can't. The final battle is approaching—"

"I know."

Chloe sniffed at the interruption. "—And I must take an active stand against the Dark. And that means you."

Adrastea sighed. "I don't fear you, Priestess. I don't hate you either. But seeing that you're still the same stiff stick I remember, I also realize that it would be a waste of breath to tell you that I've always been and still am a daughter of the Light. Will you turn me away if I were to come to worship?"

"I can't prevent you from staying here, but I will actively work against you. You gave in to the Dark God. Who knows how he's twisted you to his ways?"

Adrastea felt her temper strain. "Glory, woman! I gave in to save your wretched life. Had I continued to be stubborn, your ghost would have haunted me and blamed me for your death because I was too selfish." Adrastea moved up until she stood at the wall. The apprentices backed off, but Chloe stood her ground. Adrastea had to give her that; she had backbone. "If you wish to hold enmity between us, so be it, but you will not refer to my daughter as 'Spawn of the Dark'. She is a daughter of the Light, has been blessed by the Light and I fully intend to raise her in the Light. Her name is Harianne. Either call her that, or refer to her not at all.

"As for me, I'd really appreciate it if you didn't mention my husband again. I'm really trying to forget he exists."

She studied the priestess who got even more pinched in the face. Then Adrastea rattled her by walking through the wall. The apprentices scooted all the way to the other side of the dusty street. Even Chloe backed up a few steps. "I refuse to be intimidated by you," Chloe said, more, it seemed, to reassure herself.

Adrastea threw up her hands. "I'm not going to intimidate you." Well, not much. "That's *his* way, not mine. I'm better than that. And could it possibly have occurred to you that I dislike my husband enough to have left him?"

"How do I know you are not his pawn, come here to finish us good people off?"

Adrastea wanted to beat a head, either hers or Chloe's, against the stone wall. "How don't you know that you're a small puppy in a small pen who has absolutely no idea there's a whole world outside your little wooden walls? I doubt Mor-Lath even remembers you exist, much less knows your name. Believe me, there are millions of other people out there. Enough of them have drawn his attention far better than you. He simply doesn't care about you, whether you live or die.

"So go back to your little chapel and pray to the Light. If I see Them again any time soon, I'll express your concerns. I'm sure you, being the upright priestess that you are, will have your prayers answered soon." She waved her hand dismissively. "Now flock off, little birds, and let me get about the planning of my house. I want to get it done before the baby wakes and wants feeding."

Chloe flounced off, trying not to stomp in indignation but preserve as much dignity as she could.

When Adrastea blinked, she detected the angels remaining behind to watch her. She gave them an inquisitive look. They merely nodded their heads and departed after the priestess.

Adrastea muttered to herself about how some people had not changed. Then she bounced Harianne. The baby was awake, her dark eyes staring up at Adrastea. She smiled and reassured the baby. "I'll love you, no matter what. You just remember that, and everything will be all right."

Chapter 5

Chloe Priestess sent her two apprentices Eris and Gallian to visit Ari and Natan. If Adrastea had returned, no doubt her aunt and uncle would know. Her apprentices, young women with some sense most of the time, were given strict orders to mention the return, and then listen to what the couple had to say. If pressed for a reason behind their inquiries, the apprentices were to say that Chloe felt concern over the spiritual safety of the village. If asked to explain further, they were to express ignorance.

Chloe wanted time in the chapel to herself. Ever since it was built nearly fifteen years ago, the chapel had been her refuge from the world, a place to seek out meditation and to reconnect to her god. She had seen, first-hand, the benefits of the blessing of the Dark to protect the village. That irked her. She disliked feeling obliged to a god not her own. The chapel, with its simple wooden walls, high ceiling and several windows to allow in the light, no matter where the sun wandered in the sky, became a tangible symbol of the presence of the Light in Sacred Spring.

Chloe had also overseen the rebuilding of the shrine up on the hill and encouraged pilgrims to seek it out.

In this rare moment of solitude, Chloe locked the chapel doors and came forth to the altar of the Light.

The first and simplest ritual of the Light was the First Devotion. Chloe removed a glass goblet from its cabinet behind the altar. From the basin her apprentices kept perpetually full, she dipped the goblet and lifted it up, full of water.

After wiping the bottom of the goblet, she set it on the cloth that protected the finely-polished wood of the altar. The sun shone that day. Light filtered through the windows, making the goblet sparkle.

She knelt before the altar and raised her hands in supplication. "Oh

Light, I come before Thee to seek Thy wisdom."

Instead of following the ritual of the prayer, she bowed her head and confessed the fears of her heart. "The Bride of the Dark has returned to Sacred Spring. I fear what evil she would bring." Her hands fell until they rested on the altar cloth. She curled forward as a broken woman, resting her forehead beside the goblet. "I don't know what to do. I can't force her to leave; I have not the strength." Tears spilled from her eyes. She wiped at them with her bare hands, which served only to smear them about her face. She lifted the edge of her skirt and used that to dab her eyes. "I've worked so hard to provide a strong spiritual base for these people, to remove fear from their hearts and give them a knowledge of You." She clasped her hands before her and raised her eyes to the light shining upon her. "Please don't let her undo all my hard work."

Then she took a deep breath, the edges ruffling with emotion. "I come before Thee to seek Thy wisdom." She raised the glass into a ray of sunlight. "As the light shines through the water, let thy Light shine through me."

The light brightened. But it didn't come from the windows.

A glorious being appeared. The brightness around Her was greater far than noonday sun. The God of the Light, clad in a robe of whitest white, touched Her holy feet to the cloth until She stood upon the altar.

Chloe could stare only at those feet; the glory of the rest of Her hurt her eyes. Her hands trembled, and her arms would not move.

"Be thou at peace, child." The Light stretched forth a finger to touch the water of the goblet, bestowing it with a gentle glow. The water reached up and embraced that finger then settled happily into the glass. "Drink."

Chloe couldn't move.

"Go on." The Light waited patiently until Chloe found control of her body. She lowered the glass and sipped the water. It slid past her lips and imprinted its taste on her tongue. She swallowed and felt it slide all the way to her stomach, where the goodness from the water spread to all her limbs. An urge to finish it all took her over.

Chloe put the empty glass down but couldn't complete the ritual.

The Light didn't require it. "Thou hast been faithful child, for all thy human foibles. Now I ask that thou wilt continue in thy faith and release thy fear.

"I know of Adrastea, Bride of the Dark. I know of her sacrifice to save your village and her continuing sacrifice to save the world. Do not judge the immortals by mortal standards, for she has passed beyond the scales of such judgement.

"Knowest thou this, child of the Light. Adrastea, Bride of the Dark means you no harm. I would encourage thee to extend the hand of fellowship. Welcome her back to the village of her birth.

"I would also that thou wouldst accept the child she harbors. Raisest the child to My Ways. Teach'st her to walk in the Light, for this child is under My protection. This child of the House of the Dark is the key to eliminating the Darkness, to turn evil away and prove the worthy heart.

"Standest thou against the Darkness, but seekest not to actively thwart Mor-Lath. Thy energy is far better spent upholding the Light.

"And that will be enough."

The Light bent down and, taking Chloe's face in Her hands, gave her a kiss on the forehead.

The light of glory faded. Chloe found herself sprawled next to the altar. The goblet remained in her hand, empty. It rolled away from her fingers as she sat up. First, she touched her lips that had sipped the water, then her forehead where the holy kiss had fallen.

"Oh dear," she murmured. "And I spoke so harshly to her," meaning Adrastea. As she reflected over the words of the god—which stuck most clearly in her mind—she recalled reading once of prophecies that seemed to match this.

Then Chloe wondered, should she write all this down?

No. The answer came clear to her heart. She bowed her head. She would keep this visitation close.

But one thing was sure; she owed Adrastea an apology.

Chloe encountered her apprentices hurrying back from Ari and Natan's house. They'd gone there as ordered. Their visit had been cut short when Adrastea had shown up.

She spoke with them briefly, apologizing for her earlier chastisement. "I should never have spoken so harshly to her. That is not behavior becoming a priestess of the Light." She told them they would treat Adrastea and the child as kindly as they treated the other villagers. "And I will apologize to her immediately."

Her apprentices returned to the chapel, so they didn't have to feel uncomfortable in the presence of Chloe's humble contrition.

Ari would be at work, so Chloe knocked on the stillroom door and waited.

ⱺ◯ℛ◯ↄ

Adrastea lifted the barrel of brandy up from the cellar and set it down on the floor of the stillroom via the Deeper Power. Ari watched, arms folded.

Salle and Bitsy stared, their mouths agape. This was the first time they had seen this creature of legend use her talents. Harianne slumbered nearby in the same box Ari had prepared the night before. It would be another hour or two before she wanted another feed.

While Ari picked up the wine thief, Adrastea ran her hand over the barrel. "It's the same one." Still touching the barrel, Adrastea tilted her head and listened further to what the barrel had to tell her. "Ari, this barrel is older than you!"

Ari nodded. "The best barrels are old." Ari thumped the top, listening to the echo within. "New barrels taint the brandy with their greenness, but the old ones... they remember." Her eyes flickered towards the kitchen door. Natan.

Adrastea straightened. "I wish you hadn't said that." Her conversation with this barrel told her that the brandy within was nearly sixteen years old. Her brandy.

Ari sighed. "I hope it doesn't taint the flavor for you." She tried to work the bung out and failed.

Without being asked, Adrastea pulled it out. "Glasses?"

Ari gestured to the cabinet on the wall. Salle brought back two. She handed one to Ari who handed it to Adrastea. While they warmed the glasses in their hands, Ari dipped the wine thief in the barrel.

Bitsy stole the bung off the stone table and gave it a sniff. She made a face and slipped the bung back. She backed away to watch from afar.

Adrastea inhaled the remnants of the angel's portion and she remembered. Ari's brandy had been almost perfect before, but it was tainted by memories.

"Ari?"

"Hmm?" Ari withdrew the thief and let it dribble into Adrastea's glass.

"What memory was it that tainted the last batch?"

Ari drew a deep breath. She pulled out another thief-ful of brandy and gave it to Salle. "The day we put up that last batch of brandy was the day Natan told me he was going to stay with his apprenticeship and become Mayor."

"Oh, Ari."

Ari shrugged. "It devastated me. I cried, I nagged, I ranted until I was out of tears. I wanted to marry him. He knew it. And then he went and chose the Mayorship over me."

Adrastea wrapped her hands around the glass. Salle sniffed hers absentmindedly. Her focus was on Ari. "But Uncle Natan loves you. He always has. Hasn't he?"

Ari nodded. "And I was the greater fool for falling in love with a Mayorprentice." Ari lifted her eyes to meet Adrastea's. "And even through the pain, and the clandestine trysts—not that it was much of a secret from anyone—it all came right in the end." Ari put the wine thief on top of the barrel, where it rolled until it hit the chime hoop. "I wish I didn't have to go through so much pain before I found happiness."

Adrastea stared down into her glass. The brandy spoke to her, ringing in her memory and making her painfully aware of the lines on her face. She fought the reminiscence and focused on Ari. "So, if I may ask, when did you and Natan get together, at first, that is. As long as I remember, he's always been…"

Ari gave her a guilty smile. A small noise that could have been a chuckle escaped her. "Natan had wrenched his gut all day trying to figure out the best way to tell me he'd chosen the apprenticeship. I guess when I broke down and wept my heart out, he felt guilty and responsible. So, he was rather vulnerable at that point and," she licked her upper lip, "I guess he never had a chance."

Adrastea gaped in surprise. "Ari! You seduced him?"

Salle quickly put her glass down and covered Bitsy's ears. Bitsy squirmed, but her sister was too strong for her. "Really, Ari. Little ears."

Ari didn't care. She gestured to the stillroom back door. "Right out in that garden."

Salle wanted to cover her own ears. "I don't want to know."

Adrastea merely nodded her approval. Ari's fragrant garden under the starlight was far more romantic than a library table.

Another memory surfaced. Adrastea remembered when Ari had breached the barrel that time before. She remembered how pinched Ari seemed, and how she was sharp. The healer seemed mellower now, at ease.

"Now, Salle," Ari chided gently. "Are you telling me you've never been in love?"

Salle wrinkled her nose. "No." Salle's eyes turned to Adrastea. "What about you?"

Adrastea snorted. "Of course not. I'm married."

A knock startled them all. Bitsy squeaked.

Ari nodded to Bitsy to go open the door. Adrastea remembered she had a brandy glass. She rolled it in her hands. Salle's glass sat on the table where she put it.

Bitsy opened the door, then backed up with a curtsey. A curtsey? Where did she learn that? Adrastea never curtseyed to anyone as a child.

Chloe Priestess entered far enough for Bitsy to close it. She stood at the door, hands folded before her. "Hello, Ari." Her gaze alighted on Adrastea. The atmosphere changed. The air grew still and the whole world held its breath.

Ari greeted her. "What can I do for you."

Chloe swallowed. "Actually, I came to speak with Adrastea."

Adrastea frowned. She swirled the brandy in her glass. "We're rather busy at the moment."

"That's all right," Chloe said with a meekness Adrastea did not remember her having. "I can wait."

Adrastea turned from her and swirled the brandy once more before lifting it to her nose.

Ari was right again, just as she had been the last time. There were memories in the brandy. Adrastea smelt the apples and the spices and something deeper.

She smelled surprise and pain and the shattering of her future. When Mor-Lath had first appeared to her what seemed like so long ago and declared her to be his bride, something inside her had told her this was to be true. She never recognized it until now. "Creation always meant for me to be his Bride."

Ari had picked up Salle's glass and applied it to her nose. "So that's what it says to you?"

Adrastea realized she'd spoken aloud. "I never meant..." She closed her eyes. Creation had damned her before she was ever born.

Ari put up her hand. "I know." Her gaze flickered over to Chloe. "Sometimes our fates are not chosen by us, no matter how much we wish to be masters of our own destinies." Ari buried her nose even deeper in the glass, then tilted her head back and let the brandy run into her mouth. She held it there, then swallowed before breathing out. "It is not others but ourselves that bring us the greatest pain." She inhaled through her nose, then exhaled through her mouth once more. "But others can bring the greatest joy." She turned her head to look at the sleeping baby.

Adrastea did not drink her brandy.

Ari handed her glass back to Salle. "Come, child. You are not as bitter as we are. Drink this and don't bother remembering." She dipped the thief and emptied it in Salle's glass. Salle looked at it through the light, then raised it to her nose.

Ari glanced at Bitsy, but Bitsy gave a small shake of her head. If she'd been Bitsy's age when Ari last opened the barrel, would Ari have let her taste?

Ari invited Chloe to a taste. Chloe refused. "I'm better off not trying." To Adrastea, she asked, "Are you done?"

Adrastea did not meet the priestess' gaze. She took another sniff of brandy, trying to lose herself in the scent. It wasn't strong enough. The sharpness had disappeared, leaving only flavour. She smelled the apples, but also peaches and hot summer days. Cloves, cassia, brown sugar, vanilla... she knew the names of the spices that issued forth. The faintest-faintest aroma of toasted oak, the mustiness of a cellar, the bite of aged hard cheese. The scent of fear and surprise and loss. The scent of pain, of a pariah, of sacrifice.

"You must drink it," Ari insisted. "If you don't, the memories will haunt you. Drink, until the glass is empty. Then it will be all gone."

Adrastea looked at Ari. Is that what the older woman had done? Did she start out with a glass of brandy? Did she drink it until it was gone, then drink and drink and drink, trying to drown the memories of that first barrel?

Adrastea did not want to go down that path.

Salle tilted back her head and gulped the brandy. She choked up in surprise, then swallowed, finally exhaling to get the full benefit of the flavour. "Oh, that's perfect," she uttered.

Ari asked, "What do you taste?"

Salle thought about it. "Apples." She put her fingertips to her lips as if not sure what else there was. "And... basil?"

"What else?"

Salle shared her impressions. She, too, had tasted the peaches and the spices.

"No bitterness?"

Salle looked apologetic. "The alcohol surprised me. I thought it would be sharper. But no. No bitterness."

Ari looked to Adrastea expectantly. Adrastea shook her head. "I can't." She put the glass on the bench. Suddenly speaking with Chloe didn't seem so bad. At least she could argue back with Chloe, maybe give her a good rattling. "You wanted to speak with me?"

Chloe nodded. "Is the garden all right?"

They went through the back door. She didn't wait to see if Chloe was behind her, but strode through the garden, around the rosemary hedge, past the various plots and all the way to the stone wall. Chloe arrived later, out of breath.

Adrastea folded her arms. "This had better be good. I can't possibly imagine what else you have to say to me after this morning."

Chloe drew herself up and forced herself to look into Adrastea's eyes.

Adrastea, to her surprise, didn't see accusations in the gaze. It seemed almost mournful.

"I'm sorry," Chloe said. Then she began to waver. She wrung her hands and turned away. "I'm sorry for what I said earlier. I was frightened and ignorant and it was out of line." She said nothing for a few moments, possibly to gather her courage, and she continued. "Just because— well, you're not bad, I mean, evil. I—" Chloe hesitated. She began to pace and refuse to meet Adrastea's gaze.

Adrastea remained as she was and waited for Chloe to finish.

"I know you don't serve the Dark although he—" Chloe wrapped her arms about her. "I don't know what he's done to you. I don't know if I want to know. But it's best to let the past remain in the past. If you want to remain here, then I won't stop you. I only hope that you would feel welcome to come..." She swallowed. "...come to services." Chloe held up her hands before Adrastea could say anything. "I say that not because I want to convert you but because I don't want you to feel excluded."

Adrastea murmured, "Don't worry about needing to convert me. I've always walked in the Light."

Chloe stopped her pacing. Only now did she dare look upon Adrastea. "So we're all right with each other?"

Adrastea shrugged. "I promise I won't turn your apprentices into toads."

Chloe nodded as if this was a great reassurance. "That's settled, then?"

Adrastea, arms still folded, studied the slender priestess, whose blonde hair was still worn pulled back in the severe style she always favored. She nodded.

Chloe relaxed. "And your— the child. Has she been Annointed?"

"She's only a few days old, so no. And you may call her my daughter. Her mother, before she died, entrusted her child to me."

"So, she's not..."

"No, she's not his." Adrastea tossed her head contemptuously. "Light forbid he'd father a child on me or any woman. Too afraid his own son would kill him."

Chloe jumped at this. Her fingers shook as she smoothed her skirts.

"Oh, don't worry," Adrastea reassured her. "I doubt you'll be seeing him again any time soon."

"What? Oh, oh yes." It seemed Chloe didn't know what to do with her hands.

Adrastea sensed Chloe's increased heartbeat. The priestess made strong waves along the Lines. "Now that we've made peace between us, how about you go sit down somewhere and gather your nerves?"

Chloe nodded. She half-raised a hand, paused, then raised it completely in farewell. Then without another word, she turned and left the garden.

Adrastea felt like that brandy now.

Montrof unclasped his hands from the chapel altar. Perhaps praying had been a mistake. Too late. Montrof couldn't take it back now.

"What the hell do you want?" Mor-Lath growled at him, when he appeared seated on the altar.

Montrof swallowed and backed away as quickly as his painful old knees could take him. "Forgive me, Holiness," he stuttered. "I— I seek further guidance."

Mor-Lath wore the same cowled robe as yesterday, but minus the staff. Not that he would need any kind of weapon to thwack Montrof, should he so desire. He folded his arms and frowned. "How difficult is 'grab your things and run'?"

The priest fiddled with the coarse fabric of his own black robe. "We understand that part very well." Indeed, while it was daylight, the priests and priestesses of not just this temple, but all the temples across the

Avelian capital packed up their worldly possessions and prepared to flee. "But the laity are not so..."

"What?"

Montrof spread his hands in supplication. "They do not understand why they must flee."

Mor-Lath made a sound of disbelief. "Am I the god of idiots? I'm going to destroy Avelia. If they want to stay, they can. After they die a painful death, they can come to me personally and I shall further enlighten them."

Montrof wrung his hands. "Perhaps I did not explain myself completely."

Mor-Lath muttered. "Oh, I know what you meant to say. They've grown lax. They've forgotten who their god is. They don't want to leave their precious houses and fine things. They've forgotten who it was that gave them those pretty trinkets. They're going to find out I can take them away just as quickly."

Montrof dropped his hands and sighed. "Then many people will die."

"They were warned."

The priest raised his eyes to his god. "Must they all die?"

Mor-Lath didn't answer him right away. He seemed to consider the question for a moment. "Must a tree remain unpruned?"

The pruned tree gave forth better fruit. Montrof bowed his grizzled head. "So you would prune your people now?"

The god's temper had eased. He crossed his legs and leaned forward. "I should have done it a long time ago, but I must confess I have had some very important matters on my mind."

"More important than your people?" Montrof said before he could stop himself. Then he bit his lip, fearing the god's wrath.

Mor-Lath did not smite his priest. "The fate of the world," he offered in way of explanation.

Montrof wanted to ask what that fate was. However, one moment of cheek was enough. He didn't want the god's temper to flare again.

"The end is coming, Montrof, very soon. You just might live to see it."

"But I am an old man." The cold from the floor seeping into his joints testified of that.

"Yes, you are. And the sooner you leave Avelia, the better your chances of surviving to see that end."

"Yes, Holiness." His heart ached. He'd grown up in Avelia and had served here his whole life. He was not looking forward to fleeing his home, knowing it would be destroyed. "I worry about those who will stay and who will suffer for their lack of faith."

Mor-Lath shrugged. "Those who don't obey shall be destroyed."

"You're talking about the death of thousands of people."

Mor-Lath uncrossed his leg, pointed at Montrof. "Be grateful I am showing mercy and giving the faithful time to flee. Had I left the fate of your people to my dear wife, she would have wiped out the whole of Avelia without a single thought. The Cithrans never saw it coming. You wouldn't have either."

A lump stuck in Montrof's throat, one he couldn't swallow. He'd met the Bride in her full wrath, albeit only the once. That her hand had reft the whole Cithran army without warning, without mercy, he could believe.

Yes, he was dealing with the more merciful of the pair.

The god's temper returned. "Now stop bothering me with questions to which you already know the answer. Leave Avelia soon. If you really feel the need to save as many souls, then by all means, remain and preach until you're purple. But if you are not out of Avelia by sunset tomorrow, you will suffer the same fate as the unfaithful."

Montrof bowed his head and acquiesced to his god's command. Yet he continued to worry after Mor-Lath's departure.

Chapter 6

Adrastea lifted the glass to her lips and let the brandy slip over her tongue. She did not let it roll but swallowed quickly.

It didn't help. The finish brought back her earliest memories of Mor-Lath. How frightened of him she'd been. He seemed so powerful, so ominous, the stuff of legends made flesh.

And now... what? Adrastea looked down into her empty glass, even though there were never answers to be found at the bottom of a cup. "You bottling this tomorrow?"

Ari, who enjoyed the brandy more than the others, nodded.

"You selling it to Crossroads?"

"No." Ari put her glass down and replaced the bung. "I've got a Feowan buyer interested—" She halted, overtaken by a thought. "That is, I hope I've got a Feowan buyer. The siege might put a hold on things for a while." She considered another thought. "We'll bottle it up and recellar it, then wait and see what happens with Feown. Natan got another telegram today. The army's still there, but no action."

A timid, rapid knock came on the stillroom door. Bitsy opened it and let a younger girl in—an Innkeeper, if Adrastea guessed correctly. She wore the same type of blouse and pantaloons as the adults favored, her dark blonde hair caught up in a braid. She huffed for a moment, winded from her long run. "Mistress Ari, Ma says come quick. One o' the guests has had a turn."

Adrastea's heart thumped. "It's Lord Pennexter," according to the Lines. Ari snatched her cloak and bag from its customary peg by the door. Adrastea and Salle followed.

They arrived at the inn, where one of Martine's younger siblings guided them to the rooms guarded by the two men.

The room looked fresh and cheerful, with the curtains drawn away from the windows. A floral-printed paper covered the walls and country-style rag rugs lay on the floor.

Lord Pennexter lay propped up in bed by a few pillows. Dassie sat next to him and held his hand. She rose as soon as the two women entered the room. "He fell. He's taken a bad turn. He can't talk well. It's like half of him wants to sleep."

Ari moved swiftly to Lord Pennexter's other side. She peered at his drooping eye, his slack side of the face, then lifted his arm. It fell to his side. "Can you lift it?" she asked him.

He muttered something and turned his face away.

"Apoplexy," Ari diagnosed. "Not the worst case I've seen, but pretty bad." Her gaze met Dassie's. She motioned with her head for the young woman to follow her outside.

Dassie sighed, resigning herself to bad news. She gave his good hand a squeeze, then gently laid it on the cover before following the healer out of the room.

Lord Pennexter protested. He gestured wildly at the closing door. He tried to speak but couldn't form words with half his face not working.

Adrastea slipped into Dassie's chair and took Lord Pennexter's hand. She glanced at the man waiting by the door, but he didn't move or leave. Perhaps that was the way of lords, to be attended at all times?

"Milord," she addressed him. It was strange to call him 'grandfather'. There hadn't been anyone who bore that name for her. "I guess it's too late to ask you what my father was like when he was a boy?"

Sorrow stung her, as she realized the loss of the unknown history of her father. Who knew he was the priestly son of a lord?

Lord Pennexter made a sound that could have been laughter. He squirmed his hand until Adrastea released it. He pointed his finger and made writing motions.

Adrastea turned to the man. "Find the Innkeeper. Tell her I want the council slate. She'll know what I'm asking for."

The man looked to Lord Pennexter for confirmation. Lord Pennexter waved his hand and muttered something. The man slipped out. A moment later he slipped back in.

"Well?" demanded Adrastea.

"The child will fetch what you need."

Lord Pennexter relaxed. He waved at Adrastea with his hand again and she took it up. It was futile to attempt communication until the slate arrives, so she held his hand and said nothing.

Instead, questions about her father flitted through her mind. So many mysteries.

Lord Pennexter knew all about his son, before the wayward young man fled to the hills and disappeared. Oh, the stories he could tell. It would be unkind to rip those memories from his mind, especially in his current state.

Could she heal him? She rose and, extending a hand, asked, "May I?"

Lord Pennexter rolled his head and muttered. Adrastea took that for permission. She laid her hand on the affected side of his head, closed her eyes and delved.

As far as she could tell, there was nothing wrong there. The brain was fine. She expanded her search. To her surprise, she found a nasty bruise on the opposite side—the good side—of his head. It was a simple matter to drain away the bruising and repair the broken blood vessels.

However, when her work was done, there was no change to Lord Pennexter's condition. Maybe there was something else wrong. She didn't know much about apoplexy. Before she could think to investigate further, someone cleared his throat.

The man by the door held a slate and pencil. When had he gotten those? She hadn't been aware of anyone else coming into the room.

Once accoutered with writing implements, Lord Pennexter scrawled a sloppy message on the slate: "What happen?"

"You suffered an apoplectic fit. It's damaged you."

Below his first line, he wrote, "Why?"

Why? Adrastea wasn't sure what he was asking. "These things happen." She launched into a brief medical explanation, but he waved his hand. He pointed again at the Why on the slate.

"I'm sorry," she said. "I don't understand what you're asking. She saw a flicker out of the corner of her eye. When she blinked and turned towards it, she saw several angels hovering nearby.

Will he die? she asked them.

We all die, an angel replied.

I meant, soon?

The angel nodded.

Lord Pennexter was scratching something on his slate. "Where brother?"

"What, Mikal?"

He waved his hand in affirmation.

To the angel, Adrastea asked, *How soon?* The moment she asked, she remembered that angels and demons didn't have a good idea of the movement of time. *I mean, like, today?*

You have time to say goodbye, the angel replied.

Mikal too?

What about the people back home? The rest of the family?

The angels shared some sort of mirth between them that Adrastea wasn't in on. *You worry about the oddest things, Holiness.*

The form of address startled her. Adrastea didn't feel like speaking with angels any more. She ignored their presence. They faded from view, though she knew they watched her.

To the man by the door she said, "Fetch the mayor."

Just then, Ari returned without Dassie. "She's off crying somewhere," she explained. "I told her the facts."

Adrastea simply nodded. There was no soft way to deliver bad news. "I checked him out. He's going to die soon."

More scratching on the slate. Since he was running out of space, Lord Pennexter wrote at the bottom, but his clumsy hand knocked the slate to the floor. It slid off the blanket and clattered loudly.

When Adrastea picked it up, she read, "When?"

Ari read the same over her shoulder. "There may be a chance that with good care and therapy you may regain—"

"No," Adrastea interrupted. "I know for sure he will die soon."
Lord Pennexter accepted this. He sank back and gestured for the slate. Adrastea scrubbed the prior markings off and placed it under his pencil. "Priest," he requested.

Only after everyone assembled did Lord Pennexter inform them he meant to write a new will. As soon as Mikal read that, he pulled Adrastea to the side. "Could I see you outside?"

She followed her brother. He said, "I don't want to be made his heir."

"I don't want to either," Adrastea conceded.

Mikal scrubbed his hands through his hair. "I mean, the money would be nice, but he's asking us to go back to Feown and be lords. That means leaving Sacred Spring. I don't want to. I can't."

"I can't go either." She tapped her fingers on her chest. It felt delicate and full. Guilt for Harianne, whom she'd left back at Ari's home, nagged her. It would take some getting used to, this having a small baby. "Look at who I am. I know Jonathan doesn't like me. He won't accept me; he thinks I'm Mor-Lath's high priestess. If he found out the truth…"

"I know, I know. It's enough that we've both got plenty of reasons to say no. Besides, there are other Pennexter family members, possibly ones who'd be happier to inherit.

"So that's that. We'll go back in and tell him we're not interested."

And that's what they did. In front of Ari, Chloe and Dassie, Mikal shared their decision to turn down the offer of inheritance. Chloe and Ari stood back, the outsiders to this little dispute. Dassie sat on the chair beside the bed, watching everyone with sharp eyes. She took in much and said little. Adrastea thought she saw a flicker of worry cross her face.

Lord Pennexter chuckled then wrote something on the slate: "No choice."

"No," Mikal contradicted him. "We do. We have no desire to go to Feown. They need us more in Sacred Spring."

Adrastea added, "You've got other relatives." She pointed to Dassie. "What about her?"

Dassie looked at her cousin. "I'm not a direct descendant."

To Lord Pennexter, Mikal said, "Just because we were born to your son by chance doesn't mean you can force us to disrupt our lives for your convenience." He paced the room. "So, tell us, what would have happened if you learned your son had died and never had children? What would you have done then?"

Lord Pennexter closed his eyes and didn't remark. Mikal addressed Dassie. "Well, who would have inherited?"

Dassie thought for a moment. "It would have passed to Uncle Jonathan. But he's a priest and has no issue. After that, I don't know. My grandmother is dead."

"Where do you come in line of succession? Whose daughter are you?"

She stood up as if the extra height would add authority. "I'm the youngest daughter of Euvon, only son of Lady Adrastea, Lord Pennexter's sister."

"Lady Pen?" Adrastea asked. "I thought she was the eldest. I know she's older than Jonathan. Shouldn't you inherit?"

"Inheritances pass down, not up. That's why Uncle Jonathan's next in line for Uncle Stobol's wealth." She looked up to her new-found cousins. "Until you came along."

Mikal folded his arms. "You said, youngest daughter. What about your siblings?"

Grief crumpled Dassie's face. She sank back to her chair and dropped her face into her hands.

Lord Pennexter scrawled a single word on the slate, "Dead."

"Oh, I'm sorry," said Adrastea. "I didn't know." She put an arm around her cousin.

Dassie composed herself. She lifted her damp face. After fumbling for a handkerchief, she wiped her nose. "They all went away to war and never came back." She sniffed. "I'm the only one left, the eldest of all my cousins."

Mikal shot a quick glance to Adrastea as if to say, *See? More family.* "So," he said to Lord Pennexter, who had a line of drool descending from his weakened side, "just because you learned about us, you're going to take the inheritance away from those who were raised as Pennexters?"

Lord Pennexter turned away. Ari dabbed at the drool, restoring a little dignity.

"They were next in line, weren't they?" Mikal pressed.

Lord Pennexter didn't answer.

Mikal turned to Dassie. "We'd be taking away your inheritance."

Dassie squirmed and rose to her feet. "My grandmother has estates... it's not like we'll be poor forever."

Mikal sighed and raised his eyes to the Light. "Really," he said to Lord Pennexter. "Making us your heirs is a bad idea. And if you insist on this foolishness, I'll just turn around and deed it all back to the family.

"It's nice and all to discover who we are and where we came from, but we're grown people with lives of our own. I'm Mayor here and to leave would disrupt the village."

Lord Pennexter turned back and looked at Adrastea. He scrawled, "Child."

"My Harianne? She's adopted. And a girl. I'm barren and cannot have children of my own. I'm a dead end in the family tree."

But Lord Pennexter waved his good hand and made protesting noises. He pointed to Mikal. Adrastea rolled her eyes.

Mikal held up his hand as if to ward off his grandfather's meaning. "Mayors don't have children either."

Lord Pennexter wrote something else. "Lords do," he'd written, then circled the word Child.

"I'd prefer not to think about that," Mikal said, his voice tight. "You're tired. The turn hasn't done you well. We'll leave you to rest. Perhaps later you'll see the wisdom in our ways." He took Adrastea by the arm and led her to the door. Lord Pennexter protested loudly. He knocked the slate to the floor and tried to throw the pencil at them. Mikal ignored him but gave a look to Dassie. He beckoned ever so slightly with his head.

He had to do it twice before she got the clue and followed them out. "How about we got to my house to talk? We've got some things to discuss that are better said in private."

⁂

Back at Mikal's place, Adrastea put the kettle on and rummaged the shelves for tea. Mikal sent Jacob off to Ari's place to check on Harianne.

Before the kettle boiled, Dassie insisted to know what they wanted to say.

Mikal invited her to sit at the table, then took a chair himself. "First, it's considered polite in the country to pour the tea before discussing business. People think better with something in their stomachs. Second, you're going to need the fortitude because we're going to say some things that may rattle you."

Heeding their advice, Dassie waited impatiently, picking at the edge of the wooden table and running her fingernail along an old nick in the tabletop until Adrastea placed a steaming cup in front of her.

Dassie didn't take a sip. "What is so important you had to drag me out here and make me tea?"

"I'm hoping," Mikal explained, "that you can help us convince Lord Pennexter not to make us his heirs."

"But why should that matter? Didn't you say that you'd just sign everything over to the rest of us if he did?"

Mikal affirmed that. "However, it would be best that our names were kept out of mention entirely. Even though I'm just a country mayor, under any other circumstances I'd be sorely tempted by the offer." He gestured to

Adrastea. "This is my elder sister. She is the dangerous one."

Dassie looked at Adrastea. "Oh," she said eventually, as she sorted through the facts available to her. "The Dark priestess thing. Uncle Jonathan thinks you're one, but Uncle Stobol—Lord Pennexter—is certain you're, at worst, a country witch. I'm sure it's something we could keep silent, if you—"

"No," interrupted Adrastea. "It's a little more complicated than that." She let out a small sigh and looked to her brother for confirmation.

"She's got to find out sometime," he told her.

Adrastea nodded, then bowed her head. "I'm not a Dark priestess, as your uncle thinks. I'm something far worse."

Dassie didn't say anything, but waited, suspicion hardening her eyes, for further explanation.

Adrastea drew a breath, then called upon the Deeper Power. The aura around her intensified until she glowed. The very air shimmered about her. It felt like Creation wanted to close in and embrace her. She pulled in as much Power as she could. She risked drawing the attention of her husband. Could the others feel it? She hoped they could. She sent vibrations along the Lines that connected them.

Dassie sucked in a breath and held it. Even Mikal stiffened. He rubbed the raised hairs on his arms.

Adrastea looked at Dassie. "I'm no mere priestess. I'm the Bride of the Dark herself."

Dassie stared at Adrastea in disbelief. Her hands clutched tightly around the teacup and her brows furrowed.

"Mor-Lath, God of the Dark, is my husband. Few people outside this village know this. Your uncle Jonathan suspects my connection to the Dark God but does not know its true extent.

"I cannot be Stobol Pennexter's heir." Out of the corner of her eye, Adrastea caught a fleeting glimpse of a demon—Desideria. The dead priestess settled nearby and watched the exchange. Another demon, one Adrastea did not have time to recognize, flitted in and out. Would that one report to its master?

Adrastea released some, but not all, of the Deeper Power. She kept just enough to feel the buzz of its presence. When that happened, Mikal relaxed. Could he sense it too, being her brother—Joe and Lillybet's son? Could he have been a priest? And how much talent did Dassie have?

It was a long time before anyone said anything.

"So…" Dassie started but left her thoughts unvoiced. A small shudder ran across her shoulders.

Jacob returned before Dassie could take her eyes from Adrastea's countenance. The door banged open and Jacob waltzed in. As soon as Jacob entered the room, Dassie jumped.

"S'okay, Mikal. But the baby—" He saw Adrastea seated next to her brother and addressed his report to her. "Uh, Mistress Healer. The baby's just woken up. Salle's bringing her over now. She says she wants feeding."

"Thank you, Jacob."

Mikal gave his apprentice instructions. "Jake, Ari's at the Inn tending to Lord Pennexter, who's ill. Go ask her if there's anything she needs and then help her as she sees fit. I suspect things aren't going too well there."

Jacob looked at the three around the table. His eyes shifted from one person to another. He figured something was going on. "Couldn't Bitsy help her?"

"Bitsy's not here."

"I could go get her."

"Do that—"

"Okay!" Jacob shot for the door.

"And…" Mikal's voice brought his apprentice up short. "Check with Ari first, in case you need to help Bitsy carry anything."

"Okay." He was less enthusiastic this time. He opened the door. But before he could go through, he inquired, "Anything else?"

"Yes. Check on Uncle Natan and tell him I'll come see him later."

Jacob let out an exaggerated sight. "Oh, is that all?"

"Report back here when you're done."

Jacob didn't greet this news with enthusiasm. "Just my luck, the conversation will be over by then." He departed.

Mikal put his chin in his hand and looked at Dassie. "You realize what we've told you will have to remain a secret."

"I can keep secrets. Really."

"The reason we told you about us is because you need to help us convince Lord Pennexter to not make us his heirs."

Dassie shook her head. "But he won't believe me. He'll think I'm trying to get the inheritance for myself."

"Does he have a current will?"

"Probably. But it's back in Feown."

Mikal and Adrastea looked at each other with renewed hope. "Where in Feown?"

Dassie confessed, "I don't know."

"Would Jonathan know?"

"I don't know. Wouldn't hurt to ask."

His eyes flickered to Adrastea. His sister replied, "I'm not asking him."

"Doesn't mean I can't." To his sister he said, "Isn't it about time I met the rest of the family?" His words implied he expected Adrastea to take him there.

She capitulated. "Fine. But not today. I've got a house to construct."

As the sun set behind the mountains, Adrastea paced the length of her property. Twenty paces one way, forty the other. A quick tendril of thought into the ground revealed plenty of stone she could use. Darkness would come soon, and she could begin. Harianne, newly-fed and quiet, nestled in her sling, her hands gripping at Adrastea's blouse.

Mikal, from the other side of the wall, leaned over. "Nervous about the house?"

"No. Mor-Lath. He's upset with me."

Mikal straightened, suddenly the Mayor. "Because you're building a house? Is he going to—"

Adrastea shook her head. "No. I told him something he wanted to know. After I did, he didn't believe me. He thinks I'm holding out on him."

"Are you?"

Adrastea shivered and pulled her shawl closer around her shoulders. These spring nights were still nippy. "No. I told him everything he wanted. It was so simple, he didn't recognize it for what it was. That's why he's upset."

Mikal slid over the wall. "Now, Adrastea, if he's going to come here and make trouble, I need to know. You're my sister and I love you, but I can't have all that again."

Adrastea laid a hand on her cheek. The lines sang out her husband's wrath. Yes, it was about her, but it was directed someplace else. She could also sense a tension in him. He was holding himself back. Oh, he could have easily come here and vent his frustration upon his wife. But he didn't. Mor-

Lath had enough sense not to go down that route again. "No, he will not come here."

"I'll take your word for it." The tension did not leave him. "But the moment anything untoward happens…"

"We'll be fine." Adrastea kept her hand on her cheek. "He is well and truly distracted by something else."

Mikal swatted at a solitary mosquito. It ignored Adrastea and bothered him. Harianne, awake and calm, was swathed up in the sling where no hungry insect could get at her. Her tiny hands opened and closed against Adrastea's chest.

As the sky faded to a darkness that matched the earth, lights freckled the village as people lit lamps or candles. Soon they would settle in for the night. They'd know nothing of the night's events until the morrow when a new house would stand where nothing stood before.

Adrastea heard the footsteps before Mikal did. She observed but said nothing.

"Ah, here come the Constables." Mikal straightened and peered into the gloom.

Adrastea shook her head. "No, it's Chloe."

Sure enough, she was right. The priestess asked, "May I watch?"

Adrastea leaned against the stone wall. "If you want. How did you know I was building my house tonight?"

Mikal stretched apologetically. "I told her. I hope you don't mind." At Adrastea's sigh of disappointment, he amended, "Some people need to know what you do. Chloe's one of them."

Chloe stood there calmly, her hands folded before her. "I'm curious as to how an immortal would build a house. For some reason, I don't see you wielding a hammer."

Mikal pointed across the property to a wavering light. "There's the Constables." They came down the back way from their home.

Two stocky figures emerged from the gloom, a lantern bobbing on a stick. Evan and Janyse Constable. A couple of large dogs kept pace beside them.

"Hello," Evan called out.

"Hello," Mikal replied. "Where are the boys?"

Evan set the end of his stick to the ground. The pool of light fell around him and his wife. "Patrol. Just in case." He ordered his dogs to sit and stay.

"Oh, good grief," griped Adrastea. "I'm just building a house."

"Begging pardon, ma'am," said Evan. "It's your sorcerous ways that make this different."

"It's not sorcery."

"Now, I know that, and you know that, but the troublemakers might not. One must consider what others might think."

"I don't care about my reputation."

"I'm not speaking of reputations, but trouble prevention. Get into the head of your opponent and you can outwit him."

Adrastea felt foolish. "You anticipate trouble, do you?"

Evan chuckled. "I always anticipate trouble. Then I do something about it, so it doesn't happen."

It was a good thing the Constables were on her side. Where were they when she was trying to get out of a betrothal?

"Could I borrow your yard for a little while? I need someplace to keep my wood while I lay the foundation."

They acquiesced. While they walked around to where the others were standing, she, by the Deeper Power, moved her fifty cords of wood onto their property.

"Oh, glory," Chloe breathed. "You're glowing."

"Is she?" Mikal asked. He was rubbing his arms again.

Adrastea ignored them. Time to build a house.

She knelt and put a hand on the ground.

At her request, stones of every size came boiling up through the soil to organize into a cellar and foundation. From that, she raised tall chimneys, one on either end of the foundation. Adrastea rose and gestured to the logs. They split into beams and planks. By her will, they assembled themselves into the floors and walls of her home. For the next hour, her audience watched in awe as Adrastea constructed first one floor then another. She added an attic and a steeply-pitched roof to slough off snow in winter.

A porch ran across the whole front of the house and a matching one in the back. By the time the waning gibbous moon had risen, she added the final door.

Adrastea's home was done.

Adrastea humphed. "It is missing a few things," like metal door latches and glass for the windows. "I'm sure I can complete that tomorrow. At least all the hard work is finished."

Chloe drew a deep breath. "You didn't lift a finger."

"That's a useful talent," Janyse said.

"Not if it gets you married to Dark Gods."

Mikal ran his fingers through his hair. "I don't know if I can sleep after a demonstration like that."

Adrastea glanced north. "Jacob won't. He's been watching all this from the door to the loft." She pointed towards the Mayor's house. "He'll be glad to get his room back, after I've moved all my new acquisitions out." Her prior shopping spree to Crossroads not only included a cradle and baby supplies for Harianne, but a few needful items for herself, all stored in Mikal's attic. "I'll wait until you've warned him before removing my things here."

As everyone said their distracted goodnights, Adrastea climbed the porch and pushed open the door.

Her house. Her home, with its wide front room that took up the whole north side. It had a fireplace at one end, the other being located in the kitchen on the south side. Adrastea called forth some of the scrap wood left behind and requested a fire. It crackled and grew, the flames brightening the room.

The staircase divided the kitchen and another room from the living room. It led to a hallway and several bedrooms upstairs. For tonight, she planned on staying down here by the warm fire.

It was a good, serviceable house, perhaps too serviceable for the likes of her. She didn't build it for her, but for Harianne. Someday it would be hers.

Harianne squirmed—feeding time soon. Adrastea stepped out on the back porch and looked to the Mayor's home. Closing her eyes, she searched out her new belongings in the attic and willed them into her home.

She had bought a rocking chair and a small table to sit beside it. Harianne had a cradle and her blankets, diapers and layette. Adrastea had also purchased a trunk and a few serviceable outfits to go with it. While the country women preferred the pantaloon style, Adrastea's legs felt unclad without a skirt. She'd also procured a wash tub, several blankets, kitchen utensils, a sewing basket, some rope and other needful things.

She had debated over buying a beautifully carved bed. The headboard had vines and flowers carved into it. She had hesitated to get it, for the thought of a bed for two might bring the unwanted attentions of her husband. Mikal talked her into it, suggesting that when the winter months came, a little baby would prefer a big warm bed, rather than a small cold cradle. "My bed's a double and I don't share it with anyone. Believe me, after having to share with brothers, stretching out in a big bed alone is a nice luxury."

She hung some blankets over the window frames and laid the washing tub against the front door to keep it closed. She changed Harianne, dropping the dirty diaper in the tub. She'd wash it later. Then she settled down in her rocking chair to nurse and to spend the next eight hours wondering why the child insisted on being awake the whole night.

By the time the sun rose in the morning, she was glad of two things: that immortals didn't require much sleep, and that Mor-Lath saw fit to stay away.

Only now that the sun had risen did Harianne fall asleep for good. With relief, Adrastea dropped her charge into the cradle.

Perhaps adoption wasn't such a bright idea. She did admit one advantage to the situation—the breastfeeding meant bigger breasts. Shame she didn't have anyone to whom she could show them off. Desideria, who kept occasional silent company with her, wasn't interested.

Chapter 7

Mor-Lath stood on a hill overlooking Avelia. To the west behind him, the sun had sunk to the horizon and would soon fall behind the hills. The evening lights of the city sparkled in the approaching twilight. Beyond, the silver ribbon of the river flowed calmly. Two ships drifted on the current as first one, then the other, lost their anchor lines. Let them drift away to the sea and become lost among the currents. *Good riddance to the lot of you*, he thought. His bad mood fueled his anger as he dealt with the city that disappointed him.

Mor-Lath snapped one more line and a third ship floated down the river, taking with it its dying crew. The rats with their plague-infested fleas had already come ashore to spread their disease among the dockers.

The western gates remained open for the few departing carts. Only a few more trundled to the gate, the ones Montrof managed to convince to flee at the last minute.

And where was Montrof? Standing just inside one of the gates, ensuring everyone made it out.

They wouldn't clear the city before the sun set. Too bad.

A brightness appeared beside the God of the Dark. "So," said Phyl. "Destroying your favorite city, I see?"

Mor-Lath groaned inwardly. "Third favorite city."

Phyl shrugged. "Well, if they're disobedient, they're disobedient. You have every right to smite them." He gestured down at the tiny trail of carts waiting to leave. "Surely you aren't intending to destroy the faithful as well."

"None of your business," he growled.

"People like gods who show mercy."

Anger tightened Mor-Lath's stomach. "I've been far too permissive with them already."

"You mean you've spoiled them."

Mor-Lath glared at Phyl. "I don't recall asking Your opinion."

"I don't recall needing your permission to give it." Phyl returned Mor-Lath's look until the Dark God turned away.

The landscape faded into darkness as the sun departed for the night. Stars, one by one, appeared.

Phyl thumped him on the shoulder. "I'm sure with time you'll learn how to be a proper god. Then you won't have to go around cleaning up your mistakes."

Mor-Lath scowled at Phyl. He smacked the hand away.

Phyl punched his arm hard.

"What the—?" started Mor-Lath, reeling from the surprise attack. He drew back his fist and punched Him on the jaw. Phyl rolled with the punch. He turned back, His expression neutral, before delivering a sharp left hook into Mor-Lath's stomach.

His anger flared. Mor-Lath tackled Phyl to the ground. They rolled around, trading punches, kicks and other blows. Mor-Lath threw in a few insults. Phyl remained silent.

Phyl, Who never really let go of the Deeper Power, thrust Mor-Lath away, sending him tumbling down the hill.

When he came to a rest, he glowered at the god up on the hill. "How dare you interfere?"

Phyl only harrumphed. He came partway down the hill and sat on a rock that provided a good view of the departing people. He pointed to Avelia. "Don't you have a city you want to destroy?"

Mor-Lath wiped at the corner of his mouth with the back of his hand. Yes, he was bleeding. Phyl seemed untouched. The unfairness of it ate at his heart. What was all that for?

He turned to where Phyl pointed. With the perception of an immortal, he saw that his faithful had all cleared the gates. No more people or carts waited to depart. The last to leave was a lone man, old and hesitant, just outside the gate. Montrof. He gazed one last time upon the doomed city. Upon second glance, Montrof wasn't alone after all.

Mor-Lath swore. "What the hell are they doing there?" He scowled at the angels surrounding his priest.

"Doing what you should have been doing—succoring the faithful."

Phyl rose from his rock. "Whenever you're angry at your wife, don't take it out on your followers. Faith deserves to be rewarded. That's what feeds faith in the first place."

Mor-Lath waved his hand. "Fine. Save them if You wish."

"I hoped to save you."

"Whatever." Mor-Lath reached out his hand and snapped the telegraph wires leading away from Avelia. He took delight in their taut pings as the tension gave way, their copper singing its particular sweet tune. Let the people send the news the old-fashioned way.

"Why are you so angry at your wife?" Phyl folded His hands before Him.

Another wave of anger flushed through him. "She learned the secret that would make us a god. She refuses to give it to me."

Phyl's countenance changed. The light of recognition lit His eyes. "Has she now? How do you know?"

Mor-Lath bunched his fists and pressed them into his eyes. "I was with her when she discovered it. It was like she had the elements all along. Then they all came together, and she recognized it. 'So that's what it is,' she said, as clear as day."

Phyl leaned forward. "And what was it?"

Mor-Lath's hands flew from his face. "She won't bloody tell me!"

"Not even a clue?"

"None."

"No bargains?"

"N.. " He drew in a sharp breath. "She says she'll give it to me if..."

"If..." Phil took a step closer. "What'd she say?"

Mor-Lath shook the thought of his head. "Nothing."

The god laughed. "Oh, she said something all right. I can see it in your aura. It piques you."

"I do not like being manipulated," Mor-Lath shouted at him.

"So, what did she say?" Phyl's eagerness was palpable. "Please?"

"You really want to know? 'Give me everything,' she said. She wants me to be nice to her, make her happy, and do all those silly little things that women like."

"You mean, she wants you to be a nice husband?"

"No, she wants everything. And she meant EVERY THING. The whole courtship. All over again."

"What? Talk sweet to her?"

Mor-Lath frowned at Him.

"Share your secrets with her?"

"I don't know if I can do it."

A bright smile enlightened Phyl's face. He slapped Mor-Lath on the back good-naturedly. "Brother, congratulations! You've won."

At first, His words didn't sink in. "What?"

Before he could stop Him, Phyl hugged Mor-Lath. In his ear, He whispered, "She wants you to win. If you do everything she asks of you, she cannot keep the secret from you. It will give itself to you. You will have won." Then He hugged him tighter before releasing him.

Mor-Lath blinked. "What are you talking about?"

Twilight darkened the land. Only the twinkling lights of a doomed city shone in the darkness. Phyl gazed out over it, His mood settling. "Don't you have a city to destroy?"

Before He departed, He gave him one last piece of advice. "Try giving her a flower. Then don't expect anything in return. That's a good place to start."

Once the God of the Light left, Mor-Lath followed His departure with a few more epithets. He turned his simmering annoyance to the disobedient capital of Avelia. All that remained were the unheeding, the unbelieving. They would get their chance to reacquaint themselves with their god.

He focused his frustration as he pulled on the Deeper Power. With a cry of anger, he shook the earth and uprooted it before the closed gates, burying them under tons of dirt and rock. Then he opened the bowels of Dom-al-gol and called forth all the demons that would serve him. "Patrol the walls," he commanded. "Should any mortal seek to climb over, discourage them. Let none get past."

The demons, happy to be free of their hell, shot off to do his bidding. They would enjoy tormenting the living, if only to relieve the pinch of envy.

Mor-Lath shook the riverbed, causing the dockside of the city to settle into the banks. As a result, all the plague-ridden rats stormed into the city proper. For one brief moment, he considered shaking the foundations of the city to the ground but did not give in to the impulse. Phyl had made him a fool. He should not let it affect him. Oh, no. He had to keep calm, keep control. He would not mess up, not with the Light watching. It was bad enough They mocked him over his failed marriage. He blamed Them for that. They always were deceptive, giving with one hand and taking away with the other. He should never have allowed Them to have a say in the creation of his bride, for They had seen she grew up a follower of Them.

"Really," he spat. "A flower?" Like a flower would change anything.

Once his anger died down, he focused on the curses and prayers of the faithful. They were always there, these supplications, humming in the background of his awareness. Sometimes he paid close attention.

He heard Montrof, who'd fallen to his knees just outside the upheaval of the earth. Mor-Lath's soul twisted as he heard the words of gratitude for the mercy that wasn't his but the Light's. Really, he convinced himself, it wasn't guilt that made him ignore the thankfulness that poured towards him.

"Just bugger off," Mor-Lath muttered as he turned his attention back to the city.

Now, there was something of which to be proud. All the gates, every route of escape, including the hidden tunnels and sewers, were barricaded. Yet most of the city continued their drunken celebrations.

Wasson had declared a night of revelry to mock the priests of Mor-Lath and their warning. Those who felt they didn't owe their prosperity to the God of Wealth spent some of that prosperity in debauchery.

The people in close quarters made it all too easy.

By morning more than a quarter of the population had been bitten by infected fleas. When the people discovered the blocked gates and the flooded port district, they worried. They gathered in pubs and plazas to work themselves into a frenzy, thus giving the plague a better chance to spread its contagion. Symptoms would not present for at least another day or so, but by then, it would be too late.

As for the disobedient little king, Mor-Lath personally oversaw his death.

While the prayers of the grateful hummed in the back of his head, he heard one of pleading. If he had felt inclined to mercy that evening (which he didn't), he could have pitied the poor lost woman who barely escaped the shift of the river.

She'd not felt well these past few days, having made her home among the docks. She'd been bitten by the fleas and would soon die, one of the first casualties. With the last hope of a roof over her head destroyed by the rising waters, she had hobbled off to higher ground, not knowing where she would go, or what she would do with herself. She'd never been one much for religion, until now, turning to a god with whom she'd never been acquainted.

She was perfect. Already her symptoms presented a headache, sore joints and a cough, not that this was anything new to her malnourished body. Soon her stomach would cramp, and she'd feel feverish; that would be by morning. Mor-Lath heeded her prayers and gave her what she wanted most, a soft warm bed.

He gave her the best one in Avelia.

In the morning, as Wasson, King of Avelia finally stumbled to his room, she'd be discovered dead, or near enough as made no difference.

Now that was something that deserved his attention far more than his recent failures.

Avelia was back in his control and he would see it fall.

That, he considered a success.

Montrof stood with the faithful on the gentle slopes to the west of Avelia as dawn touched the sky to the east after they had fled the city. They had witnessed the floods streaming in through the ports and had seen the earth heave up before the gates. They wanted to get as far away from whatever destruction could be next.

Indeed, they were all weary. Fifteen thousand people had fled. Now all those people had fanned out through fields of grain and orchards of fruit to collapse in exhaustion before the rising sun. Every once in a while, Montrof thought he glimpsed the familiar face of his god, but never long enough to be sure. He chose to believe his god was with them.

Mor-Lath's priests and priestesses, those who had personally received Mor-Lath's warning of the impending destruction, stood together on the hills west of the city. They looked back to the home they had fled.

While walls of earth surrounded it and water flowed in the portside streets, the rest of the city stood tall.

"I thought it would have been completely destroyed by now," one priestess uttered.

Montrof sighed. "His Holiness never told us how he would destroy the city."

Mor-Lath spoke. "I never said I would destroy the city."

They all turned. As one, they fell to their knees.

"The people, on the other hand... Well, be grateful you are not there, for it is not a pretty sight."

"Oh, Holy One, we never doubted," cried an older priestess. "It is not the past we look to but the future. Where are we to go?"

Mor-Lath looked over his followers. "You," he said after a long moment of consideration, "shall wander. And whither shall you end up?"

His devoted looked to one another. In the end, Montrof confessed, "We don't know."

"That's right. From now on, you are to wander until I say stop." And he left them, disappearing before their eyes, leaving them to ponder what he meant.

Montrof sighed. "This is not like him." He wished Chamque was here. When she lived, she had talked at him and talked at him. Drove him spare sometimes. Despite the noise of her voice, when she finally shut up, that was when he found inspiration.

Who was going to natter at him now?

Montrof sat down on the damp earth. He pulled his knees up to his chin and wrapped his arms around his legs. Avelia was being punished because of Wasson's attack of Feown. Why was Mor-Lath favoring Feown above Avelia? Hadn't he always stood against the Glasskissers?

The older priestess who had begged their god for direction, sat next to him. She did not hide her lamenting but let the tears stream down her face. She was a wailer, this one. Montrof preferred Chamque's naggings.

Why destroy Avelia? Sure, it was wicked, but not so wicked that it should have been wiped from the earth. Nearly a third of the population had fled with the priests. Those were the faithful of Mor-Lath.

They were not the only ones to flee. All the Glasskissers had departed as well—not that they had much of a home to return to, if reports of Feown were to be believed.

Now that was an interesting development. Did they heed the Priests of Mor-Lath and think it wise to flee as well? He couldn't see that their god—whoever He was—would come and warn them at the same time. The Glasskisser god was a rather laissez-faire sort of fellow, from what he'd heard. Some doubted whether He existed at all. After all, the Avelians had Mor-Lath, who was rather hands-on.

And then there was the Cithran god, the One True. Nobody had seen him, not even his faithful. But he'd done an awful lot of ordering around. If what Mor-Lath had told him—there was no One True—then who was doing the ordering?

By now several of the priestesses had gathered about the wailing one, crowding Montrof out of the way. Their comfort came in the form of platitudes and reassurances, along with tight group-hugs and the stroking of hair.

It drew all the women to the circle.

Montrof rose and stalked off. He couldn't think with all that femininity going on.

Several smart people organized together. They sent out parties to hunt firewood. No use anyone going anywhere until they figured out a few things.

Once fires were built, people gathered about them to settle on the uncomfortable ground. Montrof found a grassy spot near a warm blaze. There he fretted until exhaustion finally overtook him. He slept, as much as one could.

The next morning, the survivors took stock of what survived. Of the religious, the priestesses numbered nearly double the priests. Priestesses were funny like that. They tended to group to the temples and stay there. The priests wandered, moving from temple to temple. Not many chose such a life. As old age wrapped itself around Montrof's bones, he had appreciated having a nice, warm temple to call home.

Even now, a hundred priests of Mor-Lath milled about the orchard, looking out to the city, the pillars of smoke tinted orange by the morning sun.

Outwards huddled the faithful of Mor-Lath, in groups of fifty or so, dispersed throughout the orchards and fields of Avelia's farms. They all hunched in misery, or lay curled up under wagons, handcarts or by the small bundle of belongings they had hastily cobbled together before fleeing on foot. Some slept in fretfulness while others stared back at what was once their home.

Were the Feowans as homeless as they? He couldn't see any about.

An earlier conversation with the god drifted through his head. Mor-Lath was punishing Avelia for Feown. Why? Why, why, why?

Montrof approached two priests who stood by a tree, their heads close together in discussion. He dispensed with the niceties of greetings and got down to business. "His Holiness told me he would destroy Avelia because of Feown. Is that what he has told you?"

Montrof recognized the older priest, Palus. The younger he had seen in passing but had not yet met. The younger priest acknowledged Montrof's seniority with a quick bow.

Palus sighed. "His Holiness told me how Wasson had taken advantage of Feown's weakened state after the Cithran war and defeated it. If you ask me, it was a legitimate military tactic. In the past there was no way we could have defeated the Feowans. But now, we have succeeded."

The younger priest offered, "Hasn't Feown always been our enemy?"

Yes, it had, but... A little spark of inspiration lit up a dusty corner of Montrof's memory.

"So," the young priest asked, "Why is our god angry? You would have thought him pleased that we defeated the Glasskissers."

Montrof put his hands to his temples. "Oh, I am so stupid! So, so stupid! I am such a fool I wonder that Mor-Lath himself did not tie me to a pillar and leave me to die in Avelia. Palus, has His Holiness ever said anything about Feown being the enemy?"

Palus thought about that, but Montrof did not wait for an answer. "Has he ever commanded us to wage war against the Feowans? Has he ever commanded us to fight the Glasskissers?"

Palus frowned. "No." A few more priests wandered over, curious.

Montrof began to pace. "For the past twenty years, what has our task been, as wandering priests? Who have we been sent to hunt? Who do we pursue?"

Palus sighed. "I had been sent to seek out Cithrans. But isn't that a moot point?"

"No," Montrof replied, his hands shaking in agitation. "It has never been the Feowans, but the Cithrans."

The young priest blurted out, "But don't we hunt them down because the Cithrans worship a false god? We do not wish the followers of a real god to be swayed by their lies. Right?"

"Yes," Palus affirmed.

"No," cried Montrof. His audience grew to a dozen priests. "Well, yes, that is part of it, but there is so, so much more." He muttered to himself. "Twenty years and you think I would have figured it out by now." He paced again, his irritated comments more for his own benefit than anyone else's. "Palus," he said, stopping before his fellow priest, "Have you ever met the Bride of Mor-Lath?"

This caused a fresh eruption of discussion among the priests. By now, nearly all had gathered, and a few priestesses as well, those who had been on the peripheral of the other group.

"I..." he started, thoughts tumbling through his head. "I'd heard of her. I didn't know if it was simply a legend."

"No legend. She is real. I have met her. Only the once, and I hope never again, but she does exist." He pressed his knuckles to his lips. "Granted, this was, oh, about fifteen or twenty years ago...

"But..." He tapped his fingers on his forehead in hopes of shaking loose old memories. "Yes, we were sent to hunt Cithrans who sent their subtle tendrils into the city in hopes of what? Not to convert the faithful. They were on a mission. They were seeking the Bride of Mor-Lath."

Palus shook his head. "But what does this have to do with Feown and Avelia?

Montrof hung his head. "I did not think anything of it at the time. Perhaps I should have. But the one time I met the Bride, I realized after the fact, her accent was Feowan."

Silence fell for a moment, then the whole group buzzed in discussion. Was it true? Was Mor-Lath's wife a Feowan? Is that why he favored the city?

Montrof saw Benadon, the priestess of his home temple, on the edge of the crowd. "Benadon! You know."

She shook her head. "I don't."

"Of course you do. Chamque would have told you."

"Yes, I know the story of the Bride of Mor-Lath. We hold her in healthy respect, but I wasn't there that day. I never saw her. You are the only one left who has."

Montrof swatted away her words like an annoying fly. "No, no. I know what Chamque and the others were set to do. I know your task. You had to remove Wacifice. Why?"

Benadon looked around. Montrof had broken a temple confidence by betraying their task, one they had been told to keep secret. "I... don't know what you mean."

Montrof groaned. Why did everyone have to be so difficult? Things had changed. There no longer was an Avelia. Her people had been scattered or destroyed. Old secrets no longer applied. "Wacifice defied the will of Mor-Lath by seeking to attack Feown." Montrof failed to mention that it has been his idea, in the beginning. "So, he had us remove him. And his son, same thing. And now, his other son, Wasson. He, too, defied the will of Mor-Lath."

Palus shook his head. "No, that can't be right."

"It has to be right," Montrof insisted.

"We didn't know we weren't supposed to attack Feown. Why should we be punished for breaking a law we didn't know about?"

Montrof knew this was true. It was a rather harsh punishment. "Three days ago, His Holiness appeared to Wasson himself and gave him a warning. He told him to withdraw his troops.

"Wasson didn't. Now Avelia suffers."

"But why?" cried one of the younger priestesses. "Couldn't he have just destroyed Wasson? Why all of us?"

Another piece fell into the puzzle. "There is something else going on, something we don't know about. That it has to do with Feown, I am sure. But does it have to do with his wife?"

Palus shook his head. "If it's to do with the Bride, why did he not smite the Cithrans?"

Montrof sat on the ground. All this thinking, all this sifting through years of memories made his head hurt and he felt dizzy. "He did. Remember about twenty years ago when the Cithran army invaded Feown and nearly brought them to their knees?"

Several of the older priests and priestesses nodded.

"They called it 'Deliverance' when the whole of the Cithran army died on their doorstep."

"So, their god was watching over them," Paulus replied.

Montrof shook his head. "No. That was His Holiness what did that, not the Glasskisser god."

A frown crossed Paulus' face. "Why?"

"Because of her."

This news rippled through the gathered priests. What had Feown done to gain the favors of their god? The more Montrof thought about it the more he wondered if the Bride was Feowan because Mor-Lath favored Feown, or that he favored Feown because his Bride was Feowan.

While Montrof had given himself over to thought, the others divided into groups. Their discussions turned into arguments. His Holiness hadn't done enough, or he'd done too much. Why was he inconsistent, or was it right to question him at all?

Montrof's head throbbed. He needed a drink of water. And when was the last time he'd eaten? Come to think of it, did he own anything other than the clothes on his back? He had been so busy making sure that the others got out he forgot to think of himself. He laid his head down on his knees. No, better to lay down on the ground before it swung out from underneath him.

Palus knelt next to him and laid a hand on his forehead. "How long have you been up?"

Montrof shook his head. "I have not been able to rest for three days. There is something else going on that we don't know about." He yawned. "So much to think about... must stop the troops before they are killed as well..."

Another earthquake rolled across the ground, not enough to damage anything, but enough to solidify fear in everyone's hearts.

Time to get well away from Avelia.

Some wanted to go west. A few wanted to return to Avelia, even on the flimsy excuse of supplies. Others wanted to head south, away from all the troubles, but Montrof would have none of it.

"No. As we are, we're vulnerable. We go north. We rendezvous with the army. Tell them what happened. Then we head west, away from Feown, away from Avelia."

Adrastea woke with a start when she heard the knocking on the door. Where was she? Ah yes, her new home. Her hands rested on the arms of a rocking chair. The fire had banked down to coals and ash. Salle's voice called out, "Adrastea?"

Adrastea stretched. Harianne slumbered in the cradle by the rocking chair. "Yes?" A wave of her hand moved the washtub keeping the door closed. The door eased open. Salle pushed it the rest of the way.

She didn't enter the house but gazed all around. "You built this in one night? I can't wait to hear what you tell everyone at Council."

Adrastea rose to her feet. "Council?" Oh. She'd forgotten. Now that she'd declared permanent residency at Sacred Spring, she had the right, and was expected, to attend Council meetings. "When's the next one?"

"Three days." Salle's countenance fell. "That is, if..." She fiddled with her fingers. "Ari sent me to tell you Lord Pennexter's slipped into a coma. He may have had another fit in the night. He's not going to last."

Adrastea sighed. She gathered up Harianne as gently as she could so the baby would remain asleep. She followed Salle to the Inn. Desideria stayed behind.

Mikal was there, with Jacob. Dassie was absent. The two men, whose names she never learned, sat attendance on either side of the bed. Ari sat at the small table, penciling notes in her book. Her elbow rested on the table and her forehead was cupped in her hand.

When Adrastea came in, Ari rose, closing her book. "He's not long for this world. If he doesn't have another fit and he continues to swallow when we give him water, he might awaken in a few days. Otherwise, he won't last the week. The girl says he wants to die at home, but the trains aren't running, I'm told."

Adrastea's eyes flickered to Mikal. "I could take him back to Feown, if needs be."

Mikal nodded. "No reason to keep him here."

Adrastea looked around. "Where is Dassie?" She rocked Harianne in hopes she remained asleep after that last feed.

Ari said, "She went to the telegraph office to see if she could get word through to the rest of the family."

"It's not like they're going far," he said. "Consider this. As long as he's like this, and the trains aren't running, they have no reason to move him. And should he die... If Feown is still under siege, they'll want to stay here because we're all the family he's got at the moment."

Adrastea lifted her head. "Dassie's back."

The young Pennexter girl entered the room, somber. "How is he?" she asked Ari.

Ari shrugged. "No change."

"So, you don't know how much longer?" Dassie looked from Ari to Adrastea.

Adrastea sighed. "To be honest, I don't think he's getting any better. If he— when he dies, what are your plans?"

Dassie gave a sad little laugh. "That was just what I had gone to communicate with the rest of the family. I'm hoping the trains will be running soon, so we can take him home. The family will want to be present for his pyre."

"And if they're not?"

Ari said, "We can have the pyre here."

Dassie scowled at Ari before replying to Adrastea's question. "I'm praying to the Light for a miracle that will enable me to take my uncle's body home. I've just telegraphed to say that we're hoping to be home soon and for the family to prepare for death."

"Oh." She looked at the unconscious old man. He seemed worried, even in sleep, with his mouth turned down like that. Would she have loved him, had she known and grown up with him? "What was he like, as a man?"

"After the death of his wife, he was involved in a few scandals, so the old Duke made him our ambassador to Cithra." Dassie wrinkled her nose.

"To Cithra?" Adrastea wasn't expecting that.

"Best way of getting rid of him." If he was to be problematic, make him someone else's problem. "He was there during the first war and Deliverance. When Feown took advantage of their undefended state and invaded Cithra, Lord Pennexter had to go underground."

Adrastea took one of the empty chairs. She settled Harianne's sling better so the baby rested on her belly. "I missed the war. What was it like?"

Dassie gave her a look that reminded her of Jonathan. "Where have you been?"

"The Dark One and I were having issues at the time. World events weren't exactly on my mind."

A moment of awkward silence fell between them all. Ari broke it before it became too uncomfortable. "Things changed after you left Sacred Spring. The call went out to gather an army, but not of men only. Women were drafted too. Any who were not mothers, or the sole supporters of their families were called to war."

"Including you, Ari?"

Ari shook her head. "I was too old. There were a few other exceptions, but it was mostly the young, unmarried women who went to war. More volunteered than was expected, possibly because they were all offered a salary and pension."

Dassie added, "It was a different war, different from anything we ever knew before. It was a holy war. We weren't out to gain land or wealth. We were out to destroy the Cithrans. They were of what they called the True Faith and they followed the One True God. They denied the Light and even the Dark. For that, we were told, they would be destroyed."

Ari nodded. "There was some dissention when we learned that our goal was genocide."

Adrastea put her hand to her mouth.

Dassie continued, "In the end, we obeyed. The Light commanded it. For their denial of the Light, the Cithrans would be cleansed from the earth, every man, woman and child. We were to spare no one." She shook her head. "But it didn't happen like that. There were those who doubted. Some took mercy on the Cithran children and spared them. We disobeyed. Now we're paying for it. We've been at war ever since.

"Those we spared were not blessed by our mercy but survived so the poison of the True Faith could sink deeper into their hearts. Fifteen years later, those poor little defenseless children we spared have grown up to be soldiers who continue to slaughter our people." Dassie toyed with the hem of her blouse. "We were fools to doubt the word of the Light. We're suffering for our lack of faith. And now, Avelia has laid siege to Feown."

This was of great interest to Adrastea. Mor-Lath favored Avelia. Did he have anything to do with the siege? Her desire to know warred with her aversion of him. If he was behind it, he would not take too kindly to her interfering with his plans.

And therein laid its appeal. Here, interference would annoy him. "I will have to do something about the siege of Feown. After all, we must return my grandfather to the rest of the family."

"Can you do that?" Dassie asked.

"Adrastea," Ari warned.

Adrastea caught her cautionary glance and changed the subject. "When the war started, how did Lord Pennexter get out?"

"He didn't," Dassie said. "Her Grace needed him there, so there he stayed, communicating with Feown by secret means. He was there for several years.

"One day he appeared on the palace doorstep. Cithra had grown too dangerous for him, so he came home. We still don't know how he did it.

"I never really saw him or got to know him until two years ago when I was sent to serve Her Grace. I think that was more because of my family connections, than anything else. But I earned the right to keep my place on my own merit," she added, proud of the fact.

"He and Uncle Jonathan advised Her Grace. Jonathan serves the Light as High Priest in Feown and Stobol knows more about Cithra than anyone else. Family Pennexter's star has risen in the heavens. I only wish it didn't take a war. While some of us are highly placed, many of the rest of us have been brought low by death."

"Will you have to go to war?" Adrastea asked.

Dassie shrugged. "I hope not. I work hard to prove I'm of more use back home than abroad."

Mikal returned, a napkin-covered plate in one hand. "I haven't had breakfast and suspect the rest of you haven't either." The warm smell of bread and bacon wafted towards them.

Adrastea's stomach tightened in anticipation. Mikal handed her a bread roll-type thing. "It's called a pasty. It's stuffed with bacon and eggs and you can eat it with one hand. War food."

Adrastea gave it another sniff then took a tender bite, so the heat of it wouldn't burn her mouth. Rather convenient way to eat bacon and eggs.

Mikal had brought enough for everyone, including Lord Pennexter's attendants. As Mikal offered the plate to them, Adrastea realized they'd not been introduced. "What are your names?"

One of them, the stockier of the two, rose and addressed her. "My name's Stepan. He's Hugh, my lady. We are distant relatives, too distant to be considered heirs, but close enough to be trusted by the family."

Fair enough. She couldn't see much family resemblance. "You don't say much, do you?"

"That's our job," Stepan said.

As they finished their breakfast, Adrastea pressed Dassie and Ari for more information about the war.

And while they were discussing things, Lord Pennexter silently slipped away.

Adrastea watched Tanat slip into the room to collect his soul. Her and Adrastea's gazes met, then she slipped out again without a word. How had Tanat judged him?

"He's gone," Adrastea murmured while Ari was speaking.

"What?" Dassie stared at her uncle.

Dassie, Hugh and Stepan gathered at the foot of the bed. Ari checked Lord Pennexter, agreeing with Adrastea that he had indeed passed on. Mikal stood by his chair, pensive.

"I'm sorry," Ari said to Dassie and the men. "Would you like me to fetch the Priestess?"

Dassie wilted. "No." Her dark hair fell before her face. "I want to go home."

Harianne stirred. She clenched her fists, screwed up her face until it turned purple, then relaxed. She'd wake soon and want a feed, after needing a change first. Adrastea looked at Mikal and he returned her gaze. Her eyes flickered over to Dassie.

He shrugged. "Your call."

Adrastea rose. "If you wish, Dassie Pennexter, I can take you home."

The girl raised her face and swiped at the tears that dampened her cheeks. "I meant Feown."

"That's what I mean. You, him," she gestured to her deceased grandfather, "and the others." Hugh and Stepan glanced at each other, puzzled. They were not privy to this deep dark family secret.

"I don't know," Dassie said, unsure. She glanced from Lord Pennexter's body to Adrastea. She drew a deep breath. "I don't think that's proper." Hugh and Stepan, their heads bowed low, conversed quietly together.

Adrastea frowned. "I don't think that's your call." Adrastea turned to Mikal. "What do you think?"

Mikal spread his hands. "I'm not the authority here. Any existing wills are back in Feown, and they were written before Lord Pennexter learned about us. You are the eldest of us, Adrastea. It would be your decision."

Harianne squirmed, turning purple once more before she started to squall. Adrastea stuck her pinky upside down into Harianne's mouth. The child sucked on it for a moment, giving Adrastea a little time to think. "Ari, could you wash and prepare the body? Dress it properly, then wrap it in a shroud. Then..." then what? How did one move a body about? For every death she knew about, the body was carried as-is to the pyre. She'd never thought about moving a body further than house-to-pyre. "We'll need a board or a box. Something in which to carry him until we get to Feown."

"He's not baggage," Dassie protested.

"Yes, he is. His soul is gone. What are left are his mortal remains. And bodies aren't easy to carry."

Dassie grew still. "That's cruel."

"No, being cruel would have been not caring about your feelings—or indeed, any of the Pennexters' feelings—and having him cremated here."

Harianne figured out the finger had no milk. She thrust it out with her tongue and began to wail. "Mikal," Adrastea said, bouncing the baby to no avail, "could you find something suitable for taking Lord Pennexter's remains to Feown? I trust you can come up with something dignified?"

Mikal nodded.

"Good. Meanwhile, I've got the living to attend to. I'll be home if you need me."

Chapter 8

Should Adrastea take Harianne with her or not? In the end, she chose to leave her behind. She and Mikal wouldn't be gone long—go to Feown, return the body to the family, and depart without much fuss. She figured that learning Josephus had had children would be too much of a shock for the family—especially when Jonathan learned she was one of them.

Ari agreed to watch Harianne until she returned, as long as the baby had been newly-fed.

With Mikal's help, she moved the body from the Inn to the stillroom, where she'd prepared it for viewing. Mikal, being the mayor, convinced the Carpenters to put together a simple box with no lid. In this box they laid his body, resting his hands upon his chest. Lord Pennexter retained the worried look. Nothing Adrastea did could erase that.

No matter what anyone said, a dead body did not look like they were sleeping. The dead looked very much dead—no mistaking it. Lord Pennexter looked even more so, lying in that box, cold, stiff, almost like wax.

Desideria, who followed her this time, told her it was called a coffin— a box for the dead. "Followers of Mor-Lath bury their dead in coffins. It's symbolic of returning to the underworld."

"Followers of the Light cremate their dead," Adrastea replied. "The light of the fire is symbolic of the Light Themselves, and the smoke from the fire drifts heavenwards."

Desideria leaned over the body. "The stench of the pyre must be terrible."

"Not as bad as leaving a body to rot."

The ghost looked up. "My body was buried. There was no funeral, nor memorial. The other priestesses gathered me together, wrapped me in a simple shroud and laid me in a grave without a coffin." She grew still, fading almost into invisibility. "I think they were ashamed. I'm certain they knew why I took my life. I thought they would have understood." Her visibility wavered.

Adraseta's heart ached. "Would you have preferred cremation?"

"I think I would have preferred that." She faded out completely.

Adrastea mused over an idea. Was it too late? Had the priestess' body moldered away completely?

Mikal came forward and looked at the body. "He looks good."

Ari touched the side of the coffin. "He looks dead."

Adrastea agreed. While they were alone, the three could speak their minds. Natan was not present. He had no desire to view the body nor felt obliged to comfort the Pennexters that didn't dwell in Sacred Spring. Dassie and the men were back at the inn settling their bill and packing for the journey back to Feown. Their instructions: bring their trunks to the Healer's home and wait for instructions.

"I'd be worried if he looked alive," Adrastea added.

Mikal sighed. Her brother didn't want to go, but she'd convinced him. "Of the two of us, you're the one with the better reputation."

"I don't have any reputation in Feown."

"That's my point."

In the end, he agreed that even a country mayor had some degree of respectability. It might be enough to carry him through. While Ari prepared the body, he slipped back home, washed up, dressed in his best and gave Jacob instructions for while he was gone.

The sound of a handcart rumbled outside. The family had returned. Dassie came in. "Where shall we put the baggage?"

"Leave it where it is." Adrastea reached out and touched the coffin. "Are we ready to go?"

Dassie nodded.

The coffin disappeared.

"What the—!" Dassie exclaimed. "By the Light! Where'd it go?"

Additional curses echoed outside. No doubt Hugh and Stepan had been equally surprised at the sudden appearance of a coffin out by the handcart.

"Come," ordered Adrastea. "We are off to Feown."

❧

Even though she had never been there, Adrastea had no problem setting everyone and their luggage down in front of Pennexter House. She followed the Lines that grew strongest when Dassie mentioned 'home'.

Pennexter House, the main residence of the family in Feown, echoed the grandeur of days long gone. One could smell the old-money of this once-prosperous family. But if what Dassie had said was true, few Pennexters remained. Even the family seat seemed devoid of life. Was this because so many of the family were dead or gone? Three stories of windows looked down on the cobbled street. The stone steps leading up to the double doors lent an even more oppressive air of domination, as did the wrought-iron fence that separated the front of the house from the common street.

The street hadn't been empty, nor had Adrastea cared. The astonishment of passers-by didn't matter at this point in time. One or two paused at the fence in vulgar astonishment.

Dassie, unprepared for the shift in location, fell to her knees and retched. Hugh and Stepan looked a touch green but kept to their feet. Both turned cautiously to Adrastea. "You're a witch," Stepan accused.

"No, not really," Adrastea replied. "Just a simple country lass." She gestured to the coffin sitting on the cobbled pavement next to the handcart. "What did you want to do with that? I am not familiar with city customs."

Hugh hastened to the foot of the coffin. "We'll carry it inside." He stooped to lift it, but Stepan had moved to the door and knocked.

Dassie, finished with her illness, rose and wiped her mouth on her sleeve. "I don't think I'll ever get used to that. Can we not do that again?"

Meanwhile, Mikal had said nothing and did nothing except cross his arms and wait. Dressed in his best, he still had the air of a country man about him. Adrastea sensed the thoughts tumbling about his head, but she did not know what they were. She wasn't sure she wanted to know. Back home, he was Mayor, and none ranked higher. Here in the city, at this House he knew nothing about, what was he?

The door opened. Stepan had a brief word with the footman. The footman hastened off as fast as his lame leg would allow, to return with several others, all women. They came out to gather around the coffin. Two of the footwomen had brief words with Dassie while the rest, with Hugh and Stepan, lifted the coffin and carried it up the steps and into the house.

The original footman limped after them.

Then the two footwomen split up. One went into the house, while the other slipped out the front gate and hurried down the street.

Dassie gestured towards the door. "Do come in. It will be a while before my uncle arrives."

Adrastea drew in a breath. "Jonathan?"

Dassie nodded. "He is the head of the family now. Also, our solicitors will be arriving shortly."

Adrastea exchanged glances with Mikal before entering.

House Pennexter looked as old and neglected inside as it did outside. It reminded Adrastea of the palace in Feown. She assumed that the fine furniture that once graced the entry hall had disappeared during the war. To the right of the entry hall rose a staircase. Along that staircase the wall was peppered with portraits of Pennexters long past. Adrastea and Mikal stared at them. Adrastea even climbed a few steps to get a closer look.

Dassie paused, her hand on a door across from the stairway. She cleared her throat, but Adrastea waved her away. "Give us a moment. This is the first time we've seen pictures of our ancestors."

Dassie sighed dramatically but she waited, her hand still on the doorknob. Mikal climbed the stairs and gazed at the portraits as well.

Adrastea studied them. A few were large, grand ones, several hundreds of years old. The portraits were newer the higher up the steps she went. Towards the top she found a cluster that looked familiar. "This one," she called down to Dassie. "This is Lord Pennexter, isn't it?"

Dassie nodded. "The one next to it, raised up, that's Lady Pen, my grandmother—now deceased. She died at the beginning of the second war. The one to her left is Aunt Fontaine who is also dead, and beyond that, Uncle Jonathan."

Smaller pictures sat under Aunt Fontaine's and Lady Pen's, presumably their husbands and children. Below that, grandchildren. Over a dozen cousins, according to Adrastea's count.

Below Lord Pennexter's was a single portrait of a young man. Adrastea caught her breath, for she recognized Joe immediately. She reached out her fingers to touch it.

"That's our father?" Mikal asked.

Adrastea nodded. Below his picture was nothing but empty wall. "And here's where we're supposed to be."

Mikal stared at the empty spots. "Adrastea?" His fingers traced an invisible frame along the wall. "What if we were never meant to be country folk? What if we were always supposed to be Pennexters?"

"Mikal, the Light put us where we were supposed to be, so we could be who we needed to be."

"Oh really?"

"Yes."

"Including that husband of yours?"

She sighed. "He would have found me no matter where I was." She went down the steps to follow Dassie through the door.

The coffin of Lord Pennexter had been placed in the middle of a sitting room, reposing on two chairs. A single couch and a small table had been shoved out of the way to make room for the coffin. Two large windows faced the front of the house. The curtains had been drawn back so the light of the afternoon filtered in to the stark room. The fireplace grate at the other end of the room stood empty.

Dassie had closed the door and sat on the couch.

Adrastea and Mikal stood. "Now what?"

"Now we sit attendance."

Mikal folded his arms. "For how long? I've got a village to run and Adrastea's got to get back to her daughter."

Dassie shrugged. "It won't be long." She avoided their gaze.

Adrastea sat next to her cousin. "We've got a similar custom. We wait with the dead while people bring us food." She hesitated. "We do get food, right?"

Dassie looked up. "I... I hadn't thought that far." She rose from the couch. "I mean, if you're hungry, I can ring for something."

"No," Mikal said before Dassie could pull a bell pull. "We're fine. We're not staying long. In fact, we shouldn't be staying at all." He took Adrastea's hand and pulled her up.

Dassie followed. "No, please. Stay. Help me explain to Uncle Jonathan."

Hugh and Stepan entered the room. They had changed from their dirty travelling clothes. They nodded to Dassie, who took her leave. "I'll be back quickly. Please don't leave."

Hugh and Stepan sat on the couch and resumed their watch, not of the coffin, but of Adrastea and Mikal. The two siblings stared back. Mikal leaned over to his sister. "I'm only staying to give closure to the family."

"Our family, you mean. Not that we owe them anything."

"Certainly not what they're asking. Besides, they don't know anything about us, so we're at least safe that way."

Adrastea grimaced. "You're safe. I've already met Jonathan."

"Who? The uncle?"

"He thinks I'm a Dark priestess."

"Does he know the truth?"

Adrastea opened her mouth, then closed it. She had no idea what Jonathan knew. The Duchess knew who she was. Had she confided that knowledge to Jonathan? They would soon find out. "He's coming." She could sense a carriage drawn by four horses racing down the street. Outriders astride saddled mares cleared the road, so the carriage could barrel along without incident.

It came to a stop outside the gate of House Pennexter. A little old man did not wait for the driver. He flung open the door and clambered out as well as an someone his age could. He hobbled to the gate.

Adrastea turned her face to the corner of the room after a quick whispered word in Mikal's ear.

Jonathan Pennexter, High Priest of Feown, stumbled into the sitting room to drape himself over the coffin of his late brother.

He pressed the side of his face against the wood and stayed there, silent for a long time.

Dassie came dashing down the stairs and burst into the room. "Uncle Jonathan—" she started, but upon seeing him prostrate against the coffin, she stilled her voice. Let him have his grief.

Jonathan eventually raised his head. "Who are you?" he asked of Mikal.

"Hello," Mikal replied. He did not extend his hand but stood there with them folded respectfully before him. "I am Mikal Mayor. I am the son of Joe Weaver, also known as Josephus Pennexter. I'm sorry we had to meet under such circumstances."

Jonathan inhaled a shaky breath. He took a few steps forward. "So young Joe is still alive?" He put a gnarled hand to his mouth. "Of course, he would be, or we all would have perished in the war—"

Mikal shook his head. "I'm sorry. My father is dead."

With this, Jonathan sagged. Adrastea wanted to rush to the old man, to hold him up, but she did not. She only watched over her left shoulder.

Mikal helped the old priest to the couch. "He's been dead a long time. I'm sorry."

"Oh," breathed Jonathan. "A son. Why did he forsake his vows?"

Mikal kneeled before his uncle. "I don't know. He died a few months after I was born." He took a breath and looked to Adrastea for permission.

Adrastea turned around and nodded.

Mikal continued. "There are two of us, brother and sister." He hesitated. "I believe you are already acquainted with her."

Adrastea stepped forward. "Hello, Jonathan."

Jonathan rose to his feet. His mouth worked a few times. "You…" He sank to the ground. He put his hand over his mouth as if to wipe away a bad taste. "Did… Please…" He covered his whole face with his hands. "I… I must know." Then he shook his head. "Oh, what have we done? He should never have entered the priesthood. We forced him to it. No wonder he turned Dark." Only then did he look up. "At least that explains you."

Adrastea fell to her knees in front of him. She gathered his gnarled hands in hers. "No. Please don't think ill of him. He was never Dark. If anything, he did all he could to protect us from it. And his protection, it worked, as long as at least one parent was alive. It was only when my mother died last… um…?" She looked to Mikal.

"Fifteen years ago," he offered in a soft voice.

Adrastea sighed. "I keep forgetting how long it's been." She shook her head. "Anyhow, it doesn't matter. Just know that he has gone to the Light. That I can say for sure."

"Why? Because you happen to know that his soul has slipped from the grasp of your master?"

Adrastea pushed back from her knees and stood up. "He is not my master. No man commands me."

She held out her hand to him. He looked up at her. His eyes watered, but the tears did not spill down his face. "Is there somewhere we could talk?" she asked. "I have much to tell you."

He studied her and then took her hand. Together they left the sitting room and the body of his dead brother. As they went upstairs, Jonathan paused and touched the portrait of Adrastea's father before he led her into a private salon.

It was there she told him her secret.

The private salon where Jonathan took Adrastea had once belonged to a woman, for the soft touches in color and remaining furniture still lingered. Could this have once belonged to her grandmother? He sank onto a couch.

Adrastea did not bother to sugarcoat her words. She sat on the other side of the couch. "I am not a Dark priestess. I am the Bride of the Dark. I am Mor-Lath's wife."

Jonathan sat there, unmoving. Had he'd heard her at all? She didn't dare say anything else.

When she feared he'd died on her, Jonathan looked up, his eyes full of sorrow. "Of course, you are. Why else would a country lass attend the Duchess of Feown?"

"She knows who I am. She calls me the Grey Lady."

Jonathan nodded. "She has spoken of you. I..." he shook his head. "I never thought that little Country Adrastea and the mysterious and illustrious Grey Lady were one and the same."

"I'm surprised she didn't tell you more."

Jonathan sighed. "Her Grace does not tell me a great many things. But she did tell me how the Grey— how you healed her." He gave a sad little chuckle. "The way she describes you... It—" He sorted through his words. He was doing a fair bit of thinking, even if she didn't know what tumbled through his head. "She described you as tall and elegant and... what was the word she used? Not intimidating, but... she held you in wary respect.

"Then you disappeared. We never heard from the Grey Lady or Country Adrastea since. Then you both reappeared a few days ago. Or rather, Her Grace saw the Grey Lady. And Dassie saw Country Adrastea." He wrung his ancient hands. "I wish I never told Stobol about you. But then, Dassie... No. This one was purely my fault."

Adrastea shook her head in bafflement. "I don't understand."

Jonathan fixed his gaze on her. He looked so, so tired, much like Lord Pennexter had after he'd discovered their identity.

"When you first appeared, I was most angry that a Dark priestess had worked her way into Her Grace's favors. But what bothered me the most was your name—Adrastea. Also, you look..." he sighed, and it turned into a sob, "very much like your father. I see it now. His hair was dark like yours.

"I put two and two together. I thought maybe, just maybe, you could have been the daughter of our missing Josephus. And the sentimental old fool that I was, I got word to my brother."

Adrastea's heart thumped as she listened to her great-uncle tell about her father. "What happened to Joe? My mother never told me anything of his life before, even if she knew."

"Josephus simply disappeared one day. He left a note saying goodbye and walked away. And we never heard from him again."

"Why did he leave?"

Jonathan gave a small shrug, his bony shoulders lifting the fabric of his robe. "Josephus was not suited for the priesthood. But of us all, he had the most talent. Oh, he could have been one of the greatest! But he was not of sober mind. His thoughts were too... I don't know. He laughed too much."

Yes, that was something Adrastea remembered about her father—his laughter. She remembered her mother laughing as well, until he died.

"But he was a Pennexter, and dearly loved by all. My brother—your grandfather—came back from Cithra and searched. A most fruitless one. We convinced him to give up after a few years." Jonathan picked at an invisible spot on his robe. "Every once in a while, we'd hear some rumor or another of someone from the country whose name could have been Adrastea, and he'd get all fired up again. But none of it came to naught, until the other week." Jonathan fixed a serious look on Adrastea. "You told our Dassie that you were from Sacred Spring. She, of course, told Stobol, and he hares off to the country that very same day.

"We never imagined he would be right."

They sat in silence, Adrastea sorry for having been so careless. Jonathan fell into a sorrow so deep it radiated off him. "I am so sorry," she offered.

A sob shuddered his body. He didn't even bother to wipe the tears from his face. "Please, if there is any decency left in you, I beg you to turn back to the Light. Not only would you be saving yourself, but the whole family."

She placed a gentle hand on top of his old one. "I have always served the Light."

He sniffed again and fumbled in his sleeve for a handkerchief. "No, you don't. Not really."

That hurt. "You don't know me. You don't know what I've been through."

"You're the wife of the Dark One, our mortal enemy." He rose from the couch. "How can you say you serve the Light when you consort with him?"

Adrastea closed her eyes. "The Light Themselves gave me to him. When we were married, it was under the tradition of the Light. Mor-Lath himself said he accepted Their authority."

Jonathan shook his head and sank back to the couch. "I can't believe that. I'm sorry, but... I can't accept that. You are Dark, even if you don't realize it."

Adrastea sighed. How could one explain if the listener did not want to believe?

A wave of tiredness rolled over her. "I've had enough adventure for one day. I believe my brother and I shall be going. We'll leave the rest of you to your grief." She reached out a hand to him, but he pulled back. It hurt to accept that, but what was said and done she could not undo. "I would appreciate it if you did not tell the family of us. Make Dassie promise the same thing. They don't need to know."

Jonathan turned away from her. "I'm afraid it's a little too late for that. When young Dassie's telegram came through—that my brother had been successful—the news spread. The whole family knows about you now."

Hm. "All they know is that we're country cousins."

"They know Josephus had issue. An heir."

Oh no. Mikal won't like this. "My father didn't care about such things. Please. I'm sure that neither he nor my brother want to disrupt the family at this time."

"Disrupt," he murmured. "Your discovery was supposed to bring certainty to a family torn by war. Like it or not, your brother is heir. And stability is once again restored to House Pennexter."

"My brother is heir? Not me, as the eldest?"

Jonathan frowned in confusion. "You are the eldest?

She nodded. "By a good ten years."

"Oh." He wrung his hands. "Oh dear. Oh, this complicates things."

She laid a hand on his knee. He didn't protest. "It doesn't have to. Your brother's will can still stand. Nothing says we have to inherit because of an accident of birth."

He raised his red-rimmed eyes to her. "The law says so."

Adrastea thought upon this for a moment. "The law does not know Mikal and I exist. Only the family knows." She scooted closer. "One thing I know for sure is that families all have secrets. Can not this be one of ours? Nobody else in Feown knows Mikal and I are Pennexters. They don't need to know. They would have no reason to think we exist."

"But I would know. And I will not lie."

A pang of guilt tugged at her heart. Here was a man who truly wished to follow the Light. He wanted to be honest and do right by all. By trying to convince him otherwise, Adrastea would not be the daughter of the Light as she claimed to be but would be of the Dark. She would be no better than Mor-Lath and his ways.

She bowed her head. "Do as you think is right. I trust you to do what's best for the family." She looked up. "Who do you believe is best to inherit?"

He snuffled again and pressed his handkerchief to his face. He considered and weighed. So strong were his feelings on this, the waves of emotion rolled through the lines of Deeper Power that connected them. "If I had my choice? I would choose your brother."

"What? Mikal? You've only just met him."

"I know enough about him to make this judgement. He is the mayor of a village. He would not have achieved that position if he did not have a certain level of integrity. Also, I feel he's a good man. Until he proves otherwise, I am willing to trust him."

"Even above the existing heirs?"

Jonathan gave her a small smile. "Since when would it be wisdom to favors the young and inexperienced over the older and wiser?"

Adrastea took a breath. "And how do you feel about me? Not as an heir, but about me as I am?"

He weighed his judgement of her carefully. "Now that I know we are family, I will never cease until I can turn you back to the Light."

Her heart swelled with a sudden feeling of warmth towards this old man. "I welcome your efforts."

Adrastea did not stay long at Pennexter House. After her conversation with Jonathan, she pulled her brother aside and brought him up to speed. "I'm sorry to abandon you like this, but it's best the family not know about me."

Mikal fretted. "I don't want to inherit. I can't."

That was an issue for later. Adrastea had more pressing matters— her aching breasts. "I need to go feed a baby. I'll return right after and stay out of the way until you're ready to return home."

Mikal folded his arms and set his face in a frown. "I'm ready to go now."

"Please. It's just for today." She wrapped her arms about her stubborn brother. "I remember when our father died. I remember our mother's grief. Here is an entire family who've not only lost their head of house but have also learned of Joe's death as well."

She stepped back and laid a hand on Mikal's shoulder. "I also remember our mother's death. That was different. That was—" Her throat tightened, as she thought back to that time. Mor-Lath had begun his pursuit of her and the village had ostracized her. Nobody wished to comfort the daughter of Mad Lillybet, a daughter about whom strange things were happening. "Please do not abandon them at this time. You've given them answers to a forty-year mystery. At least give them closure for today. We'll worry about the rest later."

Her breasts prickled uncomfortably. "Now really, I've got to go." She vanished before his eyes, startling him.

Adrastea did not surprise Ari by her sudden return, feeding and departure. Her only quip was, "I hope you don't make a habit of this."

She returned to Feown as soon as she could, going not to Pennexter House, but to the Maiden's Tower. There, she saw the true state of Feown.

Pillars of smoke dotted the city. Far too many piles of rubble lay in ruins, mostly around the outer edges of the city, where sappers had gotten in and where cannon, aimed high, had lobbed their ammunition.

Outside the walls stood the Avelian army. Annoyance filled her heart. Why were they still there?

Her first instinct was to destroy them all, as she once had the Cithrans. But that made her think of Mor-Lath. No. She would not be like him.

Her second thought was to send them back to Avelia with the Deeper Power. But would that truly stop them, or would they return to finish the job? Not unless she put the fear of the Dark into them.

She had to convince them to leave and never return. Could she do that?

Shift.

Adrastea's feet touched down outside the wall, at the edge of the army camp. Here, the remains of small buildings littered the ground and few weeds grew up between their fallen stones. A zone of exclusion lay between the walls and the edge of camp, that no-man's land where nobody wished to go. This lay in easy range of the weapons from the top of the walls.

Privates and corporals on patrol startled at her sudden presence. At their shouts, more soldiers came running, weapons at the ready.

Adrastea marveled that they all sported firearms of various kinds. Warcraft had changed since she'd encountered it last.

Several soldiers leveled their firearms at her. "Halt!" one of them ordered.

Adrastea looked at them. Up close, their uniforms were not of the best quality, nor that well-kept. Also, the soldiers gave off an air of weariness and frustration. They would be easy to intimidate.

She drew upon the Deeper Power until it filled her. No doubt every priest around—Light and Dark—would be able to feel her presence. Once sufficiently full, she advanced on these soldiers, their weapons falling away from their grasp by her sheer will alone. "You will leave this place. Leave Feown and never return."

The soldiers backed away, but they did not run. They looked to one another and although weaponless, stood their ground.

Their courage consternated Adrastea. Why weren't they fleeing?

Perhaps she was not going about this correctly. If she could find their leaders, maybe she could convince them to leave.

With a flick of her hand, she pushed back the soldiers and proceeded deeper into the camp.

The quality and size of the tents grew larger. She must be moving further up the ranks. More soldiers, some rag-tag, some dressed better, confronted her. She pushed them out of the way. As she moved, she laid her hands on the tents, and on fallen weapons, and other items left lying about. From these, she could connect them to soldiers, and to squads and centuries.

The more connections she could make, the better her chance of removing them all. She closed her eyes and pulled back to her first memories of standing at the walls of Feown, seeking out the Cithran army. She didn't know what she was doing then, and it resulted in the death of a half-million souls.

But this time, she had no Mor-Lath to deceive her. She could handle the Deeper Power with better skill. The Light absolved her of those deaths. No way she would commit such an act again.

She felt the approach of several squads before she heard their marching. Experienced soldiers arrived before her, their weapons at the ready. A man with knots on his shoulders raised a sword. "I order you to stop."

Adrastea regarded him. He was a leader, true, but not The Leader. "Where is the Avelian general?"

The man hesitated. "General Languer?"

Ah, and there was his name. Adrastea could find anyone, if she knew their name. "General Languer."

General Languer.

She sent out her thoughts along the Lines of Power until she located him at the back of the camp. That little man in charge talked at her, but she didn't care. General Languer. She found him, and her heart leapt at her triumph.

A hum of concern vibrated through the black lines on her face. She ignored it.

From the general, she found his colonels, his majors, captains, lieutenants, sergeants... all the way down to the brushboys. She sought them all out and linked them together. Her body filled with the Deeper Power until she fairly glowed.

The soldier who had come to stop her backed away. "What are you doing?" their leader called. He tried to sound brave and in control. It failed.

Another commotion rose behind the squads. Even more soldiers came forward, many of them heavily armed and plenty of them wearing the insignia of higher ranks.

"Adrastea." A familiar baritone voice spoke from behind her.

She whirled with a snarl on her face. "I don't need you, Mor-Lath."

Mor-Lath, clad in the brown robe he favored lately, kept his distance from his angry wife. "Don't do this."

She weighed his words. What did he think she would do? She could feel his concern and worry, but not his actual thoughts. "I'm not going to kill them, if that's what you're thinking. I'm sending them back to Avelia. And then I'm going to make good and sure they never return."

He took a step forward, a hand outstretched in supplication. "You can't do that." His voice remained low and pleading.

"Oh, can't I?" With a pull on the Lines, she lifted every single man of the army up off the ground. Waves of panic rolled forth from them, with shouts of terror and surprise. She left them floating in mid-air.

Mor-Lath held up both hands. "What I meant was that they can't go back to Avelia. It's not there anymore."

"What?" Adrastea let them all fall to the earth. Another collective cry rose from the army. Some did not land well, injuring themselves. Their pain flowed through the Lines. Adrastea regretted her cruelty. It had not been her intention to hurt them, only scare them.

Behind her, she felt someone coming. He rushed forward, then slowed down, approaching with caution.

"General Languer," she said, without turning around.

General Languer, a beefy man with grey at his temples and decades of experience under his belt, stopped when she spoke his name. Several armed men flanked him, weapons drawn. The General stayed well within their protection. "Who are you," he asked with caution.

Only then, did Adrastea look at him. "You made a big mistake attacking Feown." She felt Mor-Lath's hand on her shoulder. She ignored it. "I'll make you wish you—"

"Now, now, my Darklet," Mor-Lath purred, loud enough for those around to hear. "He was simply following orders. Well, the ones he chose to follow."

Adrastea swallowed as she felt Mor-Lath call upon the Deeper Power himself. He only touched upon it, but enough to give him an aura of power to intimidate the men that surrounded them.

The General stood his ground. "I don't recognize the authority of the church."

"That's what Wasson thought. He's not in a position to disagree at this point, as he's off to meet his god."

The General drew a breath. "Wasson's dead? We've heard nothing."

"They're all dead," Mor-Lath replied. "Well, all those who chose to stay."

Adrastea turned to her husband. "You destroyed Avelia?"

Mor-Lath's reply was cold. "They brought it on themselves." To General Languer, he declared, "Wasson was commanded not to attack Feown. He disobeyed. For that, he has been destroyed." Mor-Lath pointed a finger at the General. "Several days ago, you were ordered to not attack Feown, but to wait. You didn't wait, did you?"

"How do you—"

"You had a bit of the Dark One's own luck, I believe. Wet gunpowder, lost weapons, and a rather nasty plague of fleas up near the front lines."

"Who are you?" General Languer asked. "Answer me."

"I am the one you will obey, or I shall turn you over to the wrath of my wife. Even I fear my wife."

When Mor-Lath said that, Adrastea felt a momentary frission of truth through the lines of her face. Did he really fear her?

A soldier next to the general stepped forward. Adrastea only had a moment to look up when his weapon fired. She gasped and stepped back against Mor-Lath. The Dark God did not waver. His arm snaked about Adrastea's waist.

She saw a bullet stopped in mid-air, about a meter from where they stood. Her heart thrummed in her chest, fueled by panic. No way she could have stopped something so quickly. She swallowed the impulse to turn and flee.

"You're beginning to annoy me, General." Mor-Lath sounded more bored than annoyed. Only Adrastea could sense his irritation. "You are to pack up your little army and leave."

General Languer stood his ground. "No." His hand flickered. Several sergeants called, "Ready arms!"

Adrastea felt Mor-Lath's anger increase. His face did not betray his wrath. Rather, he shrugged his shoulders, released her and turned away. "Very well. Adrastea, the General is yours." *And only the General,* he added.

Why don't we just send them all back to Avelia? she asked him.

I told you. Avelia is no more. They must obey you or they will ever defy you.

Adrastea drew herself up. She breathed deeply to steel herself against the fear of those firearms. So many of them pointed her way.

"General Languer. Last chance."

"I don't recognize your authority, little girl."

Adrastea stretched forth her hand. *General Languer. Sleep.*

The General crumpled to the ground.

It took the surrounding men a moment to realize something had happened.

Almost as one, they shouted, "Fire!"

A loud cacophony of exploding gunpowder filled the air. Bullets flew forth, to stop an armspan away from Adrastea and Mor-Lath. She squeaked at the suddenness of the attack and fell back into Mor-Lath's arms.

Nothing harmed them. The bullets stopped well in front of them, falling to the ground as if hitting an invisible wall.

The soldiers fired until they were out of ammunition. When they realized their weapons were useless, they retreated.

Mor-Lath pointed his finger at another well-decorated soldier. "You've been promoted. Take your army and leave."

The newly-promoted colonel shook his head. "I can't."

Mor-Lath shook his head. "I'm not sure if you're brave or a fool."

The colonel drew himself upright. "I'm loyal to the crown."

"Does that mean you're loyal to a round bit of metal, or you're loyal to the pustule-ridden corpse that wears it? Either way, it no longer has any meaning." Only now did he allow his anger to show on his face. "Feown is mine. Leave now."

The colonel hesitated.

"So be it. From this day forth, you will never be able to take another step closer to Feown. Your feet shall be frozen to the ground unless you are walking away. You shall be doomed to ever walk away from Feown, until the prayers of the faithful release you from your curse." And with that, he sent a wave of Deeper Power through all the Lines Adrastea had connected to the Army.

"There," he murmured in Adrastea's ear. "Your favorite city is safe. Shall I return you to your funeral?"

He didn't wait for her answer.

Chapter 9

Montrof grew weary. His back ached and a chill wind blew, now that the sun had set over the fields. The farmers in this little hamlet had long disappeared. Lines of trees delineated the various farm holdings. Palus, who stood beside him, also stretched his creaky bones. "How many more are there?"

Montrof looked over the soldiers standing across the plain. In the distance, the lights of Feown glittered in the twilight. His Holiness had preferred the city of the Glasskissers. He had destroyed Avelia, a nation that had favored him in worship, though not in complete devotion.

Was he so completely besotted by his wife, that he would give over to her and neglect the truly faithful?

When scouts from the refugees encountered the first of the Avelian army, they'd learned a terrible tale of curses. "Only the prayers of the faithful could release them," the scouts reported.

Several of the younger priests went ahead to see what could be done.

Many hours later they returned, with two squads of rather contrite soldiers.

Montrof rose from his warm spot by the campfire. Soldiers? These were mere boys. "What happened?"

"Please," the soldiers begged. "Do you have any food?"

No, for trying to feed fifteen thousand refugees was a most difficult task. Still, who was he to grudge a few crumbs? It was not as if eating half his supper or all his supper would make a difference to his stomach, so little food was there.

Palus also invited the soldiers to sit. "We do not have much. We will share what little we have."

Several starving soldiers were happy to share their tale in exchange for a literal bite to eat. They spoke of a robed priest who'd warned them to leave. He was there, and a woman—most angry—who also told them to leave. "She was a sorceress," they said. "When General Languer refused to obey her, she killed him!"

Palus and Montrof looked to each other. "Did they give their names?"

The soldiers shook their heads. They looked to the elder of them, a boy only barely old enough to shave. "I do not think the man was a priest, because he called the woman his wife."

Montrof drew in a sharp breath. "Did he say anything else?" Who else had both great power and an angry wife?

"He told a colonel he was promoted and ordered him to lead the army away. When the colonel refused, that was when he cursed us." And thus, the whole army was doomed to never set a food closer to Feown. "Several of us left, hoping we could outrun the curse."

Montrof shook his head. "You could run to the ends of the earth and never escape." He and Palus exchanged glances. "You are lucky," Montrof told the soldiers. "He was most merciful to you. Had he let his wife have her way, she would have killed the lot of you where you stood."

"You know this sorcerous pair?" the young soldier asked.

Palus made a sign of protection. "I would not dare deny Their Holinesses."

A shudder ran through the young soldier. "You mean he was..." he swallowed. "I didn't think he was real."

"Oh, very much so." Offering one story for another, Palus told them of the destruction of Avelia. "Mor-Lath himself warned us to leave. The faithful obeyed and we departed. Then, as we stood outside the gates, there came a mighty earthquake that sealed off the city. Avelia is no more."

The soldiers stared at them, stunned. The eldest swallowed several times. "Has it been completely destroyed?"

"No one dares go back to see."

One of the younger soldiers sobbed. "My family was there," he explained. No one told him he couldn't cry. A few of the others failed hide their sniffles.

"So where do we go now?" the eldest soldier asked. Avelia was destroyed and Feown was off-limits.

That was a good question. Montrof beckoned to Palus. They left the warmth of the fire. "What do we do?" Palus asked.

Montrof thought about it. "I don't know. My plan was to find the army, join with them and... I don't know. I thought they'd have food and shelter." No way there was enough food to be gleaned from the countryside to support the sheer number of people.

"I say we still join the army. At the very least, we'd all be together. It's a shame about General Languer. The world will mourn the loss of his genius."

Montrof agreed. The diaspora of Avelians would need protection if they were to make their way in the world. "How many of our troops escaped, do you think?"

"You mean, how many of them had the sense to walk away from Feown?"

Montrof did not have an answer.

Palus weighed his options. "I think it is our duty to find the army and free them from their curse."

"What? And risk His Holiness' wrath for undoing all his hard work? He will not be pleased if we free the army and they go back to Feown. He just might turn the whole lot—and us, I might add—over to his wife." Montrof shuddered. "I would not wish to get on her bad side."

"From what you've told me," Palus replied, "I do not think she has a good side."

When the priestesses learned about the cursed army, they organized themselves to go out and find them. They left early the next morning taking more food than was their fair ration. By the time the priests had discovered what the priestesses had done, they were several hours ahead of them.

"This," replied Montrof, when faced with the news, "is why we do not marry."

Palus sighed and poked a foot at an empty food barrel. "Did not stop His Holiness."

"And I'll bet he regrets it every single day."

"Does he? I do not think His Holiness would remain shackled to a disagreeable wife."

"Any woman powerful enough to be the wife of a god is a force to be reckoned with. Perhaps he is too afraid to break the shackles."

Palus disagreed. "I think it is more a case that he is too wise to dare break the shackles."

While they waited for other priests to join them at the edge of camp, they discussed what they were going to do next. The priestesses were off helter-skelter to find lost soldiers and bring them back. Should the priests go to Feown and see what was left?

Montrof had concerns. "What if we are cursed as well?"

Palus didn't have an answer for that. "How about we not mention that bit."

When other priests joined them, they explained the situation—priestesses were off to rescue stragglers, whereas the priests were to find the main body of the army. "We're only a day out," Palus said. If they left the refugees behind, they might be able to reach the walls of Feown before sunset.

Alas, there were no horses for them to ride, nor wagons to carry anything. What little there had been commandeered by the priestesses. It looked like it would be shank's pony for them.

Montrof and Palus arrived at Feown. They'd not encountered any other soldiers on the way. Had the priestesses' relief society freed them, or was nobody else foolish enough to flee?

The bulk of the army still stood before the wall, albeit further back than Montrof expected. Most men sat on the ground, tossing makeshift rag balls back and forth to one another, or twiddling their thumbs in boredom. Only the ones closer to the wall stood at attention, ready to defend, should the Feowan army choose to wipe them out. They were easy targets and they knew it.

Montrof waved his hand before his face. The stench was terrible! The curse affected a man's ability to attend a latrine. "We've got to help them."

Palus stared at them. "There's thousands. No way you and I could free them all before they starved."

Montrof waved his hand to the fields behind him. "We've got a hundred priests, if we need them."

Soldiers who'd ended up turned away from the city saw the priests and waved to them. "Please free us," some begged. Others shouted news back through the ranks. The words "priests" and "saved" were used.

Palus started forward, but Montrof's hand on his arm stopped him. "Let's get organized about this first." Montrof stopped, looked at the walls and took a step forward. He took one back, then another step forward. "Good, we're not cursed as well."

Palus wilted. "Good to know." His pulse beat in his neck. He swallowed.

Montrof went up to the nearest soldier who had any kind of ribbon on his shoulder. "Where's the colonel who's in charge?"

The officer did not rise from the ground. In his lap rested a journal. He'd spent his time penciling entries. "Him? He's not in a position to speak to anyone right now." A few of the other soldiers around the officer looked away. "You best speak with General Languer."

Montrof blinked. "We'd heard he was dead."

"Nah," replied the officer. "Doubly-cursed. Not only is he cursed to walk away like us poor saps, but if he says anything against them that cursed him, he falls asleep again."

Montrof whistled. Now, that was interesting.

More shouting happened as a message passed among the men. General Languer wanted to see the priests.

Montrof found him in a tent, seated on a stool near a bucket. Various maps and papers lay scattered about, for the table in the tent was too close to the city for his use. Palus chose to wait outside.

General Languer shifted his paunch on the stool. His uniform was not crisp and his face quite unshaven. "I would thank my god you are here, if it hadn't been him who cursed me."

Montrof stroked his chin. "So, you know who he was?"

"No mortal man has that kind of power." General Languer breathed out, sinking as if all his backbone had melted. "I did not know he was married."

"We all sympathize," Montrof replied.

The general looked up. "Have you come to free us from the curse, or lecture us in the ways of our folly?" Montrof took the tone of his voice as a hint not to lecture him.

He knelt before the general, forcing his creaky knees to bend, putting them on eye-level. "I would not dream of lecturing a fellow devotee of Mor-Lath."

To this, General Languer lifted an eyebrow. "I cannot find his methods to agree with me." He outlined the curse, both the army's and his personal one. The sleep curse was an especially clever touch. "It was she who did that one."

Montrof nodded. He knees protested. He settled himself down on the trampled grass. Enough dancing around niceties. "So, you wish us to lift this curse?"

General Languer swallowed. "Please."

"You do know that if I do this, you cannot attack Feown. I will not go contrary to my god."

General Languer did not answer. He considered Montrof's words. "Why does your god favor the foreigners?"

Good question. Montrof had been asking himself that for quite some time now. "Perhaps they have been more obedient?"

General Languer stiffened. "Wasson may have been a fool, but he had an eye for opportunity."

Montrof took no joy in breaking the bad news to the general. "Our king is dead. Our people are scattered. Avelia has been destroyed."

"So, I have heard."

Alas. Montrof sighed. So much for dramatic declarations. "And yet you would still attack Feown?"

"It is the only logical course of action. Assume there is no more Avelia. Who will bankroll the army? Who will feed it, clothe it, train it, arm it? If we turn back now, we turn back to nothing. What will become of us?" Montrof had no answers. The general didn't expect any.

"The army would disperse, scattering about the land. Our soldiers would become rogue agents or thieves. That would not be good for them or the citizens. Therefore, we must persist. If we conquer Feown, we have a new source of income and a place to call home." He reached out and fetched another sheet of paper. "Now, consider: what if the destruction of Avelia is disinformation? What if Wasson was alive and well? I would not think to go contrary to his command. Thus, we persist."

Montrof was taken aback. This man had been doubly-cursed and yet he would still insist on attacking Feown? "If that is your belief, General, I cannot lift the curse from you."

He nodded his head. "Then you condemn us to death."

"Is that not a preferable fate?" He thought about what the general said about a countryless army with no place to call home, no crown to owe allegiance to.

The general blinked. "Since when is death a preferred fate to anything?"

Montrof was willing to let him find out by himself.

A man dashed into the tent. "General! I've been freed. What are your orders?"

Freed? Montrof turned around to look at the man. The ribbons on his shoulder marked this man as a lesser officer. "Who freed you?"

The soldier pointed outside. "The tall priest."

Montrof pushed himself upright. Oh, Palus. "Stay here," he said to the officer. He pointed a finger at the general. "You will do nothing until I return."

General Languer ignored him.

Montrof hurried off to find Palus.

Already, the priest had freed a dozen men. "Palus," he called. "Wait."

Palus hesitated, his hands stretched out over a man's head. "Montrof, what's wrong?"

Montrof whispered into Palus' ear, informing him of the general's goals.

Palus gave Montrof a shocked look. "He can't do that."

"He will if we can't stop him."

Palus took Montrof's arm and led him away from any eavesdropping soldier. "How are you and I going to stop a general?"

They looked around all the soldiers, some stuck, others running with joy at their sudden, blessed freedom.

Montrof's heart ached. If they freed them all, General Languer would resume his attack on Feown. If they didn't free them, they were all as good as dead.

And then, there was the bigger problem; what to do with an entire army? "We didn't think this one out very well, did we?"

Palus shook his head. "What do you think the priestesses would do?"

Montrof exhaled. "I do not think I would like their solution." He shuddered.

Palus retreated into thought.

Soldiers, still cursed, called out to the priests, their cries growing more desperate. What would he do?

Up on the tattered walls of Feown, enemy soldiers were taking great interest in the goings-on down on the fields. Montrof tugged at Palus' robe and pointed upwards. "What are we going to do about them?"

He was a priest, not a strategist. Why had his god put him in a difficult spot?

Palus put his hand behind his back and paced. "What would the priestesses do?" he posed to Montrof.

Montrof rubbed his arms as goosebumps rose. "Sometimes people 'disappear'."

Palus shrugged. "So, what if that happened here?" His voice was low, their conversation clandestine.

"What?" Montrof replied, his voice just as low. "Make him disappear?"

Palus looked side-to-side, afraid of being overheard. "Can we do that? How would we get him out of the tent?"

More shouting of joy floated over from another part of the camp. Palus and Montrof looked over. Amid the rejoicing soldiers, he saw a small knot of priestesses succoring the cursed. "Oh no," Montrof moaned. "We've got to tell them about the general."

He started towards them, but Palus grabbed his arm. "What will you tell them? 'Don't uncurse the soldiers? Or you...'" he left his thought unvoiced.

Montrof looked up at the tall, slim priest. "We can't go around without a plan."

Back at the general's tent, a familiar form caught his eye. Shereth, a priestess, slipped out of the tent, unnoticed by all but Montrof. "Oh no," he groaned. "She's freed him."

They raced towards the tent, but another soldier, this one much higher-ranked beat them to it.

"General!" he shouted, the good news elating him as he entered the tent. Montrof and Palus followed as quickly as their legs could take them. They burst into the tent, not sure what they'd find.

General Languer had toppled off his stool and laid on the floor. The officer—a colonel, if Montrof remembered his rankings right—stared down at his fallen leader in disappointment. "You'd think he'd have figured it out by now." He looked up at the priests that just arrived. "You'll have to wait to release him. He's fallen asleep again."

Palus blinked. "Again?"

The colonel backed out softly. "The general has a second curse on him, as well as the one we all suffer—suffered," he corrected himself. "When he wouldn't do as the lady wanted, she cursed him to sleep."

Montrof looked at the body. Sure, the light was much dimmer in the tent, but even he could tell the general wasn't sleeping. Death had a certain quality to it. Maybe it was his talent in the Deeper Power that spoke to him of this death. Without glancing at his fellow priest, they backed out of the tent with the colonel.

The priestess had done her job. But how did she know?

The colonel asked them to come uncurse more men. The two priests, not sure what to do next, followed.

After they'd set several soldiers free, the priestess Shereth found them.

She was a small thing, but not young. Montrof had met her a few times in his travels. She had an odd way of looking at the world.

"There you are," she said. "His Holiness sends his compliments for your cleverness, but not your timeliness. It will be at least tomorrow before anyone realizes the general is asleep for good." She folded her arms and studied the priests, whose jaws gaped open in surprise. "Oh, come now," she chided. "You knew it had to be done."

"But what about the army?"

Shereth looked about. "What about them?"

"If we free them, they'll go right back to attacking Feown. His Holiness won't allow that." Montrof's heart thumped hard. How to convince the priestesses to leave well enough alone?

A coy smile played about Shereth's lips. "They won't. We have a plan."

Montrof folded his arms. "We can't go back to Avelia."

"Don't have to. I told you, we have a plan."

"Mind sharing with me?

Shereth wandered away. "We're going to surrender," she tossed over her shoulder. "Now be a good priest and go free those defeated soldiers."

Mikal and Adrastea arrived in Sacred Spring at sunset. She set them down in Ari's back garden. Mikal knelt and kissed the newly-turned earth. "I have no desire to go to Feown ever again, either by foot or by whatever that was." Then he sat back in the dirt and looked up at the sky. The stars began to appear, one by one. "Adrastea?"

"Hmm?" She looked up at the same stars. One popped out, then another faded in. Behind them, the windows of Ari's home shone with warm light. An occasional, muffled voice could be heard, Ari's and Natan's. Adrastea liked listening to their voices from afar.

Mikal asked, "Do you ever wonder what your life might have been like if he'd never come along?" He meant Mor-Lath.

"Sure."

"What would you have done?"

She shrugged. "Ari would have grown tired of me and told me to go to Feown. Get some experience. Be a true journeyman, like she was." Adrastea sat down in the dirt next to him. "You know she went away for a few years?"

"I heard it was to get away from Uncle Natan. At least, that's what he told me."

"Huh. He said that?" She let her fingers scrabble in the cool earth. "Well, he was a mayorprentice at the time.

She scooted closer. "And what about you? Ever think of what it would be like to be married?"

"I try not to."

That surprised Adrastea. "Why not?"

"If I had a bad wife, I'd be distracted from my duties as Mayor. If I had a good wife, I might prefer to spend my time with her, rather than be Mayor."

"You can't do both?"

He shook his head. "There's too much to do."

"What if you fell in love?"

"I try not to do that as well."

Adrastea sniffed. "I'm sorry." All her lonely moments came rushing back to her. How much lonelier her brother must feel.

"Don't be. I'm happy where I am. Ooh, shooting star!" His finger shot up into the darkening sky. Adrastea saw it before it faded away. "Make a wish," he said.

They sat in silence for a moment.

"What about you, Adrastea? Do you love your husband?"

"No." Before she knew it, the words were out of her mouth: "I wish I did."

He sat up. "You wished you loved Mor-Lath?"

Had she said that? "Uh, what I mean—" she shook her head. "I wish I had a husband I loved."

"Not Mor-Lath?"

"I don't have a choice, do I? Other women do. They can leave their husbands—divorcements. They can be widowed. They can start again. I can't."

"Have you considered making the best of your situation?"

She exhaled. "That's what the Light would have me do."

Silence fell between them, broken only when Mikal chuckled. "Every time I look at you, all I see is my sister. Sometimes I forget you keep divine company. It's... you've been gone for so long. That month of courtship? It's a faded memory. I remember mother dying, then everyone else, then the invasion, then you were gone, and that was that. It's been quiet around here for fifteen years, almost as if you had never lived here.

"Well, almost never. That circle of protection does its job every once in a while. That's good for an afternoon's amusement."

Adrastea stared at him as he chuckled.

He pulled her into a spontaneous hug. "And now you're back. What happens now? Do you plan to live here until... what happens, Adrastea? I know you're immortal. What will you do for the rest of your life?"

Adrastea pondered on that. When she had been damned to Dom-al-gol, she'd given that much thought. What would happen to her, should anything happen to Mor-Lath?

"My life might not be as long as you think. Honestly, I don't know what will happen to me. In the end, there's supposed to be a great battle between the Light and the Dark. There is a very good chance Mor-Lath will be defeated. Because I am his wife, I might be defeated as well."

"Death?"

She shook her head. "Most likely destruction. Like you and your fate, I try not to think about it. It's not something I need to prepare for. Until then, I'll live here, if you'll have me, and do whatever it was I might have done, had I never met him."

She heard the cry of a hungry baby. "I should go rescue Ari." Then her breasts let down and she began to leak. She pressed her hands to the wet spots appearing on her blouse. "Oh, I really must go!" She rose up and hastened to Ari's back door.

Mikal followed. "Your husband will never stop pursuing you."

She knocked on Ari's door and folded her arms across her chest. "I know."

"Sacred Spring is not his to play with."

"I know that too."

Ari opened the door. "About time you got back." She disappeared inside and returned with a bundle that she deposited in Adrastea's arms. "You've got responsibilities now. You can't go dumping this baby in my lap every time you need to head off."

Adrastea apologized. Ari waved it away. "I understand today's a special circumstance. Don't get into the habit of it. I'm the auntie, not the mama. I've got a life of my own, you know."

And well for her that she did. "Thanks, Ari." Adrastea meant it. She latched the baby on before the milk soaked too much of her bodice.

Mikal offered to walk her home when she had finished nursing. It was not until they passed the Storekeepers that he shared his thoughts. "I know you've come here to stay, but I can't see you settling down to village life. Too much has happened to you. Too much happens around you. You're not a Healer like Ari and Salle any more. What are you expecting to do here?"

Adrastea admitted she didn't know. "All I could think about was coming home. And Harianne here." She gave the baby an extra pat. Harianne sucked contentedly on a fist. "I guess I've been selfish." When she helped Aril give birth, all she could think about was her own infertility. Maybe she should never have taken the child.

But the Light Herself blessed the adoption. She must have had a reason.

Mikal asked, "What did you do after you left? How did you keep yourself occupied?"

She sorted through her memories. "When we weren't fighting, I studied. I had free reign of the Temple library. I set up a stillroom. I spent time with the priestesses. I visited the Duchess of Feown."

"Sounds downright luxurious."

She admitted it was.

"And so, you left that life of comfort and privilege so you could come toil in a country village?"

"I was getting away from Mor-Lath."

"You can never get away from Mor-Lath."

She grimaced. "Please don't remind me."

"Just stating what I know is true. Now, assuming that you can never get away from him, either you can put up with him here, or you can put up with him there. I know what I would choose."

"You? A life of leisure?"

"A life of freedom from what I have to do, and more of what I want to do."

"But Mikal, that's exactly what I chose."

They reached Mikal's front gate. Jacob had left a lamp burning in the window, just low enough to see it. He, no doubt, had taken himself off to bed.

Mikal wasn't ready to go in yet. "Sometimes I wish I was free of all the responsibilities of being Mayor. But if not for me, the whole village would fall apart." He sat on the porch. Adrastea joined him.

"Like it or not, you are the Bride of the Dark. You are Mor-Lath's wife. He thinks he needs you very much. As much as I'd like to see the Dark One defeated in the end, until then, I would like to see you happy. My honest opinion as someone who knows his own sister? You were never happy unless you were doing what you needed to do. You talk about the Light and His blessings upon you. They want you to be where you are. Have you asked why?"

Adrastea turned from him. Harianne wailed, as she'd only emptied one breast at Ari's. Adrastea switched the baby over to the other side to resume feeding. "I really don't... I don't think about it."

"It's about time you started. The fact that the Light Himself wants you where you are tells me that perhaps that is where you need to be. What if you are the key to the Dark One's undoing? Why else would you be where you are, unless you had some key role in the success of the Light?"

"Whose side are you on, Mikal?"

"The Light's. You know that. Think upon't. Make nice with your husband, if that's what the Light wants. Remember you don't know everything. Also, speaking as Mayor, if you are on good terms with him, it'll make life here in Sacred Spring a whole lot easier for the rest of us."

Adrastea sat there with her mouth open. "I married him in the first place to save Sacred Spring!"

"Good. Stay married and keep saving it. Now go home. I'm tired. It's been a long day."

Harianne spent another night wide awake. When would the infant realize that nights were for sleeping and daytime for being awake? 'She's such a good baby,' everyone would say. 'She sleeps all the time.'

"'All the time,' my left foot," Adrastea muttered at four in the morning.

Adrastea's biggest concern was not that she wasn't getting any sleep, but that she had nothing to do but stay awake and keep Harianne occupied. Was it acceptable to pop in to the Temple and raid the library for books?

Maybe in the daytime, when others were awake and about. Would not do to get caught by Mor-Lath when there wasn't anyone around to use for distraction.

Harianne finally fell asleep about an hour before dawn. Adrastea went out and counted stars while she pulled rocks out of her future garden. She placed the stones next to Mikal's house in preparation to build an external stairway for Jacob. It gave her something to do until her library visit.

As soon as dawn came, Bitsy, Ari's youngest apprentice, came dashing up the road. "Milady!" she called breathlessly as she drew closer. (It took Adrastea a moment to figure out who she meant.) "Ari says she has work for you."

This brightened her morning. At last. Something to do.

Once at Ari's place, she learned it was a housecall. "Or rather, you'll meet the Millers half-way. Tedrick, the husband, has been injured."

Adrastea's fingers itched for Ari's medical bag and the cloak that hung on the same peg for the past thirty years. "How's he been injured?"

"Icole didn't say." Icole? Oh, his wife. "She'll meet you just outside the city limits." Ari licked her lips. "They're a strange pair. Arrived a year after you left and took over the mill. They never come into town. They say it's because Icole's afraid of 'big places', but we all know they can't cross the line."

Mor-Lath's protection still held. Even when he was at his angriest, he had never revoked it. "Can't cross? Why's that?"

Ari shrugged. "Don't right know if we should be asking. Ever since they've been here, they've worked hard and kept to themselves. Natan thinks they're laying low for some crime. Mikal's happy to leave them be as long as they don't bother us."

Fair enough. "Ari, is it all right if I 'cheat'?"

"That is why I sent for you. Mill injuries are nasty. You are the best for the task."

Good enough. Adrastea closed her eyes and called up the dormant memories she had of the mill.

Shift.

Icole had returned to the mill as soon as she'd procured help. The horse she'd ridden stood outside, its sides heaving, unrubbed. He stuck his head in the millcreek and he wasn't coming up until he had drunk his fill.

The mill looked different from what she remembered. It had been rebuilt, for the Cithrans had destroyed it when they came to Sacred Spring. The stone storehouse was larger.

Lines echoing great pain led her inside. There she found Tedrick Miller's arm stuck in gears. Icole stood on the opposite side of the mill, her arms firmly wrapped about herself and a hand tight across her mouth. The horse outside had a handsomer face than either of the Millers. Icole's was grey with shock while Tedrick's was white with pain.

Adrastea paused only to get a sense of what had happened. She laid her hands on the gears of the mill and felt along the contraption.

"Who are you?" Icole asked. "I don't know you."

Adrastea saw how Tedrick's arm had been pulled out of its socket. "I'm Adrastea. I'm Ari's... I'm a journeyman. I was Ari's apprentice. Now I'm back."

"Adrastea." Icole gasped the name. She fell to her knees.

"Hold on there," Adrastea called out. "One patient at a time."

She didn't explain or even warn. Adrastea asked the gears to move out of the way so she could free Tedrick's arm.

From across the room, Adrastea felt a wave of extreme emotion from Icole. "Don't worry," Adrastea reassured her. "He'll be fine."

She laid her hands on his arm and asked the flesh to restore itself to where it once was. It was happy to comply.

Tedrick stared at his miracled hand, too stunned for gratitude. "How'd you do that."

"Does it matter? Don't get caught again."

Adrastea had the courtesy to go outside the mill before *shifting* back to Sacred Spring.

⸎

Tedrick stared at his hand, whole and hale. Icole hadn't moved from her spot. "That was Adrastea."

Tedrick flexed his fingers. "This proves it. The Bride of the Dark has returned, after all this time."

He looked at his 'wife'. "I'll go," he told her. If he rode the horse at best pace, he might reach the telegraph office in Crossroads by sunset.

Chapter 10

Saraym, Duchess of Feown, settled in the most throne-like chair they could find. Ever since Deliverance, she'd never felt quite comfortable receiving or conducting business in the Throne Room. While the floor and pillars had been scrubbed of blood, the stains of memory could never be completely erased. Until today, it had been shut up and ignored.

She squirmed and wished for a cushion on the chair. If she had to sit in an uncomfortable room, at least her bottom could be comfortable doing it. Dozens of Feowan nobles and dignitaries lined the Throne Room to watch the spectacle of the Avelians.

The past three days had been most eventful, with the sudden cursing of the Avelian army. Jonathan Pennexter, her priest, had said nothing regarding this miracle. "I cannot claim it is of the Light."

Couldn't be the Dark. Historically, he favored Avelia, though she never knew why.

This very morning, the curse on the enemy army had been broken. Her council had panicked at the news. Would the attacks resume?

Saraym herself had gone to the wall to see this for herself. Yes, the soldiers were free, but they were rejoicing and showed no interest in picking up arms.

Their mood over the course of the day changed, as the priests and priestesses of the Dark—unmistakable in their religious robes—moved among the people, whispering, talking, and bringing a somber air about them.

What was going on?

It was not until a group of priestesses bearing a white banner came to the wall to offer parlay.

She looked over the wall at the women assembled below. They stood there, patient. If the rumors were true, and Avelia had been destroyed by its own god, they might be standing there for a very long time. She knew what it felt like to be abandoned by one's god.

"Tell them I agree," Saraym declared. She returned to her palace to prepare.

Despite the devastation of the war, Saraym's council felt she had to appear grand. They advised her on everything from treaty terms to what to wear. They even tried to argue her out of her customary mourning colors. "Really," she said to crotchety old Lady Yustibar. "Does the color of what I wear matter?"

"Only if it is a color of power," her counsellor replied.

She stood firm by her clothing choices but yielded for the use of the Throne Room. Surely the ghosts would have faded by now.

So now she sat in a fancy, unpadded chair, awaiting a delegation. Last time she was here, she faced an entirely different sort of delegation. Her hands gripped the arms of the chair. The Cithrans fought by bringing sheer force to bear. The Avelians were far subtler. They employed tactics of guerilla warfare, no doubt honed in their dense jungles. Their hit-and-run was far more effective than the siege of an army many, many times its size.

A germ of an idea planted itself in her head, one that might solve several problems.

Everything depended on what the Avelians had to say.

By her side stood two rather butch guards. Between them, in chains, was a poor Avelian corporal. He'd been captured on the second day of attacks when his sapper corps failed to escape after blowing up a government building. He should have been languishing in the cellars with the rest of his fellow soldiers, if not for the unfortunate fact that he spoke Feowan, somewhat.

Saraym knew some Avelian, enough to get the gist of things, but preferred a translator.

As she studied her POW translator, she questioned the wisdom of that. No guarantee he would translate properly.

Whatever happened, this would be entertaining.

She wasn't sure she was in the mood for entertainment.

The far doors opened, admitting a contingent of priestesses. They came unarmed, the hoods of their robes down. One priestess, a rather short woman of older years, led them. In her hand she held a small velvet bag.

She knelt before the dais and Saraym. "I greet thee, Saraym Blanqiva, Duchess of Feown." This she spoke in Avelian.

The translator's chains shifted as he shuffled forward. Saraym waved him back. She'd call him when she needed him.

The priestess said something else that Saraym didn't catch, except for the word Mor-Lath.

Now the translator could do his job. "She says, 'In the name of Mor-Lath, god of wealth, we come to...'" he paused, struggling with a word he didn't know in Feowan.

Saraym turned to him, eyebrow raised.

He flinched. "To give to, or give for..." he racked his brains, twisting his chain in his hands. "Say we lose."

"Surrender?" she offered. He thought about it and gave her a conditional nod.

She sniffed. He didn't know the word. Where'd he learn his Feowan? She studied his hands, manacled. The fingernails were short and ragged, his hands reddened. He was no scholar.

Saraym graciously bowed her head. "I greet you in the name of the Light. I will hear your surrender."

He translated.

Now, there was a lot more to a surrender than just saying the words. He hadn't said unconditional surrender. As she looked down at the priestess, she knew an unconditional surrender was not to be offered.

This is where the bargaining began. If only she spoke enough Avelian to conduct this herself. So much got lost in translation.

Several clerks lurked behind her throne. With a crook of her finger, she called one forth. "Bring stationery to draft an article of surrender. Oh, and a table and chairs. We'll be here a while. Our Avelian guests must also be fed, as long as they remain in this room. Our own people can fend for themselves." She did not have the resources to feed the lot. They should know by now not to expect such a thing at court.

The clerk and his team set off to satisfy her wishes.

She beckoned the priestess forward. If only Jonathan was here. But family must come first. It was a shame Lord Stobol Pennexter had died. Terrible shame. His talents could have been useful today. Some say he'd perished when he failed to find his lost son. When Dassie Pennexter returned from her family's mourning, she would inform Saraym of the truth. Until then, she'd made do with a lesser priest to advise her.

The priestess, flanked by two others, came forward. Saraym, sick of the ridiculousness of the chair, left it. It was better to stand on even ground.

The priestess tucked the velvet bag in her robe. She touched her forehead with both hands, then her heart, then offered her hands, palm up to Saraym. "I am Shereth, a high priestess of Mor-Lath, God of Wealth."

At least Saryam could understand that without the translator. Still, she beckoned him to come forward and join her.

Shereth, high priestess, watched the translator come forward, alarm on her face. "Please," she said, followed by something Saraym couldn't catch.

She looked to her translator. Hope illuminated his eyes. "She asks that as the war is over, I be set free."

Saraym replied, "The war is over after we agree to terms. Until then, you are still my prisoner of war."

The translator's hopes died in his eyes. He repeated what Saraym had said to Shereth.

Shereth accepted this without a second thought.

Footwomen brought a dining table and not-matching chairs. The clerks set them up with great efficiency, one of them easing a chair—padded, thank the Light—under Saraym's bottom. Shereth also sat, but her two attending priestesses were forced to stand. Still, it wasn't too bad. Two footwomen attended the parlayers at the table, offering a modest tray of fruit and sandwiches. The priestesses looked at the food suspiciously. Only after Saraym bit a sandwich, did they take the food.

Saraym watched as the priestesses devoured the fruit. Nothing like true hunger to conquer decorum. The Avelians must be approaching desperation.

A clerk settled blank paper, pens and ink and a few notes, slipped surreptitiously into Saraym's lap. These notes contained the latest intelligence. Someone had done a headcount of the Avelians outside. Even if these figures were off, there were nearly twenty thousand Avelians at her gates. Twenty thousand! What was she going to do with them all?

Before they began official talks, Shereth said, "As a token of our good will, I bring you a gift from His Holiness." She slid the velvet bag to Saraym. "A tribute and a message."

Saraym lifted an eyebrow. A message? Was she to be manipulated after all? "Go on."

"His Holiness says that as he has shown you mercy, that you are to show mercy to his people."

Her eyes narrowed. Did he think it was that easy? "He is not my god."

"He said you would say that. Nevertheless, he requests that you, a daughter of the Light," the translator stumbled over that word. ("I don't know if that's right," he added. Saraym waved it away. His translation was more accurate than he realized,) "that you be kind towards this displaced people. Let them serve to…" he hesitated again. "*Atone, atone,*" he muttered in Avelian. "I don't know the Feowan word," he confessed. "Make up, repair?"

"It'll do," Saraym snapped at him.

"Repair for what they have done."

Saraym thought about this. What game was Mor-Lath playing at? To Shereth, she said, "When was the last time you spoke with your god?"

The priestess wasn't expecting this question. "Uh, he spoke with me this morning."

Saraym harrumphed. "I haven't spoken to him for days." Her eyes fell to the velvet bag. "What gift has your god brought me today?"

Shereth's fingers shook as she undid the drawstring. She tilted out a large key, black and iron. This she gripped in both hands and brought it to her lips for a holy kiss. Her lips lingered, as if reluctant to let the key go. "This key gives you all the treasure of Avelia." Her voice caught in her throat "The God of Wealth gives it to you, if you will show mercy to his people." She placed the key on the table.

If she showed mercy. Saraym did not take it up. "What kind of mercy do you expect?"

Shereth had her answer ready. "We ask that you do not kill us. Also, do not make us slaves."

Oh, is that all? "What am I to do with you, then?"

Shereth rubbed tired fingers across her forehead. "His Holiness would have us ally with you and serve you in your war against the Cithrans."

Saraym groaned. Great. It was bad enough she couldn't equip her own people. How would she afford to feed and clothe and arm another twenty thousand?

Shereth reached out and snagged a blank piece of paper. She dipped a pen in the ink and began to scrawl, in Avelian, the words she just spoke. "Wealth… of… Avelia…" Her pen scratched.

"How much wealth?" Saraym asked.

Shereth held out the key. It reposed in the palm of her hand. "Find out for yourself. Simply touch the key to the floor, and the wealth of Avelia—now yours—will appear."

"What? By magic?"

"By miracle." The faintest glimmer of light illuminated Shereth's eyes.

Saraym's hand closed around the key. "Prove me forthwith," she muttered, as she rose. She proceeded to the center of the throne room. There, in front of the Avelian delegation and the curious of the court, she touched the key to the floor.

Like a fountain, gold and silver coins spilled forth, spreading out across the marbled floor. Gemstones, free and set, also flowed forth, as did jewelry and more. The Feowans gasped as one and moved back, afraid of this sudden tide. Among the Avelians, there were several sniffles and turned faces.

Saraym looked to Shereth. The priestess' eyes were closed, her head bowed, her heart breaking. Did she cry for the lost city of Avelia, or did she mourn the loss of gold?

So much wealth! No wonder the Avelians were attached to their god, if he had blessed them in this manner.

And now it was hers, to restore Feown, and possibly strike some powerful blows to Cithra.

The priestesses huddled together as their collective wealth was given over to someone else.

Saraym called for more food, not just for herself and Shereth, but the other Avelians as well. They looked like they needed a bit of fortification. She would have called for refreshments for everyone, but until this gold could be counted and catalogued, her coffers were still bare.

She sat back down. "Let us come to an understanding," she offered.

Shereth resumed her seat, dabbing at her eyes with the cuff of her sleeve. Saraym beckoned one of the Feowan ladies over and robbed her of her handkerchief. This she offered to Shereth, who gratefully accepted it.

While the priestess composed herself, Saraym dashed off a note to Jonathan. Yes, he was grieving, but she needed his advice. 'Am now in possession of twenty thousand Avelians. How can I ensure their loyalty?' When that was off with a messenger, she turned her full attention to Shereth. "So, tell me, exactly how many Avelians are we talking about? Soldiers? Men, women, children, elderly?"

She had to admire Shereth. From her sleeve, the priestess pulled a prepared list. Perhaps this negotiation and treaty would not be too bad.

They worked all through the afternoon and into the evening. They did not break for meals but ate while they negotiated. Most of the court grew bored after the first hour and melted away, no doubt to distribute gossip in the coffeehouses and salons. The priestesses, with nowhere to go, remained. They divided into smaller groups of four or five, chatting softly among themselves, sitting on the floor like children. Feowan soldiers kept them away from the doors or the gold.

Several accountants were brought in to catalogue the wealth and make plans for the future.

As Saraym's eyes went bleary with tiredness, a message came to her from Jonathan. He did not attend her in person, which irked her, but he did offer a solution. 'Make every one of them swear by a blood oath.' In his note, he detailed what this meant. She was to fetch some priests (other than him, was his implication), to offer a single piece of gold. Upon this piece of gold an Avelian was to place one drop of their blood to seal their oath of allegiance. Give them three chances to swear. If they did not swear, drag them away without explanation. They would be kept in the cellars for two days with no food or company, only water to drink. At the end, they would be asked once more, if they would swear.

Any who didn't were to be killed.

Saraym gave a whistle at this plan. "You are one bloodthirsty priest." But it made sense. She'd heard of blood oaths but had never seen one in application.

She looked to the pile of treasure. Were there twenty thousand pieces of gold? My, that was an awful lot. Would there be any left for spending after the oath? Any surplus would need to be put away and kept, to maintain the oath, unspent.

If it ensured the Avelians' loyalty, it would be worth it.

She sent another missive back to Jonathan in hopes he hadn't yet gone to bed.

Shereth wilted but did not quit. The poor translator had nearly collapsed so he was given a chair and a fresh pair of guards. His chains remained. Perhaps the promise of release would entice him to translate better. At least he'd learned a few new words. Sometime during the night someone had located him a dictionary. To Saraym's relief, he could read.

Coal oil lanterns illuminated the table and the steady chink of coins filled the air. Saraym's and Shereth's pens scritched as they nutted out the conditions of the surrender. In exchange for the tribute and manpower, the command of the Avelian army would fall under Her Grace. The bulk of it would be sent to Cithra. Every able-bodied Avelian woman would be trained in warfare and sent as well. Those who were unable to join the army would remain at Feown but would have to work to earn their keep. This was a city in bad need of repair. Anyone with demonstrably useful skills would be put to work in the same or similar field. Everyone else was subject to manual labor. The religious with no skill other than praying would become an advisory council, subject to Her Grace. And they had to prove their worth.

Above all, every Avelian, from Shereth down to the smallest baby would swear the blood oath. Saraym would have no dissenters in her duchy.

Shereth balked at that. She'd heard dark tales of the Glasskissers' blood oaths, those vows only breakable by death. Those tales were meant to scare both children and adult alike. She had no desire to know how true the tales were.

Saraym, being up way past her bedtime, wouldn't budge. "Seeing that your god saw fit to deliver you into my hands, consider it an exercise in faith and humility." She checked her drinking cup. It was empty. "He did want me to be merciful."

In the end, sheer exhaustion drove Shereth to accept and sign on behalf of the Avelian people.

First act she demanded: the chains be struck off the translator.

Saraym complied. "You're free," she told him, using the Avelian words she'd learned that night.

To Shereth: "I will not delay you in immediately sharing your good news with your people. Return in the morning for the blood oath and breakfast." Breakfast. What a good idea. "It may be simple fare, but far better than what you've had the past week. For each person who swears the blood oath, she shall have breakfast."

At three o'clock in the morning, that sounded like a good idea. After sleep.

Saraym slept in. She did not mean to. As she stretched herself and let her lady's maids dress her, she reflected on that. She needed that sleep. What was it, an extra hour? How that made a difference. Her energy had returned, lightening her mood enough that she didn't care what power colors now draped her body. Now she could confront thousands of Avelians.

Saraym entered the antechamber. Lady Yustibar rose from the secretary's desk. A piece of paper covered in doodles was testament to how long she'd been there. "Good afternoon, Your Grace."

Afternoon? She looked about for a clock. "Why'd you let me sleep so long?"

Lady Yustibar answered first with a curtsey. "The council thought it best. You have a busy day."

Saraym frowned at her councilor. How could she berate Lady Yustibar who knew the more sleep and food Her Grace had, the better the day went. "The Council awaits your pleasure."

They'd been informed of the treaty and the oath, to mixed reaction.

As they walked down the corridors of the palace, Lady Yustibar informed Saraym of what had happened—not much, really. There had been a few skirmishes from Feowan factions that disagreed with the surrender. Saraym sighed. "Anyone inciting to riot should be subject to the law. I assume we still have a constabulary?"

"We do."

"Good. Put them to work."

"Already have."

The throne room had been locked, the poor accountants inside along with the treasure. Only after Her Grace had shown up, were those doors unlocked.

The accountants had made tidy piles of sorted treasure. Still, there was a mountain to go. As per her orders, a pile of the lowest-denomination gold coins they could find had been separated out. The sheer number of coins made her head spin. If that was twenty thousand, there must be millions and millions more in the piles. This could take all week.

A niggle of pain started behind her eyes. "Has Jonathan Pennexter shown up yet?"

Lady Yustibar shifted from foot to foot. "His Excellency sends his regards and has sent up several priests to aid you as you require."

She put her fingers to her forehead. "I hoped he would be here."

"Family business."

This annoyed her. Lots of things annoyed her. The throne room annoyed her. "Do we have to do this here?"

Lady Yustibar looked at the piles of unsorted treasure and the busy accountants. "I recommend we not. It would be best if we secured this room."

Not quite the reason she had in mind, but it would do. "Find me a salon, preferably close to the gates. We're going to have a lot of guests."

"You promised the Avelians breakfast."

Saraym looked up. "Did I?"

Lady Yustibar nodded. "The chefs are complaining."

Saraym needed to get out of there. She turned on her heel, trying to keep her pace from looking like an urgent dash. "Have they forgotten how to cook?" Once outside the throne room, Saraym felt much better.

"They're protesting the quantity. No way they can prepare for twenty thousand in a morning."

One thing she hadn't considered in the wee hours was just how long it would take to swear a blood oath. "It's not so much that they will be feeding twenty thousand at once, but that eventually they will serve twenty thousand meals. Not all of them will be at eight in the morning." Or was it four in the afternoon? Where was a clock when she needed it?

Lady Yustibar checked her mental list. "And there's the question of supplies."

"Lack?"

"Financing."

Saraym glanced back at the throne room. "I doubt that'll be a problem. Send a clerk to procure enough funds to pay our suppliers. Do whatever you need to do to get enough food for those people." She resumed her retreat away.

Lady Yustibar followed, her small feet keeping up. "If I may speak freely?"

Since when did she need permission? "Go on."

"I do not understand why we must feed them when you can't feed our people."

Saraym slowed. "I am not feeding them. I am giving them one meal as a condition of their oath. After that, they're on their own. You can buy the loyalty of a starving man with a good meal."

"But only for as long as his stomach remains full."

"That's all I need. Promise their most pressing need will be taken care of, and a man will do anything, including swearing a blood oath."

Lady Yustibar needed an explanation of a blood oath and she got one, her eyes widening as she heard the plan. "I do not know if that is the most righteous course." Her fingers fluttered at her throat. "I mean, it's blood."

"It was Jonathan Pennexter's idea."

"Oh," she replied, her voice small. "That explains the priests. I've put them in your office."

Saraym sighed. "When you have secured a room of sufficient size, take them there. We'll start the blood oaths as soon as I'm ready. But for now, I need breakfast myself. Surely the chefs will abase themselves to feeding me?"

The salon, far more comfortable than the throne room, had just enough space to conduct a blood oath. In a show of good will, Shereth and several priestesses were present, to bless and observe.

The poor translator had also been dragged in, albeit without chains.

A blood oath, one of the priests explained, only worked if the oathmaker—that was Saraym—also contributed her blood. "Otherwise, the oath is useless."

Couldn't have that. Saraym held out her finger to a priest with a bodkin. "I hope it's sharp."

The priest was a young one, possibly no more than twenty years old. "I have several," he reassured her.

Saraym pressed her finger to the point. She hissed as it stung. As she pushed at the pad of her finger, a drop of ruby blood welled to the surface.

Another priest, this one on the other end of the age scale, held up an Avelian gold coin in his shaky, gnarled hands.

"What do I swear?" She'd not considered what her part of the oath would be.

The old priest was not helpful. "Swear by the Light."

Saraym rolled her eyes. So as not to waste the drop of blood, thus requiring another pinprick, she pressed her finger to the coin and held it, between index and thumb. She would not release it until she had thought of something to swear by.

Shereth's face wore a frown. "Your Grace?" she said in Feowan. "What you thinking?"

Saraym studied Shereth. She tapped the coin against her lips. The only thing Shereth had asked, before the treaty, was that her people be treated with mercy.

She looked at the coin. Mor-Lath had shown her mercy. Not just her, but her people.

First Deliverance. Then the ending of this war. He'd destroyed a city devoted to him, and delivered its remnants to her, including the whole of its wealth.

"I swear by the Light that I shall show mercy to these people as Mor-Lath has shown mercy to me."

Lady Yustibar and the priests cried out. "You can't swear by that," the young priest shouted.

Saraym shushed him with a glare. "I know why they are here. They know why they are here. I will have their loyalty because of it."

She threw her bloodied coin into the chest that had been provided.

The only other person in the room who approved of her oath was Shereth. She came forth and took the bodkin from the young priest. She pricked her finger and held out her bleeding hand for the coin. "I swear loyalty to Saraym of Feown, as Mor-Lath has shown her mercy." Her coin joined Saraym's in the chest. "My people will swear your blood oath."

Shereth's fellow priestesses were next. One, when her finger was pricked, saw the drop of blood well up. Her eyes rolled back, and she collapsed on the floor.

"What's wrong with her?" Saraym demanded.

Shereth bent to check the priestess. "Perrine has always fainted at the sight of blood."

"What kind of woman can't handle the sight of blood?"

"That one," Shereth explained. The poor wretch was dragged away, after her finger was pressed to the coin. She'd get her breakfast later.

As the Avelians came through the door, they offered a salaam Avelian-style to their priestess. Shereth placed her hands on their head in a brief blessing, then they moved to a pair of priests of the Light. Priests pricked Avelian fingers and pressed their blood to a coin, swearing loyalty to the Feowan Duchess.

They made their curtsey or bow, as the Feowans would, to Saraym and departed to a promised breakfast.

After several hours of this, Saraym grew weary. Also, the scent of blood grew stronger as more sanguinated coins fell into the chest. How long would this take?

At least a week.

The priests took it in shifts. Turns out, there were only ten of them left in Feown, not including Jonathan. There was only one Duchess of Feown, and she had to be present for all of it.

At the seventh day, she wanted to scream and run away. Only on this final day did Jonathan Pennexter bother to grace her salon with his presence. He didn't just attend but took over from the weary priest offering coins.

"Where have you been?" she demanded, ignoring the fealty of the final Avelians.

He waited until he finished blessing the coin of an Avelian. "I told you. Family business. My brother died."

She had never been terribly fond of Stobol Pennexter. Still, she supposed she should express some condolences to the family. "I'm sorry to hear that. I trust the funeral went well?"

"Very well. Although there have been some issues regarding his heir."

"That happens when none are left behind."

"Oh, no. We located direct heirs. There're a few legal ramifications. Our attorneys will sort it out."

Saraym stiffened. "I did not think you would be comfortable with by-blows."

Jonathan frowned. "These heirs are quite legitimate, as far as we can tell. It's their reluctance we're having issues with."

He changed the subject. "Lady Yustibar informs me there have been few problems with the Avelians so far.

Saraym slunk in her chair. "Ask me after they've digested breakfast."

"May I ask what you have planned for them?"

"Essentially? Train them up and send them to Cithra."

"You send all your problems to Cithra, don't you?"

She scowled at the thinly veiled barb. "Two birds, one arrow."

And thus, did Saraym, Duchess of Feown restore her coffers and gain addition forces.

Several weeks later, the first of the Avelian army boarded boats and headed up the Great River to atone to their god through the blood of their enemies.

Chapter 11

Upstairs in her new bedroom, Adrastea laid the sleeping baby in her cradle close to the warm chimney. Maybe tonight she'd sleep for the rest of the evening. Adrastea reconsidered her method of parenting. For the past two weeks Harianne would nurse during the day and fall asleep immediately. But come the night, she'd feed and then want to stay awake. While immortality reduced Adrastea's need for sleep, it didn't eliminate it entirely.

Sure, Ari's 'calm infant' tincture helped, but it took half an hour of her enduring Harianne's inconsolable fretfulness before it kicked in. If she had to suffer one more night of a wakeful infant, she would most likely give in and command her to Sleep.

She heard a polite knock on the downstairs door. She froze. Would Harianne wake? The sweaty little face didn't twitch. And while she was tempted to tuck the little quilt around her body, she didn't, just in case her touch roused her.

Adrastea hurried down the stairs in case the visitor knocked again. Who called at this time of night? All decent people should be in bed. Had it been an emergency, the polite knock would have been more of a desperate pounding.

She jerked her front door open. "What?" she snapped. Then she caught her breath.

Mor-Lath stood there, the late spring breeze stirring his heavy cloak. "May I come in?"

Adrastea didn't move. She searched his face for any sign of trickery or anger or anything else that would explain why, after two weeks, he chose to show up now. His expression was neutral and his voice soft. She twitched the lines on her cheeks. No deception there.

At least he had the decency to knock.

"If you wish." If he woke Harianne, she'd make him pay.

In he came. While he hung his cloak on the peg rack, she closed the door and kicked the draftstopper against the bottom of it. Still, the hint of coolness swirled through the warmth of the house. She drew her shawl tighter around her figure. "What do you want?"

He didn't answer her right away. Today he wore sturdy clothing such as a country man would wear: quilted woolen trousers, stout boots and knitted jumper over a linen shirt. He folded his hands behind his back and promenaded about her home, looking at the furnishings, the windows, everything.

It had to be for show. Adrastea knew he'd been here while she was out and had seen the house before.

"You have a cozy home, my dear."

Adrastea didn't uncross her arms or move from the door. "I like it like that."

"You prefer simpler things, don't you?"

Anger simmered in her stomach. "There is nothing wrong with my home."

"I never said there was."

"It suits me just fine."

"It does." He nodded as he approached the fireplace where the fire without any wood burned. He glanced at her as if they shared a secret. That only served to irritate her more.

He moved to lower himself to her rocker.

"Don't you dare sit in my chair."

He paused, hands on the armrests, then rose and chose the other chair opposite hers by the fire. While it had a cushion, it was nowhere near as comfortable as the rocking chair.

She didn't move.

"Please," he asked. "Come sit with me?"

"Why? You're not staying long."

An expression flitted briefly across his face. He sighed. Sorrow? Disappointment? "No, I'm not. But can we at least make my brief visit a more pleasant one?"

It was Adrastea's turn to sigh. "None of your other visits have been. Why start now?"

He took her irritated figure in for a moment. "Because one has to start sometime, even though that sometime should have been a long time ago."

Tiredness rolled over her. Babies took a lot of energy. She'd not realised how much until Harianne. Added to that, she'd been working with Mikal to install an enclosed stairway for Jacob. The last thing she wanted was for Mor-Lath to pull her into who-knows-what kind of drama. "What do you want? You never show up unless you want something."

"What good would showing up do if there is no reason?" He held up a hand before her protest escaped her lips. "The reason does not have to be a big one, or even a good one. Any little excuse will do."

She waited for him to elaborate further. On the mantle above the fireplace, Adrastea's clock ticked the time away.

"So," he said, in reply to her silence, "come sit down and I'll ask how you've been, and you can ask how I've been. We can discuss the weather, I'll share my news of what's happened out in the world and you can tell me what's happened here, and then when we run out of little things to speak of, I'll thank you for a lovely time and then after I leave, you go about your day."

She rolled her eyes. She saw no need to hide her impatience. "Why?"

He stretched out his legs towards the fire and crossed his ankles. He folded his hands across his stomach. "You wish to live a simple, country life. I am more than willing to allow you to—"

"Allow?" Adrastea spat. "Since when do I need you to 'allow' me to do anything?"

"Perhaps that was the wrong choice of words. You choose to live your life as you do, and it's not my place to pass judgment." He looked at her, expectantly as if waiting her approval.

She gave it, grudgingly. She took a few steps closer but did not sit in her chair. "You disapprove of country life?"

He didn't answer straight away. "I grew up in the country and don't miss it one bit. I prefer the city. Country towns are too small for me."

"The whole world is too small for you."

He tilted his head. "Not true. I think the world is just the right size. I'm rather fond of the world.

"So." He changed the subject. "How are you?"

"Irritated."

"Mmm. How were you five minutes before I showed up?"

"Frustrated." Her gaze rolled to the ceiling. No noise from above;

she'd know if Harianne had woken up. "Tired," she confessed.

"I did warn you."

"I don't think that's any of your business."

"Oh, do sit down," he snapped suddenly. "It must be tiring staying angry at me. You can't do it forever. Just—" He held up his hand, more to control his own irritation than anything else. "For just five minutes, let us sit and have a shallow, genteel conversation." He held his hand out, inviting her to sit in her chair.

She gave a small growl but acquiesced. Once seated, she let her fingers drum on the armrests.

"Cold weather we're having." He had restored his composure.

Adrastea didn't look at him but stared into the fire. He followed her gaze.

"It's nice to see you're staying warm and are doing well. I'm sure your little problems will soon go away. Things won't be so bad, then. Summer's soon upon us, though sooner down on the plains than in the foothills. Down by the river it'll mean plague season. I will have to do something about that. It had its uses, but I have no desire to see it run unchecked through every population." He stroked his chin as he pondered this. "Meanwhile, I assume you've given thought to your garden?"

She glanced sideways at him. "Yes. And?"

"Is there anything you'd like me to bring you? Warmer climes may have tomatoes sprouting sooner. I could bring you a few established plants to get a head start for your garden."

"No, thank you. If you can get them, I can get them."

"I know how difficult it is for you to get out and about, what with a baby and all. I just thought you might want me to do you a favor."

"No favors."

Silence descended between them.

"Ari and Natan doing fine?" he asked.

"Yes."

"And Mikal?"

"He's managing."

The clock ticked some more.

Mor-Lath folded his hands. "Berengaria and Radelisa send their regards. I saw them this morning and they asked after you."

She gave him a look of disbelief.

"They are fond of you, you know."

"Don't know why." She didn't mean to be so snippy. After all, she'd visited them just yesterday, checking on the temple, making sure things were rolling along.

He uncrossed his leg and sat up. "Ask them sometime." He gestured to his cloak hanging on the peg by the door. Something came flying out to his hand. "I brought you something." He held out a spring of honeysuckle, the lower flowers gone all orange, the newer flowers still white, with the buds on the tip still unopened. "I thought you'd like it."

He sent it floating towards her to land in her lap. She looked at it in astonishment.

"I know it's not much, but it does have one of the best fragrances. I thought you'd prefer it to the stereotypical rose."

The strong scent wafted up to her nose. She couldn't help but inhale. He was right; it did have one of the best fragrances. She lifted it and buried her face in its soft scent.

Mor-Lath rose to his feet. "I wish I could stay longer and speak of pleasant things, but I must go. Duty calls."

The honeysuckle momentarily forgotten, she leapt to her feet.

"Perhaps next time I'll stay for tea if I can. I'll show myself out and I hope you have a pleasant evening." He summoned his cloak, wrapped it about his shoulders and opened the door. "Have a nice sleep, my dear. You'll feel better for it."

Then he was gone, the soft gust of cold air from the closing door marking the spot where he stood.

That, and the scent of honeysuckle she held in her hand.

For the next several days, for as long as the blooming honeysuckle perfumed her home, she pondered upon the unusual visit of her husband.

What was that about?

Adrastea found herself back at the Temple more often than she intended. It was not so much she only went there when Mor-Lath was absent but had sent him subtle warnings through the lines on her face that she would appreciate his absence when she was there.

She had missed the Temple library. As she walked down the shelves, her fingers brushed along the spines. She longed for the companionship of these books. Her touch solicited responses from them as well. History, science, mathematics... anything she could possibly wish to read could be found on these shelves.

Berengaria followed behind, wearing Harianne's sling. For once, Harianne was awake and responding rather well to Berengaria's touch. "Is she always this good?"

Adrastea snorted. "Light, no. I only just got her into a decent routine."

"I've never held a baby before." Berengaria pressed a finger into the baby's palm. She marveled as the tiny fingers wrapped around her own. "She likes me."

Adrastea paused. "What? Never held a baby? Ever?"

Berengaria shook her head. "Never had the chance. I was a child when I came to the Temple. Priestesses don't have babies." She sighed. "Sometimes I wonder if I would have made a good mother; would I have been good with children?"

"You don't have any nieces or nephews?" Adrastea realized she knew very little about the priestesses. "Do you have any family at all?"

"I had a mother. My father died when I was young. That's why I came to the Temple. She couldn't take care of me."

Adrastea's heart ached. "Same thing happened to me. My father died young. My mother couldn't cope. I was apprenticed to Ari, while my brother, still a baby, went to a wet-nurse."

"So, you never saw him again?" There was nothing wistful or lonely in her question. Did Berengaria never see her mother? Did she even miss her?

"On the contrary. I saw him every day. I still do. He's Mayor now. Done well for himself." She realized how much her brother meant to her. They weren't that close as children, there being a good ten years between them. As adults, the age gap didn't matter so much. She came to value his insight. "Do you ever see your mother?"

"From time to time. Usually when she needs something."

"Brothers? Sisters?"

"No." Berengaria had no regret in her voice. "The Temple's my family, for good or ill."

Adrastea had a sudden flash of her first memory of Berengaria. It had been on her and Mor-Lath's wedding day. Little Garie had been the first priestess to welcome him back home. She'd been genuinely happy to see him.

"What's it like having a baby?"

Adrastea paused, her fingers on a book spine. "Busy. Full."

"His Holiness said you wanted a baby, so you adopted one."

Ah, yes. Berengaria had spoken with him recently. "What else does he say?"

"He said it'd keep you out of mischief."

"Oh really?"

Berengaria continued her investigation of the infant. Her fingers roamed over Harianne's lumpy skull. "What do you do with a baby? I mean, what do they do? They can't do anything, can they?"

"Not much."

"So, what do you do with them all day? How do they keep you busy?"

Adrastea told her. Feeding, burping, changing, playing, rocking, carrying... Babies were rather helpless creatures, so there was plenty to do.

"Huh," Berengaria replied. She ran a finger around a tiny ear. "But why would you want to do all that? What do you get out of it?"

Adrastea put out her hand and stroked Harianne's head. Her heart swelled so much, it warmed her to the tips of her toes. Her soul was so full it might spill over. It felt sweeter than pulling on the Deeper Power. It felt more like she gave back to Creation. As her heart swelled for Harianne, the Lines between them vibrated in lovely harmonies. "Because of love."

The priestess gasped. Her eyes filled up and a tear rolled down her cheek.

"Oh, Berengaria. What's wrong?"

Berengaria shook her head. "Nothing. I... I felt that. I... Oh glory." She hugged the baby tighter to her and closed her eyes. "You love her very much, don't you?"

Adrastea nodded. She stroked the baby's head again. It felt good to give her heart over completely. She planted a kiss on the little head and returned to her book browsing.

"Lucky little thing. I'd give anything to be loved like that." Berengaria looked up. An awareness brightened her eyes. "Now I understand."

"Hmm?" Adrastea wanted to find books on medicine, preferably newer ones. Ari had spoken of such things when she studied in Feown. Knowing more about medicine would help her. She remembered Mira Priestess' one and only prophecy all those years ago. She'd seen Adrastea spreading her hands and healing people. Perhaps she would always be Adrastea Healer.

Ever since her conversation with Mikal, she'd been thinking about who she was supposed to be. The only straight answer she had was a prophetic dream from the time of her birth. If only Mira was alive to tell her more about it.

"No wonder he wants you so much, if you make him feel like that. I'd marry you too, if I could."

Adrastea froze. "What?"

Berengaria ducked her head. "Sorry, Holiness. No offence." She raised her eyes. "But that's some pretty powerful love you have there. If I was His Holiness, I'd never leave your side."

Adrastea returned to the books, but her thoughts were elsewhere. Why did Berengaria think she loved him? The priestess was not ignorant regarding their disagreements. So why—

Adrastea stopped, and her cheeks flushed as a memory surfaced from where she'd hidden it away. It was only a few weeks ago. She'd tried blocking it out, but now it came back with all the insistence of a ray of sun through an open window.

She put her hands to her cheeks to stop them burning. Her eyes closed, hoping to push away the memory.

Mor-Lath had seduced her. He'd taken her moment of greatest rage and turned it around into a powerful passion. She had no idea if she had the power to resist him. The trouble was, she hadn't wanted to resist him. He had kept her occupied nearly the whole night until they dropped from sheer exhaustion. He'd paid attention to every fingertip, every inch of her skin. And she let him. No, she demanded it from him.

Creation had echoed their great passion. Did everyone with even the remotest sensitivity to the Lines know about that night?

"I was such a fool," she muttered to herself.

"Holiness?" Berengaria's voice held concern. "Are you all right?"

"She's fine," Mor-Lath replied. "Just distracted."

Adrastea looked up. Her husband browsed the shelves a few steps behind them. She hadn't heard him come in. Shame filled her heart. Had he heard her thoughts?

"Garie," Mor-Lath said. "Why don't you go show the baby to the other priestesses?"

Berengaria hesitated, looking to Adrastea for confirmation.

"No, stay." Adrastea came forward, hand reached out to Harianne.

Mor-Lath caught her about the waist with one arm and pulled her close. "She'll be fine. She's safe here."

Berengaria didn't move. "Holiness?"

"Stay," Adrastea commanded.

Mor-Lath shrugged. "As you wish." He buried his face in her hair. "Doesn't mean we will," he murmured into her ear.

Adrastea pushed his arm away. "I don't have time for this."

"But you were thinking it." He inhaled her scent. "Have you ever considered how you appear to me, Adrastea?

Berengaria deliberately turned away. She did not leave, but idled over to another row, out of sight, if not out of hearing.

He ran his fingers through his wife's hair. "You are so beautiful," he told her. His voice was low and urgent. "And so powerful. I marvel at your boundless rage. No one can hate that deeply and not feel love as strongly."

He opened himself to the Deeper Power and let it flood him. His hand stroked her face so the lines in her cheeks sang. She grasped at the edges of her will as it began to crumble. "I will not let you do this to me again," she warned.

"Oh no," he moaned. "I'd rather you did it to me. Is it not cruel to make me jealous of a baby, to want to feel such devotion myself? I see how powerful the Lines are about you. Can you blame me for craving you?" He inhaled her scent. "Fill my senses. Make me forget who I am. Imagine the power you could have over me."

Her heart thumped. The last time he tried this, it was she who felt powerless, and willfully so.

Another memory surfaced—their first time. She'd been the one in control then. How different that had been? She'd proceeded with caution, unravelling his fears.

Where were those fears now? Were they still there?

He nuzzled her neck. She laid her head on top of his and delved into him. That familiar knot of fear was still there. She sent tendrils of Power into it and began to work at it.

He froze. "Wait. What are you doing?" His walls of fear came up. He pushed her out.

"Fear," she told him. "Everything you do is motivated by fear. Even now."

His eyes met hers. "I cannot let that go."

"Why not?"

He released her. "I'm not ready."

She laid her forehead on his. *When will you be?*

He did not reply. He looked over to Berengaria, who'd politely turned her back. Or rather, he was looking over to the baby. "I see you are busy. I'll let you be."

With a faint stirring of air, he disappeared.

Adrastea let out a sigh. Was it of relief or disappointment?

"Is it safe to turn around?" Berengaria asked.

"Yes, he's gone."

The priestess peeked over her shoulder before turning around. "I don't mind if you'd much rather—"

Adrastea held up her hand. "No. It's... nevermind." She went back to her search for books. "Berengaria?"

"Yes, Holiness?"

Adrastea drew in a breath, more for courage than hesitation. "How would you like to come to Sacred Spring for a while?"

Berengaria tore her attention away from Harianne. "What? To your village?"

"Yes." She gestured to the baby. "I confess I do need some help."

Berengaria's face brightened. "For how long?"

"Don't know."

Thought crossed Berengaria's face. "You mean, leave the temple? All by myself?"

"I thought possibly you and Radelisa, if she was likewise interested."

"The other side of the mountains, right?"

Adrastea nodded.

Oh, the possibilities tumbled about in the priestess' head. The emotion rolled off Berengaria as she weighed her options. "Wait. What would His Holiness say?"

Ah. Adrastea should have thought of that. Mor-Lath might not appreciate her poaching his priestesses. "Ask him. He might say yes."

Chapter 12

The idea of a sabbath was somewhat new to Adrastea. As a child, her experience of worship occurred in semi-private cottage meetings when Mira Priestess presented the devotion rites in exchange for dinner.

Chloe Priestess had brought the idea of a more public worship service from Crossroads. Before her marriage, Adrastea wasn't sure if she had preferred the new format: more fellowshipping, less food.

Now that she had returned, she found joy in communing together with other devotees of the Light.

Chloe's sincere apology and open acceptance of Adrastea into the flock meant much to her. It made her feel almost normal.

That morning she dressed Harianne in her best clothes. She danced and sang with the infant, determined to instill the idea of the sabbath as a day of joy to the child. It was not her fault her mother was married to the Dark God. Harianne would be raised in the tradition of the Light.

Thus, they set off up the road to join with others for their devotions.

"Good morning," Mor-Lath joined Adrastea as she rounded the corner of the church, Harianne in her arms. "'Tis a fine day to attend worship."

Adrastea jumped and tightened her grip around her child. "That is what one does on the sabbath. What are you doing here?" She glanced through the budding young trees planted in front of the inn. Various people approached the chapel, yet none had turned to see her. Many were already inside. For this Adrastea was grateful, though she felt concern for the latecomers.

Because of the clarity of the weather, the air was cool this morning.

A shiver ran up her back and along her arms. She shifted the warmly-dressed Harianne in her sling and pushed past Mor-Lath. Again, he was dressed the country man, albeit in the sabbath best of a country man, down to the shiny polished boots and the felt hat he held in his hands.

"I've come to spend some time with you. One does spend time with one's family on the sabbath, do they not?"

She pushed past to the double-doors that led into the church. "I don't want to spend time with you. Not like this." She was trying to walk in the Light. How could she do that with the Dark God by her side? People would notice.

"Oh, come now." He kept pace. "Don't you wish to appear respectable?"

She halted just shy of the door. She dropped the volume of her voice but not the irritation in it. "You don't make me look respectable. It doesn't matter anyway since everyone in Sacred Spring knows who I am."

A pair of visitors on pilgrimage passed them by and entered through the doors.

"And what about others?" His gaze followed the pilgrims. "What do you think outsiders say when they see your bare left hand and the baby at your breast?"

"It's a shame I can't tell them I'm a widow."

Martine Innkeeper with her husband Willem hustled several small children past. Martine did not hide her stare. She didn't look overlong either but proceeded into the chapel.

Mor-Lath gave her a friendly nod. "Shall we go?" He took Adrastea's free arm.

"Stop that," she hissed under her breath. "I'm not going in there with you. People will see us."

"I certainly hope so."

He tugged on her arm. She dug her heels in. "I will not go."

She squeaked in surprise as he called upon the Deeper Power to lift her ever so slightly over the doorstep and through the door. "Mor-Lath," she warned.

"I promise I will behave as long as you behave." The light of day passed behind them. They entered the momentary darkness of the little foyer before emerging into the brighter interior of the church. Sunlight streamed through the high windows, illuminating the altar in the middle of concentric circles of pews. "Now everyone is looking at us. I doubt Chloe will forgive you if you disturb her service before it begins."

Nearly every pew was occupied, some stuffed to overflowing with families. Adrastea scanned about, looking for somewhere discreet to where she could slink.

Several people turned to look at them. Only the more discreet, or the ignorant, turned away.

The parishioners were all dressed in their finest, some finer than others. The new fabrics imported from the Tredan weavers with their brighter dyes provided a multihued display to rival any garden. Up at the front stood Chloe and her apprentices, dressed in the white robes of devotion. Their simplicity stood out from the sea of color.

Mor-Lath waited while Adrastea's eyes adjusted to the change in light. "Now, where do you normally sit?"

Adrastea plunked herself on the bench along the back wall.

Mor-Lath lifted her up. "Surely you don't sit with the strangers and the contrite spirits." His glance flickered up the aisle. Second pew from the front held Ari and Natan, Mikal and Jacob. "Look. They've saved us a place." Salle and Bitsy sat with the rest of the Innkeeper clan.

With his hand behind Adrastea's free elbow, Mor-Lath guided them up to that pew. He gently shoved them in and sat down, effectively blocking her escape route. Adrastea dropped to the pew and refused to look at him. Mor-Lath leaned forward and greeted the rest of the family. "Morning."

Ari, on the other side of Adrastea, gave him a puzzled look while Natan and Mikal regarded him with worried curiosity. Jacob simply stared, jaw agape. Was this his first time encountering the god?

Mor-Lath sat back and gave a small wave to Chloe Priestess. Chloe stood there, Book of the Light in hand, studying the Dark God. She did not move, nor did she breathe, but watched him, concern marring her expression. Her apprentices moved about her tending to the final touches before the service began. They had no clue as to who had just come into their presence. Chloe turned her gaze to Adrastea.

Adrastea mouthed, "I'm sorry," before Chloe turned away from them and opened her Book.

In Adrastea's lap, Harianne squirmed. Ari tapped Adrastea on the shoulder. "Want me to take the baby? Looks like you've got your hands full."

At first, Adrastea wanted to say no. Perhaps she could hide behind her child, use her as an excuse.

"Hand her over," Ari prompted. Adrastea complied. Maybe she did need all her focus to deal with her troublesome husband.

Mikal turned to her and gave her a look. Was everything okay?

Adrastea returned a look that she hoped conveyed her irritation, her caution and an advocation that nobody do anything stupid. Then she leaned over more and gave Jacob a cautionary frown. Jacob retreated behind Mikal.

Before she turned back, she caught a glimpse of the Smiths in the pew behind them. Sheelagh leaned over to Big Peter and whispered in his ear. Adrastea turned away before they saw her watching.

Only one family sat in front of them; the Constables enjoyed the front pew. Evan hooked his elbow over the back of the pew and turned to look at them. "You all right there?" he asked Adrastea.

She wrinkled her nose. "Juuusst fine," she growled.

Mor-Lath beamed at Evan. He extended his hand. "I do believe we haven't met."

Evan took the hand and shook it. "I do believe we never will."

Stop that, she chided him silently.

"Now, now, my Darklet," he admonished. "You promised no scenes."

"And that wasn't a scene?" she whispered back.

"Just being neighborly. Oh, I brought something for you." He picked up her left hand and slipped something warm over her finger. A gold ring, not too big, not too small. He snugged it down to her knuckle. "There." He settled the ring in place. "Now, nobody will get the wrong idea." He draped an arm about her.

She pushed his arm off from her shoulders. As she brought her fist up to look at what he'd shackled her with, she noticed a matching gold ring on his hand, albeit more masculine and thicker in width. Why did he wear one?

A hush fell over the whole congregation as Chloe stepped forward, crystal goblet in hand. Adrastea forced her attention to the invocation. The priestess had set the open Book of the Light on the altar and had raised the transparent goblet, full of clear water, up to the rays of light shining through the windows. "Oh Light, we come before Thee to seek Thy wisdom."

Adrastea repeated the words with the rest of the congregation. Mor-Lath didn't.

"As the light shines through the water, let Thy Light shine through us." This time, he murmured along, but his words were altered. "As the light shines before us, let Thy Light shine through us."

She elbowed him in the ribs.

Chloe continued. "May we be at peace with Thee. Forgive us our wrongs and inspire us to seek Thy Light."

He leaned closer to her. "Once upon a time it was not a glass of water the priest held up but a candle. The Light is the same, but Their rituals have changed over the years. Be a bit more tolerant."

"How about you be a bit more respectful?" she muttered back.

"How about you be a bit less angry, especially if you're going to go sip that water?"

Adrastea's gaze returned to Chloe. The first row of parishioners had risen and came forth to receive a sip of water from the goblet. As they drained the water, the apprentices topped it up.

It irked her, but he was right. One came forth with a broken heart and contrite spirit to sip of the water and to ask forgiveness for one's sins.

When the first row was complete, and the second row's turn came, she rose with the rest of them, hoping her action spited her husband. But when she came before Chloe, she whispered, "I'm sorry," and hesitated.

"What for?" Chloe replied in the same low voice. Her flickering gaze alerted Adrastea to her discomfort over the hesitation. Most people came forward and drank, nothing more. "Drink, if your heart is in earnest." Chloe tilted the goblet towards her. Adrastea cradled the goblet bowl in her hands but brought it only a hair's breadth from her lips. "I am angry with my husband." She released the goblet without taking a drop.

"That is a quandary," the priestess replied.

Adrastea moved away and did not raise her gaze to anyone, lest she see their thoughts in their eyes. She returned to the mostly-empty pew. Mor-Lath stood so she could enter. Meanwhile, Ari held Harianne up so the infant's lips could be touched to the cup. Then she quietly praised the child before sipping herself.

Mor-Lath put his arm about his wife. "What was that about?"

She flinched her shoulders away from his touch, but he would not be deterred. He put his arm back around her and held firm. "No scenes, remember?"

"Everything would have been fine, except for you," she spat, *sotto voce.*

He leaned his head close until it touched hers. *How about we discuss this later?* "Let the others enjoy their worship."

The rest of their pew had returned. Again, he rose so they could pass. He settled down next to his silently fuming wife for the rest of the service.

At the end, instead of lingering and fellowshipping, Adrastea held out her arms for Harianne, her intention being to leave as quickly as she could.

But Ari wasn't so eager to give up her grandniece. "Perhaps it's best if she come with us for lunch. Give you..." She looked to Mor-Lath who stood behind Adrastea. She didn't finish her phrase.

"What?" Adrastea said through gritted teeth.

Ari bounced Harianne in her sling. "One less thing to worry about?"

Adrastea jammed her fists onto her hips. "And why would that be?"

Ari spoke with her usual candidness. "Because he's here for a reason. He's not going to leave until he has his say."

Mor-Lath added, "Your aunt is a wise woman."

She wasn't finished. "So, the sooner he says his piece, the sooner he'll go."

"And here I thought you didn't love me." He gave Ari a big smile.

Before she pushed past them, Ari fired her parting shot to him. "Just hurry up and apologize, then go away so we can get on with the rest of our lives."

"I'll be brief, then." He slipped his hand under Adrastea's arm. Instead of guiding her out of the church, she felt the flare of the Deeper Power. He whisked them away from the midst of the congregation.

The small change of pressure under Adrastea's feet was the only difference she felt as they transferred from the church to Adrastea's home. The fire, in reaction to her presence, flared up to provide more warmth. She jerked her arm from his touch and slapped him in the face.

"Are you trying to embarrass me or something? Why were you there in the first place? The church of the Light is no place for you."

He tossed his country hat onto the table and folded his arms. "I was raised in the Light, or don't you remember?"

"That is no reason to come and mock our ceremonies."

"I never mocked. Pointed out a difference, purely out of historical interest, but mock? Never. That would be too immature, even for me."

Adrastea didn't justify that with a retort. "You won't go until you have your say? So, say it."

"All right." He sat down in his chair. "Stop being so angry." He put his hand to the cheek she'd slapped and touched it with careful fingers.

"Why don't you let me worry about how I feel and just get on with your business?"

"That's it. I want you to stop being angry with me."

Adrastea wanted to pull out her hair. "Do you have any idea why I'm so angry with you?"

He nodded.

"Unless you can go back and change the past, or you've decided you're going to give me a divorce, I'll thank you to get out of my life again."

He studied his fingernails for a moment. "I cannot turn back the clock, or even make it stand still. Sometimes I wonder if I can slow time but haven't been able to prove it. As for the other, I need you too much."

She turned her back on him. Words were wasted on his ears, but he was not yet beyond her scorn.

He rose to his feet. "I do. If I lose you, I lose myself and everything I've ever wanted. I am married to the most powerful woman in the universe, who by a simple act of willfulness, can bring about the end of the Dark God.

"The Light crafted you well. And They think They know me better than They do." He walked to the kitchen door. "I'm going to see if you've got any decent tea. I wish you had some of Ari's excellent beer."

Adrastea scurried after him. "You're not going into my kitchen."

"Feel free to stop me." He pushed open the door.

She followed him and grabbed his arm. Instead of resistance, he spun towards her and pulled her closer with an arm about the waist. He stroked her cheek with his, not unlike a cat, before releasing her. Desire echoed through her.

Adrastea didn't expect that. She lifted a hand to her face. The line on her skin hummed softly from his brief touch.

While she was distracted, he summoned a tin of tea from her cupboard. He opened it, sniffed it, and replaced it. "Mulled cider would have been nice, too."

"Why are you doing this?"

He paused, another tin open before his nose. "Because you asked me to."

"I did not ask you to come into my home, raid my kitchen and embarrass me in front of other people."

"No. You asked me to speak kindly to you, share things with you and listen to you." He paused. "All right, I'm not doing so well on the listening-to-you part, but really, can you expect me to be perfect on all points first try?"

She raised her hand to her eyes. "Mor-Lath, cut the act. I'm not falling for it."

"No, because I know you hate it when I act like, as you put it, a selfish bastard."

"Shallow insincerity isn't much better. For all I know, you could turn back any second."

He rejected the second canister. "I'm trying not to." He closed his eyes for a moment and an earthenware pot appeared in his hands. "Here. How about chocolate?"

"You're not going to win me over with gifts. And speaking of such," she tugged at the ring on her left hand. "You can take this back." She had trouble getting it off her finger, so she willed it off then threw it at him.

Her aim was skewed, so it flew past him, clattered against the wooden wall before falling to the ground and rolling in a circle.

He reclaimed it from the floor. "Yes, I know you're not terribly impressed by things." He filled her kettle from the bucket of water on her bench and swung it on a hook over the fire. "You still use a fire when most of the civilized world has converted to stoves. Your house, though well-built, is modest enough for your needs. Your cupboards are spare, your table simple and you've settled for a basic rocking chair. There is only one item here that defies your logic of simplicity.

"And that's your bed." He winked out of view. Adrastea groaned. He'd gone to her bedroom. It was situated over the kitchen in the west of the house. The warmth of the chimney kept it comfortable enough.

She stormed after him, finding him at the foot of her bed. Like the rest of her house, her bedroom was simply furnished, with undyed woolen curtains over the windows, a wardrobe in one corner, an unadorned trunk at the foot of the bed and a simple rag rug on the floor. She had a nice dressing table with an oval mirror and a plain washbasin with a pitcher of water for washing.

The bed, however, had an ornate wooden frame, carved with flowers and ferns. She may have gone overboard in her choice. It was pretty, and Mikal had talked her into an impulse purchase. Once she got it home, she couldn't see how to truncate it without spoiling the design. It was a double-bed frame. Not as big as the bed at the Temple, but it suited her. Mikal was right; it was quite luxurious to spread out in a big bed.

It didn't matter much, for having a double-bed was quite useful when one brought a cold little baby in to feed in the middle of the frigid night.

He continued his conversation as if he'd never left. "For some reason, you have a very large bed, surely too large for just one person. So, tell me. Who were you expecting to come share it?"

"That is none of your business."

"It is, if it's going to be me."

"It's not."

He sighed. "Shame. Then I ask, who would this bed be for?"

She folded her arms. "If you must know, I was thinking of my daughter." She put a heavy emphasis on 'daughter'. She did not want him to forget. "It's easy to feed her in the middle of the night in bed. I was also thinking of her future. Some day she will grow up and the bed can be hers."

He walked around to the far side and sat down, bouncing to test the tightness of the ropes. "Not bad." Then, kicking off his boots, he laid down and put his hands behind his head. "Quite comfortable.

"My parents had a bed not quite as big as this. Yet they managed to conceive all of us there."

Adrastea let out a noise of exasperation. Like she cared where he was conceived.

He continued his story. "Being country folk, we spent most of our lives teetering on the brink of poverty. We lived in a two-room cottage with a little loft not much bigger than Mikal's place. The older of my siblings slept up in the loft, the younger of us down in the kitchen and the babies in bed until they were weaned.

"When the weather was good, some of us would sleep outside at night, if only to have some space to ourselves. See, I was tenth of thirteen surviving children. Privacy was not a concept I understood until I was much older." He glanced at her still standing, arms folded. "Are you going to sit down or are you going to stand there and glare at me for the rest of this story?"

"I'm not a fool. The moment I touch that bed, you'll seduce me."

"What if I promise I won't?"

"How do I know you'll keep your promise?"

"You don't. But it would be an excellent exercise in trust."

She did not take him up on his offer.

"Suit yourself." On with the story. "The weather was not always clement, so I usually ended up inside with only a blanket to call my own and a corner I had to share with at least two other brothers.

"As soon as we were old enough to be apprenticed off or to strike out on our own, we left.

"My father never liked me for the simple fact that out of all his towheaded children, I was the only one with dark hair. He never beat my mother more than was traditional and only when drunk, but I know that some of her beatings were because of me. He was a temperamental man of many doubts when in his cups. He never thought to consider that my dark-haired mother might bear a dark-haired son. Dark hair was uncommon where we lived. Blonde and even red were what people sported.

"My grandmother was a foreign-born slave, but my mother was born free. I didn't know until much, much later that my grandfather was a lord of the land who felt no compunction over who or what he tumbled."

Adrastea let out a snort of derision. "Sounds very much like you."

Mor-Lath sat up. "Believe me, I show far more discretion and care than he did."

"Oh, really?" She thought of her seared belly. Did his grandfather sterilize all the women he touched?

He ignored her jibe and lay back down on the bed. "My mother, daughter of a slave, didn't have much choice when it came to husbands."

"And I did?"

"I at least gave you the chance to say no. You're still saying no.

"Anyhow, my mother's marriage consisted of being dropped on the doorstep of my father and told, 'Here's your new husband. Serve him well.'

"I don't think my parents loved each other, though they didn't hate one another. When he was sober, he accepted I was his son. When his reason was muddled by ale, he wondered if I was a by-blow. After all, I was the only dark one of the bunch."

Adrastea shifted her shoulders. "And were you a by-blow?"

"Definitely not. I looked far too much like him for any sane man to doubt." He shifted on the bed, adjusting the hands behind his head.

"In a society where children weren't named until they survived infancy, my parents simply didn't bother with me. By the time I'd proven I was going to live, everyone already called me the dark lad, or in the language of the time, *Moor Ladh.*"

Adrastea forgot her anger for a moment. "Really?"

He nodded. "By the time I was old enough to change it and call myself anything I wanted, I'd grown used to it. Besides, it suits me now."

"Huh." Not thinking, she sat down on the edge of the bed. "I think my name was chosen before my father was conceived."

An awkward silence descended between them. Mor-Lath looked at her and didn't avert his eyes. Adrastea realized where she was and jumped to her feet.

Mor-Lath rolled off the bed and padded to the door. "I believe that water is boiling. How about we have a nice cup of chocolate?"

Adrastea didn't reply. She folded her arms and watched him.

When she didn't follow him through the door, he looked back. "What?"

"You never do anything unless you want something in return. If you're doing all this because you think I've got some secret—"

"I've already got the secret, remember? I'm just acting on it."

She snorted. "I knew it. It's always about you. if someone else benefits while you're taking care of the most important person in the world, that's just a lucky coincidence."

Mor-Lath left her in the bedroom and went down the stairs. She followed him. "Can't you think of someone else first?" she shrilled after him.

He didn't stop until he reached the bottom. Only then did he look up at her. "Tell me. Who is more important than I am?" He waited for her answer.

Adrastea folded her arms and scowled down at him. She wasn't going to fall for his tricks. She wasn't going to enter into a contest of words where she would surely lose.

"Well?"

She pursed her mouth. "I'm not playing games with you."

He rolled his eyes in unveiled longsuffering. "It's an honest question. Who is more important than I am?" He waited while she sniffed in irritation. "You, perhaps?"

"Oh!" she squawked, throwing her hand in air. "Fine. I'll play. How about a child who can't do for herself?"

He leaned against the wall. "You mean, like the child you foisted off to Ari so you could come speak with me?"

She shook her head. No, she couldn't win. Why was she so stupid to let him taunt her into a corner?

He pushed himself off the wall and headed to the kitchen, moving out of her sight. She hastened down the stairs and turned at the bottom. "Mor-Lath."

He stopped but did not turn. "What?"

"Just because you can't think of anyone more important than you doesn't mean there isn't."

He glanced over his shoulder. "I never said there wasn't. I asked if you knew. And you couldn't answer." He turned to face her completely. "Or rather, wouldn't answer." He strolled back to her and lifted her chin with his finger. "Would you think it too arrogant to answer, 'I am more important than you'? Are you afraid I would think you a hypocrite, to denounce me thinking I'm the most important person in the world, only to declare yourself in my place?"

She jerked her face away from his touch and moved closer to the fire. "Is that your answer?"

"What? If I say you are the most important person in the world, more important than me?"

She sighed and raised her gaze heavenwards. The Light wouldn't help her in this. Or could They? How could she avoid his trickery? "And what if I considered the Light more important than you?"

She felt his hand descend on her shoulder and she stiffened. "Then I'd say," he murmured in her ear, "that you were avoiding the truth."

"I am not more important than the Light." She moved away from his touch, but he snagged her about the waist and drew her back.

"You are as important as the Light. You are destined to take Their place as the supreme god of the universe. Now, do you know how important you are?"

She pushed at his arms but he wouldn't let her go. "I don't believe you."

He released her. He raised a hand to his forehead as if he had a headache. "How can I convince you? Name it."

She spun around and hissed at him. "You want to know what you can do?" She jabbed her fingers towards her belly. "You can heal this, for a start." She stood there awaiting his answer.

He looked at her belly, then to her face. "Do you know what you're asking?"

"Oh, yes."

He thought some more. "And what would you do if you were healed thus?" His voice was soft, as if he were afraid that anyone would eavesdrop and think ill of him for considering such a thing.

"Well, I would be whole again. And you would be correcting what is one of the first of a big, long line of selfish mistakes." She poked a sharp finger at him. "If you're serious about what you say, you will do this, or you will be proven to be nothing but a lot of hot air."

He put his fingers to his lips as he continued considering her wish. "And if I do this, and you become whole again, then what will you do? I wouldn't be taking you to my bed. Would you seek out a pretty boy to entertain you between the sheets? Will you be careless and let him plant a child in the belly of another man's wife? And if he succeeds, what will you tell him? 'Sorry, I can't marry you, so your child will have to be a bastard. I hope you're not too shamed by this.'

"I know your little country beliefs regarding illegitimacy. Otherwise, you would have let everyone in the village assume the little pet you currently own was of your get.

"Then again, if your man-toy was the kind to tumble and scramble, you'd feel rejected and bitter. You don't strike me as the woman who'd trick herself out as a strumpet and take whatever unfaithful tomcat looked down her cleavage. Any mortal man you chose to take to your bed would, in the end, get his heart broken in a very harsh manner."

During his little speech, Adrastea's fists balled up. She shoved them against her stomach to prevent them from burying themselves in her husband's face. "You're one to speak of infidelity."

He took a deep breath. She could see him fighting the tension that gathered in him. He rubbed his neck to release some of it. "The last person I've had in my bed was you. There has been no one ever since."

Adrastea didn't know what to say to this. If he was lying, she had no proof. If he was telling the truth, she'd look a right fool to denounce him.

But it did give her the advantage. "There is your choice. Prove you stand behind your words and heal me, knowing that you may very well never bed another woman again. Or show yourself to be the shallow, self-centered man that—" she almost said, 'that you've already proven yourself to be,' "—who's nothing more than empty words."

He didn't reply. He gave it serious thought. "You're asking a lot."

"I've sacrificed far more for you than you're giving up for me."

He opened his mouth to say something but reconsidered his words. "Isn't there something else you want?"

"You trying to back out? That's the coward's way."

He did some more quick thinking. "What if I fail again?"

"Why would you? The last time you deliberately failed because it was all a trick to get me to release you from the table. I'm not falling for that again. You're a god, even if only a half-god; whatever you do, you can undo." She stood up straight, letting her arms hang by her side. "Now, are you going to prove that I am more important than you, or are you going to prove what you really are?"

She could tell he didn't like it. "If I heal you, and—"

She laughed at him. "I'm not bargaining with you! You started this little game. Finish it."

"If I—"

"Stop procrastinating."

"Hey," he insisted. "I've got to get something out of this."

"How about an immortal wife with the Power of Creation at her beck and call who is no longer angry at you?"

He wilted. "I guess that's the best I'm going to get. Come here."

She stepped forward. He turned her around, so he could put his hands around her and lay both low on her belly.

He rested his chin on her shoulder. "I'm not sure—"

"Mor-Lath," she warned.

He resigned himself. "So be it. But if I succeed, you will stop being angry with me." He called upon the Deeper Power until it filled him to capacity. He closed his eyes and concentrated.

His focus entered her body and explored the old scar he'd given her nearly sixteen years ago. The taste of Creation's Will made her want to call upon the Deeper Power herself. She gave in. It happily rushed into her soul. She laid her hands on top of his and observed him at work.

Mor-Lath asked the body, the smallest parts that dictated how everything was to be, what it needed to be restored to the whole, and how to do it. It gave up its secrets to the god, specifying every minute detail, what it was, where it went and what it did and why.

How complex a human being was. It never occurred to her to investigate the little building blocks that made a person. It was like how the finest sand made up the strongest rocks. When one looked closely at a grain of that sand, it was like a rock in its own way. While each small part of her body didn't resemble her the way sand resembled a rock, it did possess knowledge of how the whole body was to be. Mor-Lath read that memory, like Adrastea read a book, by requesting the knowledge from it.

That's what it reminded her of—a book. A tiny little book, complete with little words and sentences, that told the body what little blocks to make and where they went. How long had he known about that?

Mor-Lath got to work. Little by little, things began to grow, created anew. It took a great deal of energy. He put into it as much as he had, but it wasn't enough.

Help me.

She did. She let the Deeper Power fill her completely. She focused on her hands on his hands and fed her strength into his focus.

Her head spun, and her head went fuzzy. Just before she passed into oblivion, everything stopped, and the room resolved around her.

Mor-Lath's hands fell from her belly and he stepped back. *I... must sit down...* His voice faded from her mind.

He took another step backwards and, hand on his temple, collapsed into her rocking chair. His head fell back, coming to rest against a wing before his consciousness passed into oblivion. She felt him sink into the void, and he was gone from her thoughts.

Adrastea put her hands back to her belly. She summoned the Deeper Power, an infinitesimal amount compared to what they had wielded previously. She explored her own insides.

He'd done it. She discovered her womb restored and everything else that had been destroyed. She gasped as she realized what this meant. "I'm whole again."

He'd done it.

Somewhere, someone shouted her name. It came from outside. Footsteps crunched on the gravel of her pathway, then pounded up the wooden steps of the porch to her door. "Adrastea!" It was Chloe. She pounded on the door, then stopped, presumably to listen.

Another distant voice called out. "Chloe?" It was Mikal. His long stride also came up the path while Chloe rattled uselessly at the door.

Mikal demonstrated his ability to think during a crisis and, turning the knob, pushed the door that Chloe was trying to pull open.

But they didn't enter. "Adrastea?" they asked, peering in. "Are you all right?"

Adrastea looked up at them. "I'm fine."

Other footsteps pelted the pathway. Chloe's apprentices crowded at the doorway, followed by one of the Constable boys, Arn.

Mikal entered the home, with Chloe hiding behind him. "What was that?" she squeaked. "I felt that all the way from the church." Chloe's apprentices chose to remain outside.

"Even I felt that," Mikal said.

"You felt that?" Adrastea asked. "All of you?"

Arn came in, looking around to make sure it was safe. "I didn't feel whatever it was they felt. I saw them running. I knew something interesting was happening." Then his eyes fell on the figure in the rocking chair. "What happened?"

Chloe and Mikal came around to get a better look.

"Oh, Light above," the priestess cursed. "You've killed the Dark God!"

⁂

Adrastea looked back to her husband. She felt his presence, his soul; not departed yet. Other than that, he did look dead. He did not breathe. Adrastea knelt beside the chair and put her hand to his throat.

No pulse.

Chloe slid towards the fireplace while Arn Constable came forward, followed by Mikal. "Well?" Mikal asked. "Is he?"

As Adrastea was about to close her eyes and use the Deeper Power to take a closer look, she felt it: a single pulse, strong but alone. "He lives."

The rasp of metal on stone drew her attention. Chloe had lifted the kettle hook from the fireplace. She brandished it like a club. "But we could kill him. He is at our mercy." Her voice quickened in excitement. "We could destroy the Dark One once and for all." She strode forward, lifting her weapon.

Adrastea raised her hands. Before she could do anything, a bright glow came between Chloe and her target.

A pair of angels appeared. One of them held its hand out towards Chloe. "Stop, child of Light."

Chloe dropped the hook. She scooted back until she came up against the stone wall before sinking to the floor.

Arn, alert, stepped forward. He couldn't see the angels. "Priestess, what's wrong?"

Mikal moved towards Adrastea. "What have you done to her?" he demanded.

Adrastea shook her head and pointed to the angels. "It's not me. It's the Light."

He looked at her funny; Mikal couldn't see them either. She grasped her brother by the arm and passed her hand before his eyes. "See and understand."

He saw. His eyes widened, and his jaw dropped as he stared at the luminous beings that appeared before him.

Arn tried to help Chloe up, but she cowered away from him.

"Move back," Mikal murmured, waving Arn away with his hand while his eyes were still on the angels. Arn did so, not sure what was going on.

The angels spoke to Chloe. "Seek not to kill Mor-Lath, for that is not your destiny. While you fight the darkness in men's souls, leave this one to the Light. He is not of your flock."

Chloe wilted. "But he is in our power. We could destroy him now. Isn't that what the Light wants?"

"The Light will conquer evil in Their own way. Trust in Them and trust in your faith."

Chloe looked past the angels to the god whom she considered her greatest enemy. "But he's the God of the Dark."

"He is also a son of the Light."

She bowed her head. "But he's evil."

The angels regarded her, one tilting its head to the side. "Is there no man who can fall so far that he cannot come back to the Light? Conquest need not be by death."

"Chloe." When the angel spoke her name, she lifted her head. Her blue eyes spilled over in tears. She bit her lip to keep from wailing. "You have not failed in your vocation. Two hands can only do so much. One must trust the rest to the Light.

"Be at peace, Daughter. Do not run faster than you have strength."

The angels remained, waiting until Chloe came to terms with their message. After she nodded her acquiescence, only then did they depart.

Mikal let out his breath and moved forward to help Chloe. He gave the rocking chair a wide berth. Together he and Arn helped Chloe to her feet.

"What happened?" Arn asked.

Mikal glanced towards Adrastea for an explanation.

"He didn't need to know, so he didn't see," she said.

"But what about me?"

"I needed you to see."

Chloe made a few half-hearted swipes to brush the dust off her skirt.

"I still don't understand." She kept her eyes on Mor-Lath, lest he wake and startle her. "We could have killed him."

Adrastea shook her head. "Unless you're a mashiah, your efforts would have done nothing. Even I've stuck a knife in his heart and he lived. And had he learned you tried to kill him, he'd be most annoyed with you."

"He has a heart?" Chloe muttered.

Adrastea turned back to her husband. Even unconscious, he had this aura about him. She certainly wouldn't mistake him as harmless. "Please leave. I have some things I need to take care of."

Mikal ushered everyone out. "Do you want us to keep this to ourselves?"

Adrastea nodded. "The last thing I need is would-be saviors of the world waking the baby."

They left, leaving Adrastea alone, looking upon her husband. What to do with him? She couldn't leave him there, so where to put him? Should she stick him upstairs? Or what about returning him to the temple and letting the priestesses look after him?

She felt leery of trusting him into the hands of someone else. She wanted to keep an eye on him.

With a wave of her hand, she sent him upstairs, his body winking out of sight, to reappear on her bed. That would do for now until she could think of a better place to put him.

Adrastea took the stairs to give herself time to think. He'd healed her, but even then, he'd asked something in return. He told her to stop being angry.

Why was she angry to begin with? His deception—that's what angered her. He'd do something without telling her what he was doing, never mind asking her opinion. He'd given her a Hobson's choice of marriage then he made her immortal, only telling her what he'd done after the fact. She was a fool for thinking he'd be faithful. He should have told her from the beginning he had no intention of taking her to his bed. Had he done that, she wouldn't have tried to seduce him, he wouldn't have seared her womb, she wouldn't have gone on a jealous killing rampage, he wouldn't have condemned her to the underworld...

It was an old argument. She confessed her guilt in keeping the cycle going, but ultimately, it was his fault in the beginning.

As she entered the bedroom, she paused for a moment, watching him. She'd dropped him on the bed like a discarded dress. At least she could give him some dignity. Gently she rearranged him, so he lay straighter, his hands folded on his chest. He looked laid out for his funeral.

Stop being angry, he had said. It was his last request before he healed her.

Adrastea put her hand to her belly just to be sure.

Yes, her womb was there, whole and anew. She was complete. A giddy peace flowed through her veins. He'd made her whole. She threw back her head and laughed. Oh, it felt good. She spun around the bedroom, letting her joy have free expression.

Now that she had her womb back, what would she do with it? Was it simply the principle of the thing? Or did she intend on finding another man to get children on her? After all her rage and point-making over Mor-Lath's infidelity, she couldn't with all good conscience turn around and do the same. The Light would certainly frown on her breaking her vows.

At least she could stop being angry.

It proved harder than she thought. When she let go of her anger, she discovered that without it, she felt awkward. If she wasn't angry with him, how was she supposed to feel about him?

It seemed wrong to like him in the way she liked most people in her life. From childhood she'd been taught that he was evil, this chthonic god. Stories told to frighten children showed him as some dark monster who would drag naughty children down to the depths of the Dom-al-gol.

Who would have thought it to be true?

Adrastea sat on the bed, on the opposite side, where she had sat not more than half an hour ago. She brushed a strand of his dark hair into place.

"Oh, Light," she breathed. "What do I do now?"

The glow of Lucea's presence filled the room. "Let him rest," She instructed. "Give him the chance to heal."

Adrastea wanted to cling to the god like a bewildered child. Instead, she folded her hands in her lap. "What have I done?"

Lucea sat on the other side of the bed, next to Mor-Lath. She stroked his face the way Adrastea loved to stroke Harianne's when the child fell asleep in her arms. "That is between you and him. From My point of view, he simply corrected a mistake he made. Please realize this."

Was Lucea asking her to think well of him? Adrastea wasn't sure how she should take it. "He's vulnerable. He's in Your power. Yet You don't want him destroyed? I don't understand. Isn't that what's going to happen eventually? Why not now?"

Lucea shrugged. "It is not the time."

"So, what are you waiting for?" She meant it with all respect.

"A reason."

Adrastea shook her head to clear her ears in case she didn't hear right. "I thought you had a reason. He's Dark. He's evil. Isn't that reason enough?"

"Darkness does not necessarily mean evil. Sure, he is selfish from time to time. He can let his temper get the better of him. But he is much improved over what he had become and is far better than his predecessor ever was—" Lucea stopped, sighed while she weighed her thoughts. "Perhaps I should start at the Beginning."

"His beginning?"

"No. THE Beginning." Lucea disappeared from where She was, appearing immediately on the bed beside Adrastea.

Adrastea fell into Lucea's motherly arms, to be enfolded and comforted. She'd been holding on to her anxiety, keeping it under control, until her hold snapped. She had a good cry.

"I know it's hard," the god said to her. "Perhaps you will feel better once you understand his place in the universe." She settled back against the bedframe, Adrastea wrapped in Her arms like a child while Mor-Lath slept beside Them. She told her a most significant story:

"In the Beginning there was the Creator, a self-awareness who chose to create the universe. The Creator was a god, indeed, was God, a dual creature like you or Us, with two halves that we identify now as Male and Female.

"The Creator realized Their dual nature, and thought, 'If there are two of Us, could there be three? And if there could be three, could there be four?' And so Their reasoning went.

"For Their own reasons, They chose to create three children, separate beings. They created a daughter. They called Her Lucea to rule the top of Creation and direct its Power. They created a son and called Him Nazara to rule the bottom of Creation and to lift that which fell to the bottom until it could move upwards and fulfill the measure of its creation. To ensure balance between the two, They created another child and called her Tanat."

Adrastea sat up. "You are the literal daughter of Creation?"

Lucea nodded.

Adrastea continued. "I know of Tanat. I have never heard of Nazara." When Lucea stroked her hair, it comforted her. It felt good to be able to let go of one's need to stand alone and let someone else shoulder the burden.

"Nor would you. His time was long before recorded history can remember.

"I and My siblings had been conscious of Our single nature. Because I was on one end of the spectrum and Nazara on the other, We felt out of balance. Since Tanat was in the middle, she did not feel this lack. Rather, I suspect she feels partnered with the balance. She had not the desires the rest of us had.

"The Creator created Creation. They made mortals to keep Them and Us company." Lucea paused while She sorted through the history of Creation, picking out the important bits. "I can't tell you much right now, for you are not ready for such a thing. Know that Time has an ending and a beginning and the Creator exists outside of Time. You and I are slaves within Time as are the mortals. Just be aware of that and know that someday you will learn more about Time.

"Anyhow, We kept company with the mortals, placing the essence of the Power of Creation within them, then restoring the essence to Creation when they were done with it.

"I loved what I did, but Nazara grew depressed. He couldn't understand why He was unhappy. Perhaps it was that He took the souls of the living and after having shriven them, saw them depart from Him. He was lonely.

"My brother and I were single beings. We should have been dual beings, though not dual beings together. Perhaps the Creator understood this and that is why We had the mortals."

Lucea smiled. "To make a story short, I found Phyl."

Phyl was once a mortal as Adrastea was, and elevated to immortality. "And thus, We became a god and fulfilled the measure of Our creation.

"When Nazara saw this, He thought He needed to find a companion as well. He found someone who was handsome and clever and spoke very well."

"Mor-Lath?"

Lucea shook her head. "No," she said, to Adrastea's surprise. "It wasn't Mor-Lath. It was a man named Ubilis. Ubilis was far too clever for his own good, and worldly besides. I must say he was worldlier, for my brother had been raised untainted by the evil wrought in men's minds and their hearts. While He had shriven countless souls of the weight of their sins, His core had remained pure.

"His loneliness got the better of Him. He listened to this Ubilis who won Him over with sweet words. He convinced my brother to give Him his Mantle of Godhood. And so Nazara did.

"Poor fool," She said in a small voice. "It cost Him His life."

Lucea's sorrow colored with loneliness flowed over Adrastea like a summer tide. Adrastea fought it and held onto the core of herself lest she be swept away. She could not stop the tears that coursed down her face for someone she'd never met.

Lucea regained Herself. She reached out a hand to smooth away the frown lines that had creased Mor-Lath's forehead. "So Ubilis became the God of the Dark, or rather demi-god, as you know.

"He was selfish, far more than Mor-Lath ever was. He set up his pits of sacrifice. He had learned how to feed off the sins of others. He twisted not just the souls of men, but their heritage, their culture. He brought much sorrow to the world and disrupted the Balance of Creation.

"He had to be destroyed. We could not kill him, for being the God of the Light, this would be impossible.

"But that did not mean that he was unkillable.

"A mashiah has enough of a certain kind of power over Creation to change Creation, enough to slay a god, if need be, yet be mortal enough that when the time comes, they could die, and thus be shriven of their sins. Otherwise, they would have to carry that burden forever.

"That is why you were not made a Mashiah. I knew he would make you immortal and there would be a very good chance that you would try to kill him." A small smile played across Her lips.

Adrastea rose to her feet, the straw of her mattress slowly uncrumpling with little snaps. "You knew I would try to kill him?"

"I knew what you were like, even before you were born. I know what Mor-Lath is like. Sooner or later he'd annoy you enough that you would 'do him in,' as the young people say, and you would do it before you had reached the fullness of your destiny."

Adrastea folded her arms, her all-too-familiar annoyance coming back. "Which is?"

Lucea spread Her arms. "I would that you become a god."

Adrastea didn't move. "I still don't understand why—"

"Understanding will come with time." She patted the mattress beside her. "Please, let Me finish My story."

Adrastea, after a moment's consideration, sat down. "All right. So Ubilis became this evil god that disrupted Creation."

"And he had to be stopped. A mashiah could stop him. So We created them, lots of them, on the chance that once of them would find herself or himself in a position to destroy the Dark God.

"In short, one particular young man realized his talent early on for the Deeper Power. He used it to his advantage, to better his place in the world."

"This was Mor-Lath?" After her last failed guess, Adrastea didn't feel so sure of her answer.

Lucea nodded. "Indeed, it was. He had his own goals and desires. Soon his growing talent in the Deeper Power attracted the eye of Ubilis. Ubilis developed a fondness for this young priest."

"A priest?! Him?" Adrastea shook her head in denial.

"Mor-Lath craved power. The path that gave him the greatest opportunity for development of his talent was a religious one.

"Mor-Lath saw Ubilis as a way to a power greater than anything of which he could dream. But to his surprise and consternation, what Ubilis wanted from him was something Mor-Lath would much rather not give.

"But Ubilis was a god and Mor-Lath was a mortal, one whose will was bent to Ubilis's." Lucea drew a deep breath, possibly sorting through her words, choosing what would be best for Adrastea's ears.

Adrastea did not have a desire to hear what Ubilis did to Mor-Lath. She suspected this aversion was partly Lucea's fault, for the goddess did not seem to relish the thoughts She sorted.

"Ubilis had learned from Nazara that a full god was a dual being. He had chosen Mor-Lath to be his other half because he had demonstrated mighty talent.

"Ubilis asked Us how to make Mor-Lath immortal. We told him a way, one that would not impact upon Creation the way your immortality has. It was a slow path, but the best one. It had the additional advantage that it annoyed Ubilis, who was never one for patience.

"I said Mor-Lath was clever. He took advantage of Ubilis during a moment of the god's weakness. He tricked him into sharing his Mantle of Godhood. The moment he did that, Mor-Lath turned around and killed Ubilis."

Lucea stretched out a hand and placed it on Adrastea's shoulder. *I confess,* She told Adrastea, *Phyl held down Ubilis. I Myself placed the knife in Mor-Lath's hand to bring about the death of this god. Mor-Lath does not know this. I would rather he never know. Please don't tell him. I know he would be most bitter to know that We were there during the moments of his greatest shame.*

Before Lucea severed the connection, Adrastea got the faintest hint that it was not the murder of a god of which She spoke.

Adrastea looked over to Mor-Lath, sleeping silently on her bed. Her curiosity welled up. What did Ubilis do to him, that would make him want to kill him?

Lucea's hand descended once more onto Adrastea's shoulder. "Let Me finish My story," She commanded. The suggestion that she should not press the matter about Mor-Lath ran strong in Lucea's touch.

"So Mor-Lath became God of the Dark, before he was fully immortal. But that, too, came with time. He started his new reign well enough. He filled in all Ubilis his pits of sacrifice, for Mor-Lath's own dignity had been 'sacrificed' enough within them. He raised altars, after Our manner and did away with several other practices he found distasteful. Ubilis took great pleasure in sorrow and pain whereas Mor-Lath took great pleasure in, well, pleasure—quite the opposite from his predecessor.

"Mor-Lath started with such great promise. In the end, he too became a servant of his natural self. He did not ascend above base desires to become something greater." Lucea rose, hands on Her knees as if the weight of Her age made Her bones creak. "We had such hopes for him."

Adrastea followed Lucea's suit and rose. "Is there no hope for him now?" Her heart beat faster, for she knew her own fate was tied with his. If he was doomed, she surely would follow.

Lucea pulled her into one of those warm, comforting hugs that evaporated all doubt. "As long as he lives, there is always hope. And now there is you."

With that, She gave Adrastea a kiss on the forehead. "Do as you think best, Daughter. I trust in you."

Lucea left. The room became darker, despite the bright afternoon sunshine outside.

Adrastea looked at Mor-Lath. "What am I going to do?" She sat and watched him. What had he been like? What had gone wrong?

She gave up when she couldn't come up with any answers. She went downstairs, keeping a close watch on their connection, lest he stir while she was gone.

Lunchtime came and went, and nothing happened.

Adrastea's milk came in, making her breasts uncomfortable. She took a risk and left the house. She fetched Harianne from Ari, neatly evading questions.

She fed her daughter and put her down for an afternoon nap. When Harianne was fast asleep, Adrastea peeked into her bedroom.

Mor-Lath had not moved, just as she'd felt he hadn't. How long was this going to go on?

Evening came. Mikal stopped by. "How are you?" They settled into the chairs by the fire. As Adrastea sat in her rocking chair, she listened to the faintest vestiges of Deeper Power imbedded in the wood. She also felt a touch of courage.

She shrugged. "I'm all right, I guess."

"And Mor-Lath?"

She looked upwards. "I've got him upstairs."

"He's still unconscious?"

She nodded.

"How long is he going to be that way?"

Another shrug.

"What are you going to do with him?"

"Keep him, I guess."

Mikal sighed. "I suppose he is staying out of trouble."

"True."

When Mikal left that evening, Adrastea retired to her bedroom. Mor-Lath was still there. "Great," she muttered. "Where am I going to sleep?"

The next day, he was still there, and the day after that. After about a week, she realized he wasn't going anywhere. Dismissing him from her thoughts, she went about her life.

Chapter 13

Adrastea knew the rhythms of the Temple. After morning devotion, the priestesses went off for chores and other business. The high priestess remained behind for personal devotion. Desideria had spoken of her devotions, the prayers she offered and sometimes the conversations she had with Mor-Lath. Personal devotion could be quite busy for a high priestess.

As Adrastea appeared in the main chapel of the temple, she found Garsinde at the altar. But she did not pray. She knelt there, hands folded, doing not much, perhaps thinking.

"Good to see you at your devotion." Adrastea ran a hand along the polished stone of the altar. How many priestesses had prayed here over the centuries?

Garsinde jumped back from the alter. "I did not think we would see you again."

"Don't know why. I was here last week." Anyhow, she was not here for idle chit-chat. "I have news of Mor-Lath. Come with me."

But Garsinde stood her ground. "No."

Adrastea wasn't surprised. "Aren't you curious to know where he's been for the past month?"

She watched while Garsinde considered these words. For a high priestess, she showed an astounding lack of interest in her god.

"It is not uncommon for him to disappear for any length of time."

Adrastea shrugged. "If you wish. I only thought that, as his high priestess, you would want to know."

That got her curiosity up. Garsinde stepped closer. "You didn't pin him to a table again, did you?"

"No." Adrastea held out her hand. "Coming?"

Garsinde hesitated, then took Adrastea's hand.

Shift.

Perhaps she should have warned the priestess. When they appeared in the bedroom, Garsinde fell to her knees and clung to the floor until the dizziness passes. At least she did not lose her breakfast on the rug.

Adrastea helped her up. "Look upon your god."

Garsinde lifted her eyes to the prone form of Mor-Lath on the bed. Her hands flew to her face, her skin paled. "You killed him!"

"Alas, no. He merely sleeps."

Garsinde extended a tenuous hand but did not touch him. "Why won't he wake up?"

Adrastea side-stepped the question. "He will wake when he's ready."

Then the priestess fell to her knees. "I must attend him constantly."

"Oh no, you won't." Adrastea was going to have none of that. She hauled Garsinde up. "Your first devotion is to the temple."

"My first devotion is to him."

Adrastea rolled her eyes. "I know how strong your devotion is." Not. "I did not bring you here to make you an anchoress. You're here for enlightenment." She pinched the bridge of her nose. Oh, why did she bother? "Know that he is well cared for and safe, although probably not answering prayers any time soon." An ache twisted in her heart. "I know how hard it can be on a person when someone they care about suddenly disappears." Ari never forgave either Adrastea or Mor-Lath for the fifteen-year disappearance. "I do not know how long he will sleep. I didn't want you to think he'd deserted you."

Garsinde stiffened. "I will remain by his side until he wakes, or I die."

Adrastea reached out her hand to Garsinde's arm.

Shift.

This time, Garsinde did throw up, all over the floor of the temple.

"No." Adrastea felt irritated. "You will remain here and continue as you have been. Imagine how angry His Holiness would be, should he wake next week and discover you've been lax in your devotions."

Garsinde wiped her mouth. She scowled at Adrastea. "If nothing's going to change, why did you bother to tell me about him?"

Adrastea rolled her eyes. "Honestly. Why did he choose you as high priestess?" She left without saying goodbye.

She did not go back to Sacred Spring. Not yet.

In the temple kitchens, someone had to do the dishes. That was not Berengaria. Junior priestesses were stuck with the more unpleasant chores. Berengaria, having some seniority, got the lovely, clean job of putting them away.

Adrastea waited until Berengaria had put the last dish in its cupboard, before gently speaking her name.

Berengaria turned around. A light of joy brightened her face. "Holiness."

Adrastea held out her hand. "Remember how I asked if you wanted to come with me to Sacred Spring?"

The priestess nodded. Then her face grew serious. "I have not had the opportunity to ask His Holiness."

"Don't bother. He won't disapprove."

Still, Berengaria hesitated.

Adrastea's hand waited. "If you come with me, I will ease your mind."

She considered it further. Then she gave her trust and her hand to Adrastea.

"Ready?"

Shift.

Berengaria clung to Adrastea as their feet touched down on grass. The cool breeze of spring ruffled her thin priestess robes, making her shiver. They stood on a hill next to a plain stone temple and a small body of water.

"Welcome to Sacred Spring," said Adrastea.

Berengaria wrapped her arms about her. Adrastea summoned a cloak from her home and draped it about Berengaria's figure. "Sorry about that."

Berengaria looked at the mountains behind them and the plains before them. She listened to the quakies shimmer in the breeze. "It sounds like the ocean."

Ignoring the spring, she ran towards the temple. "Is this where you live?"

"No, I'm down in the village."

Berengaria looked around. "There's a village here?"

erengaria looked around the village of Sacred Spring. "Why would you wish to live here? It's so small."

"That's why I like it. Things stay quiet."

The priestess peered at the tallest building. "Not much of a suitable temple for you, is it?"

"That's the inn." Adrastea took her down a small road towards a smaller, yet well-kept place. "That is my house."

Berengaria seemed disappointed. "I thought you would have lived in more splendor."

"And what would I do with splendor? It's not as if I need it."

"But Holiness, you're the Bride of Mor-Lath. Surely that would require..." she waved her hands at the house. "Something worthy of your station."

"I'm a country lass."

Berengaria shook her head. "You are so much more than that."

Adrastea sighed and gave up. "You don't need to stay."

"No, no," replied Berengaria. "I'm happy to give this a go." Little waves of excitement rolled off the priestess, making her Lines sing.

They climbed the steps. "It's a dull life."

"Oh, I doubt that."

Adrastea allowed herself a clandestine smile as she opened the door. "Cooking, cleaning, child-minding."

Berengaria looked about as she entered Adrastea's home. "Four dishes to wash. Three loaves to bake. Two frocks to mind and mend. Compared to a temple full of priestesses, sounds like a holiday." She walked around the room, inspecting the chairs, the fireplace and the little trinkets sitting on the mantle.

"Garden to weed, water to fetch," Adrastea added.

"What?" Berengaria exclaimed. "You don't have a pump?"

Adrastea reassured her she did. "But any warm water, you have to heat it yourself."

"Oh." Now the cloud rolled over her day. "No warm baths then?"

"We'll see."

She showed her the kitchen and the cellar and everything else on the ground floor before taking her upstairs. "These northern bedrooms, one can be yours, the other is Harianne's." Adrastea had set up a small, modest bed in Harianne's room. This was where she'd been staying, as her real bed was rather occupied at the moment. The other room, soon to be

Berengaria's, likewise had a small, but comfortable bed and a table.

Harianne slumbered in the cradle near the fireplace, a cozy spot. Adrastea checked the sleeping child. "She'll be good for another hour."

Then Adrastea led Berengaria across the landing. "This room I keep sealed. No one goes in."

Berengaria looked at the door wistfully. "Yes, Holiness."

Adrastea rolled her eyes. "Now, don't be like that. I will show you what is there. But remember, only a select few know what lies beyond this door. You will need to keep it a secret and you will see why."

Adrastea drew her finger in a line down the edge of the door. Then she opened it. Berengaria followed her in.

The morning sun shone in, brightening the bedroom. "It's lovely—" Berengaria started. "Oh." She stopped cold when she saw who lay on the bed. Quickly, she averted her eyes and backed away.

Adrastea grabbed her wrist before she could vacate the bedroom entirely. "He's not dead, but asleep. Garsinde knows, and a few others here in Sacred Spring. Now you know."

Tension emanated from Berengaria. "But why? How?"

"He wrought a miracle no other could perform."

"But he is a god. I thought he was invincible." She sank to her knees and stretched out her hand to touch his. "He's still warm." She looked up to Adrastea. "When will he wake up?"

"I don't know."

Berengaria sniffed and wiped at her eyes. "Is this why you brought me here? To attend him?" Her shoulders hunched up.

"No. Sleeping gods require little. I brought you here to assist me."

That got the priestess' attention. "What? Handmaiden?" She forgot about the god on the bed. "Almost... personal high priestess?"

Adrastea ushered Berengaria out of the bedroom and resealed the door. "I don't need anyone singing my praises. I need someone to do the dishes."

"All four of them?" Berengaria crossed her arms. "Really, why have you brought me here?"

Really? Adrastea was not sure. "Company, maybe? Someone who doesn't cringe at the thought of him up there. Maybe someone I can talk to, someone I trust."

Berengaria's face brightened "You trust me?"

Adrastea thought about that. "I suppose I do."

The priestess twisted her fingers together. Her gaze fell back to the floor. "Even though..." Her voice dried up. She wrapped her arms about herself and turned away. "I can't. I'm not worthy."

That caught Adrastea by surprise. "What? Why?"

It took Berengaria a while to find her words again. "Because..." She swallowed. "When you were gone... I... He..." She closed her eyes and swayed.

Adrastea put out a hand to the priestess' elbow to steady her. "I do not blame you for being beguiled by him. I promised I wouldn't kill you because of it."

Berengaria, her eyes still closed, nodded.

Adrastea put her hands on the priestess' shoulders. "We can leave that in the past and not speak of it ever again. Would you prefer that?"

Berengaria nodded again. She sank to her knees before Adrastea. "I'm so sorry. He knew my weakness."

Adrastea pulled her up. "I know your weakness." Once she'd caught the very young Berengaria sneaking a rather erotic book back into the library. "We can't pretend it never happened, but we can not speak of it again. Agreed?"

She agreed. Her gaze roamed back to Mor-Lath, still unable to meet Adrastea's. "What do I do about him?"

Adrastea ushered her out of the room. "Absolutely nothing." She resealed the room.

Once back downstairs, Adrastea sat Berengaria at the kitchen table. A hot kettle boiled on the stove. From that, she made tea. Berengaria studied the cup.

"Tea before business," Adrastea explained. "Country custom." She sipped her own cup. "Now that you know everything you need to, I will ask you once again: do you wish to stay here in Sacred Spring?"

"Permanently?"

Adrastea considered this. "Well, for as long as I need you, and as long as you are willing to serve."

"Four meals a day?"

"Mm hmm."

"All the books I can read?"

At this, Adrastea hesitated. "I don't have many. But we can visit the temple library as often as you wish."

Berengaria didn't need to think twice. "Then I shall stay."

A great weight lifted off her heart. This must be how Ari felt having an apprentice. "There is one last formality before you officially move in." Berengaria put down her teacup. "Oh?"

After Adrastea knocked at Mikal's house, Jacob opened the door. "Yeah, he's home," Jacob replied. He didn't bother to hide his longsuffering. "Post came."

"He got a letter?" Adrastea asked.

Jacob rolled his eyes. "He got several." He looked Berengaria up and down. "Who's this?"

"Introductions later." Adrastea pushed past him. Berengaria followed, giving a tenuous smile to Jacob.

The mayorprentice sighed and closed the door.

Inside Mikal Mayor paced up and down, ranting at some poor letter he had wadded in his hand.

"In fine fettle today, I see." Adrastea remarked.

He paused only to glare at his sister. "Can you believe this?" He thwacked the page in his hand. "It seems the Pennexters have a whole army of solicitors and other toads. They pulled out Lord Pennexter's will. His unchanged will." He crumpled the letter again.

"What? The one that favors Dassie and her cousins?"

Mikal held up a finger. "Unless Josephus is located."

"But our father's dead."

"His heirs are not." He pointed dual fingers back and forth between himself and Adrastea.

She folded her hands before her heart. "So...? Mikal sighed. "Essentially, I'm the official heir."

"Oh," she replied. "It passes from male to male?"

Mikal abandoned the letter he'd been torturing. He ruffled around on his kitchen table for another. "No. Nothing so stupid."

Adrastea swallowed. "Then, I should be heir?"

He glared at her. "Officially, yes, but you're not."

"So... what?" She thought about the family structure. "Wait. I thought Lady Pen was the eldest."

"Nope." He couldn't seem to find the letter he wanted. "Gaah!" He scattered the whole lot off the table."

Jacob rolled his eyes and bent to pick up.

Mikal scrubbed his hands through his hair. "Lady Pen was merely family regent while Lord Pennexter was off in Cithra. She's second eldest. You, however, cannot inherit because there's some law somewhere about being married or descended from an enemy of Feown."

"Ah." Digging that up may have been Jonathan's work.

For the first time, Mikal noticed Berengaria. "Hello?" To his sister, he asked, "Who's this?"

To be honest, Adrastea had half-forgotten her as well. "Someone who would ask your permission to live here." She held out her hand to Berengaria, who took it. "Lord Mayor, may I present Berengaria Priestess, who would ask your permission to live in Sacred Spring for an indeterminate amount of time."

"Oh." To Berengaria, he said, "Pleased to meet you."

She gave him a nervous smile, her eyes darting to Adrastea.

"Oh, sorry." She tapped her forehead. "I forgot. She doesn't speak Feowan."

"That could be a problem."

Adrastea sighed. "I'll teach her. She does enjoy reading. I'll find some books in Feowan." Then she introduced her brother to Berengaria, in Tredan. "This is Mikal Mayor of Sacred Spring."

Berengaria touched both hands to her forehead, then to her heart, before offering them to Mikal. "I express my gratitude to you for letting me stay."

Mikal looked to his sister for translation. Adrastea obliged with, "She's glad to be here."

Jacob placed the sorted pages onto the table. He lifted one up. "Here's the letter asking Lord Mikal to attend the Pennexters at his earliest convenience." He separated it from the pile. "Here's the one denouncing Lady Adrastea nee Pennexter as an heir due to her marriage and declaring Lord Mikal Pennexter, Mayor, the sole beneficiary. What does 'nee' mean?"

Mikal snatched that one out of Jacob's hand. "A shame I can't marry, or I'd wed the first unsuitable woman to come along." He sighed. "Adrastea, what can I do? They're not taking no for an answer."

Jacob wrinkled his nose. "We don't have to call you Lord Mikal, do we?"

Mikal looked mortified. "Light, no!"

Adrastea moved towards the door. "I see we've come at a bad time."

"Don't you desert me." Mikal grabbed his hand.

Berengaria jumped. "Is he denying my petition?"

"No." Adrastea touched her arm in reassurance. "He's upset about something else—completely unrelated." At that, she gave a snort of laughter.

"What are you saying?" Mikal insisted.

Adrastea shook her head dismissively. "Sorry. Bit of a pun. Anyhow, you never did answer Berengaria's request."

Mikal looked at her. Then he really studied her. She twined her fingers nervously. "She's not one of his, is she?"

"Absolutely she is."

His brow creased. "She's not going to give Chloe grief, is she?"

"Only if Chloe gives her grief. She's been trained in self-defense."

"And a few other things, I imagine." Still, Mikal held out his hand. "Welcome to Sacred Spring."

Berengaria studied his hand, then took it, unsure. The moment their hands clasped, both inhaled deeply. The priestess looked up into Mikal's eyes. A brilliant smile lit her face. Lines of Deeper Power wrapped about their clasped hands, barely shimmering enough to be seen.

His own face seemed transfixed. "Hi," he breathed. "Yeah, she can stay."

Adrastea exhaled in relief. Thank the Light for that. "I'll take her over and introduce her to Chloe. I think it would be best that way."

Mikal tore himself away from Berengaria. "What? Oh yes, yes." With reluctance, he released Berengaria's hand. "See you later?" he said to her.

Berengaria reached out and touched her fingertips to his chest. "Thank you for letting me stay." She withdrew her hand. She turned to Adrastea. "Does he understand what I'm saying?"

"I'll teach you Feowan later. Anyhow, he's happy to have you stay. Now I have one other person you must meet and make peace with."

Worry crossed Berengaria's face. "There are two mayors?"

Adrastea didn't answer her. To Mikal, she said, "I can come back later if you need some moral support with the rest of the family." She didn't bother to wait for Jacob to open the door but willed it open. "Personally, Lord Pennexter, I think you'll be fine."

She hastened out before a wad of paper hit her.

Out in the village, Berengaria hastened to catch up with Adrastea. "The Lord Mayor seems put out about something. I think we visited at a bad time."

"Family matter. Some distant relatives want him to do something for them. It involves leaving the village, something he doesn't want to do."

"Oh." She looked over her shoulder back to Mikal's house. "He has a good aura. Is he a nice person?"

"Generally, yes. You'll get another chance to know him better."

"I'd like that." The Lines about her vibrated with happiness.

Adrastea led them across the village square to the chapel. "The next person you meet might not be as amenable."

Berengaria's footsteps slowed. "Should I be meeting him?"

"Her," Adrastea corrected. "And yes, if there is to be peace in the village."

She wrapped her arms about herself. "I don't know if I like the sound of that."

"I know. But it's necessary. Sacred Spring is a Feowan village. They walk in the Light."

Berengaria had to think about that for a moment. "Ah, Glasskissers."

Adrastea gave her a sideways glance. "You might not want to use that term in front of Chloe."

"Chloe? Is that her name?"

"Chloe Priestess."

That baffled Berengaria. "Not Priestess Chloe?"

Adrastea gave a quick lesson on surnames in Feowan villages. "Only noble houses keep a name. Everyone else is called as they work. Therefore, Chloe Priestess. Mikal Mayor, and so on."

"So, I'd be Berengaria Priestess, then?"

Adrastea nodded.

Berengaria thought some more about that. "I've never had a surname before. I've only been just Berengaria. Priestess was my title." Then she looked at Adrastea. "What are you called, then?"

"Before I was married? Adrastea Healer."

"Ah." Then it all came together for Berengaria. "Of course. You were a stillwife. What do they call you now?"

"I'm still Adrastea Healer."

They reached the doors of the chapel. "What do they call His Holiness?"

"Things one shouldn't repeat in polite company."

The doors were open, indicating Chloe was within, or one of her apprentices. As they entered the warmth of the chapel, Adrastea dipped her hand in a little basin of water and wiped it on her forehead.

"Ritual bathing?" Berengaria asked.

Adrastea hadn't thought about it but, "Yes. Water from our sacred spring."

Berengaria reached for the basin. Adrastea's hand shot out. "Wait. Just touch it with a finger first." How would it affect one sworn to the Dark?

She did as Adrastea bade, dipping the tip of her index in it. "Oh, it tingles, like when your foot falls asleep." She plunged her whole hand it, as Adrastea had. She withdrew it as quickly. "Oh, that buzzes! Is it cursed?"

"Blessed."

"And your Glasskissers drink this stuff?"

They proceeded into the chapel itself. The foyer opened up into a bright, circular chapel, the light of the day filtering in through the high windows.

"Oh," Berengaria breathed, as she laid a hand on a fine wooden pillar and stroked the backs of the finely-carved pews. "It's prettier than I thought. It's all wooden."

Adrastea called out. "Chloe? Are you here?"

Gallian came dashing out. "She'll be just a min—" She saw who it was. "Oh. It's you. I'll fetch her immediately."

Berengaria watched the priestapprentice duck out. "She seems so serious."

"Like Desideria?"

Berengaria considered this. "No. Desideria was deep. This one is more...scared."

Adrastea sighed. "I make her nervous."

Chloe came out, wiping her hands on a towel. "Gallian said you'd come." Her response was polite but cool.

"Chloe, I wanted to introduce you to someone who's come to live in Sacred Spring. Mikal's given his approval."

Chloe lifted a hand high in the air to invoke the blessing of her god, then lowered it, palm facing inward. "In the Name of the Light, I welcome you to Sacred Spring."

Like she had done with Mikal, Berengaria touched her forehead, her heart and offered her hands. "I offer gratitude to you for your kind welcome."

Chloe looked to Adrastea. "She doesn't speak Feowan?"

"Give her time."

Berengaria murmured to Adrastea, "Does she know who I am? She's being rather polite, all things considering." Instead of waiting for an answer, she put her hands to her chest, then spread them out. "I come in peace."

Adrastea translated for Chloe's benefit. "You must know that Berengaria is a Dark priestess."

Chloe's countenance darkened. "You brought one here? Isn't it bad enough we've got *him* here? Wait. Does she know about him upstairs?"

"Yes. But she's not here for him. She's here for me."

Chloe folded her arms and set herself stubbornly. "How many are you bringing?"

"Just the one." Adrastea sighed. Of all the times for Chloe to get all religious and stiff. "I need the help. You have apprentices, I have priestesses."

Chloe grumbled under her breath. "Very well."

To Berengaria she said, "Chloe's tolerant to have you stay. Welcome to Sacred Spring."

As they left the chapel, Berengaria looked backwards at Chloe, who stood in the chapel doorway, quite stern. "Are you sure?"

"Yep. Had she not accepted you, you would have been ridden out of town on a rail."

Berengaria stopped in the middle of the street, her expression betraying her thoughts of the ridiculousness of being carried out on a rail.

"Gets even better. You might have been tarred and feathered."

"Oh, now you jest."

Adrastea shrugged. "Chloe might not like it, but she has to accept that you heart is good. Otherwise, you would not have been able to come into Sacred Spring at all." She told the story of Mor-Lath's blood-oath, that protected the town from all who would come with evil intent."

"So that includes me?" Berengaria asked.

Adrastea gave her a spontaneous hug. "Berengaria, of all the people I know, you have the least guile in your heart."

Thus, did Berengaria come to live in Sacred Spring. True to her word, Adrastea provided Berengaria with all the books she could read, progressively more of them in Feowan.

Summer turned to autumn and autumn to winter. Berengaria didn't like the deep cold and snow so much. But the village had been kinder to her than she'd expected. It could have been because she treated the infant Harianne with love in her heart. This alone secured Ari's fondness for the foreign priestess.

Berengaria and Chloe rubbed each other the wrong way on several occasions. Experience taught the priestess that Chloe rubbed several people the wrong way, including Adrastea.

One person she got to know and really like was Mikal Mayor. Even the shock of learning he was Adrastea's brother didn't dampen her amiable feelings towards him.

Everyone liked him, as far as she could tell. No wonder he was such a popular mayor.

Shame he was married to Sacred Spring.

Heidi Wessman Kneale

Chapter 14

One spring afternoon, Adrastea paused over the kitchen sink, her potatoes forgotten as an awareness tickled in the back of her mind. A brief moment later, she felt it in the lines of her face.

Mor-Lath was waking up.

She dropped her knife and half-peeled potato and didn't bother taking the stairs. She appeared in her bedroom—their bedroom, really, since he'd occupied it for the past several years. As she wiped her wet hands on the hem of her skirt, he drew a deep breath. She paused her movements and sent out a brief thought to her little girl Harianne. She sat in her play pen down in the kitchen, the wooden rails blocking her in and keeping her from greater trouble. So great was her concentration in playing with her toys that her mother's absence did not distress her. Berengaria had left the house for the morning. She'd made an excuse to pick up something from the Store, but Adrastea knew she'd gone to see Mikal.

Adrastea's heartbeat increased as her husband drew another deep breath and stirred. Then groaning, he sat up and put his hand to his head. Adrastea pressed her fists to her lips and didn't dare breathe.

He scrubbed his eyes, scratched through his hair and drew up his knees while he took his bearings. He wiped his hands on the front of his nightshirt and he smacked his dry lips. His gaze fell to the dressing table opposite the bed, namely the pitcher of water there. Faster than she thought possible, he slid out of bed and padded over. Lifting the pitcher, he gulped the water greedily.

Adrastea hastened forward. "Not too quickly. You'll make yourself sick."

She had to wrestle the pitcher in his grasp. The water within sloshed back and forth, spilling over her wrists and onto the floor, leaving dark patches on the wood. Mor-Lath tugged at it and she tugged back. He didn't relinquish it easily. While her hands were closed around his, the drive of his thirst echoed through the contact. With a thought, she vanished nearly all the water before giving up the pitcher to him. He drained the rest and gasped. "I need more."

"No."

Only then, did his eyes meet hers, locked in a battle of wills. "You can't stop me."

"Yes, I can, and you know it." She stared him down until he averted his gaze.

His head dropped, and he put a hand to his forehead. The pounding of his headache throbbed through the Lines. Of course, he was dehydrated. With a touch of pity, she restored a little of the water to the pitcher, which he gratefully drank.

Once he drained that, he looked up at her expectantly. She did not give him a refill. Arguing took too much energy. He plodded his way back to the bed and dropped onto it. "How long have I been out?"

Adrastea did not sit down. She replaced the pitcher on her dressing table. "Nearly four years. It is spring now." She watched as his lips twitched slightly as he counted the time he'd spent unconscious. Then, head in his hands, he closed his eyes.

His surge of Power caught Adrastea unawares. She squeaked in surprise as a drinking glass—one of hers—appeared in his hands, full of water. He drained half of it before she could stop him.

She snatched it away, he stole it back, rising to his feet. "Will you stop that?" she snapped. He took advantage of his longer reach by holding her back with one hand while lifting the glass to his lips with the other.

Stomach full, he did not try for more water. He handed her the glass.

He studied her as if to gauge her mood, then looked to her belly. "Did it work?"

"Yes," she replied.

He turned his face away. *Happy now?*

She cradled the glass and pressed it close to her stomach. "Mor-Lath? Thank you."

"Yes, well..." He looked at what he wore. He plucked at the man's night shirt. "You borrowed from your brother?"

She didn't answer him. Instead, she moved away, to put the glass on the stand next to the pitcher. A quick thought downstairs to touch Harianne. She'd stopped playing with her blocks and had started looking around the kitchen for her mother.

She returned her attention back to Mor-Lath. She'd preferred him asleep. She had come to like him while he was in that state. "You've changed on the outside…"

"What?" He hastened to the mirror.

She was not jesting when she said he'd changed. While she'd had years to get used to his agedness, he'd only come to. It must have been a shock. His hair had threads of silver, denser at the temples. His face looked gaunter. The shadow of beard added to the hollows of his cheeks. He raised gentle fingers to pull at the corners of his eyes. He hadn't had wrinkles before. It made him look twenty years older.

He'd lost weight— his collarbones stood out. While that could be gained back, she did not know any way of restoring youth.

He put his hands on the dressing table and leaned closer. "This is what happened?"

She didn't answer.

He turned to look at her, his expression unfathomable. "Was it worth it?"

Adrastea passed thoughts across the stage of her mind, auditioning which one she would utter. Yes, he'd healed her. Three weeks later she had her proof, and every month after that. Not that it benefited her; if anything, she had returned to the inconveniences associated with womanhood.

She'd spent those years thinking about what it meant. She could, in theory, bear children now. But not by Mor-Lath. Never by him. He'd made that clear, even as he healed her.

But still…

He'd been asleep for four years. At any time she could have sought out someone to warm her bed.

But she hadn't. Why not?

Was it worth it? "For keeping a promise and giving something to someone and not expect anything in return? Yes."

He stopped and studied at her reflection in the mirror. "Now what?"

"What do you mean, 'now what'?"

He licked his parched lips. "What I'm trying to figure out is why someone who claims to hate me so much took such good care of me when she could have easily had me destroyed." His voice wavered slightly on his final word.

She shrugged. "The Light told me not to kill you."

He turned back to the mirror.

"And I had promised you not to be angry."

He bowed his head, closed his eyes and concentrated on something Adrastea couldn't fathom. She felt the tuggings of the Deeper Power.

Countless souls swooped in to the bedroom, those hungry, desperate souls who served the God of the Dark as they drew near to their master, reported and departed. They moved almost too fast for her to keep up, but sometimes she caught the edges of their bare thoughts. They were updating him on the status of the world. *So that's how he did it*, she mused. She had wondered how he knew so much about the world.

Then Mor-Lath's concentration deepened. Adrastea felt a tug as the Lines of Deeper Power congregated about him. Her head spun with the force that flowed along those Lines, so much she had to sit down. The Lines grew so bright she couldn't see him for their luminosity. She put her hands to her face as the awareness of the whole world flowed past her skin. Such a jumbled mess! How could anyone, even a god, keep all that straight?

Satisfaction, concern... These were the emotions she felt from him. Worry, even.

Adrastea blocked herself off from the overabundance of information. It made her head feel numb. Trepidation filled her heart. If she was expected to be his helpmeet, how could she possibly deal with a fraction of what he handled now? She closed her eyes and pushed the Lines away.

A cool hand touched her forehead. "Adrastea, are you all right?"

Adrastea opened her eyes to the ceiling. She'd fallen back to the bed. Did she pass out? The aura of Deeper Power had faded. Mor-Lath sat on the bed next to her.

She sat up in alarm, but it was quiet here. The world had settled back into its soft, steady hum. "How can..." She shook the last of the overload from her head.

When he reached out again and brushed back a curl from her face, she startled at the intimacy. "I— I can't do this." She leapt to her feet.

Downstairs Harianne called out, her little voice rising at the end in a question. "Mama?" Where was her mother? "Garie?"

Glad of a distraction, Adrastea hurried down the stairs and to the kitchen, to scoop up her fretful daughter. Harianne held out her arms to her mother and clung tightly. "It's all right," Adrastea soothed. "I'm here." Lines from Harianne wrapped around her as if her daughter didn't want her to go away ever again.

Mor-Lath appeared behind her. "Yes, here you are, country farmwife, in this little country house and this little country village, doing country things." He saw Harianne. "Oh, hello," he said in surprise. The baby had grown into a little girl, strong and stocky, with light curly hair and dark eyes, typical of families from Sacred Spring. "What happened to her?"

Adrastea turned away protectively. "She grew bigger. She never stayed little for long." She turned her attention to Harianne. "And she's the cleverest little thing." Adrastea gave Harianne a little tap on the nose.

"How nice." He dismissed the child as soon as he noticed her. "And what about you?"

"I'm not clever."

He folded his arms and leaned against the wall. "I dare say you're not."

She narrowed her eyes. "Oh, thank you very much."

"Or perhaps you are."

Adrastea wilted. Yes, she definitely liked him better unconscious. He kept his mouth shut, then. "Now that you're awake, I'm sure you have better things to do than stand around my kitchen and wonder where the bread is."

"Bread box." He pointed a finger in its general direction without uncrossing his arms.

Adrastea ignored this interruption. "So why don't you go and take care of what business you haven't been able to take care for the past few years and let me get on with my life."

"All right, then. How about I take care of the most important business first?"

"You do that." She restored Harianne to the playpen and returned to her potatoes. She had peeled one completely before she realized he hadn't left.

He was still in her kitchen, watching her. "Well?" she said, her back to him.

"I'm doing it."

"What?" she wailed, her patience wearing thin.

"I need to convince my wife to stop playing this silly little game, come home, and resume her rightful place."

Her grip tightened around her knife as the trepidation rose within her. Had she ever seen him tap into Creation to that degree? She pushed aside her role in Deliverance. "I am home. Sacred Spring has always been my home. I belong here." No way she could do what he just did.

"You belong with me."

She sighed again. "It's always about you."

He considered her words, possibly recalling the last conversation they had. "Yes, perhaps this time it is about me and what I need.

"I need a wife who will stand by me, who will work with me. I don't want some country farmwife who is content to peel her own potatoes, stitch her own clothes and pull the weeds from her garden by hand, a wife whose greatest pleasure in life is a comfy chair by the fire."

"But I like those things." Adrastea refused to let him bully her again.

"You don't like chopping wood.

"True."

"I want a goddess-wife."

"I'm a country farmwife."

"You're the daughter of lord, granddaughter of a noble house."

"A merchant house."

"Your uncle is the High Priest of Feown. He has the ear of the Duchess and the ear of the Light."

"I have the ear of the Light."

"And you peel potatoes by hand."

Adrastea didn't answer right away. Harianne beat against the bars of her playpen with her blocks until a flick of Adrastea's hand whisked them away from her grasp. "It's how I was taught."

He pushed off from the wall and came to her side, to lay his hands on her shoulders. "Other women, when given just the slightest bit of power, use it as much as they can. They grasp every advantage, whether for themselves or their family.

"You're the wife of a god and you wish to peel potatoes."

"I'm the wife of the Dark God."

He murmured in her ear. "Would it be different if I was the god of all Creation?" He sent a faint tendril through her. "If we were?"

Adrastea's heart ached. "Why couldn't you have been Good?"

"Goodness and the Light are not necessarily synonymous."

Adrastea felt different. She so believed in the goodness of the Light that she knew she did not need to communicate this with words.

It was Mor-Lath's turn to sigh and sink his chin onto her shoulder. "You'd rather a milksop for a husband? What kind of man is that?"

"Mama!" Harianne, possibly jealous of her mother's inattention, threw a block. It hit Mor-Lath in the leg. He scowled at her. He stretched out a hand. "*Sleep.*"

Harianne yawned and lay down.

Adrastea shoved him away. "You didn't have to do that."

"It was her naptime. We must talk without distraction."

Adrastea crossed her arms. "Why? You're not going to convince me to leave again."

He considered her words. "Indeed, I am not. By cunning or by force, I don't think I could make you do anything you didn't want." His gaze fell the sleeping Harianne. "The Lines are so strong between you and her... Threatening her, or anyone else close to you, would be moot. Anything I did to that precious little pet of yours, you would do to me tenfold." He drew her hand into his and pulled her through the doorway.

"Where are we going?"

"We can talk here, or we can go sit cozily by the fire and discuss this. It seems our relationship is based on agreeing to terms. My feet are cold, as there is a touch of draft in your kitchen. I would much rather be comfortable while I bargain elements of my life away."

She had dressed him in a nightshirt. What was her reasoning for that? Her brain had not been working too well at the time, she reasoned, because she had borrowed one of Mikal's shirts without telling him. Her brother might not like that. She followed him through the door and into the more comfortable front room. The fire flared up at her presence. "You could put on more clothing."

"You could remove some of yours to make us even."

"And what would that lead to?"

His back stiffened and he did not answer.

A smugness within her heart rejoiced. She'd scored a point against him.

As he dropped her hand, she settled into her rocking chair. He closed his eyes, held out his arms. Clothing out of the ether swirled about his being until he was fully clad. He'd chosen the style of a country shirt and trousers, as favored by the men in Sacred Spring.

He could have conjured up a more comfortable chair. Instead, he pulled the other chair closer to the fire that burned with no wood. He leaned back and thrust his feet closer to the warmth. "Ah, much better. I see you haven't reverted completely to country ways."

"Some things are easier," she conceded.

He got straight to business. "First, I must restate that I will never grant you a divorce. So, don't even think of asking. Second, I concede that this village is your choice of residence, and I will honor that. Third..." His gaze travelled to her stomach. "I affirm that I healed you from my own good will, and concede that that should not be used as a bargaining chip, nor be used as leverage of any kind. You get that gratis." His gaze turned wistful. "Since you are a jealous woman, I acknowledge that..." His words came out low. "The thought that I may never bed a woman again is painful to me." He met her gaze. "Please never mention it."

He didn't continue. When the silence grew uncomfortable to Adrastea, she prompted him. "And fourth?"

"Yes?"

She didn't expect that. "Well, what is it?"

He shrugged.

"What? That's it?"

He had a quick think before answering. "Well, a codicil to number three. As I healed you, you did promise to not be angry with me. And as I see it, ever since I came to this sleepy little settlement four years ago, I haven't done anything to legitimately raise your ire."

If she couldn't be angry with him, how was she supposed to feel about him? It wasn't right to like him.

Her cheeks tingled; he was trying to eavesdrop on her thoughts. "It's okay to like me. Lots of people do."

"Not those who know what you're really like."

A brief flicker of a pout crossed his face. "The Light like me, despite Themselves."

"They have to like you. They have to like everybody."

He sorted through his memories. "Desideria liked me."

"Not towards the end. Certainly not now." The dead priestess often conversed with Adrastea. She hadn't seen her today, though.

He scrubbed his hands through his hair. "Okay, bad example." He sought out further examples. "Berengaria has remained favorably disposed towards me. Your brother doesn't hate me."

"He tolerates you because of me. And Berengaria doesn't have much of a choice."

"She does too." He waved her memory away with his hands. "We're not talking about her. We're talking about you."

"I don't like you. I keep walking away, but you keep following me like some lost puppy."

"Puppies like me."

"Puppies are young and stupid."

His mood changed, just like that. Adrastea felt it. It was like having your hand in a bowl of warm water, then having cold water poured over it. Shocking, sudden, and very unpleasant.

"Adrastea, please stop trying to convince me that nobody likes me." He held out his hands. "Nobody else is here, living or dead. Just you and me."

He rose from his chair, knelt before her and laid his head in her lap. "And stop trying to convince yourself that you don't like me. Deep down, you do. Otherwise, why would you have taken care of me all these years?" He sat up and lifted a finger to her lips. "And don't tell me the Light told you to. I know They didn't. You could have easily dropped me off into the care of my priestesses, but you didn't. You kept me of your own free will. You wanted me close by, to keep an eye on me.

"I need you, Adrastea. I make no secret of it. I have work to do and I can't do it alone."

What was she going to do with his head in her lap? "I can't go off and do... whatever it is you do as a god. I have a child. I can't just leave her."

"Oh, find a babysitter. It's not like I must have you with me all the time—" he paused. "Well, I do, but we can compromise on that." He rose and paced before the fire. "One of my next tasks is to save a broken and remorseful people. I would greatly appreciate your help in this matter." He took her hands once more. "You want me to be better? Come see me be the benevolent god you want. Let my actions convince you. Please."

He sounded in earnest. "I will come once," she acquiesced.

"It will do." He didn't relinquish her hands.

"What? We going right now?"

"No. Spring floods aren't ready yet. And I shall require them in their own time, a month hence."

"A month? What are you going to do until then?"

He smiled and slung an arm across her shoulders. "Why, *we* are going to settle down and live a country life."

"What? You? Here?"

"I am dictated by your choice of locale. Since you won't come to the temple, I must come here."

She slunk out from under his arm. "Who said anything about living together?"

"I did."

That afternoon, Mikal Mayor found his sister on the doorstep, her arms folded tightly about her and her eyes narrowed dangerously.

Uh oh, he thought as he ushered her in. Only one thing could upset his sister. "He woke up, didn't he?"

She hissed in irritation. "Oh Mikal, what am I going to do with him?"

"Tell him to go away?"

"Tried that." She paced the length of Mikal's small cottage. Tall, lean Jacob came to the kitchen doorway, wiping his hands on a towel. Adrastea ignored him and ranted about her conversation with her husband.

Mikal listened, trying to be a brother, but kept slipping back into thinking like a Mayor. The Dark One had convinced his sister to let him stay here in Sacred Spring like common countryfolk. Trouble followed him, or rather, he led trouble to wherever he went. His sister could take care of herself, but what about the people of Sacred Spring?

Jacob remained in the doorway, listening intently, as was his job, his hand towel slung over his shoulder now.

Mor-Lath, being a god, did whatever pleased him. Long experience taught Mikal that the god did not think of others and would casually brush them aside if they attempted to interfere in his plans.

The god's obsession with Adrastea had continued. Mikal's brotherly side sympathized with his sister over her persistent husband. Had they been any other mortal couple, he would have asked Chloe, the spiritual leader of Sacred Spring to counsel them.

Adrastea flung herself into one of Mikal's chairs. "Why can't he just leave me alone?" she wailed. A floorboard creaked.

Mikal's mayorly side knew the interests of Sacred Spring were at odds with the interests of his sister. It would be such a simple matter to ask Adrastea to leave. Her husband would naturally follow. That would be the solution to this problem.

Difficult decision. His uncle Natan, when he was Mayor, had to make this same decision. In the end, he had chosen to banish Adrastea. The fact that he never had to carry out his decision must have been a great relief to him. Mikal would receive no such salvation.

Jacob spoke. "Why don't you ask him? He's standing right outside."

Mikal and Adrastea looked at him, then to the door. Adrastea put her hand to her cheek. "Go away." Then she frowned deeper.

Mikal jerked open the door. "Go away."

Mor-Lath stood there, hand raised as if to knock. He held out a shirt, clean and folded to Mikal. "My wife forgot this in her mad rush to complain to her brother."

Before Mikal could take it, Adrastea snatched it out of Mor-Lath's hand. "I was planning on washing it first." She looked at the shirt as if to find fault with it, but it seemed she couldn't. She raised it to her face and inhaled its fresh scent. "Oh, very clever."

Mor-Lath stepped through the doorway. "I know you wouldn't want to return a dirty shirt."

Mikal sighed. "Next time you wish to come speak with me, how about asking?"

"And risk you saying no?"

"It's a chance you'll have to take." This conversation was not under his control. He couldn't let the Dark God get the better of him. Mikal gave a quick nod to his apprentice.

Jacob, his expression unchanging, turned back to the kitchen. "I'll put the kettle on."

"How kind of you." Mor-Lath sank into the chair Adrastea had occupied earlier.

"Not really," Mikal replied. "You know this isn't a social call."

"I know." Mor-Lath sank down and put his head into his hands as if tired. "It's been a long night."

Mikal took the chair opposite "My sister tells me you wish to live here."

Adrastea remained standing but had not resumed her pacing. She watched Mor-Lath closely. When Jacob returned, he handed the first empty teacup to Adrastea, not Mikal. Then the Mayor was served, then a cup before an empty chair—his—before dropping one in front of Mor-Lath.

"I will go wherever my wife is."

"I thought so. You don't care one way or another about Sacred Spring—" He looked closer at Mor-Lath. Was his hair turning silver? "Are you all right?"

Mor-Lath waved away Mikal's question. "Just tired."

"You can always go back to sleep."

Mor-Lath grinned, sending the faint crow's feet about his eyes. "Can I help it if your sister's demands take a lot out of me?"

"Oh," Adrastea gasped in irritation. But she didn't say any more than that. His condition was directly caused by an incident with her. Mikal knew. Adrastea had confided everything to him. He'd told Jacob enough so that he didn't press the issue nor react to taunting. Had she told anyone else, Ari, perhaps, what had happened that day? She hadn't told Chloe. Mikal hadn't shared anything with the priestess when she had come by later seeking answers.

"I understand," Mikal replied. "It must be hard to be at the beck and call of a woman. I'm sure you'll outgrow the need to follow her like a love-sick puppy someday. Most husbands do."

Jacob returned with the teapot. He served Adrastea first. Mikal caught the tightening of Jacob's face as he suppressed his smile.

"Now that we've established just how tight your leash is, brother-of-mine, that if you wish to remain here, you will abide by our rules, or I shall take that leash and lead you away from here."

Mor-Lath raised his head. Jacob had next served Mikal and filled his own cup but had not poured for Mor-Lath. He set the teapot down within arm's reach, should the Dark God wish to serve himself. "Oh, you would, would you?"

Mikal nodded. "I would. Since you have clearly established that the purpose for your presence is due to your wife residing here, if your wife no longer resides here, then you will have no reason to stay."

"What?" squeaked Adrastea.

Mikal addressed Mor-Lath, but his words were for his sister as well. "She understands how important it is the Mayor keep Sacred Spring safe, not only from threats, but from social disruption; we do not tolerate our lives shaken up here. She understood then, and she understands now, if necessary, she will leave Sacred Spring if it means the safety of the village."

Adrastea opened her mouth. Before she could utter her protest, Mikal raised a finger. She wisely held her tongue.

"I also know how much she wants to dwell here. If I must request she leave because of you, she will not be angry with me; she will be angry with you. She will take her wrath out on you, promises notwithstanding. I know whenever she is angry with you, you suffer in rather painful ways. Perhaps this time she will succeed in dismembering your body and scattering you across the face of the earth. Perhaps she will seal you up inside solid rock, deep within the ground. Or maybe she will cast you into such a deep sleep that you will never wake up.

"Or maybe she will find the knife that can kill you."

Mor-Lath listened to this quietly. His eyes burned with resentment, but he did not speak until the Mayor was finished.

"Therefore, if you wish to avoid the ire of your wife, you will do things my way. You will follow the rules of Sacred Spring and you will follow additional ones I shall give you."

He explained the rules and laws of Sacred Spring to his brother-in-law, including respecting others' property and their rights. "And if you wish to dwell here, you cannot draw upon the commonwealth of the village unless you put something in first. While we have money, we don't exchange coins as tokens, but keep records with the storekeepers for the value of our work, or if your wife is amenable, you may draw upon her name and her account.

"I have money enough for my needs. However, I am curious." Mor-Lath turned to Adrastea. "What have you been doing to keep yourself occupied? I don't reckon Ari would be happy with you for competition."

She rose from her chair and put her teacup down on the table a little harder than was necessary.

Mor-Lath held up his hand, "No need to show me. I'll trust you if you tell me."

Mikal groaned and put his head in his hands. He wished Adrastea could see when Mor-Lath was needling her and not raise her hackles. He would have a talk with her later regarding this.

"No." She hauled Mor-Lath up by an arm. "I want you to see this."

He followed her out the door, trying to make it look like he went of his own volition and not because he was being dragged by his wife. That love-sick puppy comment must have struck home.

He and Jacob followed the pair outside. Adrastea had found plenty to do in Sacred Spring. There was only so much need for healers in the village. When Ari didn't require her help, she found other projects.

Down the path and through Mikal's front gate they went, and out into the street. Adrastea pointed to the cobblestones. "See that? I did that." She waved her hand across the whole village where every road had been paved. "I've done all that." As far as the eye could see, she had cobbled the roads with smooth flat stones that kept the dust down in the summer and prevented the muddy potholes of winter. Mor-Lath looked at the miles of paving Adrastea had done. "Impressive."

She had started after she'd built her home and before Mor-Lath had shown up. She had finished her work while he slept, working through that first winter with that talent of hers, thawing the ground just enough to place her cobblestones—again, using her talent and not grubbing on her hands and knees.

Anyone who had ever had to lay stone appreciated the value of her work.

Not everyone gave their appreciation willingly. Mikal had had his ear bent more than a few times by concerned villagers. Adrastea made them nervous, her being who she was. They accepted her grudgingly, for she was Mikal's sister, Natan's niece and she did pull her own weight in the village. That acceptance, however, would not extend to her husband.

"How about we go inside?" Mikal suggested. "I think he's seen enough." He ushered everyone into his cottage. "Why don't you pour everyone another cup?" Mikal suggested to Jacob. This time, Mor-Lath received his cup of tea from the dregs.

Adrastea sat, her chair between her brother and her husband. Jacob dutifully took the teapot back into the larder for a refill.

She leaned over to Mikal. "You're not helping."

"I can't do anything about your domestic situation. You'd have to see Chloe about that."

"I can't see Chloe."

"Then that's that."

Mor-Lath interrupted them. "You said you had rules of your own?"

Mikal gave his sister one last meaningful look. "Yes, I do. While you are here in Sacred Spring, consider yourself on probation. I will not stop you from socializing with the villagers—if they will have you—but you will not use your name or your station to gain any social advantage. You will volunteer your identity only when asked, and only if you cannot avoid it. You will not use the citizens in any of your little games nor will you cause any trouble among them. You are welcome to attend council with your wife, but you cannot suggest agenda items, nor participate in any discussions. You observe only.

"You will heed Adrastea's counsel, for she is your native-born wife. You will obey mine, for I am Mayor here. I outrank everyone, including you."

Mor-Lath sighed. "Is that all?"

"Of course not. I reserve the right to amend these rules as I see fit and will give you due notification."

Mor-Lath drew in a sharp breath but said nothing. Mikal softened his decree. "You know I am a fair man. I would not treat you with undue prejudice."

Mor-Lath, his hands curled around the cup of tea, weighed Mikal's words. When he spoke, it was not to Mikal but to Adrastea. "It seems, my dear, that your petition has been denied." To Mikal he said, "I accept."

Adrastea's eyes narrowed. Her hands tightened around her teacup.

"Your brother is wise," Mor-Lath continued. "He knows that simply ordering me to leave would be useless." He nodded. "Oh, yes, your brother is clever. For a man without a wife, he knows well where I stand."

"I have a wife," Mikal replied. "Her name is Sacred Spring."

Chapter 15

May Day had come. All day the children had roamed the forest, picking flowers. Many of them had run for hours until weariness slowed them down. Now, gathered in the Inn while their parents indulged in celebration, they would sleep, watched by a few adults.

In an upper room of the Inn, Adrastea laid the full, sleeping Harianne in the nest of blankets on the floor. The little girl's supper, followed by countless Maytime treats meant she would sleep for another few hours, possibly all night. Other young children slumbered nearby. Two who hadn't drifted off yet were snuggled in Martine's lap. She sat in a rocking chair by the window that overlooked the village green, enabling her to watch the evening celebrations while she took her turn tending the children.

A low lamp burned on a table next to her chair. Other than that, the room was devoid of furniture. Instead, piles of blankets marked squares on the floor, one for each young child. Outside, lanterns strung up on poles provided adequate illumination on the scene below.

As she tucked the last blanket about her daughter, Adrastea heard the first chords of music. "I'd better go." She felt for her recorder resting in her skirt pocket. "Thanks for doing this."

Martine nodded her head. "Just taking my turn. I don't mind missing the dancing as long as I can go maying."

Adrastea smiled with embarrassment. The highlight of the evening came after the music, after the dancing, when couples—preferably married—would pull a willow branch from the May Tree in the middle of the green. They'd wander to a secluded spot outside somewhere. By the passion of their love, they hoped to draw the luck of the Light to bless the land with fertility in the coming season. As Adrastea had no intention of going maying, she had agreed with Martine that she would return after the dancing and relieve her as sitter.

As the music started, the older children came out to dance the country dances in their clumsy youthful ways. Adrastea loved the circle dances, the line dances and other simple patterns. Martine leaned back to watch them. "Have fun."

As Adrastea emerged from the inn, the spirit of the May Day enveloped her. She loved the country festivals with which she'd grown up. She had enjoyed the dances of her youth and had learned the complex adult dances, but only had a few Mays to dance them before her wedding. She'd never been maying; no one had ever caught her eye. Her heart irked at the thought that she might never go maying, but she pushed that thought far away.

Adrastea approached the celebrations. At least the villagers accepted her somewhat, despite her husband. She scanned the gathered crowd, looking for his dark hair, his observant eyes. No matter how he dressed to blend in, she would spot him.

And there he was, leaning against the post of the general store, standing behind the latticed rail. He looked like any other country fellow, dressed in his simple breeches and shirt. The fashions had changed since Adrastea was a child. Now, men favored shirts held closed not by long, full cravats, but simple ties, no more than mere strings. For every day, they rolled up their slender sleeves. On formal occasions, they wore a dark overcoat, cut snug to the torso and with long coattails that hugged the curve of the leg.

The cut of Mor-Lath's shirt emphasized his broad chest. He wore his tie loose. His coat, the height of country fashion, he wore open at the waist, rather casual. He did not look at her but preferred to watch the crowd. She couldn't fathom his expression.

He turned his face and their eyes met. She gave him a warning scowl. He simply raised an eyebrow then returned to his spectating.

Over on the green a small platform had been erected for the housing of musicians. Little Peter Smith had saved a spot for her. He'd grown into a stocky young man, as tall as his father and nearly as big. He played a bass recorder that suited his thick fingers. Adrastea's recorder was a smaller, higher-pitched instrument, the same she'd learned on as a child. There were a few guitar players, one of whom was Gallian Priestapprentice, some drummers, and one viol player—a young man from Crossroads come up to court a certain young woman. Peter did not stop his playing but nodded in greeting.

When Adrastea was young, every child in the village learned to play the recorder. The better skilled ones would often play alongside the adults for weddings, festivals and other celebrations. As she looked over the motley band, she felt comforted that some things hadn't changed. She drew out her recorder and settled in to play.

At the far end of the green, Willem Innkeeper, Martine's husband, had breached a keg of beer.

Berengaria stood nearby, speaking with Mikal. They'd kept close company of late. She saw her uncle Natan accept a stein of beer. Ari avoided the beer table and stood chatting with some of the other women, including Chloe.

To Adrastea's surprise, the priestess laughed and shared the jokes of the other women. How odd to see the normally serious woman relax and let herself go. In contrast, one young woman—the Sempsters' daughter—hung on to the group of women, not one of the adults, yet out of place with the other youths, trying to look as if she belonged to the group. Such a homely thing, apple-shaped and shiny-faced. She stood on the fringes and listened in, laughing when she thought it was expected of her and spending the rest of the time hiding from notice, lest the adults shoo her off to join those her own age. Would anyone dance with her tonight?

As for the rest of them, Salle and a few other young women on the cusp of adulthood—the ones who hadn't been talked into nannying the children, roamed the edge of the green, openly flirting with the young men gathered there.

She saw Mikal finishing off a beer. He wiped his face on his sleeve. Leaning over, he whispered to Berengaria. She listened intently, glanced around, then sauntered off.

Oh yes, something was up there.

Meanwhile, Mikal strutted up to the group of women. Adrastea watched her brother, bold as brass, bow low before Chloe and request a dance. She accepted without her usual frown of disapproval and Mikal led her out to the green.

In the middle stood the May Tree. It was a tall pole to which branches of willows had been tied with twine. The higher branches sported paper lanterns that spread their soft glow. The circle of dancers spread at the base of the tree like a skirt.

The Mayor and the Priestess joined the circle of youths in their simple dance, laughing and enjoying themselves. When the dance finished, all applauded while they dipped their heads in acknowledgement.

Peter nudged Adrastea. "Do you know 'Over the Bridge'?" he shouted over the noise of the crowd.

Of course, she did.

The viol player counted off, and the tune began. Natan drained his beer and dashed for Ari, pulling her into the center of the party. She put up a half-hearted protest but followed her husband, nonetheless.

'Over the Bridge' was a children's dance, but one that featured greater complexity of steps. A mix of children and adults formed two lines facing each other. As the dance proper began, the two lines approached each other, and backed away. They approached once more and swung their partners before backing away. Then the even-numbered couples crossed and swerved between the odd couples until they emerged out the end, to skip along behind the lines until they reached the beginning. And then the dance would repeat again, pattern after pattern until the couples had returned to their original order.

During the applause of the song, Gallian shouted, "Too easy! Let's make them really dance. 'Round the Garden'."

Adrastea added her approval to the general shout of the band. Gallian counted it off, and the circle dance began.

The younger children passed off the dance floor as more adults and youths joined in. 'Round the Garden' was a polka kind of circle dance, where the steps themselves were simple, but as the song sped up, the steps became more difficult to execute. As couples began to flag and stumble, they'd drop out until only a few were left. The song continued until the last couple danced one whole verse alone.

Adrastea watched as Natan and Ari dropped out. A few couples later, Mikal and Chloe retired. In the end, the last couple standing was Salle and her partner the Carpenter's son. The village applauded them while they did a slower promenade around the green.

Adrastea spied Natan and Ari slip behind the May Tree and pluck out a willow branch. Then hand in hand they retreated unnoticed from the crowd of villagers, the first couple to go maying.

While the band briefly discussed the next song to play, Salle, abandoned by her last partner in favor of the beer table, approached Peter Smith. "Put down that pipe and come dance with me."

"Aw, Salle," he moaned. "I'm playing."

"Not any more you're not." She wrestled with him over the recorder.

"Oh, go on," Adrastea insisted. "She's not going to give up until you go dance."

"Yes," added the viol player. "You go dance right now, because Andie Taylorprentice will never forgive me if I don't dance with her later."

The drummer poked him in the ribs with a drumstick. "We know what you're doing later, and it isn't dancing."

This elicited catcalls from the other musicians.

But the viol player could hold his own. "We shall do nothing but dance."

This brought on groans.

The viol player gave them a cheeky grin. "Did I say it had to be vertical?"

"Enough!" cried Salle. "Play us a love song."

"Oh," replied an embarrassed Peter. Adrastea suspected he regarded Salle more as a friend than a potential lover. Knowing Salle as she did, she suspected it was the same on both sides.

"Unlikely," replied the viol player. "We're doing you a farandole."

And a farandole it was, a lively dance where everyone held hands and skipped along in a line behind the abbat-mages who, despite the priestess' initial protests, were Chloe and Mikal again. Berengaria had joined the dance, her hand slipping into Mikal's.

Adrastea didn't know this particular tune, so she sat out the first verse until she picked it up—easy enough. It felt so good to play. As she watched the line of dancers make their way around the green, picking up more and more participants as they passed, she reveled in the feeling of belonging.

This is what she'd missed—belonging. When Mor-Lath had removed her to his temple, she'd become the Bride, separate from the priestesses, and treated with a wary respect if not a barely-concealed fear by them. Then during her damnation, she was the only living person in Dom-al-gol, corporeal, powerful and, eventually, one who controlled her own fate.

Even when she returned to Sacred Spring, there were those who treated her with caution. Even those, like Martine, who'd known her all her life, maintained their distance. Fifteen years and immortality had created a barrier between them.

But here, tonight, she was just another player, whose simple recorder blended with the music of the others, and to whose music the village danced. While the music went on, she was one of them. She belonged.

The music went faster and faster until all too soon, the line of dancers broke. They dissolved into joyous laughter and breathless calls for a rest.

Salle soon returned Peter, gave the viol player an arched look before she flounced away. The viol player put down his instrument. "And now, we can play a love song, for I am going to find Andie, unless she finds me first." Then through the catcalls of the other musicians, the viol player raised a finger and pointed behind Adrastea. "Hey, unless you're here to play, get off the stage."

Adrastea turned to find her husband standing behind her. "Yes," she snapped. "Get off the stage."

The rest of the musicians fell silent. Mor-Lath ignored their silence. "I've come to steal a partner of my own." To her surprise and protest, he lifted Adrastea up and whirled her away.

Once her feet touched the ground, she pushed his hands away with a slap. "I'm not dancing tonight. I'm here to play."

"Dance with me," he said loud enough for the other musicians to hear, "or be silent if I seek another partner."

"Oh, ho!" called the viol player, seemingly unaware of the awkwardness of the others. "Seems like I'm not the only one seeking someone sweet for my arms."

Adrastea glared at him over her shoulder. "Shut up."

Mor-Lath didn't hide the humored look on his face.

But the viol player wouldn't shut up. "Play something long and slow," he told the band. "Give her time to cool her temper."

Gallian pulled the viol player down and hissed in his ear. "Do you know who that is? That's her husband."

Oblivious to what this meant, he quipped, "Then it had better be a quick dance instead, for they'll want to save their energy for maying."

Silence fell among the musicians like fallen, bruised fruit. The viol player looked around in bafflement. "What?"

"Just play," Mor-Lath told the viol player, his amused tone a contrast to the sudden iciness of the villagers.

The viol player, oblivious, nodded in agreement. "That's what I'm talking about." He picked up his instrument. Without consulting the others, he began not a slow dance, but a circle dance, not as lively as the farandole, but one of complex steps. The others joined in, one by one, their eyes upon Adrastea as if they needed her approval.

Mor-Lath dragged his wife out for a dance. "You will regret not dancing with me more than you would regret dancing with me."

The God of the Dark and his Bride entered the circle of dancers around the May Tree.

Adrastea stood there, her arms folded. "You'll look more the fool standing there when everyone else is dancing," he murmured in her ear.

She sighed and gave in. "Do you even know this dance? How do I know you won't step on my toes?"

He smiled at her and they began.

The dance involved a series of intricate steps that overlapped one's partner's feet. The unskilled dancer risked stepping on his partner's toes. To Adrastea's surprise, her husband executed the steps perfectly. They hooked arms about the other's waists and twirled in a circle, then back the other way, then join hands for a galloping spin. Then the couples divided, women to the left, men to the right, for a turn with the neighbor, then back to their original partners for one more circle.

He didn't misstep once. However, he varied the dance slightly. When Adrastea returned to him after her turn with Rop Storekeeper, instead of the handclasped circle before the sequence began again, he put his hands around her waist and lifted her high before setting her down.

The cycle began again. She heard a few people get their feet stepped on. His unexpected move had distracted them and shattered her illusion of belonging; she wasn't really one of them, not any more.

He lifted her every time, high above the other dancers. "Why are you doing that?" she asked.

"Because that is how the dance is supposed to be danced."

"That's not how we do it here."

"It should be."

Adrastea only shook her head. Yet she remained with him until the end.

The dance over, he walked her back to the stage of musicians. In his typical dramatic style, he lifted her fingers to his lips. "You dance excellently, my Darklet. A shame I could not convince you to take another turn."

She resumed her seat and took up her recorder. "Too many turns with you is dangerous."

There was no viol player to make a smart quip; he had moved on to find his sweetheart. Gallian suggested another dance, a variation on 'Round the Garden'. She counted off and the others joined in immediately to keep their hands and eyes from awkwardness.

But Mor-Lath wasn't done with his wife. "Enjoy your music, my dear. It seems to be what you prefer. Meanwhile," he pointed to the crowd of non-dancers that leaned against the latticed railing of the Inn. "See that drab little creature?"

She did. It was the same young woman she noticed earlier, the Sempsters' daughter. Miele, was that her name?

"She's been moping there all evening. Nobody has approached her. I think she is reluctant to approach others in fear of being rejected. I am going to bring a moment of joy to her life and ask her to dance."

"Why?"

He rested his hands on her shoulders and leaned forward to murmur in her ear. "Is it so hard to believe that I could bring a bit of happiness to someone? Say you'll let me dance with her?"

"And if I said no?"

"I would insist you dance with me again."

"I don't know why I would say yes."

"Because I promised I would behave myself this eve, plus I kept the last promise I made you."

Adrastea relented. She pointed a finger of warning at him. "Don't lead her astray."

He backed off and sketched a bow. "I will only lead her in steps."

Mor-Lath loved May Day, the mark of the return of fertile Spring and the night when spirits were raised, and morals lowered. He hadn't missed one if he could help it. He certainly wouldn't miss this one, albeit one marked by the first evening where he did not pursue some unwitting woman.

As he wove through the dancing couples and conversing friends, he pitied the chit of a girl whose night would end, at most, with a friendly handshake. She would miss out on the most touching experience of her life.

At least they could dance once or twice. For happy memories, that would have to do.

By now Miele had been left alone. She wrapped her arms about her waist and hunched her shoulders as she watched the dancers twirl about. She wore her sabbath best, a brown skirt with lace-edged bloomers and a matching blouse. No doubt she'd pulled her underbodice tight early that evening to give her some semblance of curves. No matter how much she scrubbed with soap then powdered with cornstarch, her face would always be shiny. Her straight hair she wore pulled back, which did not flatter her chubby chin.

If he went by looks alone, he would never have given her a second glance. But the Dark God knew better. Her sheer loneliness would make her an ideal target, easy to lure, easy to seduce.

Shame he'd promised his wife he would behave.

Armed with his charm, he approached. No coy games here, nor observance of social niceties. He sidled up to her and traced a line down her arm. She startled at being touched and gave him a cautious look.

He caught up her hand. "Come dance with me. I warrant you have practiced long and hard to master the most intricate steps."

Her mouth opened, but only the slightest of squeaks came out. The incredulous look on her face confirmed his guess. He pushed off from the lattice and drew her away. She hung back. "I don't know you."

He transferred hands and drew his arm about her waist. "The mayor has known me for many years. He will vouch for me, should you ask. Besides," he added as he led her out, "how much do you need to know about me, other than I know how to dance?"

They had reached the circling couples whirling 'Round the Garden'. It was little matter for one more couple to join in.

He was right; she had been practicing steps. With a grace surprising in one so homely, she matched him step for step. Politically, he dropped them out four couples before the end, letting Andie and her viol player win the dance. Mor-Lath and Miele applauded the winners politely. Mor-Lath glanced at Adrastea. She had watched him the whole time. She watched him now. He gave her a reassuring smile, then turned his attention back to his partner.

"Thank you, sir, for a very nice dance. I—" She twisted her fingers together. Did she wish to flee, or was she too shy to ask for a second dance?

A reel struck up. He held out his free hand, the other one still around her waist. "I hope you have enough energy for another dance?"

"Oh, yes."

They joined the line of couples. As they danced, he watched her eyes.

She smiled up at him in a horsey way, but the joy in her eyes was genuine. And there was something else there, a longing, a far hope. Ah well, he told himself. Daydreams kept many a young girl from the depths of despair.

He lured Miele into a third dance, despite her initial hesitation. Three dances in a row with a stranger? But something snapped within her. She went from a moment of hesitation to one of acceptance tinted by defiance. Defiance of whom, he wondered. Her parents? Society? Her peers? Had she been teased, that she couldn't procure a dance with anyone other than a few older relatives who would take pity on her?

The third dance was a jig, lively and only bound to get livelier.

From time to time, he glanced back at his wife. As the dances passed, she relaxed about his dancing with this young woman. Her attention turned from him. By the middle of the jig, she let the music envelop her. He watched her over Miele's shoulder. She genuinely enjoyed playing. He watched the glances she shared with the other musicians and found their intimacy and harmony a little disturbing. She had wanted to play. She had wanted to share with them, the give and take of musicians listening to each other, and building the counterpoint that stirred everyone's blood.

Musicians were lucky; when they played together, they shared something very intimate, a wordless giving and taking, an instinct that allowed their innermost souls to touch.

Miele missed a step. He brought his attention back to his partner. Her eyes were bright, and her face flushed. As her energy dropped, he slowed his steps. They dropped out of the jig.

"Oh, I've got to catch my breath." Miele wiped a hand across her damp forehead.

Mor-Lath fished a handkerchief out of his back pocket and gently mopped her brow. "You dance well. If only the others knew. But then I would have to share you with them."

She gave him an honest grin. He suggested they sit the next dance out. She welcomed a tankard of beer from the keg when he offered. He returned her to the Storekeeper's porch. Instead of loitering in front of the lattice, he led her behind it to sit on the floor boards of the porch. Here, in semi-privacy, they sipped their beers, listened to the music and watched occasional flashes of color of dancers passing by. They leaned against the wall of the store, a moment of silence to catch their breath. He crossed his ankles and folded his hands on his lap.

Miele held her hands to her stomach, possibly wishing she could loosen her bodice strings. Mor-Lath pushed away the thought that had he been a free agent, he would have cheerfully loosened those strings for her, and any other restrictive clothing she may have been wearing.

The awkwardness of the silence became too much for her. "I don't even know your name."

"Nor have you given me yours." He held up a hand as she opened her mouth to give it. "Let's not exchange names yet. Let us simply enjoy each other for who we are, and not by the labels others give us."

"Oh," she said, staring into her beer. "Oh." She put more meaning into her second one. She sat up from the wall and turned so she faced him while sitting on her knees. "I know everyone in Sacred Spring, and you're not from Crossroads."

He nodded his head. "I am from further away." He caught his breath. "I have family here."

Miele mulled this over. "You said the Mayor would vouch for you. Are you related to him?"

"Indeed I am."

She scooted closer and leaned forward. "So, you are a lord from Feown."

He had to laugh at that. "I'm not from Feown."

"Oh." She sat back in disappointment. But she wouldn't let the idea go. "But you are a lord."

"I've been called that." And a few other names as well.

Her fingers traced the stitching on his sleeve. "You have fine clothes. You must be rich."

He reached up and pushed a loose strand of her hair behind her ear. "I'm the richest man in the world."

She took this in, pondered it for a moment, then grinned broadly as if it was the greatest joke she'd ever heard. "How long are you staying in Sacred Spring?"

He shrugged. "I don't know. I might leave tomorrow, if I've no more business here."

She licked her lips. "Would you stay longer?" She leaned closer.

"I don't know. There are a great many things I must be doing. I wish I could stay here forever, but my vocation calls me elsewhere."

"Vocation..." she rolled the word around on her tongue and did not want to swallow it. "You mean you're... a priest?"

The awkwardness of the moment fell between them, then he burst out in laughter. "Oh, glory, no. I couldn't live such an austere life."

She dissolved into nervous chuckles of relief. Sobering a little, she scooted closer, nearly in his lap and took his hand. He turned his face to her, waiting for her to say what was clearly on her mind.

It wasn't words she was thinking. With some hesitation, she leaned forward, and she kissed him. It was not the nervous peck of a child, but a lingering, close-mouthed kiss of a maiden who wanted to change her status. She pulled away and observed him for reaction. "Come maying with me?"

When he didn't answer right away, she turned it into a supplication. "Please." The desperation in her voice tweaked him. Poor little, lonely, homely thing.

He did not pull his hand away but laid his head back against the way with a sigh of regret. "Oh, why must you tempt me so? If I were not a married man, I would gladly take you up on that offer. Alas, my wife does not take kindly to others poaching on her territory." He would not regale the awkward young miss with the fates of his wife's rivals.

She retreated from him. "You're married?" A chill dropped between them.

He held up his left hand to display the glint of gold on his finger. "I'm sorry." For this moment, as he watched her hopes shatter, he felt very sorry, not only for her ruined evening, but for the satiety that was not his to have.

Her breath caught in her throat. She had to swallow several times to catch it and to force back the tears of disappointment. "Is... is she here tonight?"

"Yes." He took her hand and did not release it as he urged her forward to the lattice. Then, still hunched down and completely hidden, he pointed out his wife. "She's playing with the band. She's the dark-haired woman on the end next to Peter Smith.

Miele grasped the lattice with both hands and did not notice when he laid a hand on her back. She squinted until she confirmed the identity of the woman. "But that's Adrastea, the witch."

"Mm hmm."

"And she's supposed to be married... to..." Her body shuddered with cold realization. As her gaze slid sideways, she flinched away from the god next to her. "You're the God of the Dark?" she breathed.

His direct look answered her question. For a heartbeat, they stared at each other. Then Mor-Lath's grip slid down her back to her waist.

This movement startled her. In a flurry of panic, she backed from him, scrabbling away until her back hit the wall. She pushed up against it, her gaze darting hither and yon, looking for an escape. Tears filled her eyes and spilled out in burning rivulets down her face. The god rose to his feet.

They were not alone. Mikal Mayor stood on the other end of the porch. "What have you done?" His voice was full of accusation.

The poor girl thought Mikal meant her. "I— I didn't mean it, I swear to the Light. I didn't know." Miele's words tumbled out almost faster than her tongue could handle. "I—" She sucked in a sob, turned and fled off the porch and into the blessed darkness between the store and the inn.

Mikal let out a sound of anger. "You mongrel! Can't you leave anyone alone?"

Mor-Lath drew himself up. "I have done nothing that you yourself wouldn't have done."

"I haven't led on impressionable young girls and toyed with their vulnerabilities."

Mor-Lath spread his arms in all innocence. "I tried to do her a kindness. The poor thing was left a wallflower. I simply asked her to dance, nothing more, *with* my wife's permission, I must add.

"Then, worn out by the unaccustomed exertion, we simply retired to the porch to catch our breaths and have an innocent conversation. I did not lead her on. She came on to me. She kissed me. I turned her down."

Mikal pointed an accusing finger at his brother-in-law. "You led her away then led her to believe that you meant more than one dance out of kindness."

"What? And leave her with the impression that she was no more than a charity case? That's a cruel thing to do to a young woman. She'd see through that no matter how naive. You have much to learn about the right way to treat a woman."

Mikal folded his arms. "Yeah. My sister tells me you're a genius."

Mor-Lath's expression darkened. "I have done nothing wrong. As soon as she revealed her intentions, I put a stop to it and told her the truth. She kissed me, not the other way around. You know it, because you were watching."

"Aye, I was. I wonder what would have happened if I hadn't been watching. And now I must go find the lass before she does herself a mischief."

Mikal turned away from Mor-Lath, opposite the direction Miele had fled. Before he left the porch to go whisper in his sister's ear, Mor-Lath said,

"So tell me, Mister Mayor, which would have been the worse: learning that someone who cared enough to include you in the night's festivities was married and could be no more than a friend, or standing alone on the porch for hours, watching friends dance and lovers depart, knowing that nobody, not a soul in the whole world, cared if you lived or died?"

Mikal paused, his back still to the Dark God. "Everything you touch turns sour."

"Your precious village survived."

Mikal fired a parting shot over his shoulder. "It almost didn't." Then he went to pour the bitter truth into his sister's ear before seeking out a humiliated Miele.

Mor-Lath studied the simple gold band on his finger. He looked out at the May Tree amid the few dancers left. Already many couples had plucked branches from the tree and disappeared. There were a few branches left. After summoning one to his hand, he ducked into the alleyway between Inn and Store to wait.

Adrastea found him soon enough. Even in the shadows, there was just enough light he could see the angry expression on her face. She planted her fists on her hips. "What have you done?"

He told her the whole story, fact for fact. As she listened, she relaxed. She believed him, but she didn't want to release her anger yet. Her fists remained where they were but the frown on her face softened.

He leaned against the wall of the inn. "So here I am on May Day, having turned down one perfectly willing young woman. And who would take her place?" He pushed off from the wall and slid an arm about Adrastea's waist. "My poor wife is stuck with other duties."

She pushed at his arm, but he pressed his advantage and himself forward.

"Stop that." Her back bumped up against the opposite wall.

"Now there's you, little village maid, resolved to spending May Day alone, in the service of others, and nothing for you. You couldn't spare yourself for more than a single dance and then to retire to your lonely bed."

She lifted a hand to push him away, but he moved it aside and brought it around his waist, his upper arm pinning it, so she couldn't pull free.

"You've never been maying before, have you?" He lifted the willow and brushed her cheek. "All those years you've been too young. And now you're old enough, and married enough, to pick a willow branch and steal away into the night." He lifted her chin with his finger. "Look me in the eyes and tell me you don't want to go maying."

She wrapped a hand around his and lowered it. "I can't do this. *You* can't do this. If we go off and do something stupid before you remember a certain prophecy... I won't have you hurt me again. If it means that you never touch me for the rest of our lives, so be it."

"Oh, my Darklet," he murmured. "Do you truly wish for a life devoid of passion?" He drew on the Deeper Power until it hummed in his blood. He laid his forehead against hers and let her feel the pleasantness of its song.

She turned her head away from his. "We can't do this."

"Tell me you have no desire—deep desire—to go maying."

"I can't."

"What?" he teased. "Can't go or can't tell me? Don't think I'm not aware of the stirrings deep in your belly, the yearning you're fighting." He leaned forward and whispered in her ear. "That you wish to wrap your legs around me while I stroke your soft skin, nuzzle your ears," which he did, briefly, "capture your mouth with mine..." He turned her face, so he could do just that, tasting her lips and lingering long enough to share a tendril of Power with her before withdrawing.

Her blood sang. He loved making that happen.

He released her arm he had trapped by his side, and guided it down his back, to his buttocks, and then to the back of his thigh.

She closed her eyes and shuddered. Tears spilled out as she fought the erupting emotions within. "Stop teasing me," she moaned. "You wouldn't dare touch me, lest you get me with child."

"Oh, there are pleasures we could share that would preclude any risk of you falling in the family way. I could show you such things that would have you shouting my name.

"Come maying with me." He poured his lust into her. The pleasure rippled across her skin. "Give in."

"No." Her voice quavered.

"You're safe with me." He dropped to his knees and gathered up the hem of her skirt.

She caught her breath. She tried to push his head away with her hands. "Not here."

He paused. "You're right. Maying should happen under the stars."

"What? No!"

He swapped the focus of the Deeper Power.

She protested, "That's not what I—" He summoned them away from the alley and out to a certain hillside covered in grass. "—mean," she finished, her voice trailing off.

The canyon breeze ruffled the grass and sent the quakies to shimmer in a sound not unlike rain on the roof. The gurgling of the Sacred Spring added its music to the night. In the starlight the whiteness of the temple loomed nearby, watching over them as Adrastea, no longer supported by the wall of the store, fell over backwards.

Mor-Lath caught her by the Deeper Power and lowered her gently to the ground. Before her head came to rest on the newly-sprung grass, he had her skirt up about her waist and skilled fingers undid the drawstring of her pantalets.

"Mor-Lath, I can't do this now." She reached for the waistband as he drew them down, but found that they dissolved under her touch, reforming on the ground beneath her. Essentially naked, she tried to pull down the hem of her skirt.

He held up a silencing finger. "Sssh, my Darklet. You will enjoy this." And so would he.

Oh, how he ached for sexual contact, to give such great pleasure, and receive pleasure for giving it. Many women had liked this particular skill best of all. His wife did, even if she refused to remember that long, sultry night at the Temple.

Her fingers gripped in his hair, but it was too late. "I— Oh," she breathed as his lips and his tongue touched the most intimate part of her skin. Her grip turned from pulling his head away to pushing it in more.

Enjoy it, he told her.

She gasped as he skillfully created ripples of pleasure that radiated out into her body. They washed over him, and he tried to push them aside. He could feel his arousal tightening and fought to control it. If he was not careful, he could lose himself and nothing would stop him from tearing away his own clothes and burying himself in her. It would be good, to stroke against her, entering her time and again as their pleasure mounted until they came together.

Don't stop. He caught her thought, so strongly it rolled across her mind.

He didn't. He licked and nuzzled and sucked until she reached an orgasm that sang throughout her body and caught him in the backlash. Not quite as good as experiencing it joined to her body, but satisfying, nonetheless.

She laid back limp, her hands still entwined in his hair. "Oh, that was exquisite." She let him up. He crawled up next to her body, smoothing her skirts down over her legs.

He laid next to her and cuddled up, cradling his head in one hand while laying the other across her belly. "Perhaps you can return the favor some time." He went to nuzzle her ear, but she sat bolt upright.

"Oh, I am a fool," she exclaimed. "I promised Martine I'd relieve her." She rose to her feet and shook out her skirt. "Why did I let you distract me?"

He sat up, resting a hand across his knee. "Because you wanted me to."

"No, I didn't."

He smiled. "Tell me that with a straight face."

Adrastea growled at him before winking out of his sight, no doubt returned to the village for the benefit of Martine.

He jabbed the willow branch into the ground where they'd lain, as custom dictated. He rose, gathering up the remains of the clothing she'd left behind in her haste. He turned to the temple there. "See, I told you I could win her favor."

Phyl stepped out from behind the columns. He did not hold a willow branch. "Perhaps. But only genuine intent can be maintained forever."

Mor-Lath didn't respond to this. "Well." He flicked his fingers together. "I've got some horses to put away." And he disappeared for the village green.

Only then did Lucea come out from behind the pillars. "It hurts me to think that he may perish."

Phyl put an arm around His wife and She leaned onto His shoulder. "There is still time."

"But very little. So precious little."

"Enough to change."

"Enough for Mor-Lath to change?"

A drastea eased the door open to find an irate Martine standing in the middle of the room, sleeping infants surrounding her. "Where have you been?" she hissed in a whisper.

Adrastea brushed a strand of hair from her face, tucking it behind an ear. "I'm sorry. I got distracted."

Martine looked her disheveled form up and down. "I'll say. Your ankles are bare."

Adrastea looked down. Sure enough, they were. She'd left her pantalets by the spring. She tugged at skirt which seemed too short now.

"I thought you weren't going maying, Adrastea."

"I wasn't, that is, I didn't mean to." She sighed. "All I wanted to do was play music and enjoy the evening. I didn't even intend to dance."

"You danced?"

"Just the once, then I put my foot down."

Martine yawned. "You were never any good at saying no."

Adrastea let out a squeak of indignation. "Martine!"

Martine did not look apologetic. Instead, she stretched then seemed to wilt. "I hope you had a good time, enough for both of us. I'm too tired for my own fun.

Adrastea thought for a moment. "Here, something for your troubles." She reached out and applied her hands to Martine's temples. Martine perked up, took a deep breath and exhaled in amazement. "How'd you— Ah, of course. Shame you couldn't do the same for Wil. Some joker let all the horses out of the stable. He and a few others had to gather them up again."

Adrastea felt guilty. If she'd shown up when she'd promised, Martine and Willem would have been gone before the trouble started. She closed her eyes and sent out tendrils of thought, to find the horses and bring them home.

Half were returned to the stables, and the rest out roaming still, some spooked, others wary. Before Adrastea could command them to return home, they all turned and headed back to the stables. She felt the surge of Power that caused the return.

"Hm," she said aloud. Since when had Mor-Lath ever been helpful for no reason?

"What?"

"The horses are returned. Go find your husband." Adrastea took her place in the rocking chair by the window. "No rush back." She would be there past dawn.

Berengaria had little experience with horses. Yet that night, as they were chasing them about, trying to return them to the stable, she discovered they liked her. One rather sedate old mare had trotted her way in the darkness and stuck her nose in Berengaria's hand. Alas, she had no carrots, but could grasp the halter and lead it back to the stables.

As if they'd all tired of their midnight run, the horses returned at once. Surely that hadn't been her doing, or anyone else's that she could see.

Once every horse had been accounted for, the villagers returned to the green. A few lanterns still glowed, bathing the green in a gentle light. The musicians were gone. A few souls lingered by the beer barrels, guaranteeing the last of Ari's excellent beer did not go to waste.

But many of them had gone to the maying tree in the middle of the green. One by one, they plucked willow branches and carried them off. Fertility, Adrastea had explained. Couples would take the branches and plant them somewhere else.

"They don't grow, do they?" Berengaria had asked, wondering at the scarcity of willow trees in Sacred Spring.

"No," Adrastea had replied. "But everything else does." A coy smile tugged at her lips.

Sounded like a lovely tradition.

Most everyone had dispersed. Still, the maying tree had a few branches left, higher up the tree. Berengaria reached up as high as she could, to pluck one for herself.

"What are you doing?" Mikal asked. He'd been one of the corallers of the horses. After spending the night dancing and horse-chasing, he looked tired.

Berengaria jumped. She hadn't heard him coming. "I thought I'd take one. Adrastea said they were planted about the village to bring good luck and fertility for the year."

He folded his arms. "So, who's the lucky fellow?"

"Fellow?" Was she missing something?

"The willows are for couples, not singles." His shrug could not hide the stiffness in his shoulders. Something irked him.

She twirled the willow in her fingers. Couples. Fertility. "Oh, I see." She sighed and replaced the willow branch. "I didn't understand. This is the first maying I've attended." She'd missed out on the first one and had volunteered to babysit the second. It had never occurred to her to ask more about this village custom of the Light.

Mikal stopped her hand. "You've plucked it. You might as well go find somewhere to plant it."

The branch didn't feel right in her hands. She handed it to Mikal. "You plant it. I don't know where to go."

He took it. "Out in the woods somewhere is a preferred spot. Some braver couples find an empty field." He moved away from the tree.

"Does it matter where it's planted?"

Mikal shook his head.

Berengaria followed. "Where have you planted it before?"

He hesitated. "I... never have."

"What?" she declared, possibly louder than was prudent. "Never?"

He gave an embarrassed shrug. "I'm the mayor. Mayors don't do that sort of thing." He turned from her.

She laid a hand on his arm. "Why not?"

"A wife and family can distract a mayor from his duty. Sacred Spring is my wife. I care for her and devote my whole life to her."

Her voice caught in her throat. "So, you can never have a family? Never have children?"

"I try not to think about it."

"A priestess' life is much the same. No husband, no children. Only devotion." She ran a hand down his arm. "But haven't you wondered what it's like?"

She felt a tremor run through him. The heat of his blush radiated in the dark. "I try not to think about it."

"So, you said." Her hand slipped into his. "Now that I understand the custom better, I will tell you I have seen couples slip off that I know were not married. What is the consequence for them?"

"Ah, well," he prevaricated. "There have been several marriages that have arisen from, ah," he struggled for words, "well, mayings."

"Is it wrong?"

He took a deep breath. "Are you trying to put me in a difficult position?"

"Not at all." She hooked her arm in his. "I'm merely trying to understand the custom better. If I had known that one did not have to be married to go maying, I might have scouted out a lovely young lad."

His arm tightened under her grip. "I would not have recommended that."

"Why?" Her question was most direct. She pulled him along, away from the dying torches and lanterns.

"What if you got pregnant?"

"Ah." Sadness touched her voice. "I can't. Not shouldn't, not won't, but can't." She sighed. "Until I came to Sacred Spring, I never gave it a second thought. But for you country folk, you Feowans, fertility is everything. It's like you're obsessed with it."

Mikal drew in a breath. His fingers toyed with the willow wand. "I never thought about it that way. I guess it is pretty important to us."

She pulled on his arm. "Let's go plant this willow branch. We'll honor your custom, then we'll retire to bed."

He hesitated. "Separate beds, right?"

That took her by surprise. "Are you suggesting something else?"

"No," he replied, hastily. "I'm just making sure you weren't."

"I have my principles."

He relaxed. They walked along the dark road, letting starlight and distant lanterns nibble at the curtain of night. Berengaria listened gently as Mikal explained more of various festivals and rituals. She directed him back to maying if he strayed too much.

They found a copse of trees not too far from the village. No other sound issued forth, warranting a safe and unoccupied place.

"Here." He stumbled over brambles. Berengaria clung to his arm and followed in, her voluminous pantalets snagging on fallen branches.

They reached the middle of the copse, where a bed of last autumn's leaves covered the ground. "This'll be good." Mikal knelt and brushed away a few leaves. She knelt beside him, expectant. He jammed the willow branch into the earth. "There. That's that."

Berengaria peered at the tilting branch through the gloom. "What. That's it?"

"Well, that's the end. We skipped the beginning."

"Oh? What beginning?"

He squirmed. "Well, you are supposed to indulge in a bit of fertility stuff. You know. Intimacy."

Her voice was measured. "How much?"

He made to rise. She grabbed his arm and pulled him down. "How much?" she insisted.

"I've never asked."

"What? All the way?"

"No!" He tried to rise again. She wouldn't let him. In one fluid swoop, she settled herself over his lap, so he could not rise. "How much?" she asked again. "Will a little do? Or are we talking full on—"

He put his hands on her waist. "I think we've had enough—"

"No, no," she insisted. "We're going to do this right, or it might not work." Without warning, she took his face into her hands and kissed him.

He pulled back.

"Come on," she urged. "I've learned from the best."

He froze. "What did you say?"

Berengaria's heart thumped hard in her chest. Had she really said that? "I mean..." She did some quick thinking. "The temple library has a certain collection of books— That is to say, it has every kind of book, including some more... intimate than others." She laid her hands on his shoulders. "My biggest sin in life is that I would sneak those books out of the library and read them in forgotten closets. I was only caught once. That was by Adrastea. She'll vouch for me." Oh, why did she say that? The last person she wanted knowing what she was doing was Her Holiness. She groaned in regret. "Don't tell her I said that."

His hands, still on her waist, slid around to her back. "Even though you've never be able to use that knowledge?"

"It wasn't like I had prospects in that direction." She bit her lip before she could let slip anything else. "Tonight is not like any other night. You said that. The rules are different tonight, aren't they?"

"Maybe I should not have been the one to tell you about this."

She twined her arms about his neck. "You and I are not a danger to one another. I'll bet you have regretted being left out, even peripherally."

"I've danced. I participated." Well, that was an evasion.

"You danced with Chloe." She did not attempt to hide the contempt in her voice.

"Nobody questions the mayor dancing with the priestess."

"Nobody would question the mayor kissing a priestess." She leaned forward and did not take no for an answer.

Mikal was not giving no for an answer.

Berengaria proved her theoretical knowledge to him that night. She made a promise to herself that she would never tell him how she had gained her practical knowledge.

Nobody need ever know that, ever.

Chapter 16

Adrastea sat up the whole night, fighting her memory of maying. Perhaps Martine was right; perhaps she couldn't say no.

It could be quite difficult to say no to Mor-Lath. Curse him for making her blood sing!

She watched sleeping children that whole night, comforting those who woke, and waiting for the dawn.

They all stirred when light touched the window. No doubt their parents were all still fast asleep, hopefully some of them only just making it back to their beds.

Harianne woke and came straight to her mother. "Mama, I'm hungry."

Adrastea shushed and rocked her child. "I'll get you breakfast later."

"Want bre'fas' now."

Wakeful children were going to wander the inn soon. She sure could use someone to help her. No doubt Martine would not be showing up any time soon.

She risked abandoning the children for a moment to locate Berengaria, safe in her own bed. "Wake up, sleepy head. I need your help." She shook the priestess awake. "I'll see you at the Inn in five minutes."

And back to the children. Most of them had woken. She roused the others.

Five minutes later, Berengaria showed up, breathless and avoiding her gaze. Her straight black hair was unbrushed and rolled into a sloppy bun.

Something must have happened last night. She would not pry, unless she had to. "Let's get this lot downstairs. Martine stuck some porridge on the night hearth last night. We'll get them fed and find their folks."

"Yes, Holiness." Berengaria was awfully contrite this morning. Did she stumble across a maying couple on her way home? That could have been a shock.

Most of the children had been fed and returned. By now, Martine and Willem had woken up and come downstairs. Martine's skin glowed and Willem looked pretty satisfied as well. Adrastea was glad she had not completely ruined Martine's night.

Mikal entered the common room of the inn. He got about three steps in. His eyes saw Berengaria and he blushed. Was that Berengaria's secret? A smile tugged at Adrastea's lips.

He tore his gaze away from Berengaria, who was doing her best not to acknowledge his presence. "Adrastea, we need your help. We can't find Miele."

⁓❦⁓

Outside on the porch, she pulled her brother aside. "What do you mean, you can't find her?" A tendril of ice shot through her gut.

"She never made it home."

Several possibilities flashed through her head, most of them involving her husband. Adrastea laid a hand on Mikal's arm and closed her eyes. *Miele*, she sent out along the Lines of Deeper Power.

She felt an echo. "She's not far."

Shift.

In the woods, high above Sacred Spring, Adrastea and Mikal found Miele in the company of Mor-Lath. They were behaving most proper, fully clothed, sitting more than an armspan apart on a fallen log.

Mikal wavered from the translocation. "Warn your brother next time, will you?"

He straightened when he saw Miele. "There you are. Your parents are most upset with you."

She'd been crying. Her nose was red, and her eyes were puffy. Her hair was a mess and her clothes caught with twigs and dirt. "I'm of age. What do they care?"

Mor-Lath, still dressed as the country gentleman, looked not a hair out of place. He answered her question. "Because they care. Parents do that."

She looked away from him.

Mikal folded his arms. "How long have you been here?" he directed at Mor-Lath.

"Half an hour," he answered honestly. He looked to his wife and held out his hand.

She folded her arms, looking very much like her brother.

Instead of compelling her, Mor-Lath stood up and came to her, slipping an arm about her waist. "Miele and I have settled a few things between us," he murmured in her ear. "We've come to an understanding."

Miele sniffed, scrubbing at her moon face. "I'm leaving Sacred Spring."

Mikal dropped his arms. "What? Because of this?" He sat down next to her.

"Because," Mor-Lath explained, "of everything else that led up to this."

"Nobody appreciates me." Miele dabbed at her eyes.

"Not true," Mikal replied.

Miele gave Mikal a pointed stare. "Did you dance with me?"

Unfair question. "I only danced with Chloe. I always dance with Chloe. I'm Mayor."

She looked away, abashed. "Well," she stuttered. "Somebody could have danced with me."

True. Adrastea's heart went out to the poor social outcast. She sent a silent apology to her husband. He had shown the girl kindness, nothing more.

If Adrastea had been a boy, she would never have looked at Miele with the intention of dancing. Now that she thought about it, the poor girl had had it hard growing up. Not wanted by any other trade, she had apprenticed to her parents. Now she'd come of age. What was her adult life to be? Certainly no husband or children in her future. Doomed to be a spinster under her parents' thumbs until what?

Miele rose to her feet. "I'm not staying. I'll become a journeyman and leave Sacred Spring."

Mikal shook his head. "You're not ready yet."

Mor-Lath interceded. "As long as she stays, she'll never be ready. For her own good, it is best she leaves."

Mikal turned on his brother-in-law. "I don't think that's your call."

The god stood up to the mayor. "Tell me I'm wrong."

Mikal drew in a sharp breath in consideration. "I'll thank you to not go about putting such ideas into young girl's heads."

"Too late."

Adrastea gave her husband a pinch. *Behave yourself.*

He looked at her and raised an eyebrow in amusement.

He released his wife and went to Miele. He put a hand on her shoulder before sitting next to her. "Look at it this way: you are one of the very few people in the world to have danced with the Dark One himself." He leaned in closer to whisper in her ear. Adrastea could barely hear his words. "If I saw something in you worth asking to dance, who would the rest of the world be to counter my judgement?"

He released her, an awe of look on her face. He rejoined his wife.

Mikal folded his arms again. "I don't think she's ready to be a journeyman yet."

Mor-Lath shrugged. "Why not transfer her apprenticeship to Crossroads? You know it's been done before. Do her a world of good."

"Had many apprentices, have you?" Mikal put his arm about Miele. "Come, child."

"I'm not a child," Miele retorted.

He paused. "You're right. You're not. Still, there is much to be discussed before you decide to go haring off to the big, wide world." He walked her back to the village, shooting a warning glance back to Mor-Lath.

When they were gone, Mor-Lath sank back to the log and pulled his wife into his lap. She offered little resistance.

"I don't know if you've done a good thing or a bad thing," Adrastea said.

Mor-Lath shrugged. "I did a different thing. Poor Miele is suffocating here. If she stays in this village, she will shrivel up and fade away."

"You can't guarantee she won't suffer the same in another village."

"If she does, wife-of-mine, it will be because of who she is and not because of her past. Unburdened by that, who knows? Maybe she will blossom and shine. She is a skilled dancer. Who knows what else she might pick up?"

Adrastea had her doubts.

Mor-Lath turned her face to his. "And now, how about you? How are you feeling?"

She let a frown wrinkle her forehead "About what?"

"About you. And me."

She drew a breath. Normally, her anger would ignite in her chest and she'd want to shove him into the nearest pond. But today, things were different. Yes, she'd been angry with him last night, over Miele, over being out-manipulated in front of her brother, and his insisting he dance with her. She'd been trying so hard to be a simple country wife.

She wasn't. Maybe she never would be. She could never be a Martine, never an Ari. Chloe's life was too austere, Mikal's too lonely. Miele was lonely too but had the option to leave.

"I don't know what to say."

"How about you come out with me today? I planned on going out anyway. I would prefer your company."

She gave him a skeptical look. "And do what?"

"Remember how I destroyed Avelia a few years ago."

Oh, she remembered all right. The army fled their doomed city and attacked Feown. "Yes." One couldn't forget that, nor the treaty that brought the refugees under the protection of Feown. Then, off to war for three years.

"I think it's time to finish all this. Today, I am going to cleanse what is left of Avelia, in preparation for her peoples' return."

"How do we do that?"

He gave her a mysterious smile. "You'll see. I've set several things in motion to aid us. You ready?"

Adrastea looked back towards the distant village. "Berengaria needs to know I'm going."

He concentrated for a moment. "There. I've left her a note. She'll be fine."

Mor-Lath opened himself to the Deeper Power, letting it fill him and flood into her. Adrastea gasped when its sweetness enflamed her senses. She wanted to give herself over to it.

"Come, my Darklet. Let us be off."

He did not take them directly to Avelia. Instead, Adrastea found herself in her apartments at the Temple. "What? Why?"

"Because you look like a country wife. That is hardly awe-inspiring."

Mor-Lath and his love of drama. "What did you have in mind?"

He brought her before the full-length mirror. "This."

A wave of his hand clothed them instantly in the ceremonial black robes like what his High Priestess wore for ceremonies. The robes were straight, falling to the floor with nary a line out of place. The upright collar, simple, austere, lent an air of authority to the pattern. The robes had hoods, which trailed down their backs.

Adrastea drew in a slow breath. They were impressive. As she looked at the woman of power in the mirror opposite her, she understood why Mor-Lath wanted her to change. The image that looked back was no country farmwife.

Mor-Lath drew the hood up over his head, casting his face in shadow, giving him a mysterious, almost menacing air. One did not question a god who looked like this one.

He did not touch her but stood slightly behind her. It made them look like a matched set, equal in power and authority.

They looked like the God of the Dark.

She almost believed they could conquer the God of the Light.

A burning thought entered her mind. "May I try something?"

Mor-Lath pulled back his hood. "What did you have in mind?"

Adrastea looked at them in the mirror. She drew upon the Deeper Power and changed the color of their robes.

That surprised him. Mor-Lath stepped backwards, then resumed his place, a slight frown adding to his character lines. She had clothed them in white, as the Light favored. "Why this color?"

Adrastea studied them a bit longer, trying to envision them as not just the God of the Light, but the God of All Creation.

The urge to cry rose within her. She liked herself like this.

Mor-Lath, on the other hand, looked uncomfortable. She gave him back control over the color of their robes. "I just wanted to see what it was like."

He darkened their robes, not completely to black, but softened it. He wore brown and she was clad in her customary grey. Grey Lady. That was how the Feowans knew her.

"If we—" how to say it without it sounding bad? "If we win, you know, in the end, could you—would you—become the God of the Light?"

He did not touch her. "Is that what you want?"

She did not answer. How could she? She did not know how to answer without insulting him. She couldn't look at him.

He put a hand on her shoulder. She didn't flinch away. "I would be the same person. Is that what you fear?"

"I don't know if fear is the right word."

He weighed his words. "Is your prejudice because I am the God of the Dark and you were raised in the Light?"

"In the beginning, yes."

"Title aside, as a person; how did you feel about me then?"

At least about this she could answer. "You were the Dark, the enemy of Light. I wouldn't allow myself to feel anything else but prejudice."

"That changed." He stepped closer, his hand slipping down her back. "I dare say there were times I thought your feelings weren't so unilateral."

"Before or after?"

He knew she meant their marriage. "Before. And sometimes after. Though you had to work hard to keep up that prejudice. Light forbid you might come to like me."

With one hand on the small of her back, he lifted the other to stroke her cheek and turn her face to him. Her lines sang. She met his eyes and studied them. She'd grown so used to his eyes, dark green at the moment. Everything about him felt so familiar it comforted her.

Perhaps... if only it didn't mean what she was certain was great sacrifice, perhaps he could become... Adrastea forced back her wild dreams. Sure, triumph would be sweet, but not if it meant the destruction of Lucea and Phyl.

Tilting her face to his, Mor-Lath gave her a gentle kiss.

Apples, Adrastea thought. Warm vanilla. A ripple ran through her as he drew upon the Deeper Power, to his full capacity.

"Join with me," he murmured. "And let us redeem Avelia."

She called upon Creation to fill her with its Power, to sing in her blood and complete her soul. She raised her hand and pulled his face to hers. He did not resist.

*S*hift.

He pulled away and gasped, surfacing from the passion that threatened to overwhelm them. "Work first," he said, his voice ragged. "Or I would lose myself in you forever."

Adrastea moaned and dragged at him to turn his attention back to her. Gently he pushed her back. Before he stepped away from her completely, she caught his first and last thought: *I can't now...*

She put her hands to her cheeks to still their song and turned from him. She took her mixed feelings about him and shoved them into a tiny box in the back of her mind. She would sort them out later.

Adrastea took her bearings. They stood on a hill that towered over what remained of Avelia. The early morning rays illuminated the dead city, some buildings fallen, others their walls stained with smoke, and an awful stillness that made her skin crawl.

All around the city were great mounds of earth, like a wall, separating the city of the dead from the rest of the living world. Outside those walls lay human habitations, small villages of impermanent houses. The land about was given over to farms, and the jungle to its fruits. But they city lay barren, free even of vegetation. It was as if nothing dared live among its cursed stones.

Adrastea saw the souls that haunted those earthen walls, keeping out the living. "That is Avelia? What happened to it?"

"My wrath."

"Why?"

He took even longer for his second answer. "They had grown wicked, many of them beyond living redemption."

Adrastea wanted to reach out and touch him, but he had folded his arms tightly against his chest. "You regret having to destroy them?"

He vacillated, not sure how to respond to her statement. He regretted the destruction of an entire city, possibly an entire culture and people. Why, that she did not know. "I should have been more diligent as a god. I..." His gaze fell upon her. "I let myself be distracted by... obsession."

At first Adrastea didn't understand. As per their earlier conversation, she remembered what she had learned as a child about the Dark—that evil being who helped men in their descent into wickedness and sin. Mortals who passed on with their souls in debt were sent to the Underworld, a place of darkness and eternal misery.

But now that she had met the God of the Dark—had married him— she had learned a few more things.

True, souls in deficit were sent to Dom-al-gol. But it was not Mor-Lath's role to ensure their eternal torment.

The lord of Dom-al-gol was to redeem them, to shrive them of their sins and then send these penitent souls to the Light. "You're not supposed to be evil, then?"

"I never claimed to be."

"But, why the legend? Why the reputation? The God of the Dark is supposed to help souls from their darkness and send them on. Why all this enmity between you and the Light?"

Mor-Lath turned away from her. "Can we talk about this later? We do have a flood coming."

She felt disappointed at this avoidance of the subject, but he had opened to her. He had been honest with her. She did not want to press the matter and lose the chance of him being honest with her again. "Flood. Right. What must we do here?"

Mor-Lath took her hand. They hiked about the hill until they came to a clearing that gave an unimpeded view of the city and the river. He found a thick tuffet of grass and sat down. "Come sit with me."

She sat next to him. He sighed in disappointment.

Without any warning, he scooped her up and settled her between his knees, to lean back against him.

She squeaked in protest. "I thought you said we didn't have any time for—"

He held his finger to her lips. "Shh. Remember, work." He wrapped his arms about her waist and laid his chin on her shoulder.

Adrastea settled into the familiarity of his embrace. So. Work. "What do we do next?"

"Call upon Creation to fill you."

Adrastea opened herself to the Deeper Power. She let it flood in, filling every corner of her being. It came to her eagerly, as if it wanted to dwell inside her. It felt clean and satisfying, like a good meal when one was famished.

Mor-Lath's warm breath filled her ear as he sighed in pleasure. Then he called forth the Deeper Power.

For Adrastea, when the Power came to her, it flowed from all corners of Creation. It came from outside, to fill her inside. But with Mor-Lath, she felt a tiny spark within him ignite. From this, the Deeper Power expanded, until it filled him. From him, it then flowed outward towards Creation. She had never noticed that before. No wonder he was always able to surprise her, if his connection to Creation came from within. Was it a Mor-Lath thing? A male thing? A god thing?

No matter. When they were both open to the Deeper Power, it made her feel complete. She laid her head back against Mor-Lath's shoulder. Is this what Phyl and Lucea meant for her? If only she could stay like this forever.

Suffused with the will of Creation, they turned to the city. Far below them, on the outskirts, the villages were well and truly awake, having been up and working since before dawn.

We must preserve the surrounding life, Mor-Lath's thoughts echoed in her head. *Command them to leave.*

Adrastea sent out her thoughts along the Lines of Deeper Power. She saw the smoke from the cottages and imagined the people down there. Farmwives by fires, children about, farmers in the fields, their farm animals and the wild animals of the jungle. They were connected through the land and their experiences. "*Leave,*" she said, her command rumbling through the Lines, to echo in the ears of every being.

Waves of acknowledgement rolled back through the Lines, basic, primitive, instinctual. The animals responded to her command. Down below them, the forest stirred. Leaves rustled as if by an invisible wind. At one of the nearer villages, she could see the disturbance of a few penned donkeys as they kicked at the railings that held them corralled.

She felt the humans pause. Unlike the animals, they did not move, but considered her command. She could feel confusion, bafflement, doubt. Then they shook off the feeling and resumed their lives. Some did notice the disturbance outside. Others forgot the strange impression as their attention was distracted by unsettled animals.

Mor-Lath sniffed her hair. "This will take a while." He settled back in the grass, taking her with him.

They stared up at the fluffy clouds in the sky. She asked about how they were made, and he answered. Dust and water didn't seem very romantic. Their conversation drifted here and there as she inquired into the nature of the world.

From time to time, he toyed with the curls of her hair, stroked the backs of her hands and nuzzled her neck. However, he did not let himself get too distracted. He kept a firm grip on the Deeper Power and urged Adrastea to maintain her reservoir.

They passed a pleasant, if lazy morning. She kept an eye on the happenings down in the valley and plied him with questions. He kept his attention on her and used his answers to maintain his focus.

Animals, birds and insects, unfettered by sentience and the noisy confusion it can bring, heeded her word and fled away from Avelia. Many of the people marveled at this and felt fear. They had lived in the shadow of the cursed city for several years. They'd grown complacent. But now their superstition and their caution came to the fore. If the animals were fleeing, should they?

As the sun reached noontime, Mor-Lath stirred himself and tightened his arms about Adrastea. "Time to send them a second warning." He concentrated. *Danger. Leave.* He did not speak aloud, but the resonance of his baritone rippled through the Lines of Deeper Power, to shake the foundations of the living souls.

The wiser of the people heeded his word. They gathered their valuables, loaded up their wagons and followed the fleeing animals. Some people whispered of a curse arising from Avelia. Others spoke of tales of animals fleeing in the face of natural disasters.

And then there were the remainder, ones who loved their worldly wealth—what little there was—far too much to abandon it. Others were plain stubborn, dismissing the supernatural warning as figments of their imagination, or the ale they had drunk the night before, or perhaps the stew that had tasted a little gamey this morning.

Adrastea worried over these reluctant few. "What if they don't leave in time?" She could sense the spring floods, still hours away, up-river.

"If they are not smart enough to recognize that they need to bug out, then they shall perish in the flood. The collective intelligence of humanity will rise somewhat."

"We're talking people here. Individuals. Surely we can't let them all perish."

Mor-Lath toyed with her hair. "We have given them fair warning and plenty of time to leave. They can come back to their farms and goods in the morning."

Irritation tugged at the edge of her temper. "Will those farms still be there in the morning?"

He shrugged. "More or less. Nothing they can't rebuild, if they wish." He nuzzled her neck. "Can I distract you?"

"No." Adrastea's concern for the people fed her irritation.

He didn't accept her answer. "I can be persuasive." He teased her earlobe.

"Didn't you say, 'business first'?"

"Mmm hmmm." Clearly, his thoughts were not on the valley below. His hands roamed up to her breasts. She pushed them away.

He sighed. "If it makes you feel better, we are giving them one last warning. I'll add a sweetener to it. A little extra convincing."

She nodded. It would do.

He chuckled. "Distraction managed."

As the afternoon warmed, she allowed him to distract her, though he always stayed on the safe side, not letting his loins run away from his logic. This convinced her that he was thinking of the people below, keeping them in the back of his head.

By midafternoon, not a single living creature was within a league of Avelia, barring the remaining stubborn humans. Even then, they began to feel uneasy about the unnatural quiet about them. Mor-Lath let their unease grow and worry to nag at their intestines.

He gathered up his wife. "Shall we give them one last warning?"

She nodded and focused the Deeper Power. There were not so many life forms left in the valley. "*Leave.*"

Leave. Now. Mor-Lath's voice echoed her own, to ring in the heads and hearts of the remaining people.

He also sent tendrils of Power down into the earth, seeking out the deep cracks and giving them a shake.

The earth rumbled. Hearts trembled. Everyone had been convinced it was time to go. Even the reluctant ones hesitated and thought to flee to the hills.

Adrastea relaxed. They would be saved. She cast her thoughts upriver, to where the rolling flash flood of sudden snowmelt drew even closer. The actual flood front was no taller than a child, not doing as much damage along the banks of the Great River as Adrastea had expected. She expected a mighty wall of water to wash everything out of the way. What did Mor-Lath have planned?

"You'll see," he replied, clearly privy to her thoughts.

They watched the sun drop to the hills behind them, to kiss their rolling summits. It fell behind the skyline. The flood approached.

"Now, we cleanse Avelia," he murmured in her ear. He sent her images of the land below, of layers of different bedrocks and the fractures between them. Adrastea followed his lead in sending Power down to convince them to open.

They obeyed. She watched as the earth shook and trembled. The doomed city of Avelia sank within its earthen walls. The remains of buildings collapsed to piles of mere rubble. Dust rose so thick it obscured the other side of the river, the departing rays of sun coloring it blood-red.

The bedrock settled, to move no more.

An evening breeze blew, pushing back the dust. Adrastea looked down into the pit of destruction, a dark scar amid the greenness of the earth. Just in time.

The flood came.

A small wall of water surged forth from the river, to roll over the collapsed bank and flow into the remains of Avelia. Twilight came. Mor-Lath and Adrastea remained on the hillside. Above, she counted the stars as they came out. Below, more water splashed into Avelia, turning the former city into a lake.

Hours, it took, until the lake filled to the earthen walls.

There they stayed on the hill until Avelia was no more. The waning gibbous moon rose, sending a silver path across the water.

Adrastea asked, "Is Avelia cleansed at last?"

"It is clean. I'll bring the Avelians home." He lifted his hand and commanded the land to rise once more.

The earthen walls collapsed inward as the land tilted, urging the water back into the river. It would not be until tomorrow when the earth, completely washed clean, would emerge from its deluge. Sorrow welled in Adrastea's heart. "There will be nothing here for them." What would they say when they found the land flat and new?

"There will be a new beginning."

Chapter 17

The next morning Adrastea watched the sun rise. She stood on her front porch, looking out past the stables, out across the plains. The rays of morning peeped over the horizon. Mor-Lath watched the sun rise with her, wrapping his brown-robed arms about her grey-clad waist. "Yesterday wasn't so bad," he murmured in her ear.

"You were distracting me half the time." She'd expected a wave of guilt over having enjoyed her time with him. It never came.

He nuzzled her neck. "You loved it."

Indeed, she did.

In silence they watched the sun clear the horizon.

"Would you like to come watch the sun set on the Cithran Empire?" he asked.

A thrill of excitement communicated itself through the lines on her face. He was looking forward to whatever it was he planned.

"Oh?"

"It will involve some rather unpleasant business."

That dampened her enthusiasm. "What?" Her heart thumped.

"We are going to oversee the destruction of the Cithran High Council."

"What?" she balked at that. "More death?"

His expression was serious. "This is war. Whoever the One True god is, he's built an empire of the faithless. If they have their way, they will all live and die in serious peril. Not to mention their direct threat to the rest of us." There was something else lurking in his heart; Adrastea could feel it.

"And what else?"

He looked away from her and didn't answer that question. Instead, "Are you prepared to allow our soldiers to slaughter the wicked?"

She hesitated.

"We are not killing innocents. These men are responsible for the destruction of many, including your own people."

She thought back to the Cithran siege of Feown, also of Deliverance. "The same ones who killed the Duke and his children? The same ones who raped and tortured the Duchess?"

"These are the men who ordered that done."

A spark of outrage lit in her heart. It burned and grew until it filled her with wrath. "Yes. This is war."

⁓❦⁓

Adrastea had never been to Cithra, least of all to a quiet little shop in the slums of Nyabern. Small and dingy it was, with shelves and shelves of small wooden drawers, each numbered. But as she inhaled, her heart lifted. Herbs, tonics and more rushed in. Felt like home, back in Ari's stillroom, or deep in the cellar with so many potent things. "An apothecary?"

An older woman squeaked when they appeared, clutching at the counter before her.

"They are forbidden to work in a bakery."

Before Adrastea could ask who 'they' were, and why bakeries were forbidden, the woman cried out, "Holiness!" She hurried away through a door to the back of the shop.

Oh dear. Adrastea hadn't meant to frighten her.

"You didn't," Mor-Lath replied to her unvoiced thought.

As quickly as she'd left, the woman returned, and not alone.

A good dozen women pressed into the shop, their eagerness driving them. "Is it time?" they called. "Is it time?"

Adrastea studied them. Their clothing appeared to be Cithran, and several of them had blonde hair, but, "You're Avelian," Adrastea said. The shape of their faces gave them away. So, this is where the diaspora ended up.

Caution rolled over the women like an icy fog, their enthusiasm freezing.

Mor-Lath brushed Adrastea's cheek with a kiss. "Astute, my dear."

Light of realization dawned in one woman's eyes. "Your Holiness?" she addressed Adrastea. She dropped to the filthy floor in genuflection. The other women followed suit, making Adrastea squirm.

"Now, now," chided Mor-Lath. "No time for formalities."

Adrastea reached down for the hands of the nearest woman, raising her, confusing her.

Her gaze could not rest on Adrastea's face. "Forgive us, mistress. It's…" She wanted to pull her hands away, but she didn't dare. "We've heard such stories."

Mor-Lath replied, "And most of them are true." He waved them up. "You're not the only ones I am to gather. We fight our final battle today. I need everyone. Collect your knives and your poisons."

Their caution not quite forgotten, they hastened away to arm themselves for battle.

Meanwhile, Mor-Lath departed, leaving Adrastea there alone. He did not go far, only a few streets over, to where another cell of sleeper soldiers awaited his call.

As the women returned, she studied the Lines about them. These weren't just women, they were priestesses, every one. With their god gone their caution increased.

At least one was bold enough to speak. "Are… are you to fight with us?" she asked of Adrastea.

Fight? Is that what Adrastea intended? Is that what Mor-Lath wanted her to do? She could not see herself going up against a Cithran in hand-to-hand combat. She looked to the grey gown Mor-Lath insisted she wear. Not exactly her first choice for battle wear.

Mor-Lath himself was not accoutered as a soldier. Again, he'd chosen the plain brown robe of a priest. Then again, a god did not need to wield a sword. She sent a quick thought to him, hoping he'd give her a clue.

His sure reply gave her the words she needed: "We are here to lead you into battle."

Something tugged at her awareness. Adrastea spread her arms to gather her chicks. "It is time. Let us go." A nudge of the Deeper Power urged the priestesses to gather close. Adrastea transported them away from that shop, to the streets outside the Rotunda. Dampness darkened the pavement below their feet. The tall dome of the Rotunda loomed over them, fading in and out in the haziness of smog. The sudden chill made Adrastea shiver once. Everywhere was grey and quiet, as if Nyabern was holding its breath. Did it know the Avelians were coming out?

When they arrived in the square, the priestesses clung to her in surprise. Perhaps she should have warned them.

The wan light of dawn had not yet pierced the smog. Adrastea sensed, rather than saw, the approach of many knots of Avelian soldiers, their clothes little better than rags, but their weapons sharp and well-oiled. "Bit early for wandering the streets," one group said as they approached the women cautiously.

One replied, "Best to wander about before the day grows too warm."

At that exchange, the soldiers relaxed and stood about, waiting.

One of Adrastea's priestesses fell to her knees to cast up her accounts into the gutter. Sometimes transport could affect one in that manner. Adrastea laid a hand on the poor woman's head and eased her nausea.

One priestess gasped. "You can do that? I thought…"

"Thought what?"

"Are you not the goddess of destruction?"

That took her back. "What makes you think that?"

None of the priestesses could meet her gaze.

"I've always been a healer."

Their murmurs of surprise carried through the lightening smog. "But what about all those deaths?" another asked. "Did you not destroy the whole Cithran army?"

Inwardly, Adrastea groaned. Was she never to be free of that? "I did it to save other lives."

"Feowan lives," someone muttered.

Before she could rebut, Mor-Lath reappeared, scooping an arm about her waist. "I hope you have not terrorized my poor priestesses too much. I would hate to think they feared you too much to come to you for healing should they get injured."

A few dozen other women appeared behind him, coming forth to embrace their Avelian sisters. The smog swirled about them.

He grew serious. "This morning we invade the Rotunda," he told his priestesses and approaching soldiers.

The Lines between these Avelians and Mor-Lath thickened with the anticipation of open battle. Adrastea's thoughts rode along those Lines. There were hundreds, no, thousands of soldiers. So many! How did they all come here?

She looked up to the stone Rotunda, a veritable fortress. They were going to storm that today?

"I give you but one order. Kill all within who are not of us. Spare no one."

His command rippled through the crowd. Mor-Lath stretched out his hand in invitation. The nearest soldier came forth, taking it. A priestess also came forth, laying her hand on the soldier's. In a susurrus of a quiet ocean of death, every Avelian present came forward to rest a hand on the arm or the back of his fellow soldier. Once they were all united, Mor-Lath took them all, in the blink of an eye, into the center of the Rotunda itself.

The Council never knew what hit them until it was too late.

The secretary cursed himself. He should have seen it coming. As he lurked in the marbled corridors of the Rotunda, the echoes of angry soldiers rang out, reverberating back and forth. Invasion. One could not tell from where they came. Were they coming down this hallway, or that hallway? It was as if they oozed out from the stone walls.

This foreign guerrilla army had invaded the Rotunda itself, surprising the entire High Council.

The whole skirmish had been well-planned. Who could have known the High Council was meeting today? He'd only sent the notes out last night. No general, no matter how clever, could have staged an attack like this on such short notice.

The army—Avelian by the looks of them—laid waste to the High Council. They streamed in from all sides, these ragged, mismatched berserkers. Truly barbarians. Their unshaven faces and dark ragged hair made them look like the monsters of children's stories. Some wore tattered, stained uniforms, but most simply wore whatever ragged thing they found lying in the street.

The Ministers, soft from idleness and too much wealth, were too-easy targets. The Avelian monsters chased their fatnesses down, tackling them to the ground before slitting their throat, or simply shooting them in the back. Their junior ministers, assistants and secretaries did not escape.

This secretary had slipped out along a small, unguarded passage. Now, as he ran through the deserted corridors, he came to a set of doors. All he had to do was open them and flee.

Locked. They would not budge. Frustration, and maybe some fear, rose within him. He risked connecting himself to Creation and called upon just enough Deeper Power to manipulate the lock.

The lock itself fell away. But the doors would not open.

It was as if they were held there by some sorcerous power.

The secretary quickly cut the Lines he had formed. Maybe that was it. The Avelians were notorious for harboring sorceresses. They'd brought many of them with the army when they invaded Cithra. These evil, amoral women had earned a savage reputation. First, they'd seduce good citizens, then slaughter them in their sleep, either by slitting their throat or poisoning them.

They were very good at hiding out in the open, adopting Cithran clothing. Some even bleached their dark hair blonde.

Perhaps one of them had sealed the doors?

If he wanted, he could call upon enough Deeper Power to translocate himself away from the Rotunda, but why risk discovery unless one absolutely had to? That said, it was easier to use then sever from the Deeper Power. Ever since that cataclysmic event so many years ago that had destroyed the entire Cithran Army, he'd found the Power snapped at the mere thought of severance. It was as if Creation itself was fracturing.

Shouts sounding alarmingly close spurred him to motion. He slipped up a stairway to an upper gallery.

The gallery was rather dark and full of columns, a perfect place to scout out the Rotunda.

He peeped over the edge. Below, the wholesale slaughter filled the air with terrible sounds—the cries of dying Ministers, the ring of weapons on stone, the heathen shouts of the Avelians. While some of the ministry had a few pathetic weapons, they were not lasting long against the trained soldiers.

Even then, the occasional junior minister got in a lucky blow.

Not far too the secretary's left, he heard a shout of surprise. A small group of undersecretaries and message boys had encountered a few of the Avelian sorceresses. The skirmish had been quick, nasty and rather one-sided. How could a handful of women defeat a larger group of men so quickly? One of the sorceresses cried out, "Mistress!"

He felt a shift in the Deeper Power. A lady in gray appeared out of thin air. Her curly hair she'd wound up in a bun to keep it out of the way. Two black lines marred her cheeks. Her bronze skin announced she was no Avelian. The secretary ducked behind a pillar, so she could not see him. Another Feowan, perhaps? There had been a few.

A tightness grew in his chest. Lines of the Deeper Power wove their way about her, swirling as in an eddy. It came and went as she commanded.

He watched surreptitiously as she, with a wave of her hand, sent the undersecretaries running. She knelt and with a touch of her sorcerous hand, healed the Avelians. Once free of their injuries, the women took off in pursuit of the undersecretaries.

That was no mere sorcery! No one he knew could command that much power except for...

The gray lady leaned over the gallery and shouted, "There's more up here."

The secretary edged to the gallery and risked a look down into the Rotunda. In the midst of battle, a single man stood out from the rest. Robed in brown, he did not run or shout or fight, but moved through the chaos as if observing or maybe directing. General?

No. Worse. Master Non's heart thumped. That was Mor-Lath. The Lines bent toward him as if his very presence warped Creation itself.

He looked up at the woman who'd called to him. "Find them." He lifted a finger and pointed in several directions. "Some there, and there." His finger swung around until he pointed at the secretary. "And one there."

The secretary slunk back. He'd been too careless; he'd been spotted.

Melting off into the shadows, he watched her look around, peering into the darkness. At a single whim, she summoned several glowing balls. These illuminated the gallery.

His head swam, and he felt to faint. Only one woman had that kind of power—the Bride, here before him.

What were the chances?

She'd swatted those undersecretaries like they were dandelion seeds. She'd healed the sorceresses with a mere touch. How was he to claim her?

An idea popped into his head. A certain underminister indulged in a certain addictive habit. He'd taken advantage of some of science's advances, employing it for his own obliviated pleasure. In his office, hidden in a back drawer sat a bottle of ether, which he often enjoyed inhaling whenever he sought an escape from reality.

Somewhere across the gallery, something drew the attention of the Bride.

The secretary slipped away. A quick errand, some spontaneous plans tossed together, and the Bride would be his.

A drastea," said a tenor voice behind her. She turned, wondering who spoke her name.

A hand pressed a sweet-smelling damp cloth over her mouth and nose while a strong arm wrapped about her waist. Her first instinct was to gasp, but that only drew in more of the stench of the cloth. It smelt not unlike fermenting pears. Her stomach turned. Her head spun as well, causing stars and the echo of that voice calling her name to swirl around inside. The walls faded into blackness. She lost her balance.

Adrastea. Her name echoed in her ears, ringing about her head until she wished it would escape. She fell.

At least someone caught her. She drew on the Deeper Power—too late. Someone else called upon it as well. There was that familiar shift between places which only increased her nausea as her body settled down on something flat.

Her name still swirled around her head. Someone grabbed it as if it were a thick rope connecting her to something.

That someone cut the rope.

As the connection snapped back into her, she cried out. It stung. At least her head stopped echoing, though stars swirled before her vision. She struggled against the hand that pressed against her face. She held onto the Deeper Power she'd called upon earlier but treated it more as a rescue rope than a weapon. She had to figure out what to do with it first, once she got control of her nausea.

Fear shoved reason out of her. She struggled to find something that made sense. Lines kept slipping away, or were they cut?

Wife. Daughter. Sister. Friend. Niece. Granddaughter. Apprentice. Master. Neighbor.

She felt other snaps on her soul as if someone was flicking her with a willow switch. What were they? At least they grew less painful with time.

She began to float, as if she'd become disconnected. Something peeled off her face. Not her skin, but... what? The cloth was still there.

Were her eyes open? If so, all she could see was darkness. She felt the hard surface beneath her back—wood, if her hands didn't betray her. She gripped it as it tipped one way or another. The pressure on her face continued even as she tried to shake away the wet cloth. She didn't know what the sickly-sweet smell was. It was one she'd certainly remember.

Ooh, she was going to slide off the... table? Floor? Her hands scrabbled in front of her, looking for something to hold on to.

A lifeline of the Deeper Power came to her. She clung to it as if it was the only thing she knew. Other Lines slipped from her grasp—vague acquaintances, someone she knew only a short time. Rain, she heard. The Power within her bonded to it. She could not have separated the Lines even if she wanted to.

She didn't want to. Anything, to keep from sliding away, from falling off. She'd been in a fathomless darkness once before, though she couldn't say where. This reminded her of it.

But now she had her lifeline. She clung to it and got the impression of falling rain, droplets spattering on the roof, a soothing sound that reassured her.

A thought of a cottage suggested itself, a modest little place, clean and simple, with a garden in the front and a picket fence. She lived in a village under wide open skies where white clouds scudded along and the sun fell warm upon her freckled country face.

She drew in a deep breath of dusty air. Something suggested to her that it was time to *sleep*.

The smell of blood never excited Mor-Lath. His soldiers, on the other hand, the more blood they spilled, the more they craved. It streaked the floors and made it perilous to run. With half the Council gone, the rest attempted escape, but he knew each of them by name. He knew exactly where they hid.

His people guarded every door and every window. None could escape. Even those secret passages they thought hidden from the world were known to Mor-Lath. The stones themselves betrayed their secrets.

The marble corridors of the Grand Council echoes with berserker shouts.

He transferred his awareness to his priestesses elsewhere in the city. While the council were being slaughtered here, their families also perished, victims of more subtle methods—poison, garroting, or the silence of a stiletto gently slipped between the ribs of the sleeping. The priestesses had taken rather quickly to these dark arts. Their speed and their silence made them effective assassins, all in the name of their god.

In the morning, the Cithran government would be shattered.

One by one, Tanat weighed these souls and delivered them to Mor-

Lath. "I wish you would shrive them," she'd say every time a new death happened. "They should not be left unshriven."

"Answers first."

"They cannot give what does not exist," she snapped. "If the One True is a man, as you believe, surely we would find him by his name."

"'One True' is not a name, it is a title, and one he does not deserve. Thus, I cannot find him. But he exists."

Tanat sniffed. "Only in the collective imagination of the weak-minded."

But Mor-Lath would not be swayed. "You have judged these people and have been judging them since the beginning. Everything they have done has not been the product of a collective imagination. Only a single mind could be so devoted to a single pursuit for so long. I need more clues."

"You would know," she replied. "I look forward to judging your soul. I would see why you are so driven."

He dismissed her. "Another councilor has died."

Tanat did not need to be told.

Somewhere, Adrastea reached out to the Deeper Power, but it did not answer her call.

Mor-Lath paused. What was she doing?

Adrastea?

His connection between them snapped.

"Adrastea?" he called out as his connection reeled back into him, physically knocking him to the ground. His head spun with the sudden instability. An emptiness blossomed in his gut. *Where was his wife?*

"Adrastea!" he called out as his vision went dark. He reached out for her across Creation and found... nothing.

"Holiness?" came a concerned voice.

Mor-Lath struggled to rise. Gnarled hands gripped his and helped him to stand. "Holiness?" asked Palus. His voice shook.

The dizziness left, to be replaced by terror. "Stay here," Mor-Lath ordered. "Terminate every Cithran soul in this building. Gather every single head and leave them in the Rotunda. When this is done, you all will leave, scattering far. Do not regroup for three days. Do you understand?"

Palus nodded. "As you command, Holiness." He hesitated. "Are you—"

"I have something very important to do. Do not wait for me but obey me." Before Palus could bow his head, Mor-Lath disappeared.

❦

"Raine?" Someone chafed her hand. "Are you all right?"

Raine's consciousness coalesced, her wits gathering from the nebulous regions of her mind. The throb of a headache ran along the lines of the gathering wits. She groaned. Her other hand felt the patterned stitches of a quilt. She drew a deep breath—smoky and familiar— and opened her eyes.

Raine lay on a bed in a small cottage. *This is your home*, the echo of words suggested in her head. Was it? Why did she need to be told?

Surrounding her bed were still-faced people, watching her. They were of various sizes and age, from a plump housewife who did not look happy to be here at all, to a stout man in frilly robes of a type she was sure she had seen before. A few others stood by, dressed in what looked to be their country best. They watched her with expectant gazes.

The only person who showed any enthusiasm was the man who held her hand. He sat on the bed next to her, watching her intently. It was not that he looked familiar, for Raine was certain she'd never seen him before, but he felt familiar. He certainly was handsome enough, in his way. "I know you." Didn't she?

He was a thin man, with blond hair that hung in line with his jaw. His eyes were dark. They glinted with alarm. Then they softened. "Of course, you know me."

He was the only person she knew. The other faces were those of strangers. How disconcerting. Who else did she know?

Nobody.

"My head hurts."

"The smoke was too much for you. You fainted half-way through."

"Half-way through what?"

The people who stood at the foot of her bed glanced at each other.

"The ceremony. If you're feeling better, we can finish."

Raine attempted to sit up. "Finish what?"

"The ceremony," he insisted. "Can you stand?"

She nodded. Raine swung her legs over the side of the bed. Ooh, how her head ached! Little tendrils of pain radiated behind her eyeballs. "Hold on a moment." She put her hands to her temples. Her senses began to explore the inside of her head, chasing the little rivers of pain back to their sources. "I need a drink."

The unhappy housewife delivered a dipperful of water so quickly she left trails of water across the wooden floor. Raine took the dipper from the woman and drank.

Once the water hit her stomach, she felt much better. Still, "More." The housewife obliged.

But Raine caught the quick glance of permission exchanged between the housewife and the man on the bed. While the housewife fetched, Raine gave a quick study of all the people there. Not a single one, other than the man on the bed, seemed happy at her recovery.

Who were they? Why were they uneasy? Raine sensed something... not proper.

The housewife returned. Why was a dipper and not a cup used? The water did her some good. The pain retreated into simple tension. She made a note to investigate this further.

Yes, the smoke smelled funny on her clothes and hands; yes, she felt a bit dizzy; yes, the water helped. Something else that told her Something Wasn't Right.

Hm... patchwork quilt, blues and pinks and mostly white. She'd never seen it before. And the bed seemed awfully small. "All right, let's try this again." The man from the bed followed as she rose. The straw tick crunched as she pushed herself to standing.

That, she regretted. Her head swung about. Raine had to sit down once more. "Bad idea."

The man took her hand once more as if he had all the consideration and caring in the world. He also had a gentle smile on his face, one that Raine felt he was trying to keep there. Underneath he was annoyed, she sensed that. He refused to let it show.

It was as if she could almost see what he was thinking. Almost. Raine lifted a hand, letting a few fingers stroke his face. She was supposed to be able to see the wheels turning in his head but couldn't. No. It was more like she could hear them turning but didn't know why. "You were saying?"

At this, he came alive. The man took both her hands in his in a most romantic gesture. "It would have been a shame for you to have missed your own wedding day."

Ah. Something irked inside her. It was not so much the thought of missing it that bothered her, but for some reason, she objected to having been married in the first place.

Yes, that was it! Regret. She regretted being married.

Raine looked up into the blond man's eyes. "But we're not married yet. Were we?" The last question triggered some sort of doubt. Something inside her told her she'd been married for a while, yet here was a man saying that she'd fainted during the ceremony.

He rose, pulling her up with him.

She felt somewhat better. Her head did not spin so much.

The bedroom of the cottage was a modest place. The quilt was clean and fresh. The straw of the tick as well, for it had crunched and shifted every time she'd moved. There was a bureau of drawers along one clapboarded wall and a plain runner covered the top. Upon this sat a bowl and pitcher. Everything was free from dust.

At once glance from the man, everyone filed out of the bedroom.

There was a hope chest at the foot of the bed. She hadn't noticed it before. Odd. She had the feeling it was empty.

The man guided her out of the bedroom, through the modest front room of the cottage and out into the village. He escorted her out, his hands still holding both of hers.

"Who are you?" She asked it quietly, for she didn't want the others to think her odd. They seemed to know who she was. They weren't too happy about it. It wasn't that they disapproved of her. She could sense that much, but they were unhappy about something.

It was something to do with this man. They'd all watched him. They'd taken their cues from him. Essentially, he ran the show. Mayor?

Everyone else streamed past the gate of the picket fence and through the village dust in a solemn procession past cottages with fresh-thatched roofs along to what looked like a little church. Raine had seen a little church like that recently. For some reason, she imagined it to be bigger.

While the others departed, Raine and the man stopped. He lifted her hands, one at a time, to be pressed against his lips. "Call me Master Non. In a few moments, you shall become my Mistress. I know how long you've waited for this day. You've been so excited. No wonder you fainted." He brushed back a stray wisp of her hair, tucking it behind her left ear. "You seem all right now. Come with me to the church."

It wasn't that he gave her much choice. He put his arm around her waist and pulled her towards the little building.

By now the man in the frilly robes—Raine figured he was the priest—unlocked the door of the church. In silence, everyone filed in. The priest and a few others lit candles until the place had enough glow. Inside, the wooden church did not look too different from any other barn, except there were low-backed benches, about six. Did the village not have many people?

By now Raine was able to get a good head-count. There were only sixteen people there, from a sallow-faced slip of a young woman to a few motley adults and a couple of crones. The unhappy housewife had chosen a back-row seat and sat alone. The rest huddled together in groups of two or three on the other benches, but nobody sat in the front.

The priest in the frilly robes stood before an altar. He lifted his hands as if to beckon forth the "happy couple".

Master Non tucked Raine's hand into the crook of his arm and brought her before the altar.

"Shall I start again?" the priest asked.

Mayor. That must be it, reasoned Raine. Master Non must be the Mayor of this village. Should he have been getting married?

"No," replied Master Non. "Continue with her vows. If we start from the beginning, she might faint again."

Raine turned her head to look at him. He'd cracked a joke, albeit a poor one. His mouth widened in a grin which did not touch his eyes. The priest gave the obligatory chuckle. Some of the people behind her stirred. Were they expected to laugh? Did they want to, but didn't because of the sanctity of the place? Or did they not want to, but felt they had to play up to Master Non?

She snuck a backwards glance to the people. All eyes were forward, but not on her. They all watched him. A few of them glanced at her, but their attention returned to this man by her side. He seemed handsome enough, but any beauty was missing from his eyes.

Why was she marrying him?

Those eyes ignited with a fire when he looked at her. He wanted her. Did he want to consume her? He had taken her hands again. His arms twitched as if he wanted to embrace her fully.

Did she love him? She couldn't remember. She looked into his eyes, hoping to see her own mirrored in there.

There was something she wanted of a man, but she couldn't remember what.

The priest spoke. "Raine, will you receive this man to be yours, who shall walk by your side at all times, who shall hold you up and guard your heart as his own?"

At the sound of his voice, she turned to the priest. "I'll what?"

Master Non prompted her gently. "Say yes. This time I'll be sure to catch you."

"Why?" replied Raine. "Am I going to faint again?"

A moment, then Master Non broke into the first genuine smile she'd seen on him. He gave a brief laugh then recovered. He hadn't been expecting that, she could tell. "I hope not."

"We're getting married." This was more to herself, than to anyone in particular.

Master Non, more relaxed now, nodded. "Well, not until you say yes."

"Oh." Raine turned back to the priest. "Yes, I guess."

Her answer seemed to be the correct one, for a tension in the priest melted. He breathed out a sigh of relief and possibly thankfulness. "I say to you and these witnesses that you are husband and wife."

Husband and wife. Something tickled in the back of Raine's mind. She'd done this before. She didn't recall it being so pleasant.

Is that why she fainted?

Master Non threw his arms around her, startling her. He pulled her in to a great big bear hug, swinging her around in his enthusiasm.

"Mine," he sang into her ear. "My wife!"

He seemed really pleased, or rather, triumphant.

For Raine, it didn't matter either way to her. "Now what?"

He didn't hear her. He turned her loose and presented her to the people present. "Congratulate us," he commanded.

The all bowed their head and murmured, "Congratulations."

Such a solemn assembly.

Why did weddings never go right for her?

Hers was the dullest wedding feast ever. All afternoon Raine sat at a head table with Master Non. He kept looking over at her, touching her, more, it seemed, to check that she was real, rather than through any possible lust. He seemed excited enough. He kept bouncing like an eager puppy. Anticipation. Yeah, that was it.

Hmm, she thought, wedding night. She racked her brains over what she was supposed to do. The basics she knew. But there was something else, something that kept flitting through the shadows of her memory. Something powerful. Her heart seized when she tried to touch those thoughts, but they proved elusive.

She looked over to her husband, who gripped her hand in excitement.

No, that wasn't it. Ah well. It would come to her, she hoped.

During the interminably long courses of tepid and uninspired food, Raine had a chance to survey the surroundings. There were no mountains. There should have been mountains. At least the weather was clement, for there was no village inn or other public meeting places here.

The village itself was small, about a dozen houses and a barn of a church surrounding the village green, which wasn't much more than a meadow. In fact, that's how it felt; the village seemed to have been plunked down in some accommodating field somewhere. There weren't any roads, paved or otherwise, leading from the village. How strange.

A small band played for them, mostly a few viols and pennywhistles and one lap drum—standard village fare. They kept it up all afternoon, repeating their small repertoire over and over.

Two of the songs were dance tunes, but nobody got up and danced. For the most part, everyone sat around and picked at the food before them and murmured low conversation. Most of them did not want to be here, but here they stayed. Did they do it as a favor to Master Non? The priest seemed happy enough. He enjoyed his food more than the others. He'd not shed his frilly robe and ignored when food crumbs dropped into the frills. Perhaps his joy was in that his part of the wedding was over, while the other guests still had to fulfill their roles.

Raine had no desire to speak with her new husband. She'd asked a few questions earlier and got some gentle but inane answers back. Was it too early to regret marrying such a stellar conversationalist?

Most of his conversation tended towards commenting over how good the food was, how well the band played, how beautiful Raine looked, and waxing on about how wonderful their life would be together. He told her how he'd take her away from this little village to see the world. He spoke of cities whose names she did not know and places she'd never been.

"But most important," he stressed, "we'd be together, and that's what matters."

Raine cupped her chin in her hand and studied her new husband. She didn't say anything. What was there to say? She should have said something, but what was that?

The tablecloths were standard calico, all dyed blue. The food was served on matching crockery. Even the forks and knives matched. How nice.

The main course featured a half-pig, pit-roasted. Many of the vegetables, carrots and potatoes and parsnips and the such, had been roasted in the same pit.

Later puddings were brought out, real country fare thick with fruit. Raine simply pushed her serving about her plate, as she had done with her meal for the past few hours. Once she excused herself to the outhouse. After a few minutes of wandering behind several cottages, she gave up ever finding one and obliged a lonely field.

In the end a fruit was served, along with some plain sort of farmhouse cheese. Raine poked at it. I've made better, she thought. Then she wondered when had she made better?

That she had once made cheese, she remembered. She'd made lots of things. She knew how it worked. That someone had helped her, she remembered also, but who that was...?

It was like only blank-faced people inhabited her past. She knew they were supposed to be there but could not pinpoint who they were. She could remember a baby's face, though. Curly blonde hair, dark eyes. Large for her age and chubby. She could see the child standing behind some wooden bars—a pen of some sort, in a comfortable house with wooden floors. A warm house, inviting.

Harianne, that was the child's name. How odd. Why didn't she remember before?

The sun dropped its lazy red way to the edge of the earth.

Master Non leaned over as he had so many times that day, but instead of making some unremarkable comment, he muttered, "Now is our time to slip away."

"Oh, thank goodness," Raine replied, more to herself than to him. She'd been racking her brain all day to figure out why everything was so odd and getting nowhere. Maybe it was just the company.

Master Non smiled, his eyes lighting up once more. "I did not imagine you so eager."

"Eager for what?"

Master Non didn't explain himself. For a moment, Raine saw a flicker of something across his face before he drew his mask of patience over it. He simply breathed in a sigh. "Tradition states we must slip away unnoticed."

Raine looked across at the other two tables. All day the guests had been slipping furtive glanced in their direction. "I doubt we'll escape unnoticed. Why don't we just leave?"

"Tradition," he replied, his voice harder.

"And what if they do notice?" She studied him, direct and without subterfuge. Everyone else cringed in fear of him, but she didn't. Sure, she sensed he had a temper he was keeping under tight reign. No doubt someday something would shatter his control and his temper would flare like the hottest of blacksmith fires, but Raine didn't fear even that. *I'm married to... Who?... and I am afraid of no man,* was the thought that flitted through her head.

No, that wasn't right. She looked over at the man called her husband. He just wasn't that scary. He was like the one handsome village lad who all the younger girls sighed after and the older girls had grown tired of, for his company was little more than him basking in their short-lived admiration. Did she want to slip away with him?

"Seven years' bad luck." He answered her question.

"Oh. And nobody had the courtesy to happen to be looking away if they see us laying aside our forks and slipping away from our chairs? Terribly rude of them."

Master non pondered on this. "You're right." He gave his fingers a subtle flick in the direction away from their table. Raine felt a rush of something, like a stream of water flowing in her bones. It startled her but stopped to listen. It was a familiar feeling.

As one, everyone, including the musicians, turned and looked away as if distracted by something on the other side of the green.

"Let's go." He took her hand.

Raine didn't bother to sneak. Oh, she was glad to leave that dreadful scene.

Master Non led her back to the little cottage in which she had awakened.

Chapter 18

In Sacred Spring, the chapel should have been a quiet place, good for contemplation and quiet conversation. It comforted Mikal to spend his afternoons there. Berengaria made his heart thump and his head swim. As much as he craved her company, there were times he needed quietude.

Chloe made good company for him, as he did for her. Sometimes she'd talk, and he'd listen. Other times, he'd talk, and she'd listen. No advice, no questions, just a good, honest ear, and maybe a shoulder as needed. Then there were the times he and Chloe enjoyed the sun and spoke about nothing.

Today his peace was shattered. Mor-Lath appeared without warning. He grabbed Mikal by the shirt. "You and I need to talk."

Shift.

Mikal's stomach roiled. His head spun momentarily.

They had not gone far but had moved to the inside of the chapel. Mor-Lath's hand still gripped the front of his shirt. "Where is she?"

"Who?" He was completely baffled.

The god gave him a shake. "Your sister. Where is Adrastea?"

Sister? It took a moment for him to realize he had one. "I don't know."

Mor-Lath's hand tightened until the fabric ripped. "Did she say anything about leaving? What do you know?"

"Nothing."

"What had she told you?" An edge of desperation sharpened his voice.

Mikal's heart thumped even harder. "What are you talking about?" The angry god's wrath rolled over him like waves of heat. His knees grew weak. He wanted to flee.

"Adrastea. She's gone."

Mikal shook his head "I don't—"

Mor-Lath put his other hand to Mikal's head. *Tell me everything you know.* Something heavy and oppressive pressed itself so hard against his skin, it felt like it pushed inside him. Tendrils of pain licked at the inside of his skull and walked through all his memories of a sister he didn't realize he had.

Yes, he did. He had a sister. He'd seen her a few days ago. So why had he forgotten?

A few days ago, yes, he'd seen her. And then...? Nothing.

The heaviness left--its remains, a thumping headache.

"You don't know," Mor-Lath muttered.

Mikal massaged his temples. "I told you that. I don't know anything." Another thought occurred to him. "But I should know something, shouldn't I? Why do I feel I'm missing something?"

Mor-Lath released him. "Ari might know." And he was gone, only a stirring of air where he had stood.

Chloe came rushing in from the other side of the temple. "Are you all right? He locked the front doors."

Mikal who had been heading for the doors, turned and went to the back. "He's after Ari. Come on!"

Together they rushed to the Healer's house. Mikal outraced the priestess, to arrive huffing and puffing at Ari's door.

He didn't bother with knocking, for he heard raised voices inside.

Salle and Bitzy were huddled in the kitchen, their frightened eyes towards the stillroom door.

Mikal threw caution to the wind and bolted through.

An acrid stench assailed his nostrils. Ari and Mor-Lath squared off, Ari's upraised hand holding a glass jar. Mor-Lath stood at the ready, should she choose to lob it at him. A dark puddle at Ari's feet lay sprinkled with broken glass, no doubt some potion she'd dropped when startled.

"Please, Ari," Mor-Lath begged. "Tell me. If she ever said anything—"

"I wouldn't tell you anything, even if there was something to tell." She threatened to throw the jar at him. "I never liked you, you mongrel."

Ari's eyes lit upon her nephew. "Mikal, remember how I once had an apprentice named Adrastea?"

Mikal blinked. He vaguely recalled someone by that name. "Yes."

"Seems she ran off."

Mor-Lath put his hands to his forehead. "I told you. She hasn't run off. She's gone. Disappeared. Vanished. Believe me, if she'd simply run off, I'd know it. But how did she...?"

"You wouldn't know if she ran off of her own accord or not," Ari spat. "You're not as good as you think you are."

Chloe arrived, just as breathless as Mikal. "What's going on?"

Mor-Lath glared at Ari. "Until five minutes ago, I've known where Adrastea was every moment of her days, from the very beginning." He began to pace. "When I say she's gone, I mean she is absolutely gone." To himself, he muttered, "What am I going to do?"

Ari lowered her jar. "You mean, <u>gone</u> gone? As in dead gone?" She grasped the counter as her legs gave out. "That poor girl..."

Mikal rushed forward. "No, surely not—"

"I'd know if she'd died," Mor-Lath snapped. "Our bond is stronger than death."

Chloe bowed her head. "May her soul go to the Light," she murmured.

Mikal swallowed. "But that's mortal death." Something tagged at his memory. "I thought she was immortal. What happens when one of you dies?"

"We don't die! The whole universe would know... Wait. Tanat would know."

The Dark God vanished without a further word.

Mikal rushed to the aid of his aunt. Ari waved him away. "I'm all right. It's just... I..."

"Sit down," Mikal ordered. He gave Ari no choice. She didn't refuse him. He called for Salle, reassuring her it was safe. "You may want to clean up whatever that is. It smells quite foul."

Salle fetched a bucket. "I thought he was going to kill you." Bitsy chose to remain in the kitchen. Mikal didn't blame her.

"Who's Tanat?" Chloe asked.

Neither Mikal nor Ari knew.

Ari wiped her nose. "Now that I think about it, I do know an Adrastea. Your city cousin Dassie was an Adrastea."

Mikal shook his head. "No. He said my sister. He's not the one to make that kind of mistake." He put his hands to his head. "Why can't I remember? What did he mean by 'Adrastea's gone'?"

A shudder ran up Mikal's back. "Not dead gone, surely."

Chloe shook her head. "Not the way we know death. Who knows what happens to the immortals?"

"Something happened to her, didn't it?"

Chloe had moved off to a corner of the stillroom. She fell to her knees and murmured prayers.

"Oh, Mikal, don't say that." Ari's voice cracked.

"But something has. I'd completely forgotten about her until Mor-Lath showed up."

Ari fell thoughtful for a few moments. She pressed her knuckles to her mouth and frowned. "It took me a moment to recall her as well." She looked up. "Could it be that when an immortal departs this world, not only are they gone, but they take their memory with them?"

Tears welled up in Mikal's eyes. "What happened to her?"

Mor-Lath found Tanat perched on the Rotunda's stone steps, sorting through souls in the Cithran Grand Council. The waning light of the afternoon shone in through the high windows, reminiscent of a chapel of the Light, only not as welcoming.

His army had done an excellent job. Not a single living human soul remained in the Rotunda. They'd left, as ordered. He felt them scattered about the city, finding dark places to hide until it was safe to reunite.

"Tanat, where is Adrastea?" Tension made his voice shake.

Death looked up, a question in her not-eyes. "Adrastea?" She considered. "Ah, your wife. Wait, that's not right."

He swallowed and wrapped his arms about his body. "I need to know. Is she dead?"

"Dead?" Her focus blurred as she looked to Creation. "No, I don't think so. I would know if someone of that name died."

He drew a deep breath. "What about... What if she were destroyed? When she disappeared, I felt something." He swallowed. "What if... what if a mashiah found her?"

She weighed this possibility. "Probably not. We both know what happens when an immortal departs this plane."

Mor-Lath knew. The last time an immortal ceased to be had been at his hand. He'd wielded the knife and his mashiannic nature had done the rest.

All of Creation cried out when Ubilis departed. It nearly tore him apart as well, if it hadn't been for the Mantle of the Dark.

Adrastea had no such protection.

He grew impatient. "Do you, or do you not know if she's alive?"

Tanat shrugged. "If she were gone, or merely dead, I would know. She has not passed on." She considered a few more things. "But if she were not dead or gone, one would think I could find her. I cannot."

"That doesn't help me!"

She sniffed. "I would have thought it would have helped you a great deal. At least she is not destroyed. Take comfort in that."

"Comfort," he muttered. Tanat was never any help. Before he left, he kicked over the pile of neatly-stacked heads his army had left on the floor.

How desperate was he? Mor-Lath closed his eyes and *shifted*. When he opened them, he stood before Lucea. He found her on a gently rolling hill covered with tall spring flowers. The gentle rays of the rising sun shone, and it seemed the whole of Creation didn't care that Adrastea was gone.

Lucea's eyes brimmed with tears and she held out her arms to Mor-Lath.

He did not accept her hug. "Adrastea's gone."

"I know."

"Not dead, not destroyed. But gone."

Lucea nodded.

"Where is she?"

"That," admitted Lucea, "I don't know. Already the prayers of the faithful rise to me regarding her."

His hands balled into fists. "You're the Light. How can You not know something?"

She moved through the grass and caressed the flowers that leaned in to greet Her. "I know all that is connected to Creation, I know it all by name." She closed Her eyes for a moment. "I know a name of Adrastea, but I cannot see who should be on the other end." An uncustomary frown crossed Her face. She held out Her hand. "Come here," She ordered.

He did not disobey.

Lucea wrapped him in Her arms, not as a comforting hug, but a possessive demand. He closed his eyes as the full strength of the Light flowed through him. Guilt, sorrow, shame and all his other embarrassing feelings flooded through him, making him want to cry. Also, loss and regret. These, She explored in full.

Adrastea. Her name rolled through his mind. Lucea explored the missing end. "She has been severed from you. I don't know who, but someone broke her connection to you."

A familiar darkness—anger—filled his soul.

"That is not the path you want to take," Lucea warned.

That made him even angrier. "You think I should NOT be angry about this?"

She held him firm. "Anger has always served you ill. You let it overwhelm your senses. You act upon feeling, rather than logic. You make hasty, foolish decisions that lead to failure." She brought the memories if his ignoble acts toward his wife to the surface. "You almost lost her once through your foolishness. Don't do it again."

He struggled in Her grip. "I can't not be angry!"

"Be angry then, until you learn not to be. But do not act while angry. Part of forgiveness is letting go of your anger as quickly as you take hold of it. Feel your anger. Don't nurse it. Let it go. Then plan rationally. Creation cannot tolerate a complete separation of even the smallest creature. Somewhere, somehow, she is connected to Creation. Find that link and you find your Bride."

Lucea kissed him on the forehead. "Fret not, son of the Light. You will find her."

His voice was cold and bitter. "Even if I have to take Creation apart speck by speck."

⁘

Adrastea's home lay dark and still. Night enveloped Sacred Spring with a cover of silence. Dawn had not yet threatened the horizon. It was easier to hear the world when it was not full of noise.

Mor-Lath did not desire any illumination. He lowered himself into her rocking chair and let it sing to him. It remembered Adrastea, if barely. The echo of her presence hadn't faded completely.

Only two other souls occupied the house—that child of hers and Berengaria. They were fast asleep upstairs.

Whatever Lucea did to him had let loose a great many things he'd had locked up. When he thought of his former priestess, he felt regret. She'd been so fond of him once. He'd ruined that. She'd not looked upon him the same since. Now she no longer belonged to him. In the woman she'd become, he could still see the scrawny little girl who had been given to his temple by a desperate mother.

He should have done better by her. He should have done better by them all.

Berengaria belonged to Adrastea now; her loyalties had completely shifted.

And there was a thought. Perhaps a thread still linked Berengaria to Adrastea.

In a moment, Mor-Lath stood in the bedroom Berengaria and the child shared. She'd taken rather well to the role of nursemaid, spending only part of her days in frustration. She'd adapted to village life and even learned the Feowan language without any help from him.

As she slumbered, he placed a gentle hand on her face. "Adrastea?" he asked, *sotto voce.* He sent a tendril of Deeper Power into her. Their relationship may have changed, but the Lines were still there. They sang back to him, acknowledging his presence, but no reply of Adrastea was found in its echo.

How disappointing.

What about the child? He hovered his hand over the child's face. *Adrastea?*

Nothing.

He didn't keep his hand there long for something about the child made his skin prickle. Echoes of his wife hovered over the child, an echo to the power Creation held. Whatever did Adrastea see in the creature?

He wiped his hand on his shirt and retreated downstairs to think. Hmm. Who else might have a connection to her? Saraym?

A quick journey to the palace told him no.

Jonathan Pennexter, or any of the family? He visited each of them in their beds, questing in everyone for Lines of Power.

Still nothing.

Anyone and everyone he could think of who had a connection to Adrastea turned up a dead end. Friends. Family. Acquaintances. It was as if their souls had never heard of the name Adrastea.

In the end, he retreated to the granite mountain that housed his Temple. On its pinnacle, he sat and watched the world as it slowly turned beneath a starry sky. Where could she be? Her absence ached in his heart. *I miss you,* he sent out to the whole of Creation, hoping that if she was out there, she'd hear it.

Soon, his emptiness consumed him. False dawn brightened the east, then faded away, teasing him.

He couldn't stand it anymore. She wasn't there.

Back in Sacred Spring, he had more a sense of her, for the village, the road, even the very rocks, held some memory of her. He went to the house she built. Interesting that she built a new one, rather than claim the one her parents built. Perhaps the memories were too strong there. A pang of guilt over Lillybet's death did him no favors.

Inside, he settled into her rocking chair once more. The wood spoke to him of her sitting there many an evening, rocking a baby, an infant, a toddler, a little girl. There was a memory of him in that chair too. This was where he fell, when he had undone a terrible, terrible mistake. It didn't kill him, but it took everything he had and more.

Mor-Lath found he would give it all again, if it would bring his wife back.

Without her, he was as good as dead. He might as well sacrifice himself to the Light if she were not with him.

He gave himself over to the Deeper Power. He might not be able to find her by name, but maybe he could find her by something else. Adrastea had dark hair, lighter on the ends, and curly. He sent his senses out into the world to look for every single dark-haired woman he could find.

Preferably one without a name.

Berengaria's was straight. Ari's was more silver than dark. So on and so forth, as quick as thought, he sorted through them all.

Outside, the birds began to sing, hailing the arrival of dawn. Upstairs slumbering occupants stirred. This part of the world woke up, greeting the rising of the sun.

Someone was awake. Voices came from upstairs. Mor-Lath ignored them as he sorted through the people of the world. His hands shaded his eyes as he concentrated.

Little feet came down the steps. "Garie, I'm hungry," said a little voice. Then silence.

"Yes, yes." Berengaria, speaking Feowan. "I'll get you something. Come on." Then her feet slowed. "Oh." Her steps resumed. "It's okay. That's just Mor-Lath."

At the sound of his voice, he looked up. *Just* Mor-Lath? Berengaria had reached the bottom step and moved toward the kitchen.

The child remained on the steps, peering out between the railing. She kept a close, cautious watch on Mor-Lath.

"C'mon, Harianne," urged Berengaria.

But the child didn't move. "I want Mama."

Mama.

It was as if the sun dawned in his mind. All this time he was searching for the name of Adrastea. But the child didn't know her as Adrastea. To her, she was named "Mama".

Mama. In that moment, a familiar ping echoed through a Line of Deeper Power.

He'd found her!

He dashed from the rocking chair so fast it tipped over. He called upon the Deeper Power, as much as he could hold and raced to the stairs.

Berengaria caught the movement out of the corner of her eye. She whirled around, hands outstretched. "Harianne! No!" she cried out in terror.

But Mor-Lath made it there first.

The child shrieked in fear but was not fast enough. He snatched her up. His first thought was to know everything.

That was a mistake.

*B*ack at the cottage, Raine looked for a candle while her new husband, Master Non, locked the door. The sun had sunk lower, casting the whole village in shadow. The cottage inside had fallen even deeper into gloom. He fumbled the key in the lock until it turned with a certain click. Then he tugged the curtains of the windows closed with sharp movements.

Why was she looking for a candle? She knew a better way. Raine called upon... something, and a glowing ball of light appeared above her hand. This flooded the cottage with a sudden warm light.

"Oh, by the—!" her husband started, jumping. He dropped the key. It clattered on the floor. This he swiftly retrieved.

Raine sensed the flaring of a temper that flowed through Master Non's body until she thought his muscles were going to snap. Then, with a few deep breaths, he gained control over it. Ooh, this was a dangerous one.

Why did she marry him again?

Raine used the light long enough to find a candle. How odd. Not that there was much of anything in this tiny little kitchen.

A wooden table dominated the room, with two benches the only seating available. A small cabinet stood against one wall. In her search for candles, she'd peeked inside.

It was empty. How very odd. Was this cottage simply a temporary shelter for them until they could return to their real home? What was that? Why couldn't she remember anything?

A lamp stood on a shelf next to the door that led to the bedroom. But when she picked it up, it had no coal oil in it. "Well, that's useless."

"Forget the lamp," he snapped. Then, taking her by the wrist, pulled her into the bedroom.

Now here, there was a candle. He struck a match.

The blue and pink of the quilt faded out under the light of the candle which he set on the small table beside the bed.

His countenance changed. Raine felt something greasy flare inside him. She didn't know if she liked it.

"Now, my dear wife," he murmured as he took her by the arms. No tenderness here. It was more like seizing a possession. "We have but one more thing to accomplish, for us to be truly husband and wife."

Raine's stomach clenched up. *Not this again*, was the thought that moved through her head.

He loosened the tie from his neckline and pulled it out with a snap. He tore at the buttons of his shirt, then grabbed her once more and planted a harsh kiss on her lips. Then he began to taste her like he was trying to eat a toffee apple. Raine found it wet and sloppy. Was she supposed to kiss him back? How? He wasn't doing it right.

Finally, she turned her head aside, so she could catch her breath.

Then he began to undo the buttons of her dress. Then more of that sloppy kissing again while he finished his button fumbling. He pushed the dress off her shoulders. She had to struggle to get her arms free. Failing that, she simply willed them free of the dress.

The sleeves fell apart at the seams and dropped to the floor.

Master Non jumped. "I wish you wouldn't do that." All at once, many little somethings about her snapped back as if being struck by little willow branches.

He freed the last button at her waist and the rest of the dress joined the sleeves, leaving her standing in just a shift.

Still trying to kiss her, his hands moved to the fastenings of his pants. His breathing quickened, and his heart beat sped up. He might be getting excited, but she didn't feel the same enthusiasm.

His pants came loose and slid down his legs. He yanked off his shirt and, despite a moment of awkwardness with the cuffs, soon divested himself of it, leaving him naked.

Master Non bore Raine down to the bed. His eyes burned with desire, with possession. Raine might not remember much, but she knew she did not like that look.

Then more of the sloppy kissing, including her whole face and neck. Meanwhile, his hands ran up her thighs, pushing up her shift. His fingers found the innermost part of her, but instead of stroking her gently, as she somehow expected, he quickly rubbed them up and down the slit of her labia.

It was not a pleasant sensation. The motion chafed. Then his fingers slowed as they explored. Then he climbed on top of her and fumbled at her while he guided his erect penis into her.

A raw pain radiated out as he tried to thrust in her. "OW!" she cried, and with a force she didn't know she had, pushed him off.

He flew off her, off the bed and across the room until his back it the wall.

"That hurt," she hissed. A burning sensation flared out about her vagina. Was she bleeding? She wet the tips of two fingers with her tongue and gently probed down there. Oh, that stung! And yes, she was bleeding. "You're doing it wrong," she spat. Wait. How did she know?

Her husband, having slid down the wall after impact, studied her, a scowl deepening the creases of his face. Then he brushed the blond hair out of his eyes and stood up. "You're a maiden?" The same look of possession he'd had before returned to his eyes, but then there was something else. Triumph? "You're a maiden! After all this time."

"Of course, I'm a maiden," Raine shouted back. She fetched the remains of a gown sleeve from the floor. She pressed it to herself and wished for some aloe vera. "Why wouldn't I...?" She caught her breath. Was she a maiden? Something told her she wasn't supposed to be. "Why wouldn't I be?"

Again, some vague memory flitted around the edges of her conscious thought. She had the notion that once upon a time her maidenhood had been a problem, one she had solved. She'd been on top. But... when? Who?

"I told you you were doing it wrong."

Master Non had moved back to the bed. "And how would you know? He— You've never been touched." He crowed as if this was a good thing. "Hah! You're a maiden. Of course, you are." That thought pleased him more than she expected.

Raine checked the wad of cloth. She wasn't bleeding too much. But oh, how that had hurt. "And if that's unmaidening, I'm happy to stay an old maid for the rest of my life."

He sat on the bed and loomed over her. "I'm afraid that's impossible. We must consummate the marriage. Then he grabbed her and attempted to lay her back down.

But Raine fought back. "I don't think so."

She felt his temper flare up. This time, he did not try to control it. "You are my wife now. We have to do this."

That, she knew, was true. One was not truly married until that marriage was consummated. She huffed a breath. "Fine. Whatever." At least she was able to lick her fingers and carefully moisten herself first.

He grabbed her by the hips and started thrusting before she had a chance to remove her hand.

"Hey!" The friction burned already delicate skin.

Once, twice, then several times really fast he pumped as she watched him lose all of himself to the moment. She was about to call upon all that mystery strength she had to push herself away when he stopped and shuddered. He pulsed hard inside her as he came.

Then all the energy flowed out of him. He lay back on the bed, breathing hard.

What? That was it? Raine eased herself away from him. Oh look, she was bleeding again. "I certainly hope you don't want to do that again anytime soon. That was disappointing."

He turned his head to look at her with dark, possessive eyes. "You're mine now." Triumph, as if he'd won something. He even laughed as the thought delighted him.

"Yeah, whatever." She tucked her pad back between her legs until the bleeding stopped. Then she rose from the bed. "I'm going for a wash. Is there a well or pump outside?"

He didn't answer her. He seemed too caught up in his own possessive delight.

"Master Non," she insisted.

He looked at her as annoyance flickered across his face and through his soul. "I don't know. Why are you asking me?"

Was he really that daft? Great. She'd married an idiot as well as a selfish boy. Yes, they'd consummated their marriage, but it still felt like they'd done it wrong. It felt shallow.

"Never mind. I'll find something."

Raine never did. There was nothing in the kitchen. As night had fallen, she had no desire to go outside and look in the dark, especially with nothing but a shift to wear.

She returned to the bedroom. Already Master Non had climbed into the bed, into the side without a blood stain on the quilt, rolled over and gone to sleep.

Raine sighed. She climbed into her side of the bed and lay there. Would sleep never come?

As Mor-Lath snatched up the child, his first wish rolled over them both. *Tell me everything.*

An aftershock of the Deeper Power flushed through the child and washed back over him. So powerful was the reflection, it nearly knocked him down the stairs.

Someone tugged at his arm.

The echoes rebounded in his head. One of his biggest fears blossomed in his gut. It touched on memories and patterns he'd thought banished. Something resonated with the core of his self, his mashiannic self.

The child was a mashiah. Terror flushed through him and he failed to fight it off.

His vision darkened. He dropped to his knees, to fall against the wall. A wave of prophecy overtook him. Someone else clung to him. She gasped.

Images, almost too fast to recognize, flashed through his head. He saw the child, a knife in her hand, covered with his shimmering blood. He saw the child again, this time a pistol in her grip, aimed at him. Another time he saw her older, an adolescent, her face distorted with rage, a bastard sword in her hands, swinging down towards his head.

He saw her a child again, holding out her arms to him, a smile on her face. He saw her, again an adolescent, sword in hand, but defending him. He saw her, a grown woman, holding her hand out to him, begging him to grasp it. "I'll pull you out," she cried. He saw her, angry, pushing him. "Die, you bastard!"

Image after image came, flickering between child and adolescent and adult, between love and hate and indifference.

Only after the prophecies ran their course, did he regain his senses.

He found himself at the bottom of the steps. Berengaria laid next to him, semi-conscious. Her hand reached up to images only she could see. Prophecy touched her as well. He made her comfortable and sat next to her until her vision cleared.

She looked up at him and tears formed in her eyes. "What was that?" Her voice was weak and thready.

"Prophecy," he replied. "The child is a mashiah."

Her expression was one of perplexion. Then as the import of the statement hit her, her eyes grew wide and she sat up. "Oh no." She scrambled to her feet. "Harianne!" She scrabbled around for a child that was no longer there.

No answer.

Berengaria shook Mor-Lath. "Tell me you didn't kill her! Please."

Mor-Lath shook his head. "Relax. She's in the kitchen." She fled there, frightened, looking for her mama. At least, that's where he felt her. Now that he'd identified her nature, he couldn't help but know where she was at all times.

Berengaria dashed off to rescue her charge.

Mor-Lath sat on the bottom step and put his head into his hands.

A mashiah. All this time. How did he not know? Not realize? Had Adrastea's connection to the child been so strong he never saw the child's individual potential? Had her significance in Creation been masked by Adrastea's?

The child was also the only one to have a connection to Adrastea. So be it. He'd use her, then he'd decide later what to do.

But something would have to be done. Too many of those contrary prophetic visions spoke of his destruction—at the hands of a child, no less. He could not take the chance.

For now, it was time to find his wife. He strode into the messy kitchen. Items has been pulled out of the pantry. Jam smeared the floor from a fallen pot. He lifted a corner of the tablecloth to find them both under the kitchen table. "Come on, you two. Let's go find Adrastea."

Berengaria, who had been cleaning up a jam-smeared Harianne, snatched up the child. "No. I won't let you touch her."

"I'm not going to hurt the child." At least, not yet, anyway. "She's the only one who can find my wife."

"You promise you won't harm her? I know how you treat mashiahs. I've heard—"

He grew impatient. "I've not got time for this," he roared. This startled the child, who wailed loudly.

"Stop it," Berengaria shouted at him. "You're not helping." She resumed her wiping of the child's face with a wet cloth.

"Oh, for all that's holy..." With a wave of his hand, he banished all jam stains from the child's face, hands and clothes. The table itself also disappeared.

Berengaria abandoned her rag and stood up, her arms wrapped possessively around the distressed child.

Mor-Lath drew in a breath and calmed his anger. Maybe the Light was right. He shouldn't act rashly when angry. He closed his eyes and counted to ten. When he opened them, he knew what to do.

Gently, he approached the wary pair. He crouched down to be on eye-level with the child. "Harianne?" He used the child's name for the very first time. "Do you know where your mama is?"

The child turned and buried her face in Berengaria's shoulder. She might not know where her mama was, but Mor-Lath found the string that linked them both.

It was uncut!

He wrapped his arms around both Berengaria and the child. "We're going to Cithra."

"What?" cried Berengaria.

Shift.

W hat?" cried Berengaria, her grip tightening around Harianne. That sickening, stomach-turning shifting between locations made her dizzy.

Immediately, she felt cold air against her skin. The light was also different.

They stood in a bedroom, the bed unmade, the curtains around the open window billowing with the late morning breeze.

On the other side of the bed stood a familiar, dark-haired woman. She wore nothing more than a shift that didn't cover her knees and an angry expression. Berengaria watched as she slapped an unfamiliar blond man across the face. He dropped the bedsheet he had wrapped about his lower region, revealing his nakedness. Berengaria looked away.

"Mama!" Harianne cried out. Berengaria recognized the woman. Adrastea? Why did she feel strange?

The woman—Adrastea—at Harianne's demand, looked up. Her countenance softened. "I know you."

The man, a hand to his cheek, looked about. "What the—" he started, then he shouted in panic.

Mor-Lath launched himself across the bed. The man scrambled out of the way, but he was not the Dark God's target.

"Adrastea!" Mor-Lath cried out.

He startled her. She drew upon the Deeper Power but did not move fast enough. As he tackled her, both she and Mor-Lath disappeared.

"Mamaaa!" Harianne wailed.

Berengaria's heart thumped. She tightened her grip around Harianne.

The man stood up. He rewrapped the bedsheet around him and pushed his lank blond hair out of his eyes. "Well. Who have we here?" At least he spoke Feowan, albeit with an accent. Cithran?

Harianne turned from the stranger and buried her face in Berengaria's shoulder. Berengaria clutched at the child. Something in her told her this man—whoever he was—was very dangerous. "I... I should ask you who you are."

"Whose child is that?" the man demanded.

Berengaria fought the panic that rose in her chest. Where was Mor-Lath? She searched for an escape. The man stood between her and the only door. She looked to the window. Would she be able to get both herself and Harianne out before he caught them?

"It can't be hers. She was a maiden."

A maiden? Adrastea? Hardly. Berengaria and Radelisa had walked in on her and Mor-Lath one morning several years ago.

It was after Adrastea had pinned Mor-Lath to the library table with a knife, supposedly to leave him there for the rest of forever. Then, for reasons Adrastea refused to explain, she'd let him go, took him to her bed and there'd been a very different kind of pinning going on. Maiden was the last thing Adrastea was.

"Give me the child."

"No," replied Berengaria, her voice beginning to shake. "She's mine."

The man shook his head. "You're a terrible liar." He walked around the bed. He seemed to be listening to something. "That *is* her child! Not by her body, but it is hers." A terrible light made his eyes too bright. "The one thing I did not think to check for." A nasty smile crossed his face.

Berengaria retreated. *Mor-Lath!* she cried out in prayer. Tears filled her eyes. To the blond man, she asked, "Who are you? What do you want with any of us?"

A vicious look darkened his countenance. "I want my bride back." The man moved towards her, hand outstretched.

Something strong gripped her from inside and threatened to turn her inside out.

The whole room wavered and disappeared, to be replaced with the familiar surrounds of Adrastea's house.

Harianne retched. Berengaria sank to her knees and let her panic loose in an almighty scream.

Chapter 19

Raine screamed in terror. Before she could gather her wits, this stranger had tackled her and whisked her away.

Whatever sorcery he used had made her dizzy. The light changed. Instead of the starkness of a sunny morning, a muted glow lit the chamber. The stranger let her go and she stumbled away from him.

Where was she? There were no windows here, only strange glowing balls. Were they in a cave? How large it was. The stone walls curved ever so gently upwards. Fine furniture gave the room a comfortable, lived-in feeling. That was a change from the cottage. The floor, despite being stone, warmed her bare feet.

Then her eyes settled on a large, ornate bed, its posters draped with diaphanous curtains. "Oh, no. No, no, no." She looked nervously over at the dark stranger and backed away. "I am not doing this again." The thought of having yet another fumbling, bumbling man pawing at her in a most disagreeable way filled her with anger.

It was like a liquid anger that flowed into her the angrier she got. It was thick and malleable. It seemed like she could take it and use it to push away this stranger who'd kidnapped her.

Away! Before she could think twice, he flew backwards across the room. Before he hit a stone wall, he stopped and settled to his feet. "Easy now. I just saved you."

"What? For lunch? I don't think so."

He held up his hand.

She took offence at that. "Don't you shush me—"

He wasn't paying attention to her. His focus seemed elsewhere. She felt the same rush of warm liquid something gather in him, then depart.

Only then did he pay attention to her. "Sorry. You're not the only one who needed rescuing." He mulled over something. "Though I have a feeling I might be the one needing saving from the doghouse later." He dusted his hands and approached her. "Now. You're welcome. You can thank me later once you remember why it is you're thanking me."

He held out his hand in invitation. She had only a moment to feel that same warmth gather about her before he drew her into a tight hug. A sob shook his body.

When he held her like this, it was almost as if she could hear his thoughts. Certainly, his feelings. Right now, he was terrified out of his wits.

She struggled, mainly because his arms were too tight. "Let me go."

He shook his head. "I'm never letting you go again."

She tried pushing him away again and failed. That mysterious source of inner power slipped from her grasp. "I don't know who you are."

He eased up on his embrace. "I know. Do you know who you are?"

Silly question. "My name is Raine."

His breath caught. "What? What kind of name is that?" She felt a fresh wave of fear roll through him.

"It's mine."

"Uh, no, it's not."

"I think I know my own name." Annoyance pushed out the fear in her heart.

He leaned closer to her ear. "Who gave it to you?"

She opened her mouth to answer and found she had none. Surely, she knew who named her. Parents...? No. Um...

She frowned. Why couldn't she remember.

He placed a kiss on her forehead. "Can you remember yesterday?"

She shuddered. "My wedding day."

He let her go. "Your... what?"

She crossed her arms over her thinly-clad chest. "Don't remind me." She felt quite naked. Why did she have to be wearing only a shift when kidnapped by fearsome strangers? She shivered and turned from him, trying to hide her body. That bed over there didn't bode well for her future, if this is where he brought her. "I wasn't terribly impressed."

He stepped back from her, held out his arms as if to receive something. She felt another rush of whatever that warmth was. A soft garment fell into his waiting hands. It was a robe or cloak of some sort, soft and cream-colored. "Here." He held it up for her. "This'll make you more comfortable."

She let him drape it about her shoulders. "Thank you." She grudged a kind of gratitude. Really, she shouldn't let him sweet-talk her.

On the other hand, he was being a bit kinder than Master Non, her husband.

He looked worried. "You said it was your wedding day. Did you... did he...?"

She felt him draw more of the warm stuff—what was that? It wrapped about her leaving her feeling clothed yet naked at the same time. The warmth left her as soon as it surrounded her. A hard expression settled on his face. "Did you enjoy your wedding day? And after?"

And what? The consummation? The wedding day itself was a dour waste of time. The wedding night not much better either. At the very least, perhaps she should thank him for sparing her from more of her husband's unwanted attentions. "Not really. I'm never doing anything like that again, if I can help it."

His expression warmed. His fear eased up somewhat. "Not terribly impressed, then?"

She began to squirm. "No."

Did she see a smile tug at the corners of his mouth? Was he laughing at her? "Why are you doing this?"

"Because I know who you really are." He didn't hide his smile.

She shifted her feet. "And who am I?"

His spirits lifted. "Your name is Adrastea and you are..." He glanced over to the bed. "Perhaps I should let you discover your own memories for yourself. Right now, you don't believe anything I say."

She twitched her shoulders. "And how do I do that?"

"Fill yourself with the Deeper Power. Let it infuse you. Then go over to that bed and ask it give up its last memories of you."

She looked at him with skepticism.

He held up his hands and stepped back. "No tricks. That bed has some powerful memories."

She still didn't move. He backed up even further. "I promise to stay well enough away."

"I still don't trust you."

"Oh, Adrastea. You've never really trusted me." He pinched the bridge of his nose. "Just go get one memory back. I need you to know who you are. It's important."

She looked at him.

"Please," he begged.

Raine looked back to the bed. If this was a trick to lure her there, it was a rather roundabout one. From what she knew of this stranger, he had no compunction over doing what he wanted and taking what he wanted. She took a few steps forward. It was a rather beautiful bed, all carved wood and canopied. She called on the warmth—the Deeper Power, he said it was? It filled her, singing to her with happiness. She took a moment to enjoy that feeling. It wanted to dwell in her.

She laid a hand on the bed. "What is your last memory of me?" She closed her eyes.

Harianne, as a baby. She lay on the bed while Adrastea sorted through clothing of various sorts. A tiny little invisible thread snaked out from her heart and connected to the stranger. No, he wasn't a stranger. He was a husband—her husband. She was packing, she was leaving.

"Wait. I'm leaving you. I've left you." She snatched her hand from the bed. "I left you. We were married, but I left."

He ran a hand through his hair. "Not quite the memory I was hoping you'd find. Go back and find the one before."

She couldn't shake the bitter feelings of that last memory from her hand. "Why? It seems to me there was a very good reason for me not to want to be your wife." She didn't want to be anyone's wife. More tendrils connected between them. It's like her memories were trying to find who they were remembering.

He shook his head, as if giving up. "You'll get that memory back soon enough. Please. Go back one more memory. It's important."

"Fine." She slapped her hand back to the bedpost. The warmth of Deeper Power came to her.

Feown at war. The news from the priestesses. Radelisa and... Berengaria. She knew that name. "Wait. Berengaria. She was the woman with Harianne. She was with you when you kidnapped me." Raine looked around. "Where is she now?"

"They're safe. Keep going."

She turned her attention back to the bedpost. "The priestesses. They came to tell me you'd been set free." More came to her. "Your name is Mor-Lath."

"Go on."

Darkness. Nighttime. And... "Oh!" A million tiny lines woke up with some very powerful memories of sensuality and yearning. They bound the both of them together. She couldn't help but take a step towards him.

He sighed with relief. "Welcome back. Now do you remember who you are?"

Raine didn't reply. She sorted through all those memories of tangled feet. He cheeks burned bright. She put her hands up to her face. She compared this newly-discovered memory with her only other memory of the act of marriage. Could two experiences be so completely different?"

"I don't understand. When Master Non married me, I was a maiden—painfully so."

"It doesn't have to hurt if done correctly." He took another step towards her. She retreated. He did not pursue. At least his words rang true. There was no unwelcome pain in the memory from this bed, at least, not for her. His experience under her hands was a different story. Still, she had no desire at this moment to get tumbled again.

Mor-Lath, her true husband, if he could be believed, frowned. "Master Non, you said? That is his name?" His voice grew darker, more dangerous.

Raine hesitated. "That's what he said, but I didn't believe him."

He closed his eyes for a moment, then shook his head. "It's a label, at best, not his true name." Then an idea occurred to him. It came together through their connection. She glanced over at the bed, its memories still singing to her soul. She scooted a little bit further away.

"But you." He approached her. "You are Raine to him. You would not be such if you didn't still have a connection to him." A light sprung up in his green eyes that rattled her nerves.

"Wait." She backed up. "You're not going to use me to find him, are you?"

"That's exactly what I'm going to do."

She felt the rush of Deeper Power gathering to him. It flowed out of him like the tide. It drew her in when he did this. He reached for her. She couldn't help but move toward him.

"Raine," he said, calling upon her name.

A Line vibrated within her, connecting her to someone else. It was not a harmonic hum but buzzed unnaturally.

Found you! she heard, though not with her ears.

He sent the whole of that Deeper Power along that Line until it reached the end. What echoed back was a flood of panic. She recognized its flavor—Master Non.

Mor-Lath pulled her into his arms as he gathered his power.

Then from the other end of the Line, something snapped.

The connection between her and Master Non was severed. It recoiled back to her so hard she lost her legs and sagged against Mor-Lath.

"What?" he roared. "No!" A wave of his frustration enveloped her.

The world grew dark and she sagged. A faint buzz nagged at the corners of her consciousness. She heard a voice, but it didn't make any sense.

Someone stroked her forehead. "Adrastea?"

Yes. Adrastea. Her consciousness gathered back again.

"Adrastea," Mor-Lath said.

"Yes." Another memory rose to the surface of her mind. "When we first met, the first thing you did was call me by name."

Relief spread across his face. "You remember!"

"Only bits and pieces." More settled into place. "As I recall, I didn't want to marry you then, either." She had been so frightened of him, at first.

She realized she was lying on the bed and Mor-Lath sat next to her. She pushed herself upright. "Oh no. None of this nonsense either." The fresh memories of their unbridled night of passion brought a blush to her cheeks. He'd called her by her name many times that night.

Mor-Lath rolled his eyes. "You fainted. I wasn't going to leave you on the floor."

More came back to her. "I also recall you trying to get me into bed."

"Only because I promised you I would." He grinned at her.

She folded her arms. "I don't remember that."

"I do." He poked a finger in her thigh. "You were not so aloof, always. I also remember how angry you once got when you tried to get me into bed and I refused you."

"No, I didn't."

He nodded. "Several people lost their lives because of it."

Something tugged at her memory but didn't resolve itself. "I… don't remember much of that."

His smile faded. "Well, maybe some memories are best left forgotten."

She sat on the edge of the bed. "So, now what?" The restored memories only highlighted the empty gaps in her head. So many empty gaps.

Mor-Lath sat next to her and drew her hands into his. "Adrastea, I know you won't like this, but I won't take no for an answer. It was too easy for Master Non to kidnap you. From now on, I am going to be by your side constantly."

"What? All the time?"

He nodded.

That made her squirm. "Well, what if I want a bath?"

"Then I shall scrub your back."

"What if I want to go to the outhouse? You going to wipe as well?"

"Don't get ridiculous. Everyone who knows you and loves you will agree with me. Several of them are angry with me for not keeping you safe. From now on, I am guarding you with my life. Because, frankly, without you, my life is forfeit."

And here was another hole in her head. She vaguely recalled him desperately needing her, but not the reason. "Why?"

He held her hands against his chest. "You and I have a grand and glorious destiny. But we can only arrive there together."

"Oh? What is it?" Why couldn't she remember?

He smiled "In time, my Darklet. First, let us get your memories back." He rose and held out his hand to her. "How about we start Memory Lane from the beginning?"

*S*hift.

They came to a pool of a small creek, nestled in a hollow of quaking aspen. The leaves shimmered in the gentle spring breeze. The creek, cold and pure, burbled its own music.

"It's lovely here," Adrastea replied. She hitched up her soft cream robe and knelt by the cool water. Her hand dipped in and brought up the most refreshing drink she could remember. A vague memory of dirty laundry tugged at her.

"You weren't dwelling on its beauty at the time." He plucked at his country shirt. "And I was dressed with more elegance." He stepped back from her, held out his arms, closed his eyes and concentrated.

His clothing changed color and texture until it was fine and dark. A black cloak settled upon his shoulders. "That's better."

Adrastea's heart skipped a beat. Her hand touched the water once more. "I was washing here. Someone told me to go to the spring, but I couldn't see why. I stopped here instead." She looked up at him as he opened himself to the Deeper Power. It rushed up from within him as if born there. All of nature bowed towards him. Even the trees drew close as if to embrace him. "Adrastea, I am Mor-Lath, God of the Dark. I am destined to be your husband, if you will have me."

She drew in a deep breath. "The Dark One?" More memories sorted themselves out. "But I follow the Light."

"More or less."

She swallowed. "Why me?"

"Because you're far too noble for your own good." He held up a finger. "You did agree of your own free will. I did not trick you or force you."

"So, we were married, were we? And then I left you." Must have been a good reason. Maybe correcting the mistake of having married him in the first place?

Honestly! The God of the Dark? What was she thinking?

He ran a hand along the pale bark of a quakie. "You came back to me. You forgave me all the terrible things I did. I convinced you to let go of your anger. We finally worked together, as it should have been from the very beginning." His eyes grew dark. "Then this happened. And now we must start all over."

More memories came. Mira Priestess had told her to bathe in the Sacred Spring. Uncle Natan had rescued a small boy from drowning and she'd rescued him. "I have family."

"Yes. More than you realize."

"Can I see them?"

Adrastea wondered if she'd ever get used to that sudden transportation, the being in one spot, then being in another. Mor-Lath seemed to like this sudden moving around. Was he in a hurry for something? He had his arm about her waist. She shook it off.

They stood on the porch of a modest home in the middle of the village—Sacred Spring. She had been here, she remembered.

The sun reached its zenith. She heard various sounds of village life.

Across the square was a tall building her memories called the inn. Someone leaned out a window and shook a rug. Next to that building she recognized the storehouse where a couple of women stood talking at its door, and the Carpenters' workshop, and Mira's home— no, wait. Mira was dead. New priestess? Someone thin and disapproving. Adrastea turned. On the other side of the square stood a chapel of the Light.

Her hand touched the railing on the porch. "Uncle Natan's house. He's the Mayor."

"Was the Mayor," Mor-Lath corrected. "He retired when his health grew worse. Your brother Mikal is Mayor now. He'd be most happy to see you."

Mikal. Wasn't he a boy? Mayorprentice. Wait. He was grown now.

Another Line of memory wrapped itself around her. The more she remembered, the more solid she felt. It was as if the world was welcoming her back. She shuddered. What had happened to her before? She remembered being grabbed and suffocated and disconnected.

Mor-Lath's arm settled on her shoulder. "It'll be all right."

Of course, it would be. She was home now. She knocked on the door.

"Who is it?" called an irritated male voice. Oh, it sounded wonderfully familiar.

"Mikal?" she called out.

Something crashed inside the house. The door wrenched open. A tall, dark-haired man barreled out the door, to nearly knock her over with an embrace. "Adrastea!"

"Easy there," she squeaked. But as he held her, all his worries and fears washed over her, then evaporated. She felt more warm Lines, fueled by his joy, wrap around her. Even more memories came. Family. She'd stayed with him when she'd returned to Sacred Spring. He'd stood by her as she...? Oh, the memory wasn't complete. His body shuddered with a sob. "Are you crying?" she teased.

He released her and held her at arm's length. "We never thought we'd see you again. What happened?"

"I'm not sure."

Mikal looked to Mor-Lath.

The Dark God only shook his head. "She's back. That's all that matters."

Mikal gave her another hug, then looked at her again. "Adrastea. Your face. What happened?"

Her hand shot up to her cheek. "Why? What's wrong with it?"

His gaze flickered between Adrastea and Mor-Lath. "Where are the lines?"

"Casualties of war," Mor-Lath replied. His tone suggested the subject be dropped. "Come. You have more family to meet."

He disengaged Adrastea from her brother and guided her off the porch. Unlike before, he was content to walk down the street. He kept an arm firmly around Adrastea.

Mikal caught up, draping his arm about his sister. "Mor-Lath, what happened?"

"Her memories were wiped. We need to get them back."

"Wiped by whom?"

"Not me, if that's what you're asking."

Adrastea had to hasten her pace to keep up between the two men. "Where are we going now?"

"Your aunt," Mor-Lath replied. "Perhaps she will finally forgive me."

Mikal replied, "Unlikely."

It was not Ari but Salle who opened the stillroom door. Adrastea remembered her as soon as she saw her.

When Salle saw who stood on the porch, her hands flew to her mouth. "You're back." She shrieked with delight and launched herself at Adrastea with a great big hug.

Mikal stepped inside. "Where's Ari and Natan?"

Salle let go of Adrastea. "Natan's at the telegraph office. Ari's asleep. She was up all night with worry." She gave a pointed glance at Mor-Lath.

Mikal scrubbed a hand through his hair. "Should we let her sleep?"

Salle considered her professional opinion. "May be best for now." She confessed, "I dosed her." To Adrastea, she said, "Where'd you go?"

She shrugged. "I'm not sure." Until she knew more about what happened to her, perhaps it was best to keep it close.

"I'll get Natan," Mikal offered and left without hearing anyone else's opinion.

Salle didn't mind. She squealed again with delight. "You had us all worried. I sent Bitsy back home. I sat up with Ari as late as I could but fell asleep at the table. When I woke the next morning, she was still sitting by the stove, wide awake. Finally convinced her to take something. Talked her into bed. She's been there ever since. Natan got some sleep but got up early. He took off and only came back for a bite to eat."

A new voice joined them. "What the hell is all this noise?"

A very groggy, washed out Ari stood in the doorway. Her eyes were dark and sunken and her skin pale.

Adrastea's heart leapt when she saw her. "Ari, I'm back."

Ari had to blink before she could believe her eyes. She sagged against the door frame. Adrastea leapt to help her. As soon as she lifted up her aunt's thin frame, another warm bundle of Lines wrapped around her with powerful memories. Ari, who'd been there for her from the beginning, who had snapped at her as much as she'd praised her as a child, who stood up for her against all comers, even the God of the Dark. Ari, who'd loved Uncle Natan, even when it was impossible to be anything more than an illicit secret.

Adrastea guided her aunt to a chair by the stove. Ari's hands gripped hers. "We thought you were dead, girl. Nobody knew where you were." Her eyes flickered toward Mor-Lath. "Not even him."

"It's all right, Ari. I'm back now."

"What happened to you?"

"I'm not quite sure," Adrastea confessed. "My memory's quite spotty. In fact, I don't remember much of anything or anyone."

Ari's eyes screwed up in thought. "I may know something that will help."

Adrastea lifted the glass of amber liquid and let the afternoon sun shine through it. As Adrastea inhaled its fragrance, memories rushed back.

Ari turned her own glass, regarding the color of the brandy inside. "I saved a few bottles from the last batch a few years back. Brandy remembers, you know."

Adrastea inhaled again. Then she took a sip. The brandy, the smoothest of any she could recall, slipped down her throat. As it caressed her tongue, it was as if the whole world opened to her. Everything came back to her. She remembered returning to Sacred Spring with Harianne.

"Wait. Where's my daughter?"

Mor-Lath, who'd declined a drink, answered. "She's safe at home with Berengaria."

Adrastea drained her glass and set it down. "I need to go home."

Permission or not, she bolted out the door. Mor-Lath followed. She ran down the street, the soft cream robe flapping about her naked ankles. Her body knew where she was going. She passed a big bear of a man, shambling as quickly as his old body could take him. When she ran by, he called her name.

She ignored him. Harianne needed her.

The double-story home that sat behind Mikal's was hers, she knew. Even more memories came back as she dashed down the road. She'd built that house herself, a home for a new little baby.

Mor-Lath beat her to the porch by that translocation trick of his. "Adrastea, wait." He held out his arm, blocking her way.

"No."

He struggled with her. "There's a very angry priestess in there." A wave of trepidation rolled through their contact.

"Why would she be angry with me?"

"Not with you," he confessed. "With me. So just... let's be careful."

Adrastea shoved him out of the way and burst through the door. "Harianne?"

Mikal stood by the fire, his arms around a short woman with straight black hair. She'd folded into his embrace, pressing her face to his shirt. At Adrastea's entrance, she looked up. "Adrastea. Mikal said you'd returned."

Behind the couple, a child sat playing on the floor. When she heard her name, she looked up. "Mama."

Adrastea fell to her knees, gathered up her daughter and held her tightly.

Harianne squirmed. "Mama..."

"Oh, my beautiful baby. My little girl!" She was never letting go again.

A gentle hand descended on her shoulder. "I'm glad you're safe," said the black-haired woman.

Adrastea looked up. "I know you." It took a moment while the Lines of familiarity tied Adrastea even more to reality. "Berengaria. You're a priestess."

The expression on Berengaria's face froze.

A male voice—Mor-Lath's—spoke from the doorway. "Her memory's a bit spotty."

Berengaria straightened, her face changing to rage. "I am furious with you," she spat at Mor-Lath. Anger filled her form and the tension vibrated to her fingertips. The woman's anger rolled off her in waves that lapped over Adrastea. "You left me there. He could have killed me." She advanced on Mor-Lath, her fists balled.

Was she going to give him a thrashing, this petite little firebrand? A tiny corner of her memories told her he deserved it.

Mikal got to Berengaria first. His hands descended to her shoulders. "Let it go, Garie. He did not abandon you. True, you were not his priority, but he did rescue you and Harianne."

Mikal's touch calmed her somewhat, but she did not abandon her anger altogether. She pointed a finger at Mor-Lath. "I'm still upset with you."

Mor-Lath nodded. He glanced over his shoulder. "We have a guest, my dear."

The big bear man that Adrastea passed lumbered up on the porch. Ari, still wan and pale, came with him. Mor-Lath stepped aside and let him enter the house.

"Adrastea." He came forth and enveloped her in a huge hug. Harianne squeaked and slipped away from the embrace.

As his Lines wrapped around her, she got a whole lifetime of memories from him. This was the man who had jumped into a water tank to rescue a drowning child. This man had held her when she was a child, pacing back and forth while he wondered what he would do with her. Joe was dead, and Lilly given so far over to grief she couldn't rise from bed. He gave her into Ari's care.

"Uncle Natan," she said, muffled against his large chest.

He didn't release her. "Welcome back, girl."

Ari draped her thin self over Adrastea. Natan included her in the hug. There they stood for the longest while, not wanting to let go.

The more she felt their love, the more Lines connected her to the life she had before.

Lines. Adrastea remembered Lines. When she blinked or looked askance at the world, she could see everything connected by Lines. She'd always seen them. It wasn't until Uncle Natan needed rescuing—or was it the little drowning boy—that she learned she could touch them and make them obey her command.

Her touch on the Lines of Deeper Power (that's what Mira called them) is what alerted Mor-Lath to her presence.

She looked over to him. He stood in the doorway, arms folded, lost in thought. Shouldn't she have known what he was thinking, or at least, feeling?

Something was missing. What was it?

Finally, Natan let her go. He had to sit down, he said. Ari told Berengaria they all needed tea.

Everyone moved. Harianne followed Berengaria into the kitchen, as did Mikal. Natan and Ari settled into the two chairs by the fire.

Mor-Lath had not moved from the door. He stood apart from the family, keeping his distance.

Adrastea noticed. Why was he holding back? Was he not her husband? She approached him.

He looked up at her, concern in his green eyes.

Lots of Lines joined them, more adding to the connection all the time. They were not complete. "There's something missing." She stroked her face in hopes of remembering. "It feels like there's a wall of glass between us. I can see you, but I can't feel you. You know, in here." She laid a hand on his chest. "Am I supposed to?"

"In the beginning," he explained, his voice low, "I embedded a little bit of me in you. Master Non found that and removed it." He stroked her other cheek. "I should put them back." His hand moved down to her shoulder. "Maybe someplace less noticeable."

She ran a finger over her face. As she thought about the lines, her memories returned. "Those lines hurt when you put them there. Burned for a day. Maybe you should be the one to wear them."

He took her comment far more serious than she meant it. "That's not a bad idea." He took her hand. Easing the door open, he led her outside, away from everyone else.

Out on the porch, the sun shined down, promising a lovely spring afternoon. Across the road, horses whinnied in their paddocks next to the stables. The village was so lovely and peaceful. Adrastea didn't want to leave it, ever.

Mor-Lath undid the laces of his shirt, baring his chest. "Right here," he indicated.

Adrastea lifted her finger, then hesitated. "How do I do this?"

"It's like pressing your essence into my skin. Imagine leaving some of you behind."

She reached out and drew a line down his sternum. Nothing.

"Deeper Power?" he prompted.

Ah. Of course. She closed her eyes and invited it in. How could she forget something like that? It filled her, that sweetness. It wanted to obey her will. It wanted to draw her closer to him. She marveled in its warmth.

"Don't get distracted." His voice brought her back to reality.

"Right." Now properly infused, she touched her finger to his chest and drew a line.

A black streak appeared under her touch. It felt like scraping the skin off on a hot iron. From Mor-Lath's hiss, it didn't feel too good for him either.

Once the line was in place, all his emotions rushed into her head, like the opening of curtains to the rising sun. Oh, so much was going on in his heart! Fear, a new fear, dominated it all. There was also a familiar knot of niggly fear. Also, he radiated relief and a hungry yearning he kept firmly in check. If this is what one felt when embedding lines in someone else, did that mean he had felt everything she did this intensely? No wonder their anger and rage played off each other.

He dabbed at his new line that marred his perfect skin. He did up his shirt. "Where do you want yours?"

"You mean I can choose?"

"Only fair."

Where to put a line? Definitely not her face again. Being so obviously marked gave her difficulties before. Unlike Mor-Lath, she had no desire to spoil her décolletage. "Here, on my shoulder." She loosened her creamy robe just enough to ease her shift over her left shoulder.

"Right here?" he asked, his finger drawing along the curve of her shoulder.

"Yes." Adrastea braced herself.

Mor-Lath's finger was swift and painful. She hissed and blew on it when it began to burn.

He bent down and gently kissed the mark, bestowing a blessed relief. The pain fled.

"I didn't know you could do that." Adrastea felt cheated now. Why couldn't he have done that the first time he'd marked her thus? Her first line burned for days.

He turned her face to his. "There's not much I can't do."

Before he could kiss her, Ari's voice called out, very scared. "Adrastea? Adrastea!"

"Out here," she replied, before ducking back in. Through her new line on her shoulder, she felt Mor-Lath's frustration.

Inside, Ari hugged her again. "Warn us before you disappear," she scolded. "If you go missing one more time, I think it'll kill me."

Mor-Lath had followed, closing the door quietly behind him. "She will never go missing again." He stood behind her, resting a hand on her back.

"You can't watch me forever," Adrastea replied.

"Yes, I can."

Mikal came out of the kitchen, hands outspread, empty teacups pending from his fingers. "Tea," he announced, as if it was the most important thing in the world. Berengaria followed, carrying a large teapot.

Adrastea relieved her brother of two teacups. "You'll get bored," she murmured to her husband.

"I'll get used to it."

She looked at him. The more time she spent around him, more memories were restored. "You don't handle boredom well. Also, don't you have a war to run?" She held out both teacups for Berengaria to fill.

"The war is practically over." He accepted a full teacup from her. "I don't know if you remember, but we'd finished off the High Council for good." His voice was low, keeping their conversation private.

Her heart beat faster. Memories of a slaughter flitted at the edge of reason. Avelians, carrying out one final act before they were allowed to go home. Only, "We destroyed Avelia." She remembered sitting on a hill, Mor-Lath at her back, and a giant lake, washing the last hint of civilization away.

"I destroyed Avelia. We cleansed it." He sipped his tea. "My people will not be returning to the Avelia they knew. It's time they started afresh. Like us."

Mikal cleared his throat, interrupting their conversation. "Now that we are properly served, we must discuss a few things."

Of course. Tea before business.

"What are we going to do about Adrastea?"

It took her a few moments to realize her brother was talking about her. Her name still didn't fit right. Would it ever settle? A worry nagged at the corner of her heart. "What about me?"

Mor-Lath answered that question. "She is staying here in Sacred Spring, where it's good and safe. She cannot be harmed here."

Immediately, her ire rose. "Oh, and what will you be doing?"

"I will remain with you."

Their conversation earlier this morning refreshed itself in her memory. "Oh, not this again."

He took her arm. "I can't let you out of my sight."

She pulled her arm away from him. "You said I would be safe here."

"And I know you well enough to know you don't do as your told, nor do you stay where you should."

"I can't stay here forever."

"It's only until the final battle." He inhaled sharply. "Or I kill Master Non."

Mikal asked, "Who's Master Non."

Adrastea waved her hand dismissively. "Oh, some... Uh...?" She had a vague impression but couldn't quite place his face. The only thing she did remember was that he was terrible in bed.

"He doesn't matter." Mor-Lath dismissed him rather sharply.

"Oh, I think he matters very much," Mikal replied, "if you're willing to banish both your wife and yourself to Sacred Spring because of him."

Berengaria stood next to Mikal, finishing her tea in little quick sips. Her eyes remained alert. "Is he the Cithran god?"

"The Cithrans have no god," Mor-Lath snapped. He waved his hand and his teacup disappeared.

Berengaria looked askance. "That's what you let us believe about the Glasskissers," she replied in Tredan. Another sip of tea.

"He's a pretender," he growled. "One I shall put down if he annoys me again." He drew his arm about Adrastea's waist.

She pulled back but could not escape his grip. "So, what? We wait around here until... what?"

"Works for me." His anger calmed down a bit. "He can't get to us here."

"Do you honestly think you can stay here indefinitely?"

"Great," muttered Ari, gripping her teacup.

Adrastea ignored her. "And what are you going to do while you're here?"

"Meddle," Ari added, quietly. Natan gave her a pointed look. She avoided his stare.

Mor-Lath ran his hand through Adrastea's hair. "Work on you and me." He pressed his forehead to hers. *We are not yet a god.*

Did he say *god?* What? Him and... her? She was no god. She was... what?

His heartrate increased. A tendril of excitement ran through him. *Do you remember the secret?*

What secret? Try as she could, she couldn't remember any secret, much less the particular one he referred to. Holes riddled her memory. They were like grey clouds that resided over the place where something should have been.

He sighed. Disappointment was the first thing she felt from him. But then his emotions were muddied and mixed. Then as a ray of sunshine bursting over the horizon, everything cleared up. A smile played across his face. "No matter," he concluded. "We are more than content to remain here." He inhaled the scent of her hair. "Oh, you need a bath, though."

Adrastea (*Raine*) looked down at her hands. Lines of grime, embedded in her palmprint, brought back memories. She'd slapped someone this morning. Who? And last night. That she could not forget. That was her own blood on her hands. A shudder rolled up her back and over her shoulders. She definitely needed a bath.

Mor-Lath's arm settled around Adrastea. "My wife and I have much to discuss. Garie, I'm sure you can see to our guests."

At his words, everyone stopped. They all looked to Adrastea.

"What?" she said. Why were they looking at her?

Berengaria's look of disapproval radiated off her quite strongly. "Must he stay here? I live here too, you know. And what about Harianne?"

Adrastea's daughter, who'd been curled up on Natan's lap, looked up at her name. She looked around, self-conscious at all the quiet adults.

Mikal studied the leaves in his teacup. "This is your house, Adrastea. You have the needs of your household to consider."

Ah, so that's what they were waiting on. She looked between her family and her husband. The others did not approve much of Mor-Lath. That she could sense. Even Berengaria, thought she got the impression the priestess should have been the best inclined towards him.

She blinked. Many Lines connected Berengaria to Mikal, far more than she would have expected. Something was going on there.

Ari's disapproval was visible to all. Her mouth was set firm, her eyes hard.

As for the two mayors, as she considered their opinions, memories flooded back. Natan once shouted at Mor-Lath to leave the village. A fortnight ago, Mikal laid down the law to her husband, warning him to have a care for the others in the village. He didn't banish the god outright. Why?

Not that Mor-Lath would have acknowledged such banishment.

Her head ached. "I need time to think."

Mor-Lath called the Deeper Power a moment before he scooped her up, settling her in his arms. "Don't know what there is to consider. Mikal said I could stay in Sacred Spring. I have chosen to remain with my wife, something Chloe Priestess would very much approve of." He spoke in Tredan to Berengaria. "Don't think I don't know what you've been up to, girl." Then, in Feowan, he said, "I recommend you speak with Natan, Berengaria. You will need his advice."

The blood drained from Berengaria's face. She retreated a step.

Then his eyes settled on the child in Natan's lap. "But yes." His voice grew low and cold. "There is something I must deal with later."

Adrastea felt the wave of alarm from Berengaria. The priestess stepped between Mor-Lath and Harianne. "Don't you dare," she warned in Tredan. She gripped the teacup in her hands as if it were a weapon.

What was going on there? Interesting how the priestess swapped back and forth between languages. Openly discussing secrets? At least she understood the words, if not the meaning.

"Business for another time." As if she was as light as a feather, Mor-Lath carried Adrastea up the stairs. "I have more pressing issues at the moment. Behave yourselves," he flung down at them.

Chapter 20

"What is going on?" Adrastea demanded as Mor-Lath took her into a bedroom—her bedroom, her memories said. Their bedroom? The door slammed behind them and he put her down on the bed.

Unpleasant memories of another man on another bed last night caused her gut to grip. Powerful memories from another, fancier bed from this morning overwhelmed her sense with quite the contrast in emotion.

He hesitated, his hands lingering on her limbs. Desire rolled under his skin, to echo in hers.

Her emotions of passion and fear battled each other, with panic winning out over them all. She scooted away from Mor-Lath. "No, I am not doing this again!"

"I'm not going to tumble you after you so recently—" Rage flared within him, though not directed at her. The new line on her shoulder communicated that quite clearly. His anger was for the other man. Was he angry that she was with another man, or was he angry that that man had hurt her? Her loins stung from last night's mistreatment.

Mor-Lath summoned her washtub from the kitchen. Water appeared in it. He knelt over the tub, touched the water with his fingers and murmured something low. The water warmed, issuing steam.

"I was a maiden last night. Why?" It didn't make sense. If those other, powerful memories were true, then why had she been intact? If even a fraction of those memories were true, she should have been very much open. Heat rose in her cheeks. She pressed her hands to still her blush.

"Can we not talk about this right now?" The irritation in his voice betrayed his inner battle against the passion she'd never meant to stir in him. "Otherwise, I'm going to end up doing something I really shouldn't."

He walked away from the tub and stood at the window. "Let us focus on getting you clean first."

Adrastea drew her robe tightly against her and stood before the tub. Dirty. Yes, that's how she felt. How could water wash this away?

Once he'd settled his insides, he turned around. "Maybe it was too early for imprints." He laid a hand on his chest.

Adrastea felt age-old patience flow into her.

"Kneel by the tub," he said. "Let us wash your hair first."

Her hands hesitated over the robe. Then, before she could think twice, she removed it and dropped it to the bed. She knelt before the tub, still wearing her shift.

She felt a rush of Deeper Power. A bottle appeared in Mor-Lath's hand. He unstoppered it and inhaled its fragrance. "Bend over the tub."

She complied. Warm water poured over the back of her head, soaking her long, curly hair. Then something cool and slippery poured over her head. A pleasant, familiar scent filled her nostrils. "I know that. That's from the temple."

"I know." He rubbed it into her hair, massaging her scalp, scrubbing away the memories of last night. He poured more warm water over her hair.

"Now, into the tub with you."

She rose, her head still bent over the tub. He helped remove her shift and aided her into the pleasantly warm water.

She remembered the bathing pool back at the temple. One could stretch out and float, so big was that pool. And here she was, cooped up in a little washtub. Still, the water was nice. The aches and pains of her night and day ebbed away.

"Blessed water from the Sacred Spring. I never thought I'd be so grateful to the Light." He added, almost contrite, "Don't tell Them I said that." He gave her a flannel wash cloth anointed with more of that fragrant liquid from the bottle. "Best you wash yourself." She could feel the tension behind his voice.

Still, he knelt behind her, combing out her wet hair. He'd kept a thread of the Deeper Power within him. That gave him strength. Strength? For combing out wet hair?

They said nothing while she cleansed away every last thought of yesterday, clear back to when she woke in a strange bed, apparently having fainted. An unpleasant, sweet pear smell tickled her nose.

A large barrier lay between now and her memories before. What had happened, where she had been before that, that was all a mystery. She had to strain to see past that giant blankness to what she had been before. Even then, it was only the memories of memories, as if she couldn't remember what happened, but only remembered that she remembered it happened.

Voices floated up from downstairs, but she couldn't make out what anyone said.

Mor-Lath coiled her damp hair up on her head and secured it with a few pins.

When finished, she rose from the bath. He enveloped her in a soft towel, helping her to dry and dress.

Country clothes, from a simple cotton shift and long stockings to the pantalets and skirt, a short-sleeved blouse and an outer bodice. These clothes felt right, although the skirt was too short. While she slipped on a pair of shoes, he went and listened at the door. "A few more minutes, then we'll have the house to ourselves."

The pleasantness from the bath evaporated. "Why?"

Mor-Lath didn't answer her. He remained, ear pressed to the door. "Take the child," he muttered. "There you go."

She felt his relief. He turned to her. "The most important thing we need to discuss is that child of yours. Did you know she was a mashiah?"

Adrastea stared at him while her thoughts gathered back into their rightful places. Harianne. She remembered her origin. Aril giving birth, Adrastea crying out to Lucea, the Light blessing the child. Harianne had a lovely little quality about her that drew Adrastea to her. She thought it was a mother's love. "I wouldn't know how to recognize a mashiah."

"They have a certain, ah, harmony about them. It's the way they sound along the Lines of Deeper Power. A kind of strong hum." He placed his hand on his chest. As he closed his eyes, he called forth a powerful memory of his from that morning—Harianne.

Adrastea gasped as she saw the image of Mor-Lath snatching the child from the stairs, and the rush of visions. They went by too fast for her to see them, or he wasn't letting her see them. She recognized her daughter's aura. To her, it was simply Harianne. She shook her head. "I still don't see it?"

He called forth another memory. This one was of a young boy, a little older. He felt different from her daughter, but there was a familiarity.

Adrastea shrugged. What was she looking for?

Another memory, a young woman this time. Ah, that must be it, that familiarity. It was as he said, like a buzz, low down like a bass fiddle.

Mor-Lath was a mashiah. She let the essence of him into her sense. And there, in all the power and familiarity, she felt that low hum, that harmony that flowed quite nicely with the Deeper Power, almost driving it.

"If she's a mashiah, does that mean she's got talent?"

"No." He dropped his hand from his chest and the memories faded. "While being a mashiah means a greater chance of affecting Creation, it's not necessarily by conscious will. Likewise, not everyone with a talent for the Deeper Power will be a mashiah."

She frowned at this rather vague explanation. "I thought they would have been the same thing, or at least, hand-in-hand." More thought, as memories returned to her. Why do I have the talent but am not a mashiah. I'm doing a pretty good job of changing Creation."

Mor-Lath knelt by the tub and stirred the water with his fingers, round and round. "You are not a mashiah because you do not need to change Creation. You are already what Creation needs you to be."

Her fingers toyed with the quilt on which she sat. The bed creaked as she shifted her position. "I recall being terribly unhappy about not getting to choose my destiny."

He continued stirring the water, also listening to it. What was he looking for? "You've always had a choice."

"We've had this conversation before, I think."

"Yes, somewhat. Your destiny is still up in the air. You once came to a realization of a destiny, one you considered pursuing. You even told me what I needed to do."

Her fingers traced some stitching. "Did I? When did I do that?"

"Few years back."

"Don't remember."

He shrugged, his fingers still in the water. "Don't worry about it. It'll come to you eventually."

"What are you doing?" How odd he was so fascinated by her bathwater. Was he always this strange?

He stood up. "I'm going to take out some trash. Then I'm throwing out the dirty bathwater."

Without a warning, he disappeared, leaving Adrastea with more questions than answers.

Master Non did not know if he should consider his morning terrifying or a disappointment. As for Raine, should he consider it a triumph that he'd married her, bedded her, and possibly impregnated her, or a disaster that the Dark God had found and rescued her?

He'd returned the easily-manipulated villagers to their home. He'd paid them enough money to pretend. And after, when everything went pear-shaped, he'd severed their ties to him and burned the potemkin village he'd thrown together. Nothing would be left by which to trace him.

He had returned to the Rotunda to find a heap of rotting bodies and a pile of dismembered heads. The Avelian terrorists who'd managed to sneak in and destroy Cithra's governing body in one fell swoop had disappeared traceless.

His secretarial office had not been ransacked too much. It was here he retreated. The simple desk had been swiped clean of its files and overturned. He righted this, found his chair and sat down.

She'd been a maiden when he'd taken her. In hindsight, he might have realized this. The Dark God may have found the Bride but as the world hadn't ended yet, perhaps whatever it was she was supposed to do hadn't happened yet.

It certainly didn't happen with him. Maybe there was more to it than claiming the Bride. Some secret she possessed, perhaps?

Of course, there was. If she hadn't been forced to give it to the Dark God, maybe she could give it to him.

His desperation to possess the Bride tore at his heart. He needed better plans.

Something tickled in the back of his head as a connection to Creation was forged to him.

He had just enough warning before a wrathful god appeared.

Master Non jumped up from his seat as Mor-Lath, very dark and angry-looking, appeared on the other side of the desk. With a single wave of the god's hand, the desk cleft in two and fell away. The Line of Deeper Power grew thicker between them.

Mor-Lath didn't bother with words. He grasped Master Non by the arms. As he did so, the god hissed and let him go as if burned.

Ah, so the Dark God realized what Master Non was. He was right to be frightened. Master Non had taken his Bride. Soon he would take his throne.

But not today.

"Who are you?" Mor-Lath demanded.

Before the Dark God could grab him again, Master Non separated the Line that connected them. It snapped back into him like a gentle string on the breeze, absolutely no pain at all. Once upon a time, that severing would have snapped his soul like a willow switch.

Mor-Lath flinched as he felt the severing.

Before another Line could be forged, Master Non made a different connection to Creation and willed himself away from the office.

He chose a little back alley behind the Rotunda. As soon as he arrived, he severed that connection as well. No good having the Dark God after him.

As he strolled past the litter and occasional casualty of war, he sunk himself into deep thought. Of course, the Dark God would use any trace he found on the Bride to find him. How careless of him, to think that he'd severed all links.

Next time, he'd make sure he got them all.

But first, he needed a plan to take back the Bride, maybe a better organized one than last time. Granted, that was spur of the moment.

Master Non congratulated himself on his quick thinking earlier. During the slaughter of the High Council, she practically delivered herself into his power. How arrogant of her to show up at the Rotunda and flaunt her status.

The chances of that happening again were slim to none. If he was to reclaim the Bride, he would have to go after her.

A factlet niggled in the back of his brain. Was she well and truly back at her little village?

No matter. Whether or not she was there, Master Non could guarantee that there would be someone there she cared about.

Really, he'd been far too arrogant himself. He'd lost an entire army when he pursued her earlier. Maybe he should have approached the matter in a more clandestine fashion.

With no one to summon or order about, with the governmental structure in complete chaos, it would be best to set off and get things done personally.

What was that little Feowan village called? No matter. He would find it eventually.

❧

Chapter 21

Back in her bedroom, Adrastea jumped as an angry Mor-Lath reappeared. "I almost had him!" he shouted, more at the walls than her.

She rose from the bed and brushed out her skirt. "Had who?"

He paced the room. "The bastard who did this to you." He pressed his knuckles to his lips as he paced, thinking.

She sat back down. "What happened."

Mor-Lath muttered to himself before answering her. "He has a way of disconnecting himself from Creation. That's why we haven't been able to sense him."

"Surely he can't disconnect himself entirely. He breathes. He eats. His feet touch the ground."

Only then, did he stop. "So how do I find him, then? What do I look for? How do I tell him apart from the millions of other people who eat and breathe and haven't yet learned how to fly?" He resumed his pacing.

She folded her arms and scooted back against the headboard. "I'm sure there's something about him. Maybe not anything unique, but something that'll narrow the field."

Mor-Lath stopped. "There is something. He's a mashiah."

"Another one?"

He scowled at her. "I'm serious. You don't know how dangerous they can be."

"Do tell."

He didn't elaborate. "It makes sense," he said, more to himself, as he resumed pacing. "A being with the power to change Creation... of course he can sever the Lines of Deeper Power. Isolate himself and hide, until he's strong enough." He stopped and crawled onto the bed. "Adrastea, we can't have you leave this village. It's too dangerous out there." She leaned back from him as he came forward. "He's a mashiah. He has the power to kill you."

"I don't think he wants to kill me."

He considered this. "No, I doubt he will be that kind to you."

"Could he kill you?"

Mor-Lath thought about this as well. "Yes."

She took this in. "I thought immortals couldn't die."

He stopped. "We can."

"But how? I stuck a knife in you."

"You are not a mashiah."

She growled in frustration. "I still don't know how that works."

He sat next to her and took her hands. "Believe me, I speak from experience when I tell you a mashiah can kill an immortal."

"So, we're both stuck here."

He shrugged. "Is that so bad?"

"I don't know. You tell me."

He gave himself over to more thought. He sorted through ideas faster than she could keep track.

She closed her eyes, let the Deeper Power flow into her, and focused on the one thing she had—his name.

Master Non?

Mor-Lath shook her. "What are you doing?"

Her eyes flew open. "Just seeing if I could find him."

He drew on the Power and connected with her, following the request she'd sent out. Nothing.

"First of all, that was very foolish for many reasons. Second of all, we don't want him knowing you're here."

"I thought you said Sacred Spring was safe."

"It is. But do you want him standing just outside the village limits, pacing, waiting? Do you want to imprison everyone else here? Because that's what you'd be doing, if he knew where you were. What if he decides to use those you love against you?"

She frowned at him. "You mean the way you did?"

That caught him by surprise. How would he respond to that? "It is a very effective method. You're vulnerable like that." Another thought tumbled in his head. She wished she knew what it was.

Through the line on her shoulder, she felt a ripple of concern. "We need to go back downstairs." He took her hand and pulled her off the bed and out of the bedroom.

"Why?" They went down the stairs.

When they reached ground floor, Adrastea saw her family standing together, standing firm. Mikal, Natan and Ari stood shoulder-to-shoulder, facing them. Berengaria stood behind them, Harianne wrapped protectively in her arms.

Mikal spoke. "I have decided you can't stay here."

"What?" cried Adrastea. "I can't leave."

"You're fine," he brother told her. "It's him who can't stay."

Mor-Lath folded his arms and stood his ground. "Recanting your word, are you, mayor?"

"Not at all," Mikal replied, unruffled. "I said you could stay as long as you weren't a threat to any villager." He glanced back at Berengaria. "It has come to my attention that you pose a very serious risk to a villager. I won't have that."

"Who?" Adrastea asked, completely baffled. Surely Mikal didn't mean her. Then her eyes settled on Harianne.

A flood of memories came rolling back, as strong as if she was there. Amarice Poulter's death. Mor-Lath killing a newborn baby. She remembered the violence and the rage as he ripped the soul from the mashiah child. The vision he shared with her regarding the man the child would have grown to become, the violence he could have inflicted on her. She fell to her knees, clutching her belly. She retched and fought to keep her stomach where it belonged.

"Adrastea?" came Ari's concerned voice.

If that was Mor-Lath's vision of Amarice's baby boy, did that mean he'd seen something of Harianne? Surely, he wouldn't kill her too.

She pulled on the Deeper Power and climbed back to her feet. Her anger burned within her.

Mor-Lath took one step back before she slammed him into the wall. Her hand pressed against the side of his head. "Give me your memories," she demanded, her focus on the thought of her daughter.

A shudder of pain rippled through him. Images of Harianne, a thousand of them, a million of them, poured into her. Images of a child wielding a knife. A girl with a sword or a rifle, a snarl of hatred on her face. A young woman, desperate, reaching out: "Take my hand!" Harianne, at various ages, armed or not, standing before an unknown foe, defending the god.

Somewhere, Berengaria cried out. Adrastea stared inwardly at the memories she'd stolen. Harianne as a child, a pistol in her hands, pulling the trigger. Or Harianne, giving Mor-Lath the gun. As an older girl, tightening a rope about his neck, sticking a knife into his belly, swinging an axe at his head. So many possibilities!

She shook the images out of her head. They all couldn't be true. "Which one is the real future?"

Mor-Lath, still slumped against the wall, frowned at her. "Any of them. All of them."

"None of them?"

He shook his head. "You don't understand the power of a mashiah."

"I understand the power of destiny." She put her head into her hands. "I know that destinies can be chosen and changed. You yourself told me I could have said no, for the rest of my life, until the very end. You didn't have to kill innocent babies."

"No. I killed hardened, heartless warriors would have cleaved your skull as readily as mine."

Adrastea stared at him. She pointed to Harianne. "Is that how you saw the last one you killed?"

"That was who he was."

Adrastea weighed all the futures for her daughter. "You were wrong."

He gasped. "What?"

"You only showed me one possible future. You didn't show me the rest." Her hand was still outstretched to her daughter. "But she has multiple futures. Not all of them end in your death."

She felt his anger boil up inside. "You cannot think—"

"I am not finished," she snapped. "I am not going to let you kill my child on a mere possibility of a whim."

"You cannot guarantee she won't kill me later."

Ari squeaked. "She could kill him?" There was optimism in her voice.

Adrastea dismissed her with a wave of her hand. Her attention was on Mor-Lath. "But you can. Don't you realize you could influence how she thinks about you. Haven't you considered winning her over to your side?"

Mor-Lath looked over to the child. Adrastea followed his gaze.

Ari had wrapped her arms about Berengaria and Harianne. Adrastea wasn't sure if Ari's gaze was pure fury, or if there was a little triumph woven in there. Great. Now she'd have to deal with her aunt, assuming she was able to convince Mor-Lath to not commit infanticide today.

"You have your choice, God of the Dark. Spare my daughter's life and influence the outcome of prophecy in your favor or kill my child and face certain doom." Adrastea rose and came up right into his face. "Because if you kill her, or do anything that would lead her to harm, I will turn against you. Without me, you are as good as dead."

Terror rose within him and spilled out, washing over her. His eyes filled with tears, before streaming down his cheeks. "Why did you ever bring her here?"

"Because you would have never gotten a child on me."

His hand cupped the back of her head. He pressed his forehead to hers. "I couldn't have. Too risky." *A child of the House of Mor-Lath will destroy him.*

The prophecy echoed in her head, pushing all other thoughts out of the way. She swallowed.

His voice shook. "Don't you realize you've brought our destruction into your house? You've nurtured it, you're raising it. She will turn on us."

Adrastea's throat tightened. "No. I cannot believe that. She was blessed by the Light."

"The Light would see us fail," he insisted.

"The Light would see us succeed," she countered. "Why can't you see that?"

"They play games with us." He indicated Harianne. "Really. A mother happens to die, leaving a helpless child for you to rescue, who happens to be a mashiah? Did you think that was coincidence?"

"I doubt the Light would choose this roundabout way of destroying us. They've had far too many easier chances." They could have destroyed him when he was pinned to the table. They could have not created her in the first place. They had to have a reason for what They'd done.

"Oh no," he replied. "They've got a plan."

"Oh? What?"

He didn't answer her.

She pushed away from him. "How do you expect to win in the final battle if you cannot beat them in something like this?"

He looked at her. Then he looked over at her family, ready to guard Harianne with their lives, if necessary. She felt more thoughts tumbling through his head, although she was not privy to their contents. Finally, he asked, "What would you have me do?"

Adrastea had been doing some thinking too. "A *son* of Mor-Lath might very well have destroyed you. How would you have treated a son? Kindly? Gently?" She shook her head and turned away.

Ah, Harianne. Adrastea's heart swelled when she thought of her. It did not matter that she'd not borne the child of her own belly. She bore her in her heart. Could he not see that? "But how would you treat a daughter?"

His response was cold. "She is not my daughter."

Adrastea did not argue with that. "What if you could influence the outcome of prophecy? I saw many possibilities. Not all of them ended in your death."

Ari stood straighter. "Pity."

Adrastea looked at Mikal, brother and mayor. Here was a man who would never have children of his own. Yet he treated Harianne with the warmest of hearts, as Natan had given Mikal and herself great love.

"Do not kill my child, Mor-Lath." It was both advice and warning. "Find another way."

He leaned back against the wall, his head bowed. "You are a harsh woman, Adrastea."

Adrastea came up to Harianne, still enveloped in the arms of women who cared, guarded by men who loved her. She kissed her daughter on the forehead. "Garie, can you take her for a little walk? I'll bet Aunt Ari's got a biscuit in her pantry she can have."

Ari frowned, but she released Berengaria. "Will you be all right?" she asked her niece.

Adrastea nodded. "Everything will be all right."

She got a spontaneous hug from Ari. "Sometimes I don't know one day to the next if I'll ever see you again, girl."

"It looks like I'll be spending a lot more time here."

Natan came forward and enveloped his niece and Ari with a bear hug. "You will come see us tonight," he ordered. "We will need your regular reassurance."

"I'm not leaving," Adrastea replied. "I'm just going to sort out a few more things. I'd prefer not to have an audience."

Mikal had put his arm about Berengaria and Harianne. The three of them went out the kitchen door. Ari and Natan followed, the aura of their concern wafting in their wake.

Only after everyone was gone, did Adrastea approach her husband. "Something else is on your mind." She put a gentle hand to his face.

He did not look up. "I do not like a mashiah in your life. I do not like having to share you with a child. I do not like that another man—" He swallowed. "I should have never healed you. I do not like the possibility that you might be with child. He was also a mashiah, your abductor. That frightens me very much."

She cupped his face in both hands but did not raise it up. "Your life is ruled very much by fear. I do not know how you can handle it."

She called upon the Deeper Power. He did not respond. Gently, she sent a few tendrils of thought into his heart. It was not hard, thanks to the connection he'd forged between them earlier.

He did not resist but let her work.

She found the knot within him. one line at a time, she unraveled it. Like always, it fought her attempts, wanting to tangle back up into a bundle of worry, but she wouldn't let it.

She wanted to snip the lines, like Master Non had disconnected her, but the lines refused to be cut.

No matter. They would always be there. If she could convince it not to retangle, it wouldn't matter.

That knot kept wanting to tie back up. "Give yourself over to me," she requested.

He laid his head on her shoulder. "I can't."

"You can." She teased the knot loose and kept it that way. Her arms slipped along his shoulders. She drew him close. "You need to trust me."

Another memory bubbled to the surface. Once, when Harianne was just born, they'd had a similar engagement. He'd given her all his fear and rage—thousands of years of it. He hadn't let go of it. That's when she'd realized what they needed to do. "Trust in me. Trust in this one thing."

His arms slid around her waist, pulling her in tight. She felt sorrow flood through him. It spilled out over her. She had to fight to keep it from influencing her.

For the rest of the afternoon she held him, with his broken heart and contrite spirit, keeping that knot of fear free so his soul could heal.

As the sun descended to the horizon, she felt Berengaria and Harianne returning. It would be suppertime soon.

"Trust me," she finally said. "Believe in me and let me lead in these things."

He looked at her. "I'm not fully convinced leaving a mashiah child is the best course of action."

Nervous footsteps, hesitant, mounted the porch. She couldn't blame Berengaria's nerves.

"Please, try it my way first. Can you do that?"

"Do I have a choice?"

She smiled at him. "You always have a choice. You don't like the consequences. That's all."

A tenuous knock rang out on the door.

"In a moment," Adrastea called out.

Mor-Lath slipped from her embrace. "I'll wait for you upstairs. I have no desire to see either one of them."

Only when he was gone from sight, did she open the door.

Harianne rushed into the house, heedless of any danger present. She headed straight for the kitchen. Soon, Adrastea hear her rustling about the pantry. It was hard to think of the world turning for other people. For them it was dinnertime.

Berengaria did not cross the threshold. "Is he still here?"

"Yes," Adrastea replied, honest. She glanced upwards.

Berengaria still hesitated. "Is it safe?"

"I stake my life on it."

She had to consider this. "I have your word?"

"You do."

Only then, did Berengaria come in. "I hope you are right."

An uneasy truce fell over Adrastea's house and, to some extent, the village. After Harianne fell asleep that night, oblivious to the precariousness of her future, Adrastea cheated. She sent a gentle request of *sleep* to Berengaria, so the priestess dropped off much sooner than she normally would have.

Adrastea held her promise of visiting Natan and Ari. Mor-Lath shadowed her but remained outside. Once her aunt and uncle were reassured, she returned home, husband in tow.

He had brooded all evening, saying very little. At least the knot she'd loosened had not completely retied itself. The occasional poke kept it at bay.

Adrastea was rather tired. "I have had a very long day," she admitted, when they were alone in the bedroom. She changed into a long nightgown and clambered into the bed.

A wave of worry rolled through him, but also one of relief. "I nearly lost you." He joined her, after kicking off his boots. He spooned her and wrapped a protective arm about her waist.

Bits of her memory had been returning. She'd pieced together most of the past few days. "What happened with the High Council?"

"Dead, every one. The Cithran government is in disarray."

"And...?" Who was it who fought for them? "Our people?"

He let out a sigh as if he was tired as well. "Three more days of hiding, then they'll all leave Nyabern and regroup. I will bring them back to Avelia. The Tredan battalion can take care of the rest of Cithra."

A shudder ran through Adrastea. "I thought we weren't leaving Sacred Spring."

He didn't answer her.

"Mor-Lath?"

"It'll be fine," he eventually replied. "I am a god, after all."

She would have to be satisfied with that answer. She changed the subject. "You wouldn't have left Berengaria, would you?"

His answer was swifter. "No. But you are more important than she."

"I don't think she would like to know that."

"Sometimes we are confronted with facts we do not like."

Adrastea shifted position. "She is not happy with you."

"I know."

She drew in a deep breath. "I would like it if you could make up with her. It would make for a harmonious household."

He pressed his face to her hair. "If I promise to make it up to her tomorrow, will you sleep tonight?"

It was the best she'd get.

And she was tired. Now that she thought about it, she could not stop the yawns.

"Sleep," he suggested, without a trace of Power. "I will watch over you."

Adrastea had no idea if he slept that night or not. She spent the rest of it completely dead to the world.

The next morning, Mor-Lath sat in Adrastea's kitchen, his back to the door. While his wife slumbered upstairs, he'd explored every nook and cranny of her home. She'd built it well, despite her claim of simplicity. No drafts snaked about his ankles. The window glass was thick and clear. Although plain, the fixtures were of excellent quality, even her crockery.

A cup of chocolate sat before him, chocolate he had to summon from the temple. The small bottle of milk he'd fetched from her cellar. Again, she'd cheated with the Deeper Power there, as a certain corner was cooler than the rest. There she kept perishables like milk.

The bottle sat on the table, hardly bigger than his hand. He'd used more than half already. He might have used the whole bottle, had he been more inclined to thirst this morning.

Adrastea still slept. The rest of the household stirred.

Little feet pattered on the floor above. He listened to them. The mashiah child. Everyone else might have been fooled by her innocence in youth, but Mor-Lath knew better. Childhood was but a blink of an eye. Soon she would be older, with thoughts and opinions of her own. And attitude.

Larger feet, not as fast, joined the little feet. They followed as the little feet scampered down the stairs.

Ah, he was about to have company.

Berengaria's voice called something out to the child. The child never slowed. She came down the stairs, sprinted through the living room, and burst through the door of the kitchen.

She was clad only in a nightgown, her blondish hair askew, the energy of the morning radiating from her limbs.

Once in the kitchen, did she pause, surveying her scene. Her eyes focused on the bottle of milk.

So up on a chair she went to reach it. Without a second thought, she lifted it to her lips and drank.

Berengaria came through the door, "Harianne, we need to—" She froze. Unlike the child, she did see Mor-Lath. Her heart froze for a moment.

"No!" she cried, snatching Harianne off the chair and backing towards the door. The bottle of milk slipped from the child's fingers. It hit the edge of the table, fell to the wooden floor and shattered. White milk splashed out.

Mor-Lath lifted his chocolate and took a sip. "Calm yourself, Berengaria." He used his most gentle voice. "I'm not going to kill the child today." With a wave of his hand, the bottle reformed itself, the milk retreated back to its home. He set it on the table.

The door closed behind Berengaria, blocking her escape. Her back hit against it and she struggled with the doorknob. Harianne picked up on Berengaria's panic; how could she not? She wailed her concern, breaking the fragile morning peace of the kitchen. Berengaria shouted for Adrastea as she pulled at the door.

"She won't hear you." Mor-Lath traced the edge of his cup with a finger. "Let her sleep."

Berengaria raced around the perimeter of the kitchen, knocking things off the edge of the sink on her way to the outside door. "I'll not let you kill this child."

But Mor-Lath had locked that door as well.

He held the cup in his hands. Hmm. His chocolate was a bit cold. A little channel of Power and it warmed up again. To Berengaria, he said, *"Calm."*

The Deeper Power wrapped around the priestess. Her mood evened. Her stern expression did not leave her face. In her arms, Harianne calmed down as well.

Despite this, Berengaria stood her ground. "I will not let you manipulate me. I will defend this child with my life."

He sipped from his cup. "I believe you." She'd changed, since coming to live here. He saw his wife's influence in her defiance.

She tried the back kitchen door again. It wouldn't open. "Let us go."

"How about we talk first?"

She scooted closer to the kitchen sink, hoping for a knife or something in there. "No."

He looked up at her. "Please?"

Harianne squirmed. "Garie. I'm hungry."

"Later," Berengaria murmured to her.

"But, Garie." She wriggled until the priestess dropped her.

"Wait—" she cried, but it was too late. Harianne climbed back up on the chair and reclaimed her bottle of milk. She sat back in the chair and drained the lot.

Berengaria threw her hands up in the air.

As Harianne drank, she studied Mor-Lath with her dark eyes. When she finished, she sighed and wiped her mouth with the back of her hand. She continued to observe him. "I want Mama."

"She's asleep," Mor-Lath replied.

Harianne looked at him then turned to Berengaria. "No. Where's Mama?"

Mor-Lath didn't give her an opportunity to answer. "Berengaria. Please, sit down. We need to set some things straight."

Berengaria stood by the sink, her arms folded tightly around her. "I can't think of anything we have to say to each other."

He shrugged. "I would have thought you plenty to say." He gestured to the chair opposite himself.

After some consideration she sat at the table across from him. "Really? You want to hear how angry I am with you?"

Harianne, no longer the center of attention, got up and raided the pantry. Berengaria didn't care. Her anger towards Mor-Lath radiated in waves. "Where shall I start?"

"With you," he replied.

She inhaled sharply through her nose. "All right. How about you breaking a centuries-old rule?" She put her fingers to her temples. "Is there a single temple priestess you didn't molest?"

Molest was such an ugly word. And rather inaccurate. "Honestly? Most of them."

"Oh, so just a select few. Me, Radelisa, Iocaste…" She weighed the names she knew, and her speculations. "Garsinda too? Is that why she's high priestess?"

He shook his head. "Not her. Never her." He shuddered. There was something about her that didn't mesh. There was no chemistry. Her orderliness made for an adequate high priestess, but her blood didn't burn. Also… He noticed a pattern in the priestesses he chose. "I chose those with fire in their hearts."

"You chose those closest to your wife."

Meanwhile, Harianne brought over jars and bottles and random things, piling them on the table. Berengaria simply shoved them aside.

"You should never have done it." She waved her hands in frustration. "Sometimes I think you are the god of idiots."

He reached out and caught her hand. "Berengaria. I am sorry. I did behave badly."

She wasn't finished. "You have been a neglectful god. How often have you been to the temple to succor the faithful? Adrastea has gone at least once a week. I say she's been a better god than you."

"In my defense, I've had the whole world on my mind."

She wasn't buying it. "You've always had the whole world on your mind. And yet you always made time.

"Then suddenly, you bring home a Bride and your brain turns inside-out. If I didn't like her so much, I'd swear that was the worst mistake you've ever made."

"No. My worst mistake was not listening to her."

Berengaria considered this. Her rage cooled somewhat. "Are you listening to her now?"

"She wants me to make peace with you."

"Yes? How?"

He studied his cup, which had gone cold again. "She didn't offer any particular suggestions. I believe she would have me ask you what would make you happy."

Berengaria didn't answer right way. She grew still, weighing his words. Thoughts tumbled through her head, though what they were eluded him at the moment. Her gaze roamed to the child.

She rose from the table in a burst of energy and tidied away all the bottles and jars Harianne had brought out. "What are you doing?" she chided the little girl.

Harianne stood there with a bottle of peaches. "Mama needs bre'fast too."

"She's asleep right now."

Harianne frowned. "Mamas don't sleep." She looked over at Mor-Lath. "You're supposed to be asleep. Mama says you're not supposed to wake up."

Mor-Lath blinked. "Oh, really?"

Berengaria closed the pantry. "It was a lot nicer when you were asleep." Her eyes looked upwards. "She was much happier with you asleep." She considered her words. "It's the first time I ever saw her not mad at you."

He pushed his cup of chocolate away. "I've been awake for weeks."

"And she is distracted."

He held up a finger. "But not angry."

"Annoyed," Berengaria countered.

"Not as much as you think."

"I disagree." She took the jar of peaches from Harianne and sat down at the table. Harianne protested.

Berengaria sighed. She rose from the table, opened the peaches, scooped some into a bowl and set it down for Harianne. "There. Eat that. We'll feed your mama when she's awake."

The child accepted the bowl of peaches. She scooped them into her mouth with a too-big spoon. "Mamas don't sleep."

Once the child was sufficiently distracted, Berengaria turned her attention back to Mor-Lath.

"You like this domestic kind of life, don't you?" he asked her.

"I do. It's peaceful. I wish you'd go away so we can have peace once more."

He shook his head. "I'm not leaving Adrastea's side ever again."

Berengaria's fingers traced the edge of his chocolate cup. "I doubt she'll like that."

"I say she will."

"She won't." Her fingers teased the cup her way until she could hook it with her finger. She lifted it and sipped delicately.

"Hey. That's mine."

Her eyes met his over the rim of the cup. "Not anymore." She had to goad him, didn't she?

"I'm not leaving." He leaned back, hands behind his head. "Then we have no choice but to make peace."

She looked away as she finished his chocolate.

Silence fell between them, broken only by Harianne's noisy slurping of canned peaches.

Mor-Lath studied his former priestess. "You never told me what you wanted."

"I'm not bought by a few trinkets."

"You never were, Berengaria." He spoke her name low and gently.

She put down the cup. "I want for nothing. I also know if you threaten me in any way, you will bring the wrath of your wife upon your head." She gestured to the child. "Threaten her as well, same thing."

"Ah," he replied. "Is that all you want?"

"I'm not expressing any wishes. I'm stating facts." She leaned across the table. "You know what I want more than anything else? I wish I had the old Mor-Lath back. The one you were before you got married. But I know that will never happen. She's changed you permanently and I am sorry for it."

He folded his hands across his chest as he considered her request. "And who was the old Mor-Lath to you?"

"You were reliable. You were kind. You were thoughtful. Sometimes strict, but fair."

"Is that what you want me to be?"

She tilted her head. "I don't know if you can ever be that again. I've seen too much of your dark side to be able to believe, even if you were."

It hurt she'd lost such faith in him. "I can't be any different from what I am."

"No, you can't. But you can treat her better. You once treated us well. I know it's in your power."

He sat up. "What? That's it?"

"It is everything. The only problem in this house is you. You are disruptive. If you must stay, stop being disruptive." She looked wistfully at the empty cup. "Her Holiness treats me well. I would do anything for her."

His voice was low. "You would die for her?" Yesterday he'd discovered Harianne's mashiannic qualities. Berengaria had placed herself between him and the child. He had terrified her. Regardless, she had stood up to him.

A shudder ran up her back as the memories of yesterday filled her heart. Tears welled in her eyes and spilled down her face. Sobs wracked her body and she collapsed to the table in grief. Perhaps there was some relief, but her delayed fear nearly drowned it out.

The child didn't expect that. She stopped slurping the last of the juice from her bowl. "Garie?" Her voice echoed alarm and concern.

Berengaria gathered the child into her lap, to hug her tightly. There she rocked and she cried, until the first wave of her fear ebbed.

Mor-Lath waited. He could not rush her.

Finally, she pulled herself together. "I truly expected you to kill me. I know how much you fear this child." She stroked Harianne's head. Likewise, Harianne gently patted Berengaria's arm. "If you wanted her dead, nothing would stop you. I know that. I would still stand between you and her."

He swallowed. "You honestly thought I would kill you?"

She nodded. "One way or another. Had you simply brushed me aside—" Her throat choked up.

He finished her sentence for her. "You would have attacked me. That would have been a grave sin." His voice took on a dangerous tone.

She confessed. "Before, something like that would have been unthinkable. But had Harianne died and I lived, I could not have faced Her Holiness. That," she moaned, "would have been worse."

He traced the woodgrain of the table with his finger. "I understand. I fear her wrath as well."

"Oh no. She's never been angry with me. It's her disappointment I could not bear." She sniffed and wiped her nose with the back of her hand.

It hurt that she was more loyal to his wife than to him. "You put me in a difficult position."

She sniffed again. "Not I."

She was right. He looked at the child, safely ensconced in her arms. Was this how the mashiah child would destroy him, by turning everyone against him? He should never have let his wife keep the creature.

She rose from the table, the child still in her arms. "I thought you had figured out the secret of a harmonious marriage. Still looks like you have some ways to go."

She went to the door, but it refused to budge. Berengaria sighed. "Why won't you let me go?"

He followed her. "Are we at peace with each other?"

The steel returned to her backbone. "Are you at peace with me? Are you at peace with your wife, that you can respect her wishes regarding Harianne? Are you at peace with yourself that you are not threatened by a mere child?" Her breath still shuddered in fear, but she would not let that fear conquer her.

He considered her questions. She had been hanging out with his wife too much. "One miracle at a time."

He unlocked the door. It creaked open.

Berengaria did not go through it. "I will have your word, God of Wealth. I do not want to have to be looking over my shoulder constantly. You will not put me in a hard place. If you do, I will choose her over you."

He stood. She did not withdraw. He drew closer, almost close enough to touch. "I do not think you are in a position to bargain. And you are still my priestess."

"I am both your priestess. You two should be united in purpose. Give me your word."

"And if I don't?"

"Then you are still the great fool who would act counter to his wife."

"You have so little faith in me?" Why did she insist on taking Adrastea's side?

"Right now? Yes."

He retreated. She was not to be intimidated. "I did not think a god had to earn his faith."

"Prove to me I can trust you once more."

Something upstairs tugged at his awareness. His wife stirred and would soon wake. "Faith and trust are two different things."

"They're connected. Prove to me I can trust you. My faith will follow."

He considered this. How bad did he need this priestess' good will? As she seemed to be a particular favorite of his wife, he needed it very much. "I promise I will not kill the child today."

"Not good enough." Oh, she was pushing it.

"It's the best you're going to get. Ask me again tomorrow." Adrastea was going to wake any minute. He did not want her to find him gone. "Don't think this discussion is over."

She drew in a fortifying breath. "I am nowhere near finished with you," she replied.

"I'll take that as a comfort." Without a further word, he vanished.

Chapter 22

Adrastea woke with Mor-Lath's head on her belly. Her heart beat hard for a moment as the echoes of her bad dreams faded away. She relaxed when she recognized her husband. "What are you doing?" She stroked his hair. His knot of fear had tightened while she was sleeping.

"Shh," he replied.

She obliged for a few moments. "Hear anything?"

"No. But it might be too soon."

She put her hand to the line on her shoulder, feeling his concern. "What is it?"

"Nothing, I hope."

She sat up, the bedclothes sliding over his head. He put a hand on her thigh to steady himself. "Are you quite finished?" she asked.

He confessed, "I don't know what I would do if there was another man's child in your belly." His voice quivered at the end.

A similar wave of concern rippled through her soul. She slid out from under his head. "I doubt I'm pregnant. I can tell you for sure in a day or two." She climbed out of bed and checked the water in the washing bowl. A touch of Deeper Power warmed it up nicely. No, she needed hot water. Lots of it. She had to wash her face, her arms, her legs, everything.

He followed her. "You can't know that."

"Sure, I can." She pointed her finger at the door and drew a line straight down. Once the door was locked, she pulled off her nightgown and gave herself a thorough wash. Perhaps she should bring up the tub. Maybe a full bath would be better. A dip in the spring? Even the bathing pool at the temple called her. Shame she couldn't go.

Mor-Lath kept himself busy by pacing. "You must let me know as soon as possible."

"Oh? Why? You've got nine months to panic if I am." She pushed away those small tendrils of concern that threatened to grow around her chest.

He froze. "Surely you wouldn't consider keeping it."

Adrastea rolled her eyes. "I'm not pregnant." Finished with her ablutions, she toweled herself dry before dressing. "Besides, he was so incompetent, I doubt anything would have stuck." That's what she told herself. A shudder ran through her.

"Competency has nothing to do with it."

She settled her skirt about her hips before lacing her bodice. "And you would know, because...?"

"Don't mock me, woman." A niggle of fear echoed between their connection.

Once properly clad, she slid her arms about his waist. "Are you all right?"

He wrapped his arms about her and pulled her close, burying his face in her hair. "You're mine. I wish I could erase everything about him from you."

"He's already done a pretty good job of that." Her soul still remembered the sharp pings of the Lines snapping back into her when they were severed.

"I..." he drew in a deep breath. "I can't help but worry."

She pulled back from him. "Well, stop it. Don't you have a war to distract you?"

"That's something I need to discuss with you. Tomorrow the Avelians are leaving Cithra. I need to go instruct them."

A slight frown of worry creased her forehead. It deepened as memories of her time as Master Non's prisoner came back to her. She'd been such an easy target. "I can't go with you."

He buried his lips in her hair. "I don't want you to."

"Do you have to go?" Nerves tugged at her stomach. As annoying as his presence was, his absence terrified her. Her arms tightened about his waist.

"I'll be back soon. He can't get you as long as you stay in Sacred Spring."

She fought her anxiety and lost. It welled up within her and overwhelmed her senses. She buried her face in his shoulder and cried.

"Adrastea?" Her tears surprised him as much as her.

She could only shake her head. Her body shook with sobs and her knees gave way.

Mor-Lath scooped her into his lap as he sat on the bed. His confusion and worry flooded through the line. She felt worse. He sorted through her fear, her stress, her anxiety, her rage—yes, there was rage in there, rage at being kidnapped, at being naive enough to let it happen, at Master Non for kidnapping her.

"He can't get you here," her husband whispered in her ear. "He simply can't."

That may be so, but she still wanted to cry. Her cheeks burned under hot tears. "It feels like he's still in here." She thumped hard on her head with her fingers.

He captured her hand and brought it back down. "He's not. I would know if he was."

"How can you?" she snapped.

He laid his forehead against hers. "Give your thoughts to me?" It was a question, not a command.

Adrastea hesitated. Then she nodded.

Now it was a command: "Give your thoughts to me." He couldn't have gotten in any other way.

The pain of him entering her head made her gasp. Why did it have to hurt so? She held out against the pain while he roamed her memories. The sickly-sweet pear essence. The black table where all the Lines were severed. The mock-wedding. As Mor-Lath sorted through her memories, Adrastea recalled everything, except her kidnapper's face. When it came to him, it was a blankness, like a nebulous gray shadow that lurked only out of the corner of one's eye.

He's very good," Mor-Lath commented. Wherever he looked, nothing remained. *He has completely severed himself from you.*

Mor-Lath pulled out just before the bedding. A shudder ran through his frame.

Immediately, Adrastea felt alone in her head. Very alone. Without Mor-Lath, she went over the consummation, only there was no face. It was as if he wasn't there. "Don't you want to know everything?" she asked.

He shook his head, a tight movement. "I don't want to know." The conflict that warred in him was strong enough to echo to her.

"What?"

A brief frown wrinkled his brow. "How do you feel?"

She drew a ragged breath, then another, more even one. Other than a headache? "A little better."

He stroked her face and bent in for a gentle kiss. "I have work. I'll see you later."

❦

The next morning, with Mor-Lath gone, Adrastea was out of sorts. She wanted to kick the washbucket, she wanted to hurl a jar of jam against the wall, she wanted to scream at everyone. She even toyed with the possibility of finding Master Non, just so she could bash his head in. This was his fault, and by the Light, when she got her hands on him, he was going to pay.

Berengaria kicked her out of the house. "Go see if Ari needs any help," she ordered, shoving her out the door.

While her first instinct was to resist Berengaria's firm suggestion, a niggle told her that she was just being a good priestess.

"Fine," she snapped. She stomped her way out of the house and strode through the streets. Several people gave her one look and moved out of her way.

When she got to Ari's place, she stormed into the stillroom. Ari sat at the bench, poring over the medicinal text Adrastea had loaned her. "Hello." Then she took another look at Adrastea's dark face. "What's that bastard done now?"

"Oh," she cried, throwing her hands in the air in exasperation. "He keeps wanting—" She composed herself. "There's something he wants to know, but I can't give him an answer. Not yet."

Ari pushed her book back. "He'll simply have to wait, then." Ari gave a satisfied smile.

Impatience gnawed at Adrastea's insides. "I wish I didn't have to wait." She rummaged Ari's shelves, looking through her bottles and boxes of herbs. "You got any powdered dandelion leaves?"

"Yeah— Wait." Ari slid off her stood. She laid a hand on Adrastea's arm. "Adrastea?" Urgency deepened her voice. "Are you...?" Ari knew exactly what one could use dandelion for in certain cases. Mix enough of it with a woman's urine, if the urine turned red, the woman was pregnant.

Adrastea pressed both hands to her mouth to hold back the tears. Ari put an arm about her.

Salle entered the stillroom, a basketful in her arms.

Ari viciously waved her out.

Salle stopped, got the clue, turned on a heel and marched back out.

The tears spilled out Adrastea's eyes and a confession from her lips. "It's a possibility." She drew a shaky breath. "If I am, it's not Mor-Lath's."

Silence fell across the stillroom. Ari blinked at her former journeyman several times.

"WHAT?" she shrieked as it all came together.

Adrastea, tear-damp and shaking, told Ari the whole story of her abduction, what she could remember. "He'd completely severed my connection to everything and everyone. I had no memory of my life. There was a ceremony and consummation." She sniffed.

Ari embraced her niece. "Oh, dear child," she breathed. "I'm so sorry." All she could do was hold her until Adrastea had cried herself out. "You know, there are ways..."

Adrastea sniffed and wiped her nose on her sleeve. Ari fished out a hanky from her apron pocket. "I know." Ari had not neglected that aspect of her education. "But first I've got to find out if that sort of thing is necessary."

Ari sighed. "If it's only been a week or so, dandelion isn't going to give you an accurate result. With that, you need to be a month or two along before you could get a reading." Ari would choose to act well before dandelion told them anything. "When are you supposed to get your monthly course?"

"Tomorrow, if I'm lucky."

"What? You mean you haven't missed anything yet?" Ari rolled her eyes. "Good grief, girl. You could have at least waited until tomorrow before coming and crying to me."

"I know," she snuffled. "But I can't stand waiting." Her soul still ached from the stress of her kidnapping. Her hands shook.

"No woman can," Ari replied dryly. "Anyhow, one day will not matter either way. You want me to give you something to help you sleep?"

She turned down the offer. "I've slept enough this week."

"Want me to give you something to make him sleep?" Her voice was too eager.

"I doubt it'd work."

Ari sighed in disappointment. "You're probably right. He drinks enough of my beer and never gets drunk. Now, what kind of life is that?"

Adrastea went to the sink and washed her face.

"Feeling better?" Ari asked.

She nodded. "It hit me harder than I expected."

Ari had a remark sitting on her tongue, but she held it back. "Now, let yourself be distracted. I could use your assistance."

Adrastea gave her a small, relieved chuckle. "Sure. Nothing work can't cure, right?"

"That's what I've always said." Ari consulted the medical book. "I was thinking of attempting this burn salve. It uses aloe as a base, with poppy tar oil. I was wondering if I could use psilocybin instead."

Adrastea perked up. "You have psilocybin?"

Ari pointed a warning finger at her. "Not for you."

"Wild lettuce?"

Her aunt sighed. "Really."

"There are a few things I would like to forget."

A knock rang out on the kitchen door. "All clear?" Salle called from the other side.

"Yes," Ari replied. To Adrastea, she said, "I can't keep my journeyman out forever."

Salle came in, basket in hand. She dumped its herbal contents on the bench and headed out for more.

By habit, Adrastea sorted through the plucked leaves. "You know, m—my kidnapper? He was really bad—in bed, you know."

"What? Your kidnapper?"

She nodded. "Worst sex of anyone's life."

"Not that you've had the best experiences to judge by." Ari joined her in sorting herbery.

Adrastea looked aside, a blush suffusing her cheeks.

Ari paused, the herbs before her forgotten. "Wait. You saying that husband of yours can actually do something right?"

Adrastea conceded, "He has had a fair bit of practice."

The healer gave a snort of contempt. "Far too much, I'd say." She waved her hands. "That's something I don't want to think about. However, if you and he are going to indulge in that sort of thing, I'd prefer you take some precautions. I remember the last time you had a pregnancy scare."

It took Adrastea a few moments before she remembered her sterilization.

"I swear," said Ari. "He ever do anything like that again, I will kill him. God or no god."

Adrastea's heart, still battered from her earlier crying, lifted a little. Wouldn't it have been nice if Ari had the touch of a mashiah about her?

"You're right. Let's see what tomorrow brings."

The next afternoon, like clockwork, her cycle turned over. It's like the blood released itself all at once, soaking her skirt and the chair she sat in as she read at the kitchen table. She had never been so happy for that Time of the Month to come. But must it have come with such a vengeance?

She laid a hand over the line on her shoulder. Her husband was far away in Cithra. *Not pregnant,* she told Mor-Lath.

Two heartbeats later he appeared in front of her in the kitchen. Lifting her up by the arms, he bussed her enthusiastically on the lips. His relief, as he drew her into his arms, flowed over her like a warm shower. It was not the only warm fluid running.

Before her embarrassment over the mess peaked, he had set her down and was gone, only a faint swirl of air left behind.

At least the relief remained.

Palus and a handful other Avelians, including several injured priestesses and a few sergeants and privates, holed up in a waterfront tavern. They'd appropriated it from the previous owners just before the final assault on the High Council. The bodies of the owners they had tossed in the river, to become yet more anonymous floating corpses. Other Avelians had selected rooms here and there in the neighborhood, empty either by random chance or by the skills of the army. For the past three days, everyone had laid low, letting the chaos of a leaderless nation shake everything up.

In the tavern, the sergeants guarded the doorway, inviting in any Cithran who approached them. Once inside, they were relieved of their purses and their lives, to be tossed out, just another dead body.

Yesterday, Cithrans stopped coming.

Today the Avelians had run out of beer and hope. Tomorrow was the third day. Tomorrow, they would unite with the rest of their people. Where, when, and what would happen next were the unasked questions that hung in the air between them all.

Palus sat at a table, a bowl empty of gruel before him. Whatever meat the innkeeper had was long gone, as was anything safe to drink.

One of the privates had been sent off to locate a major, or possibly a colonel—someone who could tell them what they were supposed to do. He had not returned. The sun had long left the skies and darkness fell over the inn. One priest had lit a solitary lamp. Otherwise, the inn sat in darkness.

Had Nyabern not been torn by war, the tavern would have been filling with navvies and sailors, all looking for grog and more. But nobody had come that day. Palus liked it like that. The soldiers were restless. Some were considering slipping out and cracking open random Cithran heads. A few days cooped up with nothing to do had made them edgy.

The tavern door opened. It was not the private, but a man in a familiar brown robe. He was alone.

The soldiers came to readiness, their alertness fueled by their suppressed battle-lust. Palus rose to his feet. "Ah, a wanderer, come to drink, perhaps?" Wander. That was their password. Every Avelian had come to use that term to tell each other apart from possible enemies. Anyone who did not use the word in reply would die on the spot.

The stranger pushed back the hood of his robe. "We wander too much these days, I think."

Palus squinted at the stranger in the dim light. His hair was dark, albeit streaked with silver at the sides. His eyes burned and the aura about him drew a sense of devotion from Palus.

"Holiness," he gasped, before dropping to his weary knees. The few priestesses in the main tavern room also fell to their knees. The soldiers stiffened to attention. Only their eyes darted back and forth, gauging the reactions of others. Were they remembering the curse His Holiness had laid on them at Feown? The common Avelians, last of all, sank to their knees. Chances are, none of them had ever met their god before.

Mor-Lath, the god who had driven them from Avelia, cursed them from Feown, and led them to battle in Cithra, had come at last. "You have all done as I have asked. You have served me well. Because of this, we are going home."

"What?" cried a priestess, one of the younger ones. "Home to Avelia?"

Mor-Lath smiled. "Yes, Claudi. Home to Avelia. You will wander no more."

The whole tavern erupted in cheers.

The god held up a finger. "However..." The cheers died down. "You may not find it as you remember it."

"But we are going home?" Palus asked.

"Did I not say that?"

Palus bowed his head. "Yes, Holiness." It would not do to invoke the god's wrath.

Mor-Lath made himself comfortable at a table. He motioned for all to gather near. As he waved his hand over the table, the lamp brightened. A map appeared in the pattern of the wood. "Here is what you will do—you all will do."

The map, apparently of Nyabern, had little figures moving. Mor-Lath put his finger on a particular spot near the river. "This is you. Tonight, you shall go out and find an anchored riverboat." The map zoomed in to show better detail of the river. Everyone watched as little figures came out of the tavern and up into a riverboat. "Kill the captain, the first and second mates, but leave everyone else alive who claims they are a sailor. You will need them. Treat them well. Anyone else—passengers, stowaways—you kill."

Palus sighed. He did not mean to. So much killing, their god required of them.

Mor-Lath patted the priest on the back. "Cheer up. Most of these anchored riverboats have a skeleton crew. If you are lucky, you might only need to kill one or two useless souls."

One of the sergeants smacked his fist into the palm of his hand. "Consider it done."

Mor-Lath continued. "Now, you will hold the riverboat until tomorrow. Come dawn, people will come. You will have withdrawn the gangplank. Should anyone risk coming on board, challenge their identity. Unless they are Avelian, refuse them entry. Say, 'captain's orders'."

The sergeant asked, "What if they claim they are the captain?"

"Call him a liar and shoot him." Mor-Lath looked the sergeant up and down. "You still have your firearms?"

"Sir, yes sir. Bit short on gunpowder, though."

Mor-Lath reached into his cloak and pulled out a bag. "This will be sufficient for your needs."

The sergeant thanked him and pocketed the gift.

Mor-Lath closed his eyes for a moment, then opened them. "Your injured people have been healed."

"Thank you," replied Claudi Priestess. "I had wondered how we'd get them to the boat."

Back to business at hand. "So," Mor-Lath continued, "come sunset, every Avelian who's going home should be on board the riverboats. Otherwise, they can stay behind.

"Every riverboat will be under our control. Once the sun sets, you are to leave on the boats and head for home. Stop at Feown to pick up your fellow countrymen. No doubt they want to go home as well."

He rose from the table. "So, Claudi? Where are your sisters?"

"Upstairs." She led the way to the recently-healed priestesses.

Once His Holiness was gone, Palus whooped with joy. The others were as enthusiastic. "We're going home! We're going home!" they chanted and danced. If there had been any beer left, they would have broached that casket.

They sang and danced and sounded just like a tavern should.

Only later did Palus notice Claudi return, her mood quite a contrast to the celebrating soldiers. He took her aside. "Something's wrong."

She looked up at him with haunted eyes. "Nothing important. I'll tell you later." She took a breath and steeled her courage. "We have a boat to secure."

The soldiers were more than happy to set out. A good boat theft was a perfect way to celebrate their upcoming emigration.

Montrof had been warned to expect the riverboats. He ensured the word spread, advising his fellow Avelians to leave what they were doing and be at the docks, or risk being left behind.

No Avelian wished to remain in Feown. At least they'd learned their lesson.

He had expected resistance from the government, but when Shereth had returned from her audience with the Duchess, she informed him that there would be no roadblocks to their departure.

On their way down the Great River, the riverboats stopped by the docks of Feown where scores of Avelians awaited them. As soon as one riverboat was full, it continued on down the river. Little by little, Feown lost its indentured work force.

He'd seen Palus on the deck of one boat. He even considered boarding then. But when he saw Shereth, also making sure everyone got out, he waved Palus on and stood by the priestess. The river stank, as rivers often did. The cry of birds wheeling about the boats battled with the slap of water against the pier.

She'd looked rather green since the night they'd received His Holiness' revelation. It was she who had delivered the news of their departure to Saraym. Perhaps it was that meeting that turned her stomach.

"Are you all right?" he asked her again.

She glanced at him, nodded and waved him away.

He wasn't to be dismissed that easily. "No, really. You look like you can't afford the price of breakfast."

The private joke elicited a wan smile from her. "I'll be fine. It will be good to be gone from here, be our own people." Despite the treaty, the Feowans had not treated the Avelians well. Slum housing, menial jobs, poor food, and the prejudice, both subtle and overt. Not a single Avelian chose to remain behind.

They all should be glad to be leaving. So why wasn't she? "What aren't you telling me?"

She considered his question, staring off to the other side of the river, so far away he doubted there would ever be a bridge that could span it. "I suppose I am pondering what we will do when we get home."

The thrill of leaving this place made his heart skip a beat. "Whatever we want, of course."

"Yes..." she replied, her voice unconvincing.

He laid hands on her shoulders and turned her to him. "You're not happy and not because Saraym yelled at you. There is nothing in our treaty that says we have to stay."

"I know. I helped write it." By the time Saraym had found an adequate translator, the treaty had been ratified and accepted by both sides.

"So, what's eating you from inside?"

She laid a hand over his. "I promise I'll tell you once we leave this place. Truly, I am glad to go."

He accepted her word.

By evening, the last of the Avelians had boarded the purloined riverboats. From the deck of this final boat Montrof and Shereth watched the city of Feown retreat into the dusk. "Good riddance." While Montrof's heart wanted to curse the place, his logic told him it would not do to risk the wrath of his god.

At least his god was favoring his people once more. Yes, it was good to go home.

They riverboats chugged down the river, a giant diasporic fleet. They anchored near the shore when it grew too dark to navigate. Montrof could not sleep for several hours, so great was his excitement. Eventually he dozed off and did not wake until much later that morning, with the boat well underway. Three days they were on the boats. Montrof's excitement tempered, but never waned.

As they approached Avelia, he noticed Shereth's nervousness increase. "You've got to tell me what's wrong."

She stood at the rail, gripping it tightly. "When His Holiness came to me, he revealed we would return home today. He told me everything I needed to know to get our people out."

That wasn't so bad. "So?"

She swayed. He put out a hand to steady her. He recognized this turn of the river, those hills. It was like waking up on a feastday.

"His Holiness also informed me what we must do when we return to Avelia."

"And will you tell me? Or am I to spend the rest of my life wondering what to do?" Maybe that wouldn't be so bad. He'd find a temple with a sunny courtyard and a good cook. He'd bless the people, counsel them, share stories. It would be a good life. What better way to end one's days?

Above them, the sky was a beautiful, clear spring day. A few clouds studded across and random birds flew by. He watched the jungle lining the riverbanks pass by. Soon it would give way to farmland and then the glorious city of Avelia itself. Sure, it'd be a bit worse for wear, but home was still home.

One more bend and they entered the straightaway.

He thought it was the straightaway. Surely, he'd be able to see the buildings of Avelian by now. A few wisps of smoke rose, but not nearly enough for a city.

Hundreds of boats of all types crowded the river along the straightaway, jostling for space. Theirs joined the line of ships desperate to dispel their cargo.

"Here we are," Shereth replied, her voice full of sorrow.

"What?" Montrof asked, craning his neck. "I don't see anything."

She pointed. "There."

Still nothing. Too many ships in the way.

Their riverboat nudged a smaller craft out of the way. Now Montrof saw.

Where a mighty city once stood, a vast brown scar marred the green landscape. Avelia, as he knew it, was completely gone.

Montrof sank to his knees. He put his face into his hands.

Shereth remained at the rail. "His Holiness told me what had happened. We are to start from nothing. We are to rebuild from scratch. Perhaps next time we will not forget the god who gave us our wealth in the first place."

Montrof laid down on the deck, feeling rather green. His temple, gone. His lovely sunny nook, gone. Now what?

Shereth sighed and dusted her hands. "I guess we need to get to work."

☙❧

Chapter 23

A knock rang out on the Millers' door. When Icole opened it, a floursack needle in her hands, she frowned at the stranger. "What do you want?"

He who knocked on the door brushed his lanky blond hair from his handsome face. A shame about Icole's rather unfortunate physiognomy, he thought. He wished her face was forgettable. He shuddered. Still, she'd been a faithful servant all these years. "You may call me Master Non."

For a mill, it was rather quiet. The grindstones in the other room were silent and only the faintest sound of creaking could be heard. Had they no wheat to grind?

He gave her a bow. "I have been sent by the One True god to keep watch on the Bride."

Icole's countenance changed. She laid her hand on her heart in a sign of devotion. "May he watch over us all." She turned and bellowed into the mill. "Tedrick!"

She looked about, in case they were being observed. Who would be watching them, this far from town? Ushering Master Non in, she shut the door once he was safely inside. "Tedrick!" she bellowed again. Was this her idea of being secretive? The room held no furniture, only several sacks of flour, some open, some stitched shut. They lined one end of the empty room. One door led to the mill, the other, perhaps the rest of the house.

Tedrick, just as ugly as Icole, came in from the mill, dusting flour off his hands. "What?" He saw the stranger. "Welcome, fellow. Don't get too many guests here."

Icole hissed at him, as if in an awkward social situation. "He's from back home," she said, trying to talk without letting her lips move. "He's come to watch *her*."

Master Non resisted the urge to roll his eyes. Instead, he gave another bow. "I have been sent."

Tedrick harrumphed. "Haven't we all?"

"I've come to watch the Bride."

Tedrick shrugged. "So?"

Didn't this man care at all? "I've come to remove her."

A short ha of laughter pushed up out of him. "Good luck with that." Tedrick turned back to the mill.

Was there something he needed to know? "What can you tell me?"

Tedrick paused in the doorway. "Not much to tell. Only seen her a few times. We don't go into the town."

Oh, of all the incompetence! "I thought you were sent to watch her."

"We did." Icole jumped to her husband's defense. "She came down here once, she did."

Tedrick shot a warning glance to his wife. Like Master Non was going to miss that. "What did she do?"

Icole and Tedrick looked at each other. "Fixed summat was broken. Used her magic." Then they clammed up.

There was something else they weren't telling him. "Does she do that often?"

Icole slunk off to the other side of the room. She passed through the door, presumably to a kitchen, deserting Tedrick.

Master Non would have his answers, one way or another. "What does she fix?"

Tedrick looked away. "She done paved the roads with her magic. Laid all them stones out."

He blinked at the miller. The Bride has all this power and she's tending infrastructure? What next? Emptying the night soil? Pulling weeds? "Anything else she does?"

Tedrick shrugged. "She don't leave the town much."

He folded his arms. "Oh? So, you see her when you go to town?"

It seemed Tedrick's eyes wanted to look at something, anything, other than the man before him. Oh, you should be afraid, Master Non thought. "You're saying you don't see her there?" Had he come all this way for nothing?

The miller shuffled his feet and kept looking to see when he wife would return. "No, not saying that. Just that we don't go to town."

"And why not?" His annoyance with this little man increased. Were they so yokel they couldn't even wander into town regularly? "Too many big houses for you? Too many people?"

"We can't go into town."

His eyes narrowed. "Who has forbidden you to go into town?"

Plain, unvarnished worry replaced the nervousness on Tedrick's face. "We don't know. We tried, but we couldn't go."

Master Non sighed. The man was a complete idiot.

The wife, Icole, came through, a steaming teapot in her hands and several beakers in her apron pockets. "You would like some tea?"

Tea? At this time of day? What an odd request. Master Non didn't know if he could stomach much more of this pair.

Without waiting for an answer, she poured a beaker full of the steaming stuff and shoved it into his hands. She did not tip one for her husband. "Tedrick, the mill needs tending."

It was an excuse. The relief on Tedrick's face was so obvious, Master Non would not have been surprised had the miller clapped his hands and skipped from the room. He hurried off, happy to be out of there.

Icole turned to leave, but Master Non grabbed her arm. "Please, join me."

She looked at his hand, his long fingers tight around her upper arm. She looked about the room—anywhere but him. Why the hesitation?

She sighed, obviously unable to think of a good excuse. "The country folk here do say tea before business."

He offered her his beaker. No way he would drink anything she had not tasted first.

"Ta." She shifted the teapot to one hand. She took the mug and without guile, drank deeply.

Ah. So, it wasn't poisoned after all.

"Here." She handed him the hot teapot. He juggled its burningness until he had grip of the cooler handle. She gave him another beaker from her apron, this one chipped on the edge.

It had been a long journey; he helped himself.

"Tell me," Master Non asked, after he'd sipped the tedious brew, "how often do you go to town?"

"Don't never go. Can't get to town."

Would she be insulted if he didn't finish his horrible tea? "What? Never? Why?"

Icole shrugged. "We tried, at first. It's like the air slows you down.

You try and try, but don't never get there. Some say it's to keep out evil. Other say evil is what put it there."

Oh, was she to be as thick as her husband? "And what is 'it'?"

She shook her head. "Don't nobody know."

Or nobody's telling. He recognized witchcraft when he saw it. "I will have to see this place. Tell me: does it extend all the way around the village?"

She answered him with a slack-jawed silence.

Honestly! Of all the idiots to post watch on the most important village in all the world? He wanted to throw his cup at her head. "You never tried any other way?"

"There's just the one road going in." She gave him a look as if he were the fool.

He did not bother to hide his sigh of contempt. "And what about the other side of the village?"

"They only got a road coming out."

That was it. She was useless. He shoved his half-empty cup back at her. "I'll require a room for the night. I'm going out to investigate this mystery border. Have my room ready for when I return."

She looked at him funny, again, as if he were the fool, not her. "Him and I, we sleep up in the loft." She looked him over. "Dunno if you'd like it."

"Fine." He waved a dismissive hand at her. "I'll take some other room."

"There ain't summat but up there and down here."

"I'll sleep down here then." He was losing his patience. "Preferably near the fire."

At this, she laughed at him. "There ain't no fires inside mills. Everyone knows that. Flour explodes, you know."

He jabbed a finger at the teapot in her hands. "How'd you heat that up."

"Oh. The fire outside, of course."

He rubbed his temples. Perhaps it was easier to kill them both now, put them out of his misery. "I'll sleep there."

"What?" Icole declared. "Outside? You're not terribly bright, are you, Mister?"

After he severed his ties to Icole and Tedrick, Master Non spent the rest of the afternoon circumnavigating Sacred Spring. Unlike previously reported, there were several ways into town, most of them nicely paved if they were any wider than a footpath.

At least Tedrick and Icole told the truth when they said they couldn't get to town. As soon as he approached the border, he felt a slowness, like the air conspiring to stop him. There wasn't an exact border, per se, but a definite inability to proceed further.

He wondered, what would happen if one rode a horse or a cart. Would such a fellow be pushed off the wagon, or would the horse slow down as well?

He should have brought the horse he rode from Crossroads. He'd put the beast away in the little barn the Millers had for housing their own pony. In his saddlebags he carried, among other things, some hemp rope, two pistols and a bottle of ether. It had worked before; perhaps it would serve him well again. But first, he needed to know the lay of the land.

He walked about the village counter-clockwise, hiking up the hill first, tracing where it became difficult to walk. He ascended until he reached a place where the hill leveled off. Up here, there were more houses, well-built, though a couple of small log cabins as well, most likely outbuildings. Half the houses sat outside the border.

A few people passed through the border without any ill effect. He tried to follow and failed.

So, on he went, through a forest of some pine, but mostly tall white trees, their slender branches reaching up ever so high. Their round leaves shook and shimmered in the breeze.

He traced along until the forest gave way to a mountain meadow. Here the meadow dimpled into a pond. This must be the spring for which the town was named. On the far side stood a stone temple, well-kept. Was that the Dark God's? A stone path followed from the temple to the edge of the spring. Steps descended into its water.

In his experience, springs were terribly cold. Why would anyone would wish to bathe there?

Unless there was something different about this spring. He risked being seen and left the edge of the forest.

Here in the meadow, the tall grass was fresh and green, spotted everywhere by wildflowers. As he approached the spring, the ground round about felt muddier. Reeds grew about the edge. He went to the path—the safest route, apparently, if one did not wish mud on his boots. When he reached the water, he knelt down and scooped up a handful.

Oh, it burned! He shook the water off his hand and wiped it on his pants. Despite drying his hand, it continued to burn, even if he blew on it. He clenched his hand until the sensation went away.

Truly, these people were mad.

Perhaps this was not what he thought. If this was the temple of the Dark God, maybe this was a cursed spring, where people were sacrificed, or at least tortured. He peered into the water, but saw no bodies, floating or sunken.

He looked up at the temple. It was a simple building, mostly a round pavilion of columns holding up a stone roof.

The spring and the temple stood outside the border of the village. He would come back to it later.

He followed the strange border down the hill and around where he saw more houses, a few of them more than one story tall. There were some stables, also within the border. He followed it behind the tallest building and on until he came well behind some small cottages.

There he found one of the largest personal gardens he'd ever seen. So many cultivated plants all in a row. More the fool who had to tend this garden.

A younger woman with straight black hair, stooped and moved along, more toward this end of the garden, rather than up near the house. Her voice called out to someone. She bent down to pick up a child.

His heart skipped a beat. He recognized the woman now. That was the one the Dark God left behind when he stole Raine. And that was the child he'd used to track her down.

He wanted to dance. This confirmed it. Raine was here, in this village. This must be her house.

He might not be able to get in, but as he watched the black-haired woman, he hatched a plan.

He crouched in the scrub outside the border, watching as the nursemaid—for that must be who she was—played with the fair child. The woman was Tredan in coloring, with her almond skin and straight black hair. That made sense, as the Dark God's main temple stood in the Tredan territories.

They weren't exactly playing, as the woman occasionally plucked leaves and twigs off plants.

He continued to observe, noting every detail he could.

A door to the house opened and an older woman, judging by her silvery hair, called to them. She was too far away for him to catch what she said.

The little girl ran to the older woman. She must be another servant. The Tredan woman followed at a more sedate pace, her apron full of her gatherings. Potion brewing? Or lunch?

All three went inside. If that was where Raine lived, he was disappointed. He was expecting a grander home for one so powerful. Then again, if what Icole and Tedrick told him was true, she was a woman of simple focus and means. Perhaps a basic residence was what she was used to.

Then again, maybe these were the servants' cottages. If so, where was the manor?

Deserting his spot, he finished his circumnavigation of the village. By now, the sun approached the horizon of the mountains. He may not have spotted the Bride, but he was pretty certain she was here. He would continue his investigations tomorrow.

He returned to the mill. After checking on his horse, he knocked on the door of the house. Icole answered, looking tired. "What do you want?" Ah, ever so polite, she was.

He bowed. "You may call me Master Non. I have been sent by the One True god to learn more about this village."

Her eyes widened. She laid her hand over her heart. "May he watch over us all." Then she turned around and hollered, "Tedrick!"

Master Non groaned. There they went again. Ah well. When he departed in the morning, he would sever the Lines of Deeper Power that insisted on binding him to anyone he spoke, but only after he'd delivered his true opinion to them. It was a shame they'd forget. "I believe you have a letter announcing my arrival?" This morning, before he had severed the Lines last time, he'd given her a letter and told her to read it. She'd better have obeyed.

She nodded. "Tedrick must have brought it in." She stood out of the doorway and jerked her thumb to the interior. Such an elegant invite. "I've made supper. Hope you like bread. We eat a lot of it."

He pinched the bridge of his nose and entered the mill. Surely, he would not have to put up with this much longer. As soon as the Bride was his, he'd kill the Dark God and become supreme ruler of Creation. Then he'd show them how to behave.

In her kitchen, Adrastea stirred honey into her cup of tea. She enjoyed the stillness of the evening, after the world went to bed. She carried her cup into the front room by the fire and sank into her rocking chair. While sometimes she wished she could sleep more, for nights like tonight, she enjoyed the quietude.

Mor-Lath was somewhere, gently pleased with himself. Ever since he'd restored the Avelians to their home, and the Tredans were cleaning up Cithra, he'd been in a rather cheerful mood. For an entire week she and Mor-Lath had not argued once. She quite liked him when they were not at odds. The fact that she wasn't pregnant by that horrid little Master Non had been a big relief for him.

She confessed to herself, she was also pleased. While a baby would be most welcome in her heart, she would not welcome one of that bastard's get.

The burning ball in the fireplace issued a pleasant warmth. Spring might be half-way to summer, but nights still had a touch of chill, especially when the breezes rolled out of the canyons.

She felt Mor-Lath return a moment before he appeared. "Here." He dropped a pile of books into the other chair. "I've brought you something to read."

Adrastea rose. Books were good, if not for herself, at least for Berengaria. What a surprise for the priestess tomorrow. Adrastea herself couldn't leave Sacred Spring. While Adrastea did not mind, Berengaria had chafed a bit. Adrastea had been her connection to the outside world.

Mor-Lath picked one up and studied its spine. "This one's a medical text—rather dull stuff, if you ask me." He handed it out to her while he looked over the stack.

Adrastea took the book. "I like medical."

He dug through the pile. "Here's another history, as requested." He added it to the pile in her hands. "And a couple of others you might want."

He lifted a smaller volume. "I also brought you some fiction. This one is called 'The Barnyard Maid'." He flipped through it quickly. "Spoilers: she's no maiden, if you know what I mean."

Adrastea shook her head. "Why'd you bring something like that?"

"All work and no play will drive you mad." He slipped past her and sat in her rocking chair.

Dropping the books back on the stack, she put her fists on her hips. "That's my chair."

He grinned. "I know. Shall I read you a bedtime story?" He held his hand out to her. She felt the usual tug that existed between them. He wasn't compelling her but inviting her. She came over. He pulled her into his lap, hooking her legs over the armrest. "It's a perfect chair."

"That's why I like it."

He raised his eyebrows. "But I like it for different reasons." His hand slid down her back to her bottom, cupping it appreciatively. The other roamed over her thigh. "We can have a bit of a canoodle. But it's too crowded for anything risky." He buried his face in her hair. The connection between them came alive as his passion ignited.

Adrastea groaned. Should she fight it or give in? When he started nuzzling her neck, her resolve broke. How could something so lovely be so dangerous?

He willed her bodice strings to loosen.

"Hey," she protested, her hands going to her dropping neckline. "I thought you were going to read me a story?"

He took advantage of her distraction to slide a hand up her skirt. "I thought you didn't want to hear 'The Barnyard Maid'?"

She gasped when he stroked her skin. "This is not a good idea," she groaned.

"I know." That he sent suggestive thoughts through the connection between them didn't help. A hunger opened in her belly. She wished he had a thousand hands. She wanted to be touched everywhere all at once.

His lips sought hers, teasing, playing, delivering. His tongue ran along her lower lip, tempting her to open wider.

She felt her bodice loosen. The hand on her back slipped up under the bodice, under the blouse and sent shivers up her spine.

It wasn't enough. She wanted more.

He buried his face in her bosom. She twisted so she could press closer to him. Her leg pressed against the back of the chair. How inconvenient.

He felt her frustration. "Now, now, my Darklet. You can't have everything."

She growled. But he was right.

Behind the passion he fed her, she felt that firm control. Nothing untoward would happen. She also felt that knot of fear, ever-present. What a shame. She tugged at it, loosening a few lines, relaxing him.

Meanwhile, he tugged at the drawstring of her pantalets. She'd like to see him succeed at getting them off her, without cheating.

His lips sampled every inch of exposed skin. He eased her blouse off her shoulder and ran his tongue along the line he'd drawn into her skin. Oh, how it sang!

She pulled at the laces on his shirt and ran her fingers over his line.

It was electric. He arched under her finger. An echo of the same delight came through her line. It left more of the hunger in its wake. She stroked the line again, getting better results. It made her blood race to see him react so to her touch. She raked her fingernails over his whole chest. A shiver caused his skin to prickle.

His shirt was in the way. With a word, it parted to her whim. She stroked her hands over everything. They glided over his stomach and down lower.

He grabbed her hands. She felt that knot tighten, and his wall of control come back up. "Careful," he admonished.

"Why?" She bent over and breathed a warm breath of air over the line. The hair on his chest stirred. His arms weakened. His hands let go of her wrists, sliding up to cover her breasts. She gasped as he played with her erect nipples. Currents rippled within her, shooting downwards to her loins. Oh, they burned.

She tried to shift to straddle his lap, but he wouldn't let her. Oh, that infernal knot of control!

While he made her skin beg for more, she focused on that knot of fear, loosening it bit by bit. She also took that yearning that burned in her belly and between her legs and fed it back to him. That knot of fear about his heart was in the way. In her frustration, she tore it away entirely.

Without warning, he lifted her up and out of the chair, bearing her down to the rug before the fire. He flung her skirt up and slid her pantalets off. She cried out when he buried his face between her legs. It was exquisite. The hunger within her exploded to an obsession, making her blood burn. It felt as if the power of the whole of Creation resolved into her. She refocused that energy onto the last of the knot of fear within him, tearing it completely apart.

She didn't know what she needed but she needed it. Bad.

Mor-Lath came up for a breath before he slid up her body. He needed it too. He captured her mouth in a punishing, salty kiss. His tongue explored the inside of her mouth just as it had been exploring her nether regions moments ago.

He wore too much clothing. At her insistence, their clothes dissolved into shreds. She wanted his skin against hers. She wanted his skin to be hers, to melt into the whole of her being.

He wasn't in her enough. She wanted to possess all of him, to bring every last speck of him within her.

She wanted to consume him completely.

He slid into her. She wrapped her legs about his waist, so he could never leave.

More! She needed more. She demanded more.

He was willing to give it to her. It was as if his very soul sent tendrils into her, to take root and feed the insatiable hunger driving her, moving her body with his.

Give it all to me, she urged him.

He didn't reply, so lost was he in her gloriousness.

Almost, almost there.

It happened. He couldn't stop it. His body took over. Their passion culminated all at once. It flowed through her veins, making her blood sing. His arrival rolled over into her. She gave herself over to the most exquisite pleasure she'd ever known.

He breathed her name into her ear: "Adrastea..."

Realization cut through the beneficence like a stream of frigid water. The good feelings shattered and evaporated. Adrastea opened her eyes as Mor-Lath pulled away from her. "What have I done?" he gasped, his gaze meeting hers in cold realization. He pushed himself backward. She felt, through the line on her shoulder, the knot of fear return.

Oh no. She was having none of that. Filling herself to capacity with Deeper Power, she dragged his protesting self back to her.

He fought her. Their wills battled, evenly matched.

"We are not finished," she insisted.

Despite her efforts, he pulled away.

She pushed herself up, leg akimbo, her skin icy at the loss of his contact. "Wait," she cried, her hand outstretched. "We were almost there." Almost... where? While the mutual pleasure had been a completion, one last tendril of hunger remained, burning a hole of frustration into her heart. Something had almost happened, possibly a greater level of satisfaction, of completeness, if that was even possible?

She leapt at him, pushing him back to the floor. She would have him, even if she had to consume him bite by bite.

"Adrastea, wait. We can't do this." He gripped her wrists, fighting her.

"We already have," she cried, trying to get free.

His breaths were ragged. "No. It's... I can't— we can't." A tear spilled out from his eye. "I should never have—"

She cried out in frustration. "Why do you always do that?" Why did he let fear rule him? Her heart ached with desire. Once more, that hunger blossomed. She stopped his mouth with a kiss. Perhaps she could stir him again.

The knot multiplied. His whole concentration resolved on his fears. The return of his control washed every last vestige of passion from him. That same rationality spilled over into her.

She stopped fighting him. He released her hands and turned away.

Adrastea knelt beside him, her hands on his naked shoulders. "Mor-Lath. Please."

"I'm such a fool," he muttered. "I thought we would be safe."

"Safe?" Her voice elevated. "Safe? With you and me, there is no such thing as safe. We do not want to be safe." An echo of the song her blood sang murmured to her. "There was something. Something was about to happen. You stopped it."

"Adrastea!" He gripped his hair in his hands. "You cannot— you must not get pregnant."

Pregnant? "Is that what you thought was going to happen?" The idea settled into her head. "Is that what was going to happen?" She retreated from him, to sit cross-legged on the rug. Is that what a conception felt like? Part of her still cried out for that completion.

It made sense. That had not happened the other times. The first time wasn't long enough. The second time, she was quite sterile. But this passion, this climax. It left the others far behind.

She still wanted it. She whimpered as she collapsed to the rug. She was a starving woman with a single morsel to eat when she wanted to feast.

"I don't know," he confessed. He scooted closer to her but didn't touch her. His blood also sang in memory. "It's never been like that before." More to himself, "It's never been that good." He laid back onto the floor. "You have ruined me."

She reached out, but he flinched away from her touch. "Too dangerous," he explained.

Her hand clenched into a fist. She wanted nothing more than to press her body to his. No, she also wanted the taste of him. She gasped as the memory of him buried deep inside her flushed through her head.

He must have felt her emotional reaction. Mor-Lath leapt up and moved away. "We need some time apart."

That broke her heart. "But…" But what? She knew he was right. If he stayed, either she'd draw him back into compromise, or he'd resist her, and, in their frustration, they would argue. Their arguments never went well.

She felt the Deeper Power wrap around her. He transported her into her bedroom, setting her gently upon the bed. In the dimness of the bedroom, she saw him standing there. As he held out his arms, clothing wrapped itself around him.

He sat next to her and leaned over. "I will return tomorrow. I can't stay tonight."

"I wish you would."

"You know I can't." His voice cracked.

She sat up and reached for him. He moved just out of range of her fingers. "Don't do anything stupid, Mor-Lath." Her heart beat fast. "Just… don't."

"Don't worry." His voice was calm and even. "I'm going to have a cold bath."

He still felt it, despite his best efforts. "Sacred Spring is cold."

"Yes. I know."

He leaned over her, his lips almost brushing her skin. He murmured a single word: "*Sleep.*"

Never had Adrastea been of two minds to embrace oblivion.

Chapter 24

Master Non was a patient man. Ever since he'd arrived at the village, he had sat in this copse of weeds and watched Raine's house—her real house. After more reconnaissance, he had discovered where she lived. How disappointing. The whole of the world at her feet, and she chose a pathetic little cottage?

Today he saw the nursemaid leave with her charge. Where would they go today? Usually they went to the house with the giant garden, or the smaller house behind Raine's.

Today, they chose a different path. They bypassed the smaller house and walked past the chapel. They followed the paved path up into the woods.

His heart beat faster. There were no houses in that direction, only the spring and the temple. Outside the protection of the village. He tripped over his feet as he pushed his way out of the weeds. If he followed the path past the constable's house, he might make it up there before them.

He checked his supplies—two revolving pistols, fully loaded, his bottle of ether with a cloth, and the rope. His plan: secure the child, wait for Raine and ambush her. He'd scouted an ideal location within the woods. Lure her there, surprise her when she rescued the child, and disappear. This time, he would make sure every single Line between her and everything she loved was severed. Once he had her, she was the key. She would make him immortal. Then he would use her as bait to lure the Dark God to his destruction. A ripple of pleasure made him sigh. Oh, it was perfect.

He pushed his way through copses of trees, panting out of breath as he headed uphill.

They'd reached the meadow before he did. There they played,

warmed by the sun. The little girl ran through the grass, picking every wildflower that caught her fancy. The nursemaid followed at a slower pace, letting her charge run about.

He paused at the forest's edge to catch his breath. He was on the wrong side of the spring. His planned location was over on the other side of the meadow, closer to where the child played.

Now, how to approach them without spooking the nursemaid?

He studied the child more. She sure liked her wildflowers.

Women liked flowers, didn't they? The tendrils of a cunning plan came together.

Leaving the woods, he gathered wildflowers.

The sun shone, the bees buzzed, and a gentle breeze rippled along the tops of the grass. The nursemaid gave in to such a lovely day. She laid down on the grass and stared up into the sky.

The child's exuberance waned. She sat by the reclining nursemaid and sorted through her multitudinous flowers.

Too easy, thought Master Non as he approached them.

The nursemaid heard his approach. She sat up, startled.

"Hello." He held forth an armful of flowers.

The nursemaid did not react as he expected. Her eyes grew wide, her hands flew to her mouth and she screamed. She scooped up the child and fled.

That didn't go to plan. Of course; she remembered him. Her rescue last time had been so swift he'd completely forgot to disconnect her Line. How could he have left such a loose end? He pulled out his revolving pistol and pursued her.

No burdened woman can outrun a man. He caught up with her before she fled the meadow. He grabbed her arm, spinning her around. The child fell from her arms to bounce in the soft grass. Typical of small children, she cried.

Again, the nursemaid surprised him. With an unexpected strength, she pulled her arm free, then returned his assault with a punch to the jaw.

She scrambled for the child while he shook the stars from his head. The bitch would pay for that. He lifted his pistol and aimed straight for her back.

He fired.

A loud report echoed about the meadow. Birds startled and rose from the forest. The woman fell, her dark hair billowing out as she collapsed.

Serves her right. Master Non nabbed the wailing child by an arm and headed in the direction of the forest.

⚜

Adrastea sat on a bench in Ari's stillroom, reading aloud to her from a medical book. The text was Tredan, so she translated for Ari's benefit. Switching between languages could not completely distract her from the thought of her husband. His presence buzzed under her skin like an itch she could not scratch.

He sat safely on the other side of the room, feet propped up against the wall, paying especially good attention to a cold bottle of Ari's beer.

Adrastea wasn't fooled. The same itch that annoyed her also pestered him. He couldn't hide it. He repeatedly pressed the cool bottle against his chest. That didn't work.

Honestly, she didn't know how much longer she would be able to resist. She turned her focus to the book. Keeping her eyes on the page, she fought off the Deeper Power. How easy it would be to let it fill her. It wanted to spill into her soul and make her burn.

A memory of her legs twined about his danced through her mind.

No. Focus on the book.

Ari stood at the stove. She held a large glass mercury thermometer in a simmering pot. "All right. It's there."

"Add the honey, but don't stir."

"Really? How odd."

Adrastea tapped the book. "That's what it says here." Her hand stroked the smooth page. Her gaze flickered in Mor-Lath's direction.

Ari sighed. "Okay." She poured in the liquid honey that had been warming on the stove. "Now what?"

She fought off the urge to throw herself at her husband. Why was Creation doing this to her? Was it last night, their failure to achieve… whatever it was they'd not quite completed?

"Adrastea!" Ari's sharp voice brought her back.

She blushed. "Sorry."

Mor-Lath dropped his beer bottle as an icy fear flowed through their connection. Adrastea looked up, her book forgotten.

"Berengaria," Mor-Lath exclaimed, then disappeared. His alarm hummed through the line on her shoulder.

Berengaria? If something was wrong with her, then... Adrastea cried out. "Harianne!"

She closed her eyes and willed herself to her daughter.

Mor-Lath's heart beat in his chest. Berengaria lay face down on the grass, unmoving. He knelt and placed a hand on her back. She was dead, shot. The sticky blood was warm on his palm. He didn't want to believe it. "I'm so sorry. Oh, my little Garie." An ache throbbed in him.

What happened? He looked about for her soul.

Adrastea appeared not too far from him. "Harianne!" She ran towards the forest.

Mor-Lath looked up. They weren't alone. Adrastea pursued a man, who lumbered toward the safety of the trees. Under his arm he carried a little screaming girl—the mashiah child.

A cold rage flowed through Mor-Lath. That was Master Non. What was he doing at Sacred Spring?

He reached out his hand to grab the man, but the Lines of Deeper Power refused to obey. "What the—?" Mor-Lath exclaimed, looking at his hand.

Instead, he reached for Harianne. He sent out his will and snagged the little girl.

She jerked from Master Non's grasp, spinning her kidnapper around. He crashed to the grass. She landed not too far away.

"Harianne!" Adrastea slowed and stumbled. She fought an invisible force. It brought her to her knees. She struggled to lift a hand toward her daughter. She fought a losing battle against... what?

His heart beat even harder. What was happening? Was it Master Non? There was no Deeper Power that he could sense. Adrastea gasped as she failed to draw a breath. Panic welled in her. She couldn't free herself. She couldn't breathe.

Mor-Lath ran after his foe, roaring with rage. How dare that bastard manipulate his wife!

Master Non, sprawled on the ground, cried out as the angry god rushed him. He raised his hands and disappeared, just as Mor-Lath's hand reached for his throat.

"Damn you!" Mor-Lath slammed his fist into the earth. He almost had him.

Adrastea. He raced to her side. Whatever had imprisoned her disappeared. She raised to her hands and knees, coughing. "Harianne?" she gasped.

Mor-Lath looked around for the child. He found her by her little voice.

There she was, where she'd been dropped. Tears ran down her face as she snuffled in fear. She stood up from the ground, something shiny and metal in her hands.

Master Non's revolver. Had he dropped it? She lifted it up, her hands firm around the weapon, fingers interlaced in the trigger.

Mor-Lath's heart raised into his throat. The weapon pointed at him, wavering.

His vision tunneled until all he could see was a loaded revolver in the hands of a mashiah, aimed at his heart. Spots formed before his eyes. Surely this could not be his end!

What a fool he'd been. In weakness, he'd given in to his wife's wishes to keep the child alive. She'd all but promised that if he'd won the good will of the child, she would not kill him in anger or in the name of righteousness. Nothing had been said regarding accidents.

Could his life have come down to the moment of convincing a child he was not the embodiment of all evil?

How did he convince her? He felt for his coat pocket for sweets, only he was not wearing a coat. He could not remember where he'd left it.

What else could he offer the child? Then he remembered. A cookie appeared in his hand. Berengaria had baked them this morning. No doubt she'd taken the child from the house to keep her from stealing too-hot cookies. That child sure had a propensity for acquiring ill-gotten food.

He held out the cookie and edged a little closer. "Look what I've got for you."

No luck. She looked at him, sobs still shaking her little form, the gun wobbling dangerously on her trigger finger.

Adrastea's voice, just as shaky, said, "Harianne? Give us the pistol, sweetie."

"Harianne?" His voice betrayed his anxiety as he used her name. "May I have that, please?" He held out his hand. "I've got a cookie for you." He got even closer. He fought the impulse to flee.

His hand itched to snatch the gun from the child. Knowing his luck, it would misfire in a most unfortunate manner. That left diplomacy and more courage than he'd used in a long time. "Would you like a cookie?" He waved it gently.

She still snuffled, but her eyes remained on the cookie, mesmerized. The tip of the revolver dipped down. He brought the cookie within her reach. She sniffed.

As quick as a snake, she dropped the pistol and grabbed the cookie.

Mor-Lath's hand closed around the barrel. He moved it away from the mashiah child.

Adrastea rushed forward to gather her child in her arms. "Harianne!" She hugged her tightly.

The giant knot of anxiety that had twisted in his gut evaporated. He sank to his knees, relieved.

A change in air pressure raised the hairs on the back of the neck. Cold metal pressed to the back of his head.

"Die," said Master Non, as he pulled the trigger of his other revolver.

Adrastea froze as Master Non appeared behind Mor-Lath. A moment later, the loud bark of gunfire erupted. "NO!" She threw the child aside and scrambled towards Mor-Lath. She grabbed his outstretched hands as he fell. *Adrastea. Take it.* Something flowed from his touch into her, overwhelming her senses.

The lights faded from his eyes. As he fell into her lap, her whole world spun around. The trees melted into each other and dissolved into the sky. The sky fell, flowing into the earth and a heaviness settled onto her shoulders.

A million impossible Lines wrapped around her, passing through her skin into her soul. The universe poured into her and filled her senses with more awareness than she thought possible. It was like she could feel the whole world—ever tree, every flower, every person, every insect, every speck of dust.

The mantle of authority. He had given it to her in its entirety.

Somewhere, something rippled, urgent, panicked.

She looked down at the body in her lap. Mor-Lath. No, not Mor-Lath. This was but a shell, whose emptiness seemed endless. She bent her head down. Was there no spark of life? Where did he go?

Her fingers dabbed at the back of his head. So much shimmery blood and white fragments of skull. She called upon the Deeper Power to heal it. The fragments moved back into place and the blackened skin knit back together.

But no pulse beat. The skin remained still.

A man shouted in exultation to the heavens. "I have killed the Dark God!" he cried. "Now I rule Creation."

"Raine," he commanded. "You will come here now." He grabbed her by the scalp.

A rage unlike any she had ever felt before filled her. It welled up from within, bubbling ever bigger, without end.

Somewhere, Someone said her name, her true name.

She sent her fury into the hand that gripped her hair. That hand began to burn. It jerked and twitched as she punished it for assaulting her.

Master Non cried out in pain and let go. He wailed as he held his hand up. Before his eyes, it seared and melted, first the skin, then the flesh, then the bones. His screams rang out over the hills of Sacred Spring.

Her fingers closed over the pistol still in Mor-Lath's hand. Slowly, she rose. Her eyes burned with a holy fire. "I am not Raine. I was never your wife." She drew herself to her full height and called upon Creation to fill her. This time, it welled up from within her, filling her like a spring, enveloping her. It completed her to her very skin and beyond. The whole of Creation bowed to honor her awful glory.

Master Non, holding the stump of his arm to his chest, scrabbled back, his eyes wide with terror.

Somewhere a Voice warned, "*Don't do this.*"

She looked down upon the cowering man, this cowardly man, who dared to confront her. "I am Adrastea, God of the Dark. And I am very angry!"

She raised the pistol to Master Non's face, what could have been so handsome, had he not been so cruel.

"*Adrastea, no!*" cried a Voice.

Oh, how she loathed that face. She pulled the trigger.

His face exploded in red gore. In the middle, a black hole appeared, sucking in the edges of the wound. A high-pitched wail echoed in her ears. About her, Creation itself screamed. His whole head began to collapse inward, falling into the black hole. It sucked in air and dust and even sunlight, growing larger and larger.

Adrastea's hand shook. She dropped the pistol. What was happening?

Celestial hands grabbed her by the arms. Phyl cried, "Adrastea, what have you done?" He dragged her closer to the collapsing body of Master Non. "Help Me!"

She resisted. "I can't go near that." It was sucking in not just Master Non, but the grass near his head. Fallen leaves rolled towards it. It pulled at her, threatening to consume her.

Phil did not let go. His superior strength won. His desperation rolled over her. "It's a tear in Creation. If We don't close it up, it will destroy Us all, to the last atom."

"I can't." She fought Him, panic tearing at the edges of her reason. "Let me go!"

"No. We have to do this together, the Light and the Dark." He wrapped His arms about her, pinning hers to her torso. Wind whipped about Them as the sky darkened.

"He'll eat me." Tears streamed out her eyes, flying off towards the vortex of nothingness. The blackness of the hole grew bigger and bigger, a yawning maw ready to consume.

"You have to do this," Phyl urged, His voice in competition with the howling wind falling into the blackness. "You have to reach inside and pull it in on itself." He forced her hand up. "If you don't, We all die."

She wilted. Only His strength kept her up. "I can't."

"I will hold you." He spoke into her ear. "Adrastea." A warmth from His voice poured into her.

Adrastea. Her name was Adrastea. By that link, she was connected to Him, and to Creation. Only by her, could everything be saved. She had to trust Him.

She nodded and gave her hands over to Him. Together They reached into the black hole that had eaten Master Non's chest and the ground beneath him. As she reached in, her hands tingled, then went numb.

"Imagine grasping the bottom and pulling it up."

Adrastea nodded. She couldn't feel a thing, other than Phyl's warmth pouring into her. It flowed into her hands and disappeared into the void.

"Pull," He urged.

Did she hold onto the hole, or simply imagine it?"

"No, don't doubt. You cannot doubt. You and Me, we are the Power of Creation incarnate. If We imagine it, it can be done."

Her legs buckled. She fell to her knees. Phyl was behind her, never letting go. "I have always known your destiny, Adrastea. It does not end like this. Reach in and pull."

She must have reached the nadir. She had been to Dom-al-gol, the bottom of Creation, where all the Lines connected, and then after that, nothing.

That was the nothing she stared into once. She could face it once more. "Pull."

Phyl braced and pulled her back. She kept a hold of the nothing and brought it out into Creation, folding it back on itself. It resisted and twisted in her grasp. But she would not let go. The numbness moved up her arms to her shoulders and beyond. She found it difficult to breathe. Spots swam before her eyes.

"Let go, Adrastea, let go."

Did she let go? All she had was the thought of her hands. Did they even exist anymore? Did she exist anymore? The darkness consumed her. As she descended into oblivion, she felt a distant burning pain.

Her hands. It had to be. She focused on that pain and all its unpleasantness. It grew, coming closer and closer, bringing with it light.

Done.

Adrastea blinked. Above her spread a sky of the most beautiful blue. Also, above her was the face of Phyl. His lips may have had a smile, but His eyes were full of great sadness.

She sat up. Before her, a crater marred the meadow. Nothing was left of Master Non. "Did we do it?"

He nodded.

A quiet sobbing seasoned the air. Over, closer to the trees, Lucea mourned upon the body of Mor-Lath, prostrate in Her grief. "What happened? Why don't I know what happened?"

A hollow space opened under Adrastea's heart. Mor-Lath was dead, killed by a mashiah.

"Mor-Lath was right." Phyl fell back onto the grass, His head in His hands. "He believed in a man unconnected to Creation. We could not sense such a creature, so We thought it a figment of his imagination."

Adrastea shuddered and turned away from the crater. "He severed the Lines of Deeper Power, even his name. Every time Creation tried to reclaim him, he'd disconnect. That's what he did to me."

"We never lost you, Adrastea. We always knew you were there, even if We didn't know where.

"He didn't know about Harianne," said Phyl.

Cold realization flooded her. "Harianne! Where is she?" She leapt to her feet.

Phyl simply pointed. Further down the hill Harianne had found Berengaria. She'd crawled under one limp arm and laid there, curled up against the dead priestess' bosom, still warm. In her hands she clutched some wildflowers and a half-eaten cookie.

The ghost of Berengaria hovered over her, stroking Harianne's pale hair.

Adrastea sank down to the earth. "So much death. I can't take anymore." She crawled over to her late husband's body. He was so still. The essence that made him Mor-Lath was gone. His skin was too pale. His hair gently stirred in the afternoon breeze. It seemed disrespectful for the sun to shine so brightly.

Lucea's own light had dimmed. She sprawled across him, torrents of grief rolling off Her. Even the very flowers around Her bowed their heads.

Adrastea felt Phyl's hand on her shoulder. "It wasn't supposed to happen like this. Not like this. You two were so close. You almost convinced him, Adrastea."

"What? To share everything?"

Phyl nodded. "The key was the mantle of the Dark God. While Mor-Lath lived, the whole of that authority rested on him. He's always wanted to be a full god, to do what Lucea and I do. Only his selfishness held him back. Had he given all—his memories, his hopes and dreams, even shared his godly authority, then he would have become what he has always desired. You both would have."

Her heart ached. They had been so close. Is that what they'd felt that night, when things had gone too far? Not the conception of a child, but a transformation? "So, the God of the Dark is dead?"

"No. Only Mor-Lath is dead. Before he died, he gave the mantle to you. Not shared it but gave it completely. You are the God of the Dark."

"I know." Her senses had come alive. There was so much to the world, and she could feel it all. Was this what it was like for him? If so, no wonder he found it so easy to handle her. No mere mortal stood a chance against a god. "But only a demi-god." She brushed back a few tendrils of Mor-Lath's hair. They kept blowing over his face.

"I'm sorry," said Phyl. "More than you know."

He laid a hand on His grieving Wife's shoulder. They disappeared. But Adrastea felt Them close by.

A voice called her name in the distance, breathless.

Salle arrived at the meadow first to find the fallen priestess. "Ari," she called back. "It's Berengaria!" Salle bent down and gave the body a quick check.

Ari arrived. Salle scooped up a reluctant Harianne. The little girl didn't want to leave the body.

Ari dropped to her knees, rolled Berengaria onto her back and listened to her chest. "She's gone." She checked the priestess' back once more. Ari put a hand over her mouth and rocked back and forth.

"Who did this?" Salle tried to shield Harianne. The little girl kept reaching for Berengaria.

"We need Adrastea," Ari replied.

Another voice shouted up the hill. "Ari?" It was Mikal. He dashed up the path, followed by an out-of-breath Chloe. Gallian also tagged along. A few other people also came up the hill.

Mikal froze when he found Ari. "Berengaria!" he cried, dashing to her side. He lifted her hand and stroked it against his cheek. "Oh, Berengaria." Then he threw back his head and howled. His grief welled up loud and empty.

Rop Storekeeper, Martine Innkeeper and a few more surrounded the grieving Mayor. Still more people came up the hill, drawn by the sounds of destruction—Arn Constable and Janyse, and more, all to gather around Berengaria.

Adrastea sat in the grass and watched them. It was like a wall between them and her. She entwined her fingers with Mor-Lath's unmoving ones. So many people, so much sorrow.

Arn, ever the lawman, did not stare at the body, as everyone else, but looked about. His gaze roamed the ground in an ever-widening circle.

His eyes were the first to meet Adrastea's. Then he saw the second body. He did not say a word but tapped Ari on the shoulder.

Ari looked up. She rose. "Adrastea?" She started to move forward, but froze, when she saw Mor-Lath dead. She put both hands over her mouth.

Natan had arrived. He put his arm about his wife. Together, they approached Adrastea. Mikal never noticed, so lost in his sorrow he was.

But Chloe did. She followed, staying well behind Natan and Ari. "Is he dead? For real this time?"

Adrastea looked back to the body. Slowly, she nodded.

"Did you kill him?"

Adrastea shook her head.

Ari sank to her knees. "What happened?

"Oh, Ari!" Adrastea cried. Something within her broke. She flung herself into the arms of her aunt.

No grief is greater than that of a broken-hearted god.

A drastea sat alone in the dark, never moving from Mor-Lath's body. Down in Sacred Spring, a funeral pyre lit the village green. Mikal stood, held up by his aunt and uncle, with the funeral torch in his hand. He lit the pyre and stood back, watching the body of Berengaria burn, to send it to the Light.

Adrastea never left the hill. From where she sat, the glow of the funeral pyre shone above the treeline. Up here, it was still, silent. Alone.

His hand was now cold, as was his other hand. When she stroked his cheek, it was also chill. Was there nothing warm left?

Her memories mocked her. She was a fool to marry him. She was a fool to wait so long. She hated him. She loved him. Had she never told him that? She whispered it into his unhearing ear. "I love you."

The canyon breeze blew across the back of her neck. How she wished she could hear his voice.

For the rest of the night, she heard nothing.

A ri and Chloe came up the next afternoon. Ari brought a bottle of soup. Chloe brought an empty glass.

Ari didn't bother with salutations. "You cannot stay here forever."

Adrastea didn't answer her.

Ari held out the bottle. "At least have something to eat."

Chloe went to the spring, dipped in her glass, then murmured words of blessing over it. When she brought it back, she offered it to Adrastea.

Adrastea shied away from it. "That might be blasphemy."

"What? Against him?"

"Against myself." She looked up into Chloe's eyes. "I am now the God of the Dark."

Chloe drew in a shuddery breath. Then her steel returned, and she held out the glass with both hands. "Then it is even more important that you drink."

Adrastea shrugged. She accepted the glass. "As the Light shines before me, let the Light..." Her voice caught in her throat. She drew a shuddery breath. "Light shine through me." She lifted it to her lips.

The water was sweet and cool. It coated her dry mouth and moistened her throat. Before she knew it, she'd drained the lot. "More." She handed the glass back to Chloe.

The priestess obliged.

When Adrastea had her fill, Ari asked, "What are your wishes regarding the body?"

She looked at him. He hadn't changed since yesterday. "I can't have a pyre for him."

Chloe said, "Surely the Light won't have him."

Adrastea shook her head. Thousands of years of sin would weigh down his soul. "The tradition of his followers was burial." God of wealth, god of earth, god of the underworld. Burial was symbolic of returning to him.

Returning to her?

Chloe asked, "Will you bury him here in Sacred Spring, or return him to...?"

Adrastea shook her head vigorously. "I can't stand the thought of burying him." Deep down in the earth it was cold, dark and lonely.

Ari pursed her lips. "You can't leave his body lying around like this."

Adrastea smoothed out a wrinkle in his shirt. "I don't know what to do." That connection between them, that constantly drew her to him, and him to her, was gone. She never thought she'd miss it.

"Catacombs?" Ari suggested.

Chloe shot that down. "That's a Cithran tradition."

Adrastea shuddered, thinking of the crater Master Non's destruction had created. "I want none of that."

Ari squirmed, shifting from one foot to the other. "You could always stick him in the attic."

Adrastea only shrugged.

They fell into silence as they ran out of ideas.

Chloe tapped the glass against her upper lip. "I think I've got it. The kings of long ago were buried in tombs."

Ari shook her head. "What's a tomb?"

"Like catacombs, only above ground. Almost personal chapels for the mortal remains."

Ari wrinkled her nose. "Wouldn't that stink?"

"Perhaps that's why they discontinued the practice."

Adrastea spoke. "I like that idea."

Ari sighed. "Where are you going to put it?"

"Here," she said.

"What? By the Sacred Spring? I get my water from here."

Chloe added her opinion. "This is sacred ground."

Adrastea rose. "Are you telling a god she cannot use sacred ground?"

Chloe backed down.

Adrastea turned from her. She stood forth, looking over the meadow surrounding Sacred Spring. She closed her eyes and called upon the Deeper Power. Unlike before, it welled up from within her. She was its source.

Once sufficiently full, she sent her thoughts out into the earth, seeking for stone—good, hard granite—from which to build a tomb. It replied willingly.

From the obliging granite that migrated to the surface, she laid out the base, then a dais, almost like an altar. By her will, she lifted the body of Mor-Lath and set it upon the cold stone. Adrastea laid his hands on his chest in a most dignified position. With a sigh, she plucked at his clothing. Such a shame to bury him looking like a country farmer.

She closed her eyes and imagined what would suit him best. The clothes she first saw him in? The formal robes his priests wore? The simple brown robe he'd adopted towards the end?

She remembered the time he'd asked her to go with him to cleanse Avelia. Before they left, he'd clad them in flowing, high-collared robes. She had speculated what it would have been like to be the God of the Light.

With a wave of her hand, his clothing changed. Now his body was properly draped in a black robe of the finest fabrics.

No, that didn't seem right. She changed it to white. It had surprised him, when she'd done it for the first time, setting him off-balance.

She sighed. Not white. It was too reminiscent of lost dreams. She darkened it, not quite to black, but to gray. Gray Lady, he'd named her.

It would do.

For the last time, she bent over him and with a kiss, placed one last blessing.

As Chloe and Ari watched, Adrastea willed the stone to close up in a simple square tomb.

Thus, she laid to rest the body of Mor-Lath.

"Wake, God of the Dark." Tanat's level voice stirred Adrastea to consciousness.

Adrastea felt the coolness of a granite slab below her face. She sat up and opened her eyes to the waxing light of pre-dawn to the east. She'd cried herself to sleep, slumbering the whole night on top of the tomb. Her eyes felt dry and puffy. She stretched stiff limbs.

Tanat sat next to Adrastea. "New day, new life. You have work to do."

"I do?"

Tanat crossed her legs and tilted her head. "You are the God of the Dark. You must purge the sin from souls."

When Tanat spoke those words, deep in her heart, Adrastea recognized what she had to do. She held out her hand. "I suppose you have souls for me?" As much as she would like it to stop, the world went on, turning. People lived their lives and died, heroes of their own stories, not waiting for hers. "Such a waste of potential to have a god simply for the removal of sin from a soul."

She flicked her fingers over a pretend soul. "There you go, all clean. And you too, all clean. Off to the Light with you. Don't dilly-dally on your way there." She laid back on the cold stone. No wonder Mor-Lath had been so frustrated with the job. She began to understand his yearning for the Light's power.

Tanat did not share her wry views. "There is more to it than that. I judge the dead to see if they are ready to move to the Light. If they are, off they go. If not, they are given into your care. Souls can only go to the Light if they are ready to go. They need to be contrite, humble and willing to give up their burdens. True penitents. Your job is to get them that way."

Adrastea sat up. "Oh? And how do I do that?"

"Give them time to reflect upon their sins. Also, encourage them to introspection. Teach them to let go of their anger, their lust, their fear."

Adrastea sighed. "Mor-Lath wasn't very good at that." How many times had she tried to undo that knot of fear within him?

Tanat continued, "You were. You spent time in Dom-al-gol. You talked with the souls. Many of them listened to you. When their desire to be free—truly free—from there was strong enough, they pinned their hopes to you. You brought them out of Dom-al-gol and convinced Mor-Lath to shrive them."

Adrastea shuddered at the thought of her banishment. "I think they simply wanted out of there."

Tanat shook her head. "It is more than that. Dom-al-gol is not always a place, but a state of mind. Live under the burden of sin, unable to forgive or let go, and you carry that hell with you.

"Dom-al-gol is necessary," the immortal explained. "Here in mortality, there are infinite distractions that can occupy a soul and keep them from reflecting upon themselves. Dom-al-gol is a quiet place, free from those distractions, so a soul can progress and not get hung up on external stimuli."

Tanat pulled a handful of souls out. "Here are the recently dead." She gave them into Adrastea's care. "I judge them when they first depart the mortal coil. You work with them and you judge them after. When they are ready—and you will know—then you can purge them of their sin and send them to the Light." She selected a particular soul from the crowd. "Here is an easy one."

Adrastea cupped the little soul in her hands, waiting until it resolved into an image of who she'd been in Mortality. "Berengaria." It pleased her to see the priestess again, even if the reunion was bittersweet. She gave her life to in defense of Harianne.

The soul of the priestess looked up and smiled. "Holiness." Then her smile faded. "It happened so fast. I never saw it coming."

Ever since Mor-Lath came, Adrastea had been able to see the dead. Their thoughts had never been privy from her. But now, she could also see their history, their deeds, their sins. That was new.

Not too much burdened Berengaria. "I'm surprised she was not raised to the Light," she said to Tanat.

The immortal replied, "There has to be the desire to go, as well."

Adrastea turned back to Berengaria. "Do you not want to go to the Light?"

"Harianne needed me," she explained. "You had the fate of Creation at stake. I couldn't leave her."

"She's safe now," Adrastea replied. "Mikal's got her."

Berengaria nodded. "He's a good man. I wish I could have stayed." She gave a little hiccup of a laugh. "I got to spend the rest of my life with him."

Adrastea's heart ached. Even from here, she felt her brother's palpable sorrow. Had Berengaria lived, would Mikal have followed in his uncle's footsteps, loving a woman, yet forbidden to marry? Or would he have caved to Pennexter pressure and married after all? And then, with Berengaria being Tredan, would she have been an acceptable wife, or as a priestess of Mor-Lath, one of the enemy, disqualifying Mikal from inheriting? So many questions, none of which mattered now.

In her hands, Berengaria waited patiently while Adrastea reflected.

"Are you ready to go to the Light?" Adrastea asked her.

She considered. Within her depths, she catalogued all her errors. There were some dark moments when she had given in to weakness, but also bright times, when she stood up for what she believed in. It was not so much which god one followed that determined righteousness, but the conviction of truth.

"Did you behave the best you knew how?" That was the question to ask Berengaria.

"Yes, I believe I did."

Adrastea agreed.

Shriving wasn't so much a cleansing as an unburdening. As she was relieved of her sins, Berengaria's soul began to glow bright. She became lighter until she was completely freed.

"There. All forgiven."

She held Berengaria close for a moment more before releasing her to the Light. With unfettered joy, Berengaria flew upward and onward.

Soon, she was gone. Adrastea sighed. She would miss the priestess.

The other souls were not ready to be shriven. After Adrastea had sorted through them all, she tossed them into Dom-al-gol to reflect upon their lives. Perhaps they would see how they could improve in death. She did not envy their purgatory time. She idly wondered about Desideria. She would seek out the priestess later.

"I have one more soul for you," Tanat said. "I have no choice but to give it to you. I am sorry, for this will be a most difficult one to purge."

That intrigued Adrastea. She held out her hands. Into them, Tanat poured a soul so experienced it was an inky black. "What has he done?"

"What hasn't he done? Thousands of years is a long time to misbehave. I wish you the Dark One's own luck." She vanished without a goodbye.

Adrastea looked down into her hands. As the soul pulled himself together, her heart began to warm. "Mor-Lath."

"Am I glad to see you." He looked over to where Tanat had been. "Remind me never to die ever again. Being Judged by that one was a most unpleasant experience."

She laughed as tears spilled out her eyes. "I thought you were gone for good."

"Yes," he replied, all contrite. "Sorry about that."

ᴄ◉ঞ⑤᎑

Chapter 25

Harianne Pennexter sat at her desk and sighed over the paperwork her Uncle Mikal had handed to her. Bills, estate inventories, correspondence—the lot covered her desk, filled several cabinets and demanded her prompt attention. Had he handed over the management of the whole Pennexter family estate to her?

He had. That was the only explanation. What a fool she'd been. Of course, he had. This is what being the legal heir was about.

He'd done it ever so subtly, easing her into it over the past five years, after she'd reached the age of majority. "Harianne, could you answer these letters for me? I've got some Mayoral business this afternoon I can't put off. Harianne, could you double-check my figures in this ledger? I might have carried too many ones. Harianne, could you send a telegram to your cousin regarding our tax statements? We need to know by tomorrow, but I've got to plan the agenda for Council tonight."

Throughout her adolescence the joke about Sacred Spring was that Harianne was Uncle Mikal's "lord's apprentice". He had Jacob as Assistant Mayor and several mayorprentices besides. Nobody had offered for Harianne to apprentice in any other trade, and Uncle Mikal didn't bother pushing her off to anyone.

Yes, she had been the lord's apprentice. It was no secret that Mikal Mayor accepted the Pennexter inheritance reluctantly. Of course, he was more than happy to hand the estate over to the next in line—her.

"I am thirty-six kinds of fool," she shouted at her ceiling.

Shouting helped a little with her frustration.

Also, her mother Adrastea did not show up, much to Harianne's relief. She did that, sometimes, when Harianne was upset. Well, she used to. Not so much anymore. Was it because Harianne was older now and didn't need her Mama as much, or was it because, over the years, Adrastea got wrapped up more and more in her own occupation?

Her mother. Now there was a member of the family that needed regular management.

A knock rang out on her front door. "Harianne? You home?" It was Uncle Mikal.

She resisted the temptation to shove all the paperwork off her desk. What would he say if she asked if she could have an apprentice?

"Please don't tell me you have more paperwork," she growled as she yanked open the door.

A contrite Mikal Mayor stood on the porch with only his hat in his hands. "No," he replied. "I'm afraid I need to ask your help in something very important."

Harianne's stomach dropped. "It's Mama, isn't it? Has she been shriving souls in the spring again?"

Gallian Priestess maintained a presence at the spring to succor the daily pilgrims who came for devotion, repentance and worship. She complained to Mikal Mayor whenever the God of the Dark saw fit to spend time there. She thought it most inappropriate and highly sacrilegious for Adrastea to dabble in the spring.

But Mikal shook his head. "She's at the monument."

Ah, the monument. Other than a few tight-lipped Springers, nobody knew what the plain stone edifice was. It sat not too far from the spring itself, opposite the small temple of the Light. Some said it was an altar. Others claimed it was a plinth. Harianne knew it was the best place to find her mother.

She retreated there when the grief of her widowhood grew too much to bear. Many was the time Harianne or Mikal or even Chloe Priestess had to talk Adrastea back to the world.

"I think this time is different," Mikal confessed. "I've been there all afternoon. She..." His brow crumpled.

She... What?

He shook his head. "I couldn't do it. She won't listen to me."

Oh dear. That was bad. "How long has she been up there?"

"Gallian says days. Says she's been talking to herself. She's spooking the pilgrims."

Harianne closed her eyes. She knew exactly to whom her mother was speaking. "I'll go see what I can do."

Or rather, she suspected it was more about what her mother had to do.

arianne marched her warm way up the hill to the sacred spring. Being a hot day, sweat streamed down her face. Would it be too much to bathe her face in the spring before she confronted her mother? Gallian, holding watch in the shrine, insisted on blessing her to give her the fortitude to face the God of the Dark. Not that Harianne needed it. She simply needed a cool head.

Harianne had a plan. A very scary one. But it had to be done.

After a cool wash in the spring, Harianne approached her mother, who sat in the shade of her late husband's tomb. "Mama," she said. "You know you should not be here."

Adrastea, her knees drawn to her chest, cradled her hands as if holding something. Harianne could never see souls, could not see the Lines of Deeper Power as her mother explained them. But she knew they were there.

She knew exactly which soul her mother cradled.

"Mama?"

Adrastea did not answer.

Harianne knelt beside her. "Mama, you need to come down."

Adrastea looked up. "Why?" She brushed a tendril of curly brown hair, untouched by silver, out of her eyes. Adrastea never aged. If Harianne didn't know better, she would have thought her mother the same age as herself.

"You're scaring the pilgrims." She held out her hand.

Adrastea took it and rose to her feet, brushing the dry grass from her skirts. "Don't know why. I don't talk to them."

"That's the thing. You will murmur to the dead—whom most people can't see—but not acknowledge the living." Harianne leaned in closer. "They think you're mad. The last thing we need is another Crozie."

"Crozie wasn't mad." Not really. She had two souls in her, Adrastea once explained. Adrastea's great-grandmother, whom Crozie tried to save from death, was the other one. They were shriven some years ago. "Crozie didn't understand. She feared death. Death's not so bad. It's not the end."

"Oh really?" Harianne replied. "What is the end?"

Adrastea didn't answer.

"Mother?" she prompted.

Adrastea rolled her eyes. When Harianne used 'Mother' instead of

'Mama', she meant business. "What?"

"You're afraid," Harianne said. "You're just as afraid as he was."

Adrastea closed her eyes. "Must you keep mentioning him?"

"What? Like he's not here?" Of course, Mor-Lath was here. He'd been here for twenty years, the only soul her mother refused to shrive. "Hello, Mor-Lath," she greeted him, even though she would never hear his response.

Her mother frowned at her. She clutched the soul to her chest. "You don't know what you're saying."

Harianne sighed and looked back to Sacred Spring. Once upon a time there had been a protection over the village, where none with evil intent could come. That had disappeared with Mor-Lath's death. Sacred Spring had grown in the last twenty years from a village to a thriving town. A rail spur had come through, bringing pilgrims every day.

Things had changed. The world had changed. "I know exactly what I'm saying, Mama. We're going to talk about it. Don't think I haven't noticed you withdrawing more from the world."

"Not true."

"Oh really? When was the last time you'd been to the temple?"

Adrastea paused.

"See? Your answer should have been 'yesterday'." Harianne had been to the Tredan Temple many times as a child. She rarely went as an adult, for duty to Sacred Spring and Feown called her too often. "You should go there every day. How about you take me there now."

"I don't see why we should go. The living get on very well without me. It's the dead who need my attention."

"They can be shriven?"

"Right," agreed Adrastea.

Harianne didn't reply. She let the heavy silence do her speaking.

Adrastea drew herself up. "Now look here, child—"

Harianne gave her mother a very direct look. "Oh, I'm calling you on this one."

Adrastea looked away. "I don't know what you mean."

"Yes, you do. I am going to ask you why you are not doing your job."

Adrastea clenched her hands tightly and turned away. "That is none of your business." Her voice was low and dangerous.

Her mother didn't frighten her. "You know I am right."

Adrastea put a hand to the granite tomb and sank to the grass.

Harianne knelt next to her. "Look at me."

Adrastea looked at her daughter. She blinked several times and swallowed.

Harianne laid a hand over her mother's. "It's happening again. Like him, you're letting fear rule you."

"No, I'm not."

"You're afraid to let him go."

That got her. Adrastea wilted. The tears she'd been keeping back welled up and spilled out her eyes. She bowed her head until it rested on the cool stone. No matter how much she shook her head, she couldn't deny the truth. She gave herself over to twenty years of sorrow.

"It's time to say goodbye and you know it." Harianne put her hands on her mother's heaving shoulders. "The longer you keep him, the more you become withdrawn. I've noticed. Uncle Mikal has noticed. Even random strangers notice." She tucked a lock of hair behind her mother's ear. "The world needs you. You cannot properly shrive souls if you are not acquainted with the world. It's time to move on."

Adrastea closed her eyes. "I don't want to."

"Have you asked him?"

"I can't."

Harianne frowned at her mother. "You mean you don't want to ask."

She sobbed and raised her face to the heavens. "Not that. If I ask and he's ready to move on, I must shrive him. I cannot keep him."

Harianne said nothing.

"I— I don't know how to be a god. I can't do this without him."

"You've had twenty years."

Adrastea clung to her daughter. "Please, Harianne. I don't want to be alone."

Harianne hugged her. "You won't be alone. That's why you have me."

Adrastea looked up. "You're mortal. You won't always be here."

"My children, perhaps. Grandchildren?" Not that she had any prospects in that direction. As the Pennexter heir, the topic of marriage was a complex subject.

Adrastea only shook her head.

Harianne stood, her arms folded. "I cannot tell you what can make you feel better. I can only tell you what is right. You need to shrive him and let him go."

"In my own time."

"No, now." Harianne took matters into her own hands. She couldn't see or hear him, but Harianne would have bet the entire Pennexter fortune that Mor-Lath was also there. "Mor-Lath, are you ready to be shriven?" she said aloud, possibly louder than necessary. Her words echoed off the tomb, ringing back to her.

Adrastea froze. Her eyes grew wide and her jaw dropped. "Harianne," she moaned, her voice breaking. "How could you?" She clung to her daughter's legs.

Harianne folded her arms, more to keep her heart, which thumped uncontrollably in her chest. "Because it needed doing."

Her mother collapsed on the grass, her body wracked with sobs. "You terrible, terrible mashiah child!"

Harianne closed her eyes and sent a silent prayer to the Light. May the Light forgive her, she prayed, for forcing her mother's hand like this. "Do it, mother."

"No."

Harianne put a hand on her mother's shoulder, but she shook it off. "Do it." She did not raise her voice.

"No!" Adrastea cried. She leapt to her feet and disappeared.

Harianne sank to the grass in defeat, her back to the tomb.

She sighed.

Gallian, who had been watching from a distance, came over. Her white robes shone pure in the sunlight. "Dear child. You cannot force a god."

Harianne looked up, determination in her eyes. "Oh yes I can. It's why I was born."

At first, Adrastea fled to the village. But that was no good. Harianne could find her there.

"The temple?" Mor-Lath suggested.

At first, she rejected that idea, because of guilt over her neglect. Yes, she could surround herself with priests and priestesses, if she so chose, but it wasn't the same as having a husband at her side.

On the other hand, Harianne would not be able to bother her there.

Shift.

She walked through granite corridors of the temple, heedless of the priestesses and beguines who bowed as she passed. The bedroom had too many memories, as did the library. She went to the only place she could be assured of solitude.

In the main chapel a few priestesses attended to devotions. "Out," she ordered, waving her hand.

They obeyed, murmuring, "Yes, Holiness," as they departed.

Adrastea shut the doors and sealed them.

The main chapel was a lovely space, with tall columns and high ceilings. Countless lights illuminated the walls and the altar at the far end. Upon this she sat.

Mor-Lath's soul resolved into a figure which settled on her shoulder. "Do not be angry with your daughter."

Adrastea did not reply. She stared ahead, her brow furrowed.

"You know it was a question that had to be asked."

"I was not ready," she replied.

"You once taught me things happen when they are ready, not when you think you are ready."

"I don't remember that."

"Your mind was on other things at the time. You took matters into your own hands for something that should have happened but didn't because I wasn't ready. I should have been. After all, I'd put myself in that position."

She wasn't in the mood for cryptic philosophy.

"No," he replied, privy to her thoughts. "You aren't in the mood for doing what you need to do."

Her heart beat so loud, she thought it echoed in the chapel. "She should not have asked you that question."

"Yet it has been asked."

"Don't answer, please." She was going to cry again.

He stroked her cheek. "You know I must."

She shook her head. "I don't want to be alone."

He sighed and slid down into her hands. "I am sorry for that. I never thought it would end this way. I always thought we would either defeat the Light and be exalted together, or be defeated ourselves, both of us being utterly destroyed."

She thought of the destruction of Master Non twenty years ago. Death was the mere separation of the body and spirit. But with destruction, there was nothing left behind. As soon as she could, she'd filled in that crater and told the wildflowers to grow so that no memory of him, not even a dimple in the meadow, remained.

"Either way," he said, "We would have been together."

She clutched at him. If only she could bury him within her. Is this how Crozie felt, when her sister died? This unwillingness to let someone go? Was Harianne right?

He gently extracted himself from her grasp. "You must let me go." He moved away to stand before her, incorporeal arms outspread. "Adrastea, I am ready to be shriven. I have been, for a very long time."

Her grief pushed up through her stomach and spilled out her eyes. He reached out to catch her teardrops as they fell. They passed through his insubstantial fingers to spot her lap. "Do this one last thing for me?"

Her head sank in defeat. She nodded. One last act of service. She gathered him into her hands. Thousands of years of regretted sin and bad choices, of fear, anger, rage and indifference evaporated from his soul. She watched it fade away, flowing off into nothingness.

As she shrove him, she watched his soul brighten, as if lit from within. He returned to his pure state, a being of glorious light.

Every last shred of sin was gone. So bright was he, she could barely look at him.

Mor-Lath bent down and gave her a tender kiss. "Thank you, my love. Goodbye."

He soared up, away from her reaching hands, to disappear from her view, joined to the Light.

Adrastea watched as long as she could until her vision wavered. Around her, every light dimmed and went out. Chapel lights, temple lights, Tredan lights. Even the sun momentarily dipped its brilliance.

Abandoned, alone, hopeless, Adrastea curled up in the dark and gave herself over to utter despair.

⚜

As the leaves on the quakies turned golden, a telegram came for Harianne. One of Rop Storekeeper's horde brought it over to her house for her, all sealed in its yellow envelope. Harianne pushed her paperwork to the side and opened it.

She scanned through it, her lips twitching. She read it twice, three times.

She bolted out of the house so quickly her chair fell over and the door slammed, making the windows rattle.

Next to the chapel stood a building that housed Mikal Mayor's office. Harianne ran through the front door and past Mikal's lowly secretary. She burst into his office, heedless of who may have been in there.

Mikal sat at his desk, hands folded as he spoke with two men. "I've found her," Harianne wheezed. She handed the telegram over.

"I say," one of the men exclaimed, insulted. Who was this creature who interrupted their meeting?

Harianne ignored him.

"Honestly." The Mayor chastised his niece. Then he read the telegram. He rose to his feet, studying it. "Radelisa," he murmured.

He thrust the telegram back into her hands. "Go. Or there'll be hell to pay."

The train from Sacred Spring took Harianne to Crossroads. There, she caught another train through the mountains and beyond until she reached the Tredan territories.

Harianne knew of High Priest Radelisa. They had met a few times, when Harianne was young. Or rather, Radelisa knew who Harianne was. She had telegrammed and sent for her personally. Harianne pondered the possibility that at that moment she was the most powerful mortal in the whole of Creation. Who else in the world could convince a god to change her mind?

She'd telegrammed ahead to advise Radelisa of her arrival. When Harianne reached the Temple gates a beguine sister greeted her in the Tredan language. "Have you come for worship today?"

Harianne handed over the telegram. "I have come to see the High Priestess Radelisa. She is expecting me."

The beguine frowned at the telegram. Harianne realized it was printed in Feowan. "If you show it to her, she will understand."

The beguine sister considered this unusual request. Nevertheless, she allowed Harianne in to the outer court while she hurried off with the telegram between her fingers.

While she waited, Harianne gazed upward in awe. The whole Temple had been carved out of a mountain, with tall white pillars. It never failed to amaze her. Her mother had brought her here several times as a child. But as Harianne grew older, those times became farther between. Would Radelisa even recognize her?

High Priestess Radelisa emerged from the Temple entrance, her diaphanous robes fluttering in her haste. Several other priests and priestesses hurried after, ducklings desperate to keep up if not understanding why.

Radelisa slowed, studying Harianne's face. "It is you," she said in Tredan. To everyone's surprise, she genuflected and kissed the hem of Harianne's shirt, much to the young woman's embarrassment.

Some of the younger priestesses gasped. Who was this plainly-dressed young foreign woman, that the high priestess, who knelt to no one, paid great honor?

Harianne squirmed. "You have summoned me. Why?"

Radelisa, her age showing, pushed herself to standing. "I did not know who else to call upon. If Her Holiness will not listen to me...?"

Harianne nodded. "What happened?"

As they walked into the Temple, Radelisa explained Her Holiness' sudden appearance and the sealing of the main chapel. She gestured to a seamless stone wall. Adrastea had done a thorough job. "She's been there for weeks."

Harianne drew her hand along the wall. She laid her face next to it. "Mama?"

Nothing.

She closed her eyes. "Mother?"

No answer.

Harianne pondered this one. She knelt down, bowed her head and began to murmur.

Radelisa folded her arms. "Prayer? That won't work. I tried that already. She's not listening."

Harianne didn't move. "First, I'm a mashiah. I can change Creation.

"Second," and she let a small smile play her lips, "you haven't been praying to the correct god."

ays?
Weeks?
Months?

Adrastea didn't care. Nor did she move from the inky blackness that surrounded her on the altar. Let her wallow in her grief, her loneliness.

"Adrastea?" A gentle light brightened a chapel long in darkness. Phyl's feet touched onto the steps leading up to the altar.

She turned away from Him.

"Adrastea, you cannot stay here."

"Go away. Let me be truly the lone God of the Dark."

Phil shook His head. "I cannot. It is time."

Adrastea kept her back to Him. Time for what? Wouldn't he leave her alone?

"It is time for the final confrontation."

She sat up. "What do you mean?" Cold dread filled her soul.

He held out His hand. "Everything Mor-Lath worked for, everything he dreamed, even you, was in preparation for this moment."

She curled her lip. "Now, not only is he dead, but he is gone. Shriven and gone to the Light. Nothing left to confront."

"There is you."

She turned back from Him once more. "Not interested." Her hands trembled.

His hand descended to her shoulder. "I think you are."

"No." Her heart beat fast and her breath came rapid.

"You don't have a choice." He pulled her off the altar. "Come with Me."

Before she could voice her protest, They were at the sacred spring. The bright summer moon shone down on a night-drenched meadow still warm from the day. Even then, the moon and the myriad of stars above her were too bright.

The final confrontation. Mor-Lath had spoken about it when he was living. How close to the end they had been when he'd first came a-courting. His obsession to make her immortal as quickly as possible cost a half million lives. His focus on the upcoming battle led him to neglect her, then feel contrary to her, and in the end, banish her. When she returned, they clashed again, but then she realized the secret—share everything. By the time she learned exactly what that meant, Mor-Lath had died, taking any chance of true godhood with him.

And now here she was, a demi-god at best, incomplete. Mor-Lath had been so sure he could defeat the Light. If Only. If only he had a wife, if only they were a full god, if only he were ready.

Adrastea was not. Then, perhaps this is what the Light was waiting for—her contrition. How easy would it be to defeat a demi-god who had no desire to win?

Perhaps it wouldn't be so bad. Maybe They'd be merciful and send her quickly to oblivion. That would be nice.

Lucea waited for Them by the tomb of Mor-Lath. Her hand lay on the smooth stone.

"Adrastea," She said. "It is time."

Adrastea rubbed her arms. Autumn nights held a certain chill about them. "So He said."

"Are you ready?"

Adrastea bowed her head, willing to submit to the will of the Light. They would be merciful. How could she have ever doubted? "I am."

Lucea shook Her head. "No, you are not. You are incomplete."

This startled Adrastea. She looked up. "I cannot help that. My husband is dead."

"Yes. Dead and properly shriven. His contrition frees him from his last shackle."

Adrastea's heart ached. If only she could be freed as well.

Lucea's hand stroked the stone of the tomb. "I have a necessary gift for you, Adrastea, to prepare you for Our final confrontation.

Lucea pull upon the Deeper Power, summoning all Creation to Her. Naturally, it obeyed.

The god focused the Power on the tomb. A deep, booming crack rang out as the granite split down the middle. Two halves of the tomb fell away, startling Adrastea. She took several steps back, but Phyl held her hand. "Just watch," He said.

Once the tomb had fallen away, Adrastea saw the body of her husband, as whole and complete as the day he died. Cautiously, she came forward. She had expected moldering bones on the slab, or even dust.

"Immortals never perish, not in the way of mortal flesh." Phyl guided her up the dais.

In the moonlight, Mor-Lath's skin had a faint luminescence. In contrast, his grey robes appeared almost black. It was only reflected glory. Dead was dead.

Lucea came forth, held Her hand over Mor-Lath, and called upon the Deeper Power.

Adrastea wavered as the Lines of Creation flowed to Lucea, to wrap Her in their brilliance. So luminescent was She that Adrastea had to shade her eyes.

The Lines faded, and Lucea stepped back.

On the cold slab of the tomb, Mor-Lath drew a deep breath.

Adrastea cried out and backed away. He opened his eyes and sat up, to her horror. She collapsed on the ground, her shaking legs unable to support her.

Mor-Lath gasped a few times, then studied his hands. By habit he called forth a globe of light, by which to better look at himself. "Oh, glory," he uttered. He looked up to Lucea. "You restored me?"

She held out Her arms.

"Thank you," he cried, falling into Her hug.

Adrastea trembled on the ground. What had Lucea done? Hadn't she already lost him twice? Did Lucea bring him back just so she could lose him again?

Mor-Lath noticed Adrastea on the ground. He slid off the granite slab, his gray robes slithering with him. Kneeling down by his wife, he stroked her cheek with his hand. "Adrastea?"

His touch was warm. She drew a shuddering breath and wrapped her arms about herself.

To her surprise, he dragged her up into an enthusiastic hug. "Oh, my Darklet. Your sacrifice was necessary. I could not be truly free until you gave me up."

He laid her head near his heart. It beat strong, it beat for her. She knelt there, listening to his heart. Lub-a-dub. The truth sank into her, filling every empty place within.

Mor-Lath lived.

He lived!

He rose, pulling her to standing. He stroked her cheek once more, then buried his face in her hair, inhaling deeply. "Oh, I've wanted to hold you for so long."

The reality struck her. This was Mor-Lath. He was real, he was alive. Her breath caught in her throat. "Are you really here?"

He gave her a funny look, then bent to kiss her lips.

That old familiar thrill that had haunted her from the beginning ran through her blood. Her bones vibrated like plucked viol strings. A yearning she'd though long dead stirred within her. This is what she missed.

"Pending business," Lucea reminded them.

Mor-Lath lifted his head for only a moment. "Not now. This is the first time in twenty years I've been able to kiss my wife." It might be the last.

"You'll have plenty of time for that later."

Mor-Lath broke contact with Adrastea. "Oh? Do tell."

Phyl joined Lucea in the moonlight. He linked His hand with Hers. "First things first. Adrastea, can you share the mantle of the God of the Dark with Mor-Lath?"

Butterflies of eagerness fluttered in her belly as she realized what this meant. "You mean, we can still...?"

Lucea gave her a gentle smile. "Only if you share."

Adrastea turned to Mor-Lath. "Will you share godhood with me?"

He ran his fingers through her hair. "Love to."

A power within her flowed up and out through her hands into him. She did not feel diminished; rather, she felt complete.

He tilted her chin and laid his forehead against hers. "I give my memories to you."

In they rushed, thousands of years of experience, so fast she could not keep them straight. In the end, they flowed into her like water and she let them come. She could sort them later.

Deep within her, that itch she'd forgotten stirred. It welled up within her. The last time she felt this was when she and Mor-Lath had forgotten themselves the night before his death. Instead of fighting it, as he had, she gave in and let it wash over her. Mor-Lath's arms tightened about her waist. His head tilted back as he surrendered as well.

A billion Lines of Deeper Power enveloped them both, wrapping around and tunneling through them until Adrastea couldn't tell where she ended, and Mor-Lath began.

When the dizziness settled, Mor-Lath's arms held her. He was not as she once knew him. His hair, once streaked with silver, had turned completely white.

They had become a god.

He gazed at Her in amazement, fingering one of Her curly locks. It, too, had turned bright white. He lifted it and inhaled. A gentle smile of pleasure spread across His face. As He bent to kiss Her once more, Lucea interrupted.

"Before You get lost in Yourselves, I must ask You a question."

Mor-Lath sighed. He tapped Adrastea on the lips. "Later," He promised. To Lucea He asked, "What?"

"What do You want, more than anything else?"

Is that all She wanted to know? Adrastea turned Her husband's face back to Hers. He couldn't help but smile. Adrastea said, "I only want to be with Him."

He nodded in agreement. "I only want to be with Her."

"What about Your desire to be the God of the Light?"

As one, They turned back to Phyl and Lucea. "What are You saying?" Mor-Lath asked.

Phyl and Lucea came forward. "Do you wish to be the God of the Light."

Adrastea felt an old desire, one She thought had died with Him, rise in His heart.

Lucea tilted Her head. "Or rather, God of all Creation?"

"You would give up Your mantle?" Adrastea asked.

Mor-Lath caught His breath. "You would rejoin the two?"

"They should never have been split in twain."

Adrastea asked, "But if it's rejoined, what will happen to You?"

The best smile spread across Phyl and Lucea's faces. "Blessed rest."

Adrastea looked to Mor-Lath. "Light and Dark. Everything. The whole of Creation for Us."

"Shall we?" He asked Her.

Adrastea's heart leapt with joy. "Of course."

Together, They answered, "We accept."

Lucea nodded. She and Phyl held out Their hands to Mor-Lath and Adrastea. As soon as Their palms touched, the most brilliant Light flowed into Them. The more the Light poured into Them, the greater Their capacity increased.

It was done.

Phyl and Lucea stood arm in arm, looking rather ordinary and faded. Lucea's hair remained white, but Phyl's had darkened to a brown. They turned to each Other. As They shared a gaze, They melted together, dissolving back into the Creation that had birthed Them. Soon They faded away, leaving only Mor-Lath and Adrastea under the quiet moonlight.

Adrastea's head rang with the song of Creation.

Congratulations. The message settled on Them like the gentlest of feathers. In the back of Her, rather, Their heads, She sensed the whole of the world. Oh, it needed help.

"It'll keep," Mor-Lath murmured. He lifted Her divine chin so They could gaze into each Other's eyes. "I love you," He murmured, then sealed that declaration with a kiss.

"Come, my beautiful Wife. Creation awaits." Together, Mor-Lath and Adrastea ascended to the Light.

The End

A Note from the Author

Thank you so much for reading Bride of the Dark. I hope you enjoyed it. If you did, please leave an honest review on the site where you purchased this book. Alternatively, leave a review on a reputable review site of your choice. Reviews are not only the highest compliment you can pay to an author, they also help other readers discover great books. Share the love by telling others. Thank you!

Other Books by Heidi Wessman Kneale

Available where all good ebooks are sold.

Of The Dark series
God of the Dark
Bride of the Dark
House of the Dark

Romance Novels
A Lady of Many Charms and Other Stories
Her Endearing Young Charms
The White Feather
For Richer, For Poorer
Marry Me – A Candy Hearts Romance
As Good as Gold

Acknowledgements

So many people go into the production of a book. From the support of so many fellow authors (Hello, NaNoWriMo. SFF-OWW, Romance Writers of Australia and Write Club!) and beta readers (Jen Kilshaw and Hannah Whitehead, especially), to editors (Fontaine M Manners, and the Edit Minions) and artists (Elaen K Haras), no book is ever born alone.

Dear readers, I wrote this series for you. I released this into the world so that you could have an escape hatch from reality, even if only for a few hours. May you find a quiet moment of blessed relief from *weltshmerz*.

Finally I acknowledge the Whadjuk tribe of the Nyoongar people, past and present, who are the traditional owners of the land on which I live and write. Gratitude from this *wadjila*.

About the Author

Heidi Wessman Kneale is an Australian author of moderate repute. She is best known for her escapist fiction. Like most humans, she's got a family and a cat. When not writing novels, she can be found composing music and staring at the stars.

Socialize!

Hang out with me online:
Twitter: @heidikneale
Blog: Romance Spinners
Web: Heidi Kneale, Author

Want a free story?

Of course you do!

Get Heidi Kneale's short story "Within Her" when you sign up for her quarterly newsletter at http://tinyurl.com/heidikneale/ plus get news of upcoming releases, special deals and more.

Those in the know read the Quarterly Newsletter, because I tell my subscribers the bestest stuff first, not to mention freebies and other goodies. Sign up now to stay in the know. After all, I do have more books planned for Of The Dark.

When I've had too much of reality, I open a book.